KINGDOM COME

A freelance writer for twenty years, Carl Huberman lives quietly in Cheshire with his wife and family, four cats and his conspiracy theories.

His first novel, *Eminent Domain*, was greeted as 'a potent mixture of sex, violence and intrigue . . . a real page-turner' (*Midweek*) and was followed by *Firefall Taken* and *Welcome to the 51st State*.

Also by Carl Huberman

Eminent Domain

Firefall Taken

Welcome to the 51st State

CARL HUBERMAN

KINGDOM COME

PAN BOOKS

First published 2000 by Pan Books
an imprint of Macmillan Publishers Limited
25 Eccleston Place, London SW1W 9NF
Basingstoke and Oxford
Associated companies throughout the world
www.macmillan.co.uk

ISBN 0 330 36776 5

A CIP catalogue record for this book is available from
the British Library.

Phototypeset by Intype London Ltd
Printed and bound in Great Britain by
Mackays of Chatham plc, Chatham, Kent

For Alice, always

It was beauty killed the beast.

Carl Denham, *King Kong*

THE NIGHTMARE
BEGAN IN 1977 ...

Well, that went well, thought Ellie Jonacezk as she drove out of Didra. She rooted around on the passenger seat for a tissue, came up empty, and had to wipe her nose on her sleeve.

Just her luck. Traffic was stalled in both lanes leading west out of town, and there was a middle-aged woman staring in disgust at this repulsive action. Ellie had a good mind to wind her window down and empty her nose over the woman's Olds. Instead, she tried tuning the radio to check traffic reports about her intended route back to Portland.

It was 11.20 p.m., and she faced a long, lonely drive. She only had enough money for gas, and Jake had dumped her. Worse, her lovingly hand-carved wooden fruit had proved a disaster both in the judging and on the sales front, her damn cold ensuring she had drowned the things in scent. To her, they had been pleasantly aromatic; to everyone else they stank to high heaven, and the judges' eyes were watering long before they could consider their artistic merits. All in all, a disastrous weekend, her budding career and her affair over and finished in the same day.

Why hadn't she listened to her parents and dutifully attended State, instead of trying her hand at woodwork with that hippy charlatan Jake Colliver? She and mom hadn't spoken since she left home, and mom wouldn't have changed her attitude by now. In other words, Ellie's life was in the toilet, at just nineteen.

To cap it all, her Gremlin now started overheating, and soon – unable to see through the clouds of steam – she eased it off the slow-moving highway and parked up. What would be the best thing to do now? Why, have a good cry of course.

She hunched over the wheel, sobbing like the stupid, selfish girl she was. Why can't they just hand out big notices with STOP! THINK! DON'T! written on them, to make your right decisions for you? It would be a whole lot easier . . .

She stepped out of the car and watched the rest of the traffic crawl past. It was this little Washington State community's biggest weekend of the year: a couple of thousand woodworkers, professional and amateur, descending on the town for its annual craft competition. She doubted she'd ever be back here again.

Ellie popped the hood and breathed in oily steam. Great, just great. She leaned back against the door and lit a cigarette. Perhaps lung cancer would consume her within the next eight hours, and end her miserable existence. She looked back towards the town, all lit up like Christmas. She hadn't stayed for the fireworks, but they were due to commence about now. A green streak suddenly shot across the horizon. *That's pretty.* Then it exploded without a sound, turning the entire valley green. She shielded her eyes. *My, what a big one. But why no explosion?*

She watched the light die, but couldn't see any sparks cascading earthwards. *That's odd, surely?* Must have malfunctioned. Symbolic of her whole weekend, really. She could imagine the big firework's carcass slamming to the ground outside someone's house, scaring the bejesus out of them. She suddenly felt dizzy. Oh no, not a migraine – not now. Not with everything else I've . . .

She bent over involuntarily, as cars nearby began bumping into each other, their drivers apparently also disoriented. She saw puzzled faces, young and old. It's not just me, is it? she thought. It was as if the world had suddenly slipped sideways, and no one had any control of their movements. Only the slow pace of the traffic had prevented any serious damage.

She fell to her knees, convinced she was going to throw up. And then, just as the last traces of the failed giant green firework faded and the sky returned to normal, her nausea lifted and she stood up quickly, feeling strangely refreshed.

She glanced at the cigarette in her hand and, despite her normal craving for nicotine – she was a forty-a-day gal – she dropped it to the tarmac and ground it out. When she took another sniff, she found her nose was clear for the first time in days. Ellie knew that cigarettes could ease sore throats – by anaesthetizing the nerves or something – but they'd never cleared her head before.

Just then a chunky pick-up stopped, and an even chunkier guy stepped out to enquire what was wrong. Obviously to put her at ease, he introduced himself as 'Frank Cantrillo From New Hampshire On A Touring Vacation', like it was his full name, then asked if she too had seen that crazy light. She said she had, discreetly drinking in his good looks, muscular build and easy charm. Never had Ellie been so self-conscious of her extra pounds . . .

Flustered, she indicated the radiator, and he eased off

its cap with a rag, then topped it up with water from a plastic container stored on his flatbed. And only when the car's temperature was again normal, did he bid her goodnight and drive off.

Getting back into her car, Ellie gathered up all the chocolate bars and candy she had stashed in the glovebox, and tossed them into a ditch. No more crap for me, she vowed.

And from that day onward, with one notable exception, everything went right in Ellie Jonacezk's life. She quit smoking, reached her ideal weight, and never suffered another day's illness. She became reunited with her parents who, strangely, showed no hostility towards their wayward daughter. She enrolled in college, got a business degree, and made a career for herself as an artists' agent.

In 1989, she ran across Jake Colliver again and, despite her better judgement, they rekindled their affair. But he was killed in a freak gas station explosion before he knew she was pregnant – or before, as she later learned from his friends, her reformed lover could propose marriage to her.

Eight months later she gave birth to Tasmin, a beautiful dark-haired image of herself. A single mother with sensible investments and no family ties – since her parents had died – something now told her the time was right for one final adventure. She decided to drive across country, finally settling in a small town in New Hampshire, where she opened a gallery-cum-coffee shop, specializing in work by local artists. And she also found, to her surprise and delight, that the local sheriff was the same generous spirit who had fixed her car all those years before.

For Ellie and Tasmin Jonaczek life in Rhododendron quickly became a dream come true – quiet, safe, healthy – and it was there she eventually learned the incredible reason for her continuing good fortune.

But now Ellie – and those friends who also shared the secret of that fateful June night outside Didra, WA – would have to pay a terrible price for their intervening happiness.

SUNDAY
17 SEPTEMBER

CHAPTER 1

Boston, Massachusetts, 7.15 p.m.

Drexill replaced the telephone receiver. They were here already. It was inevitable, of course – but so soon? It was a good thing he had tipped the guy on the front desk, otherwise he wouldn't have had a chance. As it was, he was stranded in his fourteenth-floor room at the Dickson Tabula Hotel with no way out. Outside his bedroom window there was a balcony with a 150-foot drop to the street, and the room's only door opened on to a landing affording a similar drop into the vast, open lobby.

What a mess. Why couldn't computers wipe information totally when you hit DELETE, instead of just writing over it? He wondered if the Crypt Kickers had retrieved all the information. It had taken him over a year to decode Siemens's remaining files but with the technology possessed by the DECRYPT department of OCI, the Office of Central Intelligence, it wasn't a matter of *if* but *when* – and he had no idea how much they might have unravelled. Christ, they might even know of the town itself by now, but at least they wouldn't know their address, since the Carters were late arrivals there. He had to warn them – but first he must *survive*.

His attackers wouldn't come straight through the door, but would already be positioned out on the landing and in the adjacent rooms. No, they would enter from the outside balcony, rappelling from the roof. The odds would be overwhelming, and he was armed only with a Ruger 22 pistol and one ten-shot magazine. Add to this his age: although an agile six feet three, he was sixty years old, and so his physical options were limited. However, he did still possess one item that always proved invaluable in a crisis: his mind. Time for him to start evening out the odds.

First, he now knew they were coming, so they had lost any element of surprise. Second, he knew their normal tactics. And, third, it was dark outside, so they would be using night-vision and laser sights – which gave him two further minor advantages.

Switching off all the lights but positioning a table lamp nearby, he carefully slid open the glass door and peeked between the drapes. He could see Boston's Back Bay area lit up, with its office buildings and other hotels rising high, only the graceless stack of the Prudential Tower dwarfing them all. And, beyond, the constantly re-forming red neon triangle of the CITGO sign with the floodlit pool of Fenway Park to its left, the Red Sox batting vainly for a wild-card place. Then suddenly, closer to home, he saw two ropes come dangling into view, and two pairs of feet sliding down them, their black-clad owners already kicking themselves towards his balcony. As expected, they were holding sleek Glock 17 autoloaders with laser sights attached to the trigger guards, and they were wearing night-vision goggles. Soon the blue and grey décor of his room would be splashed with scarlet, and he had no intention of any of it originating from him.

Drexill backed towards the mini-bar, and extracted a large plastic bottle of lemonade. Unscrewing the cap, he emptied its contents over the couch next to him, then twisted the neck of the bottle on to the end of his pistol. This would provide an effective silencer for three or four shots at least. He next heard a stifled grunt as one of the men landed clumsily on the balcony. Pressing back against the wall in the darkness, Drexill waited, holding his breath.

A pencil-thin red beam lanced into the room, roving over the furniture. If that dot of light fell on Drexill, he would be shot instantly. Laser sights are superb for accuracy, but at night they have one drawback: by following the beam back to its source, the assailant is easy to locate. Sure enough, as the first man entered, the red beam pinpointed his position. Drexill almost tutted with contempt as he raised his pistol, aiming for a point eighteen inches behind the source of the beam, then fired twice. The makeshift silencer did its job, reducing the sound of his shots to little more than pops. As the hooded figure collapsed, Drexill knew the man would be dead before he hit the floor.

Equipped with night-vision, the second attacker could see his colleague's death as plain as day. Now he knew their quarry was ready for him but, although he retained the advantage of enhanced eyesight, this also would prove his Achilles' heel.

Drexill snatched up the table-lamp, switched it on and hurled it down on the carpet just in front of the open drapes. There was a cry and Drexill hurled himself over the corpse, firing out on to the balcony. His silencer burst with the first shot, so his next two cracked loudly across the street. But by then his blinded adversary was also dead, with three shots in his belly.

Drexill crawled outside to peer down through the

balcony railing. The invaders' ropes reached all the way to the neon-lit sidewalk below, where they coiled in circles. People were staring up but there was no way of knowing whether any were part of the assault team, so he couldn't risk rappelling down to street level. Instead he leaned outwards, snagging one of the ropes towards him. Certain he was grasping it securely, he picked up his attacker's silenced Glock, aimed the laser sight upwards at the dangling rope and fired off a couple of precise shots. The blue nylon parted as if slashed by a knife. He quickly hauled in its remaining length, tied one end to the balcony railing and threw the rest of the rope into the hotel room. He next unzipped a couple of cushions and wrapped their padded covers tightly around each hand.

'Okay, pal, let's go upset your friends,' he whispered at his first victim.

He pulled open the corridor door and, holding up the corpse in front of him, pushed it firmly out on to the landing.

At first he could hear only the normal hubbub rising from fourteen floors below, but then came the coughs of suppressed machine-gunfire – and the dead man spasmed as bullets penetrated his midriff. Drexill stepped on to the landing, and turned instantly to face the waiting gunman, still too shocked by his error to react to Drexill's sudden appearance.

Three shots from Drexill ended his misery.

Spinning, Drexill saw another hooded man taking aim with a Heckler & Koch MP5 SD machine-gun. Again Drexill fired three times, but this time his aim wasn't true. The man collapsed screaming, both knees holed.

With no time to waste, Drexill ran his gloved hands

along the rope until he judged himself to have ten feet of slack, then threw the rest of the rope over the balcony and jumped after it. The jerk almost pulled his arms out of their sockets. Now hanging thirteen floors above the marbled lobby, it wouldn't be long before he was spotted by his enemies – and then he might as well be hanging by his neck. He began to ease himself down the rope.

The luxury Boston hotel had twenty-two floors in all, nine above him, the rest below, each landing running in a wide semicircle above the crowded atrium lobby. Unable to swing straight down to a lower floor, because they tapered inwards as they descended, Drexill was going to have to edge himself down all the way.

Dozens of people were milling around the large ornamental pool and fountain, as yet oblivious to the carnage above. A piano tinkled 'Come Fly With Me', grounding its melody with glissando. Directly beneath him, a mob of blue-jacketed conventioneers were trying to check in at the over-worked front desk. Drexill could also see two scenic elevators rising swiftly, carrying those lucky guests who had finally succeeded in registering. And everywhere there was foliage – hanging from balconies, draping wide columns, patterning carpets – giving the soaring atrium the feel of a forest glade.

He was level with the tenth floor when the first shot was fired. The man he had hit in the knees was leaning over the fourteenth-floor balustrade, taking shaky aim. Either he was out of his mind or his superiors didn't care about the attendant costs of killing Drexill. Clasping the rope with both feet, Drexill sighted the pistol's laser on the man's forehead, and pulled the trigger.

At last his hovering presence was noticed: a couple of women on a nearby landing started screaming at the sight of a black-clad, white-haired man hanging only feet away from them. He was going to have to go down express now. But suddenly there was the shattering of glass, and uncontrolled machine-gun fire. Jesus Christ, they *were* desperate.

He glanced up to see that a man in the scenic elevator parked on the eighteenth floor was now firing down at him. People in the lobby screamed and fell over each other in their desperation to escape. Several fell into the fountain, and the sound of frantic splashing joined the hubbub.

Drexill took aim up at the elevator and fired six times. All his shots missed, but the gunman ducked out of sight. Glock near empty, Drexill dropped it, and loosening his grip on the rope, began sliding down.

He had dropped eighty feet before he tightened his grip and entwined his legs around the rope, friction heat instantly searing his palms and the inside of his knees and thighs. He had halted twenty feet above the lobby, hotel guests scattering under his descent and colliding into each other or abandoned luggage. Then machine-gun fire recommenced from two directions. Four innocent guests were cut down before the firing ceased.

Drexill suddenly let go of the rope, plummeting on to a cartful of luggage, spilling its contents. Discarding his improvised gloves, he rolled towards the front desk and hugged its marble front.

The counter's overhang temporarily shielded him from above, but there were bound to be back-up gunmen somewhere down on this floor. Glancing across the lobby, he could see terrified people fleeing as the hotel's shops, restaurants and coffee lounge swiftly emptied. He could maybe use these desperate guests as cover but, with his distinctive white hair, he still needed a disguise.

Just then a fat man collapsed beside him, his eyes wild, his face puce; he wore a conventioneer's powder-blue jacket and cap. Twenty seconds later he'd been rendered unconscious, his jacket now around Drexill's shoulders, the conventioneer's cap covering his head.

Stooping, Drexill let the hysterical crowd carry him towards the exit. Soon he was being swept out on to the cold street, the distant whoop of sirens promising rescue for the terrified mob. Drexill found himself forced up against an idling white Cadillac with a burly black chauffeur standing guard on it.

'Get away from the fucking car!' the man snarled.

A quick surprise chop to the throat, and Drexill was sliding in behind the steering-wheel. Honking the horn, he edged the stretch limousine away from the stricken hotel.

Suddenly, a voice piped up from the rear. 'Hey, vot is dis?'

Drexill glanced over his shoulder to see a large, tanned man crammed into a black tuxedo, his cropped hair and chiselled Aryan features instantly recognizable.

'Roland Armangetter!' exclaimed Drexill. 'I've seen all your movies.'

Just then, a police cruiser began howling behind them.

'Hang on, Roland! This could get fraught,' he warned.

The German movie star looked puzzled. 'Vot da hell does "frort" min?'

'This is what it means,' muttered Drexill, as he threw the 23-foot-long automobile through ninety degrees and roared down one-way, four-lane Boylston Street against the flow of traffic.

CHAPTER 2

Escaledo Del Dios Observatory, New Mexico, 8.40 p.m.

Roland Ward had been sidelined. There had been that little problem with his expenses in Seattle, and that big hassle over his trip to Japan, but that could have happened to anyone in his position. Just dumb luck, but someone needed to take the fall.

The intention had been to force him to resign, but the US Air Force was his life and he knew that, once he took off his general's uniform, the chances were he would be driven to try flying without the aid of wings. So when his superiors had offered him this alternative to a court martial, he had accepted it gladly. Hell, he'd have taken a posting to Greenland as Puffin Liaison Officer as long as it meant remaining in the service.

He had been enjoying the last of his annual leave in Tucson, playing golf with old air force buddies during the day and whoring at night. He was still good-looking and in fair shape for his forty-nine years, with piercing blue eyes set deep in a long, well-defined face, but his chin and hairline were receding and what so recently had been distinguished greying of the temples was spreading like a disease. He never had any difficulty picking up women but he preferred the company of hookers: like subordinates they did what they were told. No doubt this pointed to some fundamental flaw in his make-up, but he was too old – and having too good a time – to fret about it. But then he had received a phone call from Dr Alberta Gaines, and the fun was over.

Five hours later he was haring off I-25 thirty miles before Socorro, on to an unsurfaced, potholed mountain track: eighteen miles as the crow flies, but by car thirty-one miles of tortuous turns and bowel-loosening drops. He completed its dusty length nine minutes faster than ever before but, given the circumstances, his seeming indifference to crashing did boast a certain logic.

He hit the final rise doing forty and, as the grimy Shogun became momentarily airborne, the big upturned tit of the observatory itself was revealed, surrounded by a motley collection of grey block buildings. It was desert dark, so, apart from a couple of shaded windows in the main administration building, the only light was provided by the stars above and a reluctant moon occasionally peeking from behind high clouds. As the 4x4 slid to a halt and a weary Ward stepped down, a long shadow bounded from the yellow rectangle of the open observatory door.

'General, you gotta see this!' Alberta Gaines, the civilian head of WATCH, was dancing on the spot.

Excitable at the best of times, Gaines was a black thirty-something MIT graduate with a mind like a computer and the personality to match. The coloured beads in her black, shoulder-length, braided hair jigged and clacked as she gesticulated. Ward thought she looked like a refugee from an old *Soul Train* show, her voluminous red pants and floppy emerald sweater doing nothing to alter his opinion. She was thirty pounds overweight, dressed ten years too young, and always had about her the air of a pre-menstrual student on a major sugar rush. She irritated the hell out of Ward, and was adored by everyone else at Escaledo Del Dios. But any time he was prepared to admit to himself that she was attractive in a 'big' sort of way, she would spoil it with another display of adolescent overenthusiasm. Witness her current state.

'We got things to do!' she yelled. 'People to tell! Plans—'

General Ward clasped the woman's shoulders, fixing her with a stare. 'Calm down, Alberta! Look at me – and *think*. If what you say is true, what the hell is there to get so goddamned *excited* about?'

'But . . .'

'Scientists – you're all the same.' He led her back into the observatory building, his crisp blue uniform a stark contrast to her sour-apple outfit. 'Bet the guy who invented Agent Orange was real glad to get rid of his crab grass.'

The observatory computer room was long and narrow, and cramped by arrays of bright monitors, flickering oscilloscopes and winking banks of equipment. It reeked of stale coffee, old cigarettes and new sweat. It always reminded Ward of the interior of a submarine or an early Awacs plane and, though no one else ever wore a uniform, the mood was every bit as serious as if they were operating a machine of war. Tonight the usual laid-back calm had been replaced by palpable excitement. Gil Brock, fat and bearded, was seated at a VDU running a series of graphs, cursing every time a new calculation was revealed. Dreadlocked Ice-T lookalike Dan Costello was staring at twin photographs through a stereoptic viewer. And, in the corner, Jane Radinsky, six months pregnant, was clasping a mug of herbal tea. Her face was drained, her blonde hair equally colourless. This sight more than any other told Ward the readings weren't wrong. This was the real thing.

Gaines explained, 'We found it two nights ago.'

'So why the hell didn't—'

'We needed to be sure. And you were on vacation. Besides, you know the NASA protocol: wait forty-eight hours to recheck.'

'We ain't NASA.'

'But some of us *are* scientists.'

He ignored the jibe. 'And you're sure?'

'Positive. SIBYL says 99.997 per cent. So does SQUAWK.'

'Oh, Christ.' SIBYL was their own computer here at the observatory; SQUAWK was a larger computer at the Massachusetts Institute of Technology.

'How long?'

'Initial calculations put body correlation within days.'

Body correlation? Where did they get these phrases? Collateral damage for dead civilians; friendly fire for shooting your own boys. Christ, they'd even called the Challenger disaster an anomaly.

Gaines tapped a TV screen showing stars. A grid superimposed itself over the shot, followed by a thin red line tracking to the screen's bottom edge.

'And heading right this way?' said Ward, too overwhelmed by the meaning of their findings to worry about the math.

'There's no doubt,' said Brock, still managing to demolish a Mars bar despite the crisis. 'I've run the program three times, given it margins of error that would make night into day – and it still comes out in the side pocket.'

Ward waved aside their proffered papers and photographs, and instead stepped over to Radinsky. Crouching down, he slipped his arm around her shoulders. He had never been much taken with this plain Jane, but right then he wanted to comfort her. For perhaps the first time in his life, he was actually thinking of someone else.

'We gotta call people!' bellowed Costello, as a computer spat out another screed of paper.

'Yes, yes . . .' said Ward. 'Maybe it's not so bad, Jane.'

She looked up at him, blue eyes rimmed with tears. 'My son won't even get to be born,' she croaked.

'But it might—'

She stood up and tossed her Snoopy mug at the large window that looked out on the night-shrouded valley. The glass cracked, but didn't break.

'Might what?' she brayed. 'Run out of power? Take pity on us and fly off somewhere else?'

'No, but its size? The trajectory?'

Gaines spoke up. 'There's no avoiding the facts, general. Give me the word and I'll get the others on to it. Queensbury can track it next, and Fujamata can switch. Telefeuno are already lined up. We should have absolute confirmation in twelve hours max. And we need to get Spacewatch and NEAT on board.'

'No, not yet. You know *our* protocol.'

He studied the team, taking in the banks of computers, the *Contact* movie poster with its 'AS IF' graffiti, the WATCH logos stuck on each of the six 24-hour clocks registering the time around the world. He walked across to a yellow telephone inside a Perspex case. Fishing a key from his pocket, he unlocked it.

'No one says a word to anyone outside WATCH, understand?' he said, pulling out his Berretta pistol. 'Our job is only to find them. It's up to others to decide who gets to know about it. Are we clear?'

There was a stunned silence. They had been together as a team for eleven months and, although they didn't get on well with Ward, this was the first time he had shown anything other than sarcastic disdain or bored lack of interest.

He stared at his gun and laughed. 'Why do you think they put a military man in charge of all this?' He laid the weapon down, then lifted the Perspex cover. Cradling the receiver under his ear, he pulled out a sealed file from the base of the box, and unzipped it. Emptying the contents, he located an orange card. As he began to study it, someone finally answered the phone.

'*Eight* rings?' he spat. 'Eight rings on a fucking hotline! This is General Ward, out at Escaledo Del Dios. I've got a WATCH code for you.' He held up the orange card and read from it. 'Code winter six. Repeat, code winter six.'

The man at the other end of the line swore audibly.

'You could say that, son. Now tell your people to get their asses in gear, and make a decision about what we do next.'

He put the receiver down and sat back on the desk, reading through some papers.

'What *can* they do?' asked Brock.

'What they usually do,' Ward explained bitterly. 'Call a

meeting, fudge the issue, avoid telling anyone else until it's too late and . . . Well, this time they might be right.'

'Right?' said Gaines.

Ward sighed. 'Who do you know would want to be told they had so little time left to live? Give me blissful ignorance any time.'

Except now, he wouldn't be able to enjoy even that simple pleasure, would he?

CHAPTER 3

Rhododendron, New Hampshire, 9.10 p.m.

King Kong was very upset, and his impending rampage was weighing heavily on the minds of two eight-year-old sisters. King Kong was their hero: a big monkey torn from his home to be displayed in strange surroundings as entertainment. That he would be angry and trash things wasn't only understandable; it was to be lauded. If a giant ape can't stand up for himself, who on earth can?

But, at that moment, right and wrong were not the primary concerns of twins Kara and Lorri Carter. They had front row seats and simply wanted to see 'The Eighth Wonder of the World' break his chains and run amok. They knew they would be safe – King Kong was their friend – so the girls hugged their own black furry gorillas, Kong and King, and waited for the inevitable. However, just as flashes from the reporters' cameras scared the gigantic beast, a familiar voice disturbed their reverie.

'Time for bed.'

'Oh, mommy, no,' said Kara. 'Just till the end of the movie.'

'Please, mommy,' agreed Lorri, pausing the videotape.

Cheryl Carter gave her daughters one of her mommy-knows-best stares, and Kara and Lorri turned to show her their sweetest faces. This looked set for a battle of wills, both daughters having inherited as much of their mother's stubbornness as her colouring and good looks.

Just then, the girls' father came down from his soak in the tub, a white towel wrapped around his waist. He glanced at his wife, at his identical blonde-haired daughters (differentiated only by Kara's hair being cut shorter), then at angry King Kong frozen on the television screen.

'What's the problem?' he asked innocently.

'This movie, Stanley. It'll give them nightmares,' said Cheryl.

'Serve them right,' said Stanley, placing an arm around her shoulder while winking at the two little girls.

'But it's the fourth time they've watched it this week,' his wife complained, shrugging him off.

Stanley let out a loud sigh, then walked further into the room. Placing a palm on each of the girls' heads, he slowly turned them to face their mother. The girls offered sticky-out tongues and eyes disappearing up behind eyelids.

'What possible harm could watching *King Kong* three hundred and six times do to my darling daughters?' he demanded.

'Okay, but only until it's finished.' Cheryl was trying not to laugh.

A resounding 'Yeah!' reverberated from three mouths – and the girls returned their attention immediately to the screen.

Stanley sidled up to Cheryl, opening his towel briefly to flash at her. 'And there was that fascinating PBS show about mud on now . . .' he said. 'Seems we'll have to find something else to do.'

Cheryl ignored his invitation. 'It isn't healthy, Stanley; they keep watching that same movie over and over.'

'Kids get obsessed, honey. I was into the Eagles. Didn't do me any harm.'

'You haven't heard yourself singing "Hotel California" in the shower.'

'Let them watch it.' He smiled, displaying the contents of his towel again. 'It'll keep them occupied, if you know what I mean?'

Cheryl was set to give him another withering look, but instead grabbed the towel away from him and darted upstairs.

Completely naked, Stanley glanced round to see if his daughters were looking at his bare behind, but they were too engrossed in the movie, so he dashed upstairs after Cheryl.

Five minutes later, as King Kong was ripping up an elevated train in New York City, Stanley's naked chest and sweating face appeared on the TV screen, looking just as Cheryl would be seeing it now.

'Oh no. They're *doing* it,' said Kara, frowning.

King Kong reappeared momentarily, but then, from their father's viewpoint, they saw their mother's face appear, eyes closed, her large breasts wobbling as she lay on her back on the bed upstairs.

'Why do they have to do it *now*?' complained Lorri.

She concentrated hard, willing King Kong back on to the screen – only for Stanley's scrunched-up face to appear again, funny-ugly with lust.

Kara let out a sigh. Both girls then held hands, staring hard at the television – and King Kong roared back into the living room. They gave each other a high-five.

Soon their hero King Kong was on top of the Empire State Building, batting at biplanes. They watched the movie through to the end, agog.

Meanwhile, upstairs, Stanley and Cheryl were regaining their breath.

'Sorry it was so quick,' he gasped.

Cheryl stroked his thigh. He was still a handsome man, wiry and fit for his forty-four years, his thick black hair sparsely peppered with grey.

'Happy?' he asked.

'Could we be anything but?'

Stanley sat up. 'Life here isn't exactly the Daytona 500, is it?'

'I know, and I do miss the action, but look what we've got . . .'

Stanley surveyed their bedroom. It wasn't big, nor expensively furnished, but it served well – as did the house as a whole, and their way of life. They lived in a three-bedroom colonial house, at the top end of a quiet residential street on the southernmost tip of a relaxed New England tourist town. It was a doors-unlocked-cat-on-the-sill-fresh-flowers-in-the-hall-Norman-Rockwell-is-alive-and-well existence. They lived less than two miles from their own business, and during most seasons could walk to work along tree-lined streets, swapping greetings with their neighbours. Stanley loved this laid-back, idyllic existence, but knew Cheryl did not. She made a good job of hiding her frustration, but dissatisfaction would some-times nag at her, pricking at her with memories of how exciting things used to be. They weren't well off – hell, they couldn't even afford to get the radio fixed in their six-year-old Jeep

Cherokee – but, for all Cheryl's disappointment, they did have something no amount of money could buy.

'And there's always the girls,' she added.

'Those cute little terrors.'

'Yes, cute *talented* little . . . oh shit!' She sat up, clasping her forehead. 'They'll have *seen* us.'

'Not a lot we can do about that now,' he said, trying to be reasonable.

'Well, *you're* the one who's going to put them to bed,' she announced. 'We've *both* been letting our guard down more often recently.'

'You're right,' he sighed. 'But it isn't for want of trying, is it? It's like . . . it's like they're getting stronger. Or we're getting weaker . . .'

'That's silly.'

'Oh yeah? Look at this.' He rolled over to reveal his buttocks, and a bruise on his right hip.

Cheryl prodded it and he winced. 'How long have you had that?' she asked.

'I got it this afternoon; banged it on the shop counter. We don't normally bruise, not from something that minor.'

She sat up, arms across her breasts. 'Now you mention it, I had a headache this evening. That's why I was lying down. Been so long since I had one, I wasn't sure . . . I even thought of going down to Taylor's Pharmacy.'

He forced a smile. 'Would you even find it after all this time? It's almost as if we're losing our—'

'Don't even think it.' She rose, heading towards the bedroom door. 'Kara! Lorri! Has your movie finished yet?'

'Yes, mommy,' came the chorused reply.

'It's bedtime, then. Daddy'll tuck you in.'

As she heard the girls start clumping up the staircase, she retreated quickly to the bathroom.

CHAPTER 4

Danzig Cut, Vermont, 11.25 p.m.

The train was approaching. He could hear it: the 11.15 freight out of Marsden, heavy with coal. Two minutes from now it would reach the far end of the tunnel.

'Our Father which art in heaven,' he began, his throat dry with fear. 'Hallowed be thy name. Thy kingdom come . . . '

He struggled to move, but his arms were tied tight to his body. He had not been gagged, and realized this was so his screams could be heard. Well, he wouldn't give that satisfaction.

'Thy will be done in earth . . .' he whispered.

He felt a cool breeze on his sweating face – air pressure. The train had now entered the single-track tunnel. He struggled again, but it was no use.

' . . . as it is in heaven. Give us this day our daily bread . . . '

He could hear the rapid clacking of the rail joints. The draught grew stronger, too, as the locomotive pushed forward against an invisible wall of cold damp air. Only a bend in the tunnel kept the train from sight.

'Forgive us our trespasses . . . '

He could hear the engine's throaty rumble, like some threatened beast disturbed in its lair.

' . . . as we forgive those who trespass against us.'

He knew he was going to die. Even if his tormentor changed his mind, he couldn't be saved in time. So he was going to die cursing – cursing that bastard for coming back for vengeance after all these years.

The engine growled louder, its driver throttling up to maintain pace on the low upward gradient.

Oh God. Oh God. 'Save me! Save me!'

That was when he heard laughter ringing in the air above him. The cocksucker was watching, and could hear him.

'And lead us not into temptation!' he shouted. 'But deliver us from evil.'

Temptation. This was what it was all about. Being tempted, and not being forgiven by the Lord – or by that creature.

As the diesel engine clamoured round the bend in the tunnel, the victim screamed and pleaded like a little boy . . . And now he remembered just why it had come to this.

'For thine is the kingdom . . . '

Oh Lord, he could *see* it now. The light from the train, bright and white, mocking all he had hoped for, all he had preached about. *Oh God, no!* Again he fought his bonds, but they wouldn't loosen.

' . . . and the power and the glory!'

He could see the front of the engine thundering towards him through the dark tunnel mouth.

'FOREVER AND EVER!'

Laughter again, and he strained to peer upwards, past his feet – up along the rope securing his ankles, which dangled him head first above the railway track. But he could see only darkness up there.

The train's horn blared, and it was barely a hundred feet away now: a moving mountain of steel set to slam him into oblivion. His body would surely explode, turn inside out, *vaporize*.

And all because of him up there – his own son.

'Beep-beep, dad!' He heard a screech. 'Beep-beep!'

Lying along the same tree branch from which hung the rope supporting the screaming man thirty feet below, Jacob Lebrett sniggered with joy. He had waited a long time for this moment, planning it to the last detail, determined everything should be perfect. And *always* he had anticipated the imminent, glorious moment of impact when his father's body was obliterated.

That same father who, twenty years earlier, had carried out his 'good work' in the Chebbawa Woods by brutalizing his younger son, as his elder boy looked on with sadistic glee. Well, payback time had finally arrived. One second, the Reverend Nathaniel Lebrett hung there, screaming to his God for mercy; in the next he had totally ceased to exist.

As the engine, with its long string of freight cars, clattered away into the night, the driver still ignorant of his part in a gruesome execution, only the rope was left swinging in the breeze, at its lower end a single bloody shoe.

'Beep-beep,' Jacob Lebrett said softly.

He looked down towards his two companions, morons both. They had enjoyed his latest game.

He clambered down the tree and moved over to the stolen Dodge Interceptor, climbing into the back while the others sat up front.

'So where to now, boss?' said Oren Hilts, an eager young black man.

Lebrett opened an oil-stained Gousha road atlas, and targeted their whereabouts with one damaged finger. The other two leaned over, and watched as the wounded digit trailed a bloody smear from their present location down through places they didn't recognize – Littleton, Lebanon, Rhododendron, Keene, Holyoke, Hartford, New Haven . . . until it halted on Stamford, NY.

'Why there?' asked Clark Pinder, the fat man in the driving seat.

Lebrett smiled. 'Got a long-lost brother, Noah, I aim to get reacquainted with.'

MONDAY
18 SEPTEMBER

CHAPTER 5

Business in Evergreen Souvenirs was slow. The tourist season was on its last legs, and Cheryl and Stanley Carter knew they were about to enter an annual six-month downturn.

Their store sold all the usual tourist souvenirs, with a sideline in New Age paraphernalia. Neither had dreamed they would end up selling this kind of junk but, hey, a married couple's got to make a living. Once fall was out of the way they would have to rely on the local community, or on the down-shifters who lived in the tri-state area of Vermont, New Hampshire and Massachusetts. As one of their regulars had once said, 'You never know when you're gonna need rosewood incense sticks.' Quite.

Thankfully, hippies and hopheads didn't observe holiday seasons like regular tourists did. So, whilst half the store resembled any one of a thousand New England souvenir traps, with its T-shirts, keyfobs, postcards, mugs and seed packets all branded *Rhododendron, NH*, the other half boasted dolphin mobiles, sculpted candles, Native American jewellery, World Music CDs, lava lamps and assorted crystals – all priced with large mark-ups. This material was Stanley's preserve, while Cheryl dealt with the 'normal' tourist side of the business – if dough art qualified as normal. It was all quiet, predictable and safe; a lifestyle many would envy – unless they knew the reason . . .

It was mid-morning when Mrs Kobritz came in to enjoy a regular browse.

'Hello, Mrs Kobritz,' Cheryl welcomed her.

The plump, well-dressed woman was sniffing at an apple-scented pot-pourri. 'Morning, Cheryl, and how are you?'

'Fine, fine.' Cheryl was always fine.

'And the little ones?'

'Fine.' Kara and Lorri were always fine, too. 'They're up at the school, helping out on the jamboree.'

Cheryl could see Mrs Kobritz's disappointment. The older woman adored those twins as if they were her own grandchildren; and fortunately the kids tolerated her.

'They should be back here in about five minutes. Would you like a cup of coffee?' Cheryl usually kept a pot on the go in back.

'I'd love a cup,' said Mrs Kobritz with relief. She *needed* to see the twins regularly. They were so pretty, so friendly, so *calming* – like living, breathing Prozac.

Cheryl entered the cluttered back room and first slipped on a Fleetwood Mac CD, then she poured two cups of coffee from the filter machine. What little wall-space was available was crammed with photographs of helicopters, including movie posters for *Blue Thunder* and *Wings of the Apache*. The entire range of Revell model helicopters hung by threads from the ceiling. This was as near to a shrine for her own past career as Cheryl would allow herself.

Strange, maybe, for a thirty-five-year-old married woman and mother of two but, before her thoroughly fateful

and eventful meeting with Stanley Fulbright, she herself had
been a helicopter pilot. Now she was forced to lead a safe,
quiet domestic existence: no more choppers, no more risks
... no more *fun*. For such an adrenalin-charged lifestyle to
be halted in mid-flight was a source of eternal regret to her,
but her compensation was a happy marriage, two beautiful
daughters, and ostensibly living the American small-town
dream. Still, whenever she entered this back room, the pang
of regret was almost physical.

Reluctantly, she went back out into the main shop.

A couple of minutes later, while she and Mrs Kobritz
made small talk, an elderly married couple came in. Over Mrs
Kobritz's shoulder, Cheryl saw them give that oh-dear-what-
have-we-walked-into glance at all the New Age stuff. For a
moment they looked like they might just turn tail, but as soon
as Cheryl had flashed them a smile, they were hers. She knew
this was naughty and unfair, but business was business.

On this final day of their vacation, the New Jersey couple
were searching for a gift for their daughter. Cheryl ran them
through the options, steering them well clear of Stanley's wares.
She did, however, make some point of adjusting the half-price
ticket on a basketful of glass paperweights, and the elderly
woman immediately homed in on the pink, swirly-patterned
one.

'It's just perfect!' she exclaimed.

Just then a battered green Jeep Cherokee drew up
outside, and Stanley and the twins piled out.

All three customers turned as the children entered, the
gasps from the elderly couple audible.

'My, aren't they *adorable*!'

- 39 -

Kara and Lorri, more mature than their eight years warranted, took such admiration in their stride. Stanley, meanwhile, headed off in search of coffee.

As he busied himself in the small back room, Cheryl slipped in behind him and hooked her arms around his waist, whispering in his ear.

'You take over now. I've just about had it today.'

There was a sudden crashing of glass from the shop, followed by a muffled cry. Had one of the paperweights been dropped? Stanley headed through the door for a better look – to find three strange men standing over a broken vase which had contained dried flowers.

'Hey, accidents happen,' Stanley offered pleasantly.

'Yeah, they do.' One man grabbed a second vase and hurled it to the floor. Stanley sensed they were in for a rough time.

The perpetrator was a black man in his twenties, dressed in blue jeans and a brown leather jacket, with close-cropped hair.

'Hey, I think you'd better . . .' Stanley trailed off.

A second intruder – fat, white and forty, with a prominent black eye – had meanwhile picked up a large ornamental candle, and was running his fist up and down it in a masturbatory gesture. 'Any you ladies wanna oblige me?'

Cheryl had stepped out to join her husband. 'Put that down,' she said firmly.

'I'll be puttin' it *up*, before I put it down, lady,' he sneered. 'Just a question of whether it's old or young.' He looked at Kara and Lorri. 'Maybe *real* young.'

Stanley lifted the counter-top, and moved into the main

body of the store. 'Just put it down, and take your inadequacies outside.'

The black man let out a derisive howl.

The fat man stared at Stanley in mock surprise. 'My inadequacies?' He turned to the third man, standing motionless in the shadows. 'Maybe I'll just see how tight-assed Mr Tight-Ass here really is.'

Mrs Kobritz let out a strange gargle and fell sideways, Stanley catching her just in time. Cheryl slipped through the counter to help lower her to the floor, presenting her rear towards the strangers as she bent over.

'Now *that's* a sight worth comin' in for.' The black man leered.

The fat man dropped the candle and moved towards Cheryl.

Stanley stepped in his path. 'Leave, *now*.'

The fat man halted. He smelled of urine. 'You going to make me?'

'Look, why don't you three just leave us alone?' Cheryl was anxious to end this drama.

The black man toppled another vase.

The elderly male customer piped up. 'L-look, you're upsetting the l-ladies.'

'Up-upsettin' the b-bitches?' he mocked over his sunglasses. 'You ain't seen the beginnin' of upset, man.' He pulled out a knife and brandished it at Stanley.

Cheryl gestured for Kara and Lorri to move towards the gap in the counter.

The third stranger, who had remained silent so far, now moved quickly to the shop door, flipped over the CLOSED sign, and pulled down the shade. He then turned to face them in the light, revealing a scarred face with hooded eyes, a broken nose and long but patchy black hair. He stood six-two at least, and was dressed in a filthy black coverall open to the waist, beneath which was a grimy purple T-shirt decorated with some faded cartoon. He looked just like a Hell's Angel with alopecia.

Staring at Cheryl's prominent breasts, he withdrew a long, serrated knife from his thigh pocket. Then taking slow, determined steps towards her, he finally spoke.

'Beep-beep,' he croaked. 'Beep-beep.'

CHAPTER 6

'Is this information reliable?' asked Parvill Rodin.

It was noon, and he was sitting in the back of a police car parked behind trees a mile off Highway 2, near Athol, Massachusetts. He peered through his fieldglasses at a red and white shotgun shack nestling in a gully of cedars. The view had a picture-postcard quality that seemed almost unreal – particularly given his current intentions.

The nervous FBI special agent sitting in the front of the cruiser replied. 'That limo stolen in Boston was found just a hundred yards from the bus station in Cambridge. One of our guys located a clerk who'd sold a ticket to someone of Drexill's description. The ticket was a one-way to Albany.'

'So why, pray, are we sitting around here?' demanded Parvill.

'It seemed unlikely he'd go *all* the way there, so we checked every stop en route and found he got off at Athol yesterday, asking the way to Keene. The local sheriff checked for all the motels or empty houses along that road, and came up with that shack over there. It's a holiday home for some doctor, and should be empty now, but the drapes are closed and there's fresh-chopped wood out back.'

'Surely he wouldn't burn any? The smoke would give him away.'

'After dark, who's to tell out here? And night's when he'd need a fire most.'

Parvill sighed. 'Okay, I'll buy it.'

He headed back to his black command vehicle. Sliding open the side door, inside Parvill found a lone man studying several television monitors. Christie Rodin had the same blond good looks as his brother, but at twenty-nine was two years younger. They were both athletic six-footers, their muscular bodies honed through daily workouts and prescription medicines. Their handsome faces were long and finely featured, and what little change of expression they offered the world was usually conveyed with a narrowing of ice-blue eyes, and belied by a deceptively calm Mid-Western burr. There was no denying the natural charisma of each, but such a cold demeanour could be extremely daunting, not least to those over whom they had authority. 'Cold fish' was a common epithet for them, 'blond bastards' another.

Today both were wearing grey Armani suits and Police shades, in overall appearance as immaculate as the manicures of their slightly overlong fingernails.

'Found anything yet?' Parvill asked his brother.

They had already set up a number of cameras round the cabin, as well as a battery of microphones.

'There's certainly one heat source: probably the kitchen stove,' replied Christie. 'No sign of movement, but he could be sleeping.'

Parvill nodded. 'I say it's a go. So how should we play it?'

'Boom?' suggested Christie.

'Yes, boom. We've tried it straight twice already – and look at the mess that caused. Our people have been on TV so much lately they should hire theatrical agents. I say we blow the shit out of the place, then get forensics to pick up the pieces and confirm the ID later.'

'Not exactly subtle.'

Parvill extracted the Glock from his shoulder holster and offered it to his younger brother. 'Hey, you want subtle, *you* go in there and pretend to be delivering pizza.'

Christie laughed, and Parvill put his pistol away. He turned to the FBI man who had followed him over from the car. 'Get me Porky Pig.'

Five minutes later, the local sheriff was expressing his outrage. 'But you *can't* just blow the place up!'

'Yes, I can. You know I can. It's not your problem anyway.'

'But what about the owner – and that man inside?' he said in exasperation.

'Fuck the owner; he's got insurance. As for him inside, why do you think we're blowing it up? Now take your people somewhere safe and let the professionals handle this.'

As the sheriff stomped away, muttering, Parvill radioed his own men. 'Okay, people, it's the Fourth of July. Repeat, the Fourth of July.'

He donned a dark blue Kevlar jacket with a large yellow LAW insignia on the back, then crouched in waiting behind one of the six cop cars strung along the road.

As he was finally about to give the order, his cellular phone chirruped.

Flipping it open, he barked, 'This better be good,' and listened. 'You got confirmation on that? . . . Okay, it's a go. I want everything – and no loose ends. Contact me when you have what I need.'

Putting the phone away, he finally gave the signal. Seconds later came an enormous explosion. The whole building erupted, shattered by two missiles fired from opposite sides of the gully. As the sound of it rolled away down the steep-sided valley, the flaming remains of the holiday shack rained down on thirty law enforcement officers hunched in the ditch for cover.

Even before all the burning debris had landed, Parvill Rodin stood up and squinted through the dispersing smoke to where the house had been standing earlier. *No one* could have survived that explosion. It looked like it was all over for that pain in the ass Drexill.

'Get a team right in there now!' he demanded. 'First put out the fires, then check for evidence. I want teeth, I want fingers, I want a signed fucking photograph!'

Smiling, he leaned back against the debris-strewn cruiser. He really loved explosions.

It wasn't long before an excited Christie came over from the shelter of his van to join him. 'If that didn't take him out, I'm gonna have to reconsider my position on religion!'

Parvill smiled. 'He just better be dead this time. Because if he ain't . . . '

He left the alternative unsaid, glancing up at the noonday sky.

Christie followed his gaze. 'You still feel it?'

Parvill spat. 'I fucking *know* it. Those nerds in New Mexico finally found it.'

'Excellent!'

'With Drexill out of the way, we should have a clear field.'

'We might have got him to tell us where they are.'

Parvill laughed. 'Drexill's one of the old school: he wouldn't tell you his own name even if you cut off his dick.'

'But finding those two won't be easy. And we've only got—'

'Christie, please do not state the obvious.' Parvill grabbed his brother's jaw and squeezed.

Christie nodded under the pressure, then the ringing of Parvill's cellphone put an end to this fraternal torture. The older man flipped open his Nokia, and listened in silence.

'Send me the list,' he said at last, turning the cellular round so Christie could read the words scrolling across its miniature e-mail screen. 'The Crypt Kickers have got us some names of towns out of Drexill's files.'

'Eight of them,' confirmed Christie, reading down the list.

'Let's lower the odds,' suggested Parvill. 'Drexill only ran to Boston to get away from us. Now he was heading north. How many of these towns look like they lie in that direction?'

'Just three of them: Burlington, Montpelier, Rhododendron. The rest aren't even here in the east of the country.'

'Okay, let's check out all three straight away. And remember,' he said, glancing up at the sky again, 'the clock is ticking.'

CHAPTER 7

'I think it would be a good idea if you gentlemen left now,' Stanley urged the three troublemakers.

Hilts, the young black, stared at him. 'He called us *gentlemen*.'

Pinder, the fat one, laughed, pulling out a .22 revolver which looked like a toy in his large pudgy hand. 'Everyone gets to do what we want now, or everyone gets to be dead, understand?' he hissed, eyeing the sexual smorgasbord set before him. Three generations of pussy! *Whoowhee, was he ever gonna have himself a good time.* But as he stepped towards Cheryl, Stanley blocked his way, staring into his face.

Pinder aimed the gun at Stanley's chest. 'Time to get ventilated, shopkeeper.'

But Stanley continued staring him out, and after a few moments the man's vicious demeanour crumbled miraculously.

'I'm sorry,' he finally gasped in a voice like a little boy's. Dropping the gun to the floor, he hung his head and started sobbing.

The old tourist reached down for the discarded revolver, but Cheryl told him to leave it.

At first Hilts could only stare in disbelief at his companion's bizarre behaviour, then rage coursed through him.

'You goddamn pussy, Pinder! Goddamn fat pussy motherfucking waste of space!' He waved the stubby knife in his hand, as if sizing up Stanley's stomach.

Cheryl interrupted his thoughts. 'Hey, why don't you pick on someone your own size?'

The man then turned his anger on her, the fact she was taller than him infuriating him even more. 'Gonna carve my name on your tits, lady.'

'Can you actually spell "fuck face"?'

Despite the tension, Kara and Lorri giggled.

'Now look what you've made me do – bad language in front of my own daughters,' admonished Cheryl.

At this point Hilts lost control. Howling like an animal, he lunged at her. Cheryl took one quick step backwards, then stared into his eyes with renewed contempt.

He screamed, 'You fuckin' whore!' his eyes now fixed on hers. Then suddenly he went very quiet.

'Put the knife down,' Cheryl ordered.

He did so, as if in a trance, then moved across the store and slumped down beneath a gift rack of name keyrings, his eyes wide and hands shaking.

'What the—?' spluttered the old man.

The third intruder studied his two companions, then looked at the knife in his own hand.

'We have weird shit going down here in the boonies,' he said hoarsely. 'Taming them two would take powerful voodoo.'

'Are you going to leave now?' asked Stanley.

The man continued to stare at his knife. 'Eye contact,' he surmised. 'Seems to me eye contact is what this is all about.'

Stanley and Cheryl swapped anxious glances.

'I think we need some distraction now, so you two won't be staring me down, too. How's about this, then?' He turned suddenly and hurled the heavy weapon directly at Lorri.

But, even as Cheryl screamed in horror, the knife halted its deadly trajectory barely inches away from the little girl's face. It was as if it had encountered an invisible wall. After wavering in mid-air for a couple of seconds, it clattered impotently at her feet.

The ashen-faced elderly woman became hysterical, toppling back against the counter and scattering a bowlful of carved wooden fruit all over the floor. Her husband grabbed her arm to steady her, the colour already drained from his own face.

Lorri stood stock-still, plainly shocked by her narrow escape. Kara, however, charged across the room.

Cheryl hurried to intercept her, but slipped on a wooden pear and went crashing down on to her backside. Stanley also tried vainly to get between Kara and her target, but the scarfaced man lashed out with his fist and caught him on the side of his face. Stanley reeled back, stunned, leaving no obstacle to prevent Kara reaching the object of her rage.

She actually jumped up at him, small fists bunched and teeth bared. 'You don't hurt my sister!' she screamed.

He grabbed her around her tiny waist with two large hands and, laughing, held her aloft. She slapped and kicked out at his face to no avail.

'Feisty little runt,' he cackled. 'Seems like she'd make us a sweet hostage.' Clutching her at arm's length, he started to back towards the door.

Stanley was still on his knees, his mouth bloody, his

mind confused. Cheryl scrabbled amongst the wooden bananas and apples for some kind of weapon, and found eventually the black man's pocket knife. Without hesitating, she lunged at her daughter's tormentor, and plunged the blade into his right thigh, handle-deep. He let out a howl, then kicked out viciously at Cheryl, tumbling her back on to the kneeling Stanley.

'Your daughter here's gonna pay for that, bitch!' he hissed, turning to the entrance door.

But it was now Lorri's turn to take a run at him. She leapt up on his back, kicking furiously. With an animal roar, he tried to shake her off.

Kara stopped her frantic pummelling, and instead dug her fingernails into the tender flesh of his earlobes. He bellowed in pain, shifting his right hand up from her waist to her throat. By now their two faces were only inches apart – and their eyes quickly locked.

'You little shit—'

Then he suddenly loosened his grip, stopped panting, stopped yelling.

His eyes still fixed on hers, he slowly lowered Kara to the floor. Lorri slid off his back and stood shoulder to shoulder beside her sister.

No. Can't be. Can't be . . . Panic surged in him instead.

'Girls, you okay?' said Cheryl, pushing past Stanley.

'It's all right, mommy,' said Kara. 'He's not angry any more.'

Indeed, 'he' had lowered himself to his knees, his eyes never leaving Kara's. She glanced down at his thigh, at the knife still protruding from it.

Damn bitch, she's in my head. She's in my head...

Still without removing his gaze from the girl's bright eyes, he pulled the weapon out of his flesh, and raised its bloody four-inch blade to his own throat.

No, I won't. No little bitch is going to make me... No! NO!

Having finally shaken off his muzziness, Stanley approached the kneeling man. He glanced around at the other two intruders, both seeming totally uninterested in what had been happening.

'Kara,' whispered Stanley, 'what were you doing?'

'Punishing the bad man,' she explained calmly.

The 'bad' man's hand shook violently as he unwillingly forced the blade closer to his Adam's apple.

'You're going to die soon,' Kara said to him simply.

No. No. Leave me alone.

'Sheriff Frank will punish him instead,' intervened Cheryl suddenly, becoming aware of her daughter's intentions. She motioned to Stanley to ring the police.

'But he tried to kill me,' argued Kara, her thoughts still boring into the evil man's mind, slowly eroding his self-control.

'I know, baby,' said Stanley when he put the phone down, 'but this is where the law takes over.'

'That's not fair,' Kara started to protest.

Get her out of my head! Get the bitch out of my head!

'Maybe it's not,' confessed Cheryl, terrified that her daughters would succeed in their aim, 'but it is the *right* thing to do now.'

The elderly tourist was on his knees, tending to his

hyperventilating wife. He turned to the two girls. 'Go on, make him do it! Make him do it!'

Just then, a police siren cut through the quiet.

'See,' explained Cheryl. 'Sheriff Frank's coming. He'll take care of them.'

Kara looked at her mother uncertainly, then at the knife. It had already teased a speck of blood from the man's unshaven throat. This would be so easy . . .

Bitch, bitch, bitch . . .

The police car was nearer now, and they could hear excited voices outside in the street.

'Please,' begged Stanley.

'All right.' Kara and Lorri spoke together.

As if a puppet's string had been cut, the man's hand dropped away and the knife fell to the floor. He then leaned forward and retched violently.

Cheryl quickly dragged her daughters back towards the store counter as the front door crashed open. Sheriff Frank Cantrillo and Deputy Ray Fischer burst in, their .38 revolvers drawn and cocked.

'Holy shit!' Cantrillo exclaimed on spotting the dark figure hunched over a pool of his vomit. 'It's Jacob Lebrett!'

As he pulled the handcuffs from his waistband, his deputy ordered the two other intruders to lie face down, hands on top of their heads. Whatever had happened here, they were taking no risks.

CHAPTER 8

Despite Gaines's furious protestations, and her team's equally vocal outrage, the word came down from Ward's immediate superior that their figures had to be triple-checked before the panic button could be pressed.

Ward had expected as much, so encouraged them to do as ordered, privately holding on to a vain hope that they might yet find some error in their calculations. But, after waiting fifteen hours for further observations and quantifiable verification, they accepted that they had irrefutable confirmation of their initial prognosis.

Ward relayed their findings to Washington, and a helicopter was despatched to pick up Gaines and himself, and to ferry them to Lubbock, Texas, from where they were to be flown to Andrews Air Force Base in Washington, DC. It was while they were waiting for this US Marine chopper that the ever impatient Gaines proffered a few home truths to her boss.

They were sitting in his office located in a temporary building in the shadow of the main observatory. He had furnished the small room in leather and mahogany, dotting the wall with framed prints of vintage USAF jets. He had also invested in a well-stocked mini-bar – particularly handy whenever he was still at work during the small hours. It was proving of value now as he made serious inroads into a bottle of Jack

Daniels. After sipping from his heavy crystal tumbler, Ward lay back in his seat and closed his eyes. He had been awake for twenty-four hours straight, and was feeling his age. But Alberta Gaines had other ideas. Dressed now in a smart dark-blue trouser suit, she had fetched in her laptop and was running data, downing Evian water straight from the bottle.

'Ward, I don't know how you can take all this business so relaxed.'

Without opening his eyes, he replied, 'I'm tired, not relaxed – can't fight the sandman.'

'Well, you'd better try. Way we figure it now, we've got maybe five days left.'

This woke him up.

'Just five days? Less than a week?'

'Yeah. Bitch, ain't it.'

He drained his glass, and righted himself in his seat with a fart of leather. 'How come you didn't get to notice it sooner?'

'It's an asteroid, general. Comets, you see, they're made of ice, and they throw off gases, so the light from the sun gives them a tail and luminescence. Hell, you can sometimes see them for decades in advance, and they're even visible without telescopes. Look at Halley's comet in '86, and Hale-Bopp in '97. Asteroids, however, are inert lumps of rock, dark and invisible until the last moment. You only see them if you're looking for them. And, if they're heading our way, they're only visible to the naked eye when they actually approach the Earth's atmosphere.'

'Any chance of this one missing us – or burning up first?'

'It isn't going to miss, and it isn't going to burn up. The

meteors you see flaring in the sky, they're probably the size of that bottle cap.' She nodded at the bottle of whiskey resting on the table. 'Anything that's bigger than your fist is going to *hit*. Happens all the time; it's just no one notices something that small for the couple of seconds it's in our atmosphere. They reckon more forest fires are started by meteors landing than by lightning strikes. They even suspect the Great Fire of Chicago was—'

'Screw the history, it's the future we're concerned with. Tell me about *this* mother.'

Alberta smiled. 'I knew your ignorance would come back to haunt you.'

'My ignorance?'

'Come on, general. You didn't give a damn about WATCH since that day you came to introduce yourself – and called us a bunch of astrologers.'

'Hey, that was a natural mistake.'

'Only for the ignorant. I know why you were put in charge, but I thought even you would have made the effort to find out more about what we were up to.'

'I trusted your judgement.'

'Bullshit. I'm a woman, for one – you'd only trust me to make you a sandwich. I know your record. I know you're a dyed-in-the-wool macho, military lifer with one too many sexual skeletons rattling around in your locker. In your eyes WATCH represents just a twenty-month stopgap to your thirty-year pension.'

'Just what are you saying?' Ward said, staring out at the grey sky, trying to control his temper.

She continued her attack. 'If you'd just been put in

charge of a squadron of experimental fighters, wouldn't you have read their test results in advance?'

'Of course.'

'So how come you still don't know anything about what WATCH is actually looking for?'

'I do. I studied up.'

She laughed – it was deep, horsy and unattractive. 'Where do asteroids come from? Or comets? How many types of asteroid are there? How big do they get? How fast do—'

'Look, this isn't a fucking exam! We're in the middle of a crisis here.'

She leaned towards him, and whispered. 'Yes, we are. A crisis as big as they get. And if, by some miracle, we survive, your career certainly won't, not if you continue to show your goddamned ignorance.'

Ward was set to argue further, but he realized she was speaking the truth, so instead he allowed her to lecture him further.

'Listen and learn. First, asteroids are minor planets,' she explained. 'We believe they were originally formed by the collision of larger bodies. So far, we've discovered five thousand asteroids, but there could be ten thousand times that number throughout our solar system. Most of them are found in the asteroid belt between Mars and Jupiter. What goes to make up an asteroid is a matter of conjecture but, based upon evidence from meteorites, plus spectral readings from reflected sunlight, we're agreed on three basic types: C, S and M. The majority, three-quarters of all asteroids, are C-types made of dark carbonaceous rocks. About one-seventh are S-types, which are stony. And M-types, about a tenth of the total, are metallic. We believe Erebus is an M-type asteroid.'

'Erebus?' asked Ward.

'Whoever discovers an asteroid is entitled to name it. As team leader, I chose Erebus, the Greek god of darkness. He was also the son of Chaos, and brother of Night. Given the circumstances, it seemed an appropriate name.'

'You're goddamned weird, Gaines.'

'No, I'm educated. Now, Erebus is big but by no means the biggest,' she continued. 'The largest asteroids can be at least one hundred and twenty kilometres across, so they are virtual planets. Erebus, however, is approximately eight kilometres across.'

'Well, that's not so big.'

'You weren't listening, were you? It's not so much the size that counts as the speed of impact.'

She stood up, walked around his desk and, grabbing the arm of his chair, spun him to face her. She then balled her fist, leaned forward, and pushed it slowly towards his crotch. Then, pulling her hand back, she punched hard – jerking her fist back at the last moment to avoid contact. 'Get the picture?'

He jumped in his seat. 'You're mad,' he gasped.

She ignored him. 'The general consensus is that a major asteroid impact some sixty-five million years ago led to extinction of the dinosaurs, together with half of all other species on earth. That asteroid was estimated to be *ten* kilometres across. Here, let me explain the mechanics.'

She walked back to her own seat, keyed in a program on her laptop, then turned it around so that Ward could view its screen.

'This is part of a presentation I've been putting together for the annual funding committee next month. Here is a shot of Meteor Crater in Arizona. This was caused by a meteor just fifteen metres across generating a crater forty times its own size. In this shot, we see the town of Firefall, Wyoming. The meteor that struck here about six hundred years ago was probably only eight metres across. The crater it generated now encompasses a town of three thousand people. We estimate Erebus is some eight *thousand* metres across. With an impact crater only forty times that size, that's a 320-kilometre-wide crater. But the impact force is, unfortunately, geometrical; so the crater is likely to be at least double that size, and at least ten kilometres deep. That's a hole four times the depth of the Grand Canyon, and the size of Arizona, created in a millisecond. One moment everything's normal,' she smacked Ward on the thigh, 'now you've got this giant hole. All so fast it's unimaginable. The impact would be felt everywhere on earth. The seismic shock would run around the world at two thousand miles per hour. Fragile seismic structures could well be kick-started into action. So, even if Erebus impacted somewhere in Russia, the shockwave could trigger the big ones in California and Japan.'

'Could we fire something at it?'

'You've got five days, general. Standard turnaround for a space shuttle is fifty-five days. No missiles currently available can target objects in outer space and, even if you could, you couldn't *destroy* Erebus. It's too big. You might try to deflect it, but imagine the nuclear firepower required to deflect a mass the size of a mountain travelling at up to sixty thousand kilometres per hour. And, whatever you use, it would need to be launched within the next twelve hours so that the explosion would be far enough away from the earth not to contaminate us with subsequent radiation, or to rain lethal chunks of the fragmented asteroid on us.'

'In other words, we're doomed.'

She snorted again. 'Doomed is too kind a word. Fucked would be more accurate: the universe has decided to fuck us.'

Ward stared at her for several moments, hoping the woman would provide a get-out clause, but she remained silent, her full but attractive face grim.

He slowly unscrewed the cap of the whiskey bottle and, with a shaking hand, poured himself another tumbler. But, before he could pick it up, she leaned forward and nabbed it for herself, downing in one gulp the large measure it contained.

Now he knew she had been speaking the truth: Alberta Gaines didn't normally touch alcohol.

CHAPTER 9

The bad man was standing in Kara's room. She pushed herself upright in her bed, and rested the back of her head against the coolness of the painted wall. He was standing there in the corner, in the shadows. She could hear him breathing – short, sharp breaths as if he had been running.

Running all the way from the Sheriff's Office.

She wanted to wake Lorri but, glancing over, saw her sister's bed was empty. It was just herself and Lebrett.

'That's right,' said the man in a raspy voice. 'Just you and me, little girl, and I'm gonna cut you up. I'm gonna cut you up into so many pieces, your mom and dad will need a map to find all the fucking bits.'

Kara gasped, and felt her bladder loosen, leaving the mattress warm and wet. Never had she felt so frightened. All through her short life, whenever anything even slightly threatening occurred, somehow the danger of it had evaporated quickly: bullies at school, that strange man near Meadowlark, those drunken boys in the town square at carnival time – all had seemed to suddenly change their minds and leave her alone. But this man wasn't going to be deterred – and now he was here in her bedroom

She wanted to call out for her mommy, but the man just laughed. He stepped out of the shadows, and she could see his evil smile, his wide black eyes, that awful patchy hair. And then the smell of him: blood and vomit and urine.

He edged towards her, one hand raised, its fingers clawing open and shut continually.

'Gonna fuck you up so much, little girl.'

'*Stop it!*' she screamed, finally finding her voice.

Lebrett halted his menacing advance. His fingers slowly uncurled, and his arms fell limp to his side.

'Gonna fuck you up,' he repeated, but his voice sounded distant now, like some actor repeating a line he no longer understood. 'Never gonna get rid of me.'

'Go away,' she ordered firmly.

Grimly he nodded, then slowly turned and shambled back into the shadows.

'Gonna get you, girl,' he hissed finally, before the darkness swallowed him up.

At that moment the bedroom door flew open. Cheryl raced in, falling protectively over her daughter, hugging her tight.

'What is it, baby?'

Kara clung to her mother, while staring wide-eyed in terror over her shoulder at where the bad man had stood. But now the light shining in from the hallway revealed only some discarded toys, a poster of Barnie – and Lorri lying in her bed, blinking sleepily at the sudden commotion. *No bad man, no threat.*

And yet she knew he had been there with her – if not in the room itself, then in her mind. Lebrett had talked to her for real, and had told her for real what he wanted to do to her, and she knew he would do it if he could. That part hadn't been a dream but a promise.

She began sobbing uncontrollably, for the first time ever having experienced the disorientating effects of genuine fear.

Two miles away, Lebrett himself woke up in his jail cell, shrieking and seemingly unable to stop. He had dreamed of being somewhere with that little girl who had got him locked up here ... and he had been so close to killing her ... but she had somehow stopped him with her words alone. Yet it had been his own dream; why couldn't he kill her in his own fucking dream?

As he kicked off the bedclothes and sat up, slamming his fist against the wall, he knew for sure that it had been *more* than a dream. That girl was in his head, sitting inside his skull like a maggot, worming her way into his thoughts, screwing up his dreams. He had never been really afraid of anyone except his brutal father, but here he was sweating and all but vomiting – because a little girl had *ordered* him to stop threatening her. A little girl, just a fucking kid.

He stood up and hurled his body against the cold bars of the cell, feeling the metal bruise his flesh, but he didn't care. Pain, cold, the rattle of metal – these were real, not some mind-fuck caused by a little girl.

But he knew the dream was as real as pain, as substantial as steel – for he knew he now had a *second* passenger in his head. The first was the black cancerous egg which was slowly eating his brain until it would eventually consume all his thoughts. The second was now to be the girl. She had got inside his thoughts in that goddamned tourist shop, and had been riding him ever since like a stowaway. The doctors might not excise the cancer from his cranium, but he himself sure as dammit could cut out the little girl. And once she was dead, she could ride him no longer.

And then a new fury enveloped him. For she alone was the reason why he was back in a cell under lock and key; the reason why his brother Noah would now escape retribution; the reason why Lebrett would end his days strapped to a prison hospital bed, being administered insufficient painkillers until he died in agony and they burned his carcass. She had just managed to fuck up his long-planned revenge, so would have to die in his brother's place. And die slowly and painfully.

TUESDAY
19 SEPTEMBER

CHAPTER 10

It was lunchtime and Evergreen Souvenirs was closed for the day, the Carters having decided to remain at home. Cheryl was upstairs somewhere with the two girls, while Stanley sat on the back porch with Sheriff Frank Cantrillo and Deputy Ray Fischer, all three drinking Nantucket iced tea.

'Damnedest thing,' Fischer said yet again, 'the way those three assholes just gave themselves up.'

'Guilt,' offered Stanley, avoiding the sheriff's gaze.

'But that's the fourth time it's happened in your store,' insisted Fischer. 'And each time nobody gets hurt, while the bad guys surrender.'

'I'm a persuasive talker,' said Stanley, eyeing the deputy.

Ray Fischer was twenty-five, rangy and olive-skinned with sharp features, his long limbs always looking uncomfortable in his uniform. He was a complete contrast to the burly Cantrillo, whose thinning grey hair was rarely out of his cap, and whose Ray-Bans were as much a part of his face as the wide nose and thin lips. Despite his easy manner, there was an authority about his body language that seemed to come naturally to cop dynasties (his father and two uncles having been uniform cops in Philadelphia). Put simply, even in his fifties Frank Cantrillo was every inch the sheriff, while Deputy

Ray Fischer looked like an ill-prepared actor. These two formed the backbone of the town's small police department.

As they heard girlish laughter from upstairs, all three smiled. Seemed like Kara and Lorri were already getting over their recent ordeal.

'You must be a *damn* persuasive talker, Stan,' said Fischer. 'Those two other boys kept blubbing for an age afterwards.' He leaned forward. 'Have either of you noticed just how weird this place sometimes seems? It's like a kind of Stepford where everything's perfect, and nothing bad happens. Christ, the worst thing we ever suffered was that lace-bug epidemic of '91 screwing up that year's floral displays.'

Rhododendron was famous for the flowering shrubs that provided its name, so consequently a year of bad displays meant bad tourist business. Fortunately this latest year had proved one of the best ever.

'I don't call a visit by Jacob Lebrett and his gang "nothing happening",' Stanley argued, since the deputy was now treading on dangerous ground. 'And you said it yourself, Ray, this is the fourth attempted robbery we've had at the Evergreen. Another time it might just get real nasty.'

'And then it might not . . .'

'What's that supposed to mean?' interrupted Cantrillo.

'Nothing . . . Okay, Frank, when was the last time either of us saw a car wreck here involving a genuine resident?'

'Only last week Dan Fardon got hit by—'

'By an out-of-stater who pulled out without looking. I'm talking about native Rhoders being careless, or Rhoders speeding.'

'What you saying, Ray?' asked Stanley.

'I don't honestly know what I'm saying.'

'No change there.'

'No need to get personal, Frank.'

'Maybe not, but speaking of personal, I hope you weren't aiming to sell any story about Lebrett to the press.'

Fischer began to bluster, but Cantrillo was suddenly impatient.

'Ain't it time you got back on patrol, Ray? There's TV and press people all over town now. You'd better make sure they don't cause us no problems.'

'Okay.' Deputy Fischer was pleased for an excuse to leave. He raised his gangly frame from the sunlounger. 'Thanks for the tea, Stan.'

As the other two watched him leave, Stanley was the first to speak.

'You're sure he doesn't suspect anything?'

'What the hell's to suspect?' The sheriff finished his own tea. 'He ain't to know why Rhododendron's got the lowest crime rate in the goddamn Union. Or why the only hassle we get here is from outsiders – and even that don't last too long.'

'What was that crack about him selling stuff about Lebrett?'

Cantrillo sighed. 'Ray's got a gambling habit. Takes himself down to Foxwood's Casino most weekends he's free. I reckon he'll try and get money any way he can.'

Stanley leaned on the porch rail, staring out into the backyard. Colourful toys were strewn about as if a mini-tornado had hit. 'Funny how Lebrett worked it out. Leastways he knew not to look into our eyes.'

'How could he know?'

Stanley turned to face him. 'I just think he's one bright bastard.'

'I checked his prison records: IQ's 180-plus – a goddamn Einstein. Makes you wonder why he'd go round killing folk. His tally's nine that we actually know of . . . '

'His IQ didn't stop him getting caught, though.'

'That kinda personality, they get too confident. Think they're smarter than everyone else. And maybe they are, but they forget there's a lot more of us than of them – and while he may think he's some kind of one-off, we've dealt with a lot of others just like him.'

'Why's he called Beep-Beep?'

'From the Roadrunner. As a kid his only escape was watching cartoons. Saw his dad as Wyle E Coyote, and himself as Roadrunner, always outsmarting him – 'cept he never did. Got tattoos of that bird on him, wears a cartoon T-shirt. But we've only got Lebrett's word for what his father did to him.'

'Just how bad is Lebrett? I've read some stuff.'

Cantrillo settled back, and stared at the amber liquid in his glass. 'Short version: he's one twisted fuck. Claims to have been sexually abused by his father, a preacher no less, and loaned out similarly to his elder brother like a goddamn power tool. Left home in his early teens, soon fell into trouble – and he's spent most of his life since then behind bars. As far as we know, he's only killed a couple of people outside prison – the rest inside. He's cool, clever – and very violent.'

'The two outside jail? Were they women?'

'No, he boasts he doesn't do sex crimes, but that ain't much comfort for the deputy he shot in Columbus or the gas jockey he stabbed in Rutland. He's no thrill-killer, but you get in his way, you're doomed. Ruthless bastard.

'Last night he even beat up one of his two sidekicks. Claims he was trying to get rid of that little girl who put him behind bars, though why he should half-kill Pinder instead, God only knows.' He leaned forward, lowering his voice. 'He sure has got it bad for young Kara. Blames her completely for him getting caught – that really dented his pride. So damn near obsessed now, doesn't talk of anything else. But this afternoon he'll be shipped out to the State pen, and then it'll all be over for you. Besides, Lebrett's not long for this world.'

'He's dying of something?'

'Brain cancer, inoperable tumour. He escaped from the hospital while they were running a CAT scan on him. He's got a couple of months left at most. Course, that makes him even more dangerous: it'll either send him crazier than he is, or he'll want to take it out on the whole world. Hell, what's he got to lose? I doubt he's the kind who'll suddenly find God.'

'Kara *told* him he was going to die,' mused Stanley. 'Back in the store, I thought she meant she was going to make him kill himself, but maybe she could somehow tell . . .'

'Wouldn't surprise me. Those two girls are as smart as whips.'

'And getting smarter.' He ran his tongue over his cut lip. It would normally have healed by now. Cantrillo saw him wince.

'Your lip still hurting you?' he asked.

'Not really, but that's the strange part: it was just a cut lip so should have been gone in a few hours. This thing is like *ordinary* people suffer.'

Cantrillo leaned forward. 'I been noticing stuff, too. My back's been hurting the last few days, like I pulled a muscle. And a couple of nights back, I had me a beer, and puked like a teenager . . . Well, we normally don't drink, do we? Not ever. But it shouldn't affect me like that.'

'If I didn't know better, I'd say we were losing it.'

Just then, Cheryl came out through the back door, dressed in a yellow T-shirt and red shorts, her voluptuous figure evident through the thin material. Cantrillo whistled appreciatively. She gave him a knowing smile and a little twirl, then settled herself on the arm of Stanley's chair.

She held up her right hand, the nail of her third finger sporting a large black spot. 'I heard what you were just saying about us losing it. I caught this in the car door a couple of days back, and thought nothing of it. Now it hurts like a bitch and it looks set to split. Something's definitely not right with us these days.'

Stanley was concerned, but not so much for themselves. 'Well, if we're losing it, what about the girls? We might not be rich, but at least we've passed on to them the ability to get through life without being bothered by nuisances and injuries. What if they don't even have that any more?'

Cheryl shook her head. 'You saw the knife; and the way they controlled Lebrett. If anything, *their* powers are getting stronger. And Kara told me something else . . .' She glanced up at the girls' bedroom window, then hunched towards the two men, whispering.

'She said Lebrett came right into her bedroom, threatening her, last night. Now, I dismissed that as a nightmare after what happened yesterday. Christ, I had nightmares too!

But when I overheard you talking about Lebrett freaking out last night, too, I felt sure a guy like him couldn't just be dreaming. So I think . . . I think Kara *was* actually inside his head.'

'Like when she was trying to influence him to stab himself?'

'Yes, they somehow got into his mind, and were *forcing* him to harm himself. We've never been able to do anything like that ourselves – and I've never seen *them* do it before either.'

'So, if they're getting stronger and we're getting weaker, what the hell does it all mean?'

Cantrillo stood up and stretched. 'If I didn't want to rain on our own parade, I'd say they were drawing it away from us – towards themselves. I've heard rumours that some other kids are also getting more powerful. Tasmin Jonaczek is one. Doc Morrow tells me she broke her leg in two places just a couple of weeks back, but it's almost healed already and she'll be out of her cast in days like it never happened. And I just heard her mother Ellie's gone down with the flu. Now, *that's* a first for any of us adults.'

They fell silent, each lost in their own thoughts. They had been so accustomed to the protection their unusual condition engendered, it would be very difficult now to adjust to its loss. But, more worrying than that, what exactly was happening to their children?

Suddenly there was an eruption of distant gunshots. Cantrillo was up and running through the house before the noise had ceased.

He bounded down the front steps to climb into his Explorer, Stanley and Cheryl hurrying after him.

Cantrillo leaned out of his car window. 'Damn radio's dead, but those shots came from the north side of town.'

The Sheriff's Office and jail lay in that direction.

Stanley ran over and jumped into his Cherokee, but his hand refused to turn the ignition.

Cheryl leaned through the window. 'What is it?'

'Can't switch it on,' he groaned. 'Something's working in my head.'

The sheriff pulled up alongside them. 'Keep out of this!' he shouted.

Cheryl suddenly pulled open the back door of Cantrillo's Explorer, and dived inside.

'Get out!' he barked.

She slammed the door. 'Just drive, Frank!'

There were several more gunshots.

'Holy shit!' He accelerated away.

Stanley leaped out of the Jeep, as if to run after them, but soon realized it was pointless. He looked back towards the house, to see Kara and Lorri on the doorstep.

'Come on, you two, get inside.'

'Where's mommy going?'

'To help Uncle Frank.'

Yet more gunfire.

Stanley ushered his daughters inside, but something was worrying him more than the distant shooting. Why the hell had Cheryl got into Frank's cruiser? Normally she would stay well clear of trouble, not head straight into it. Something was different, seriously different.

CHAPTER 11

Kara and Lorri played in their monkey-themed bedroom, under Stanley's anxious eye. As yet another shot rang out, startling him, he flipped on their portable television. A Tom and Jerry cartoon – perfect. He turned up the sound of comic crashes and bangs.

'What are you looking at?' he asked, when he noticed them both staring at the window overlooking the empty backyard.

'Sheriff Frank and those *bad* men.'

'But he's not out there.'

'We can see him. He's in his car, and mommy's down on the floor behind him. They're driving down Main Street, and the bad men are standing outside the Sheriff's Office, with Uncle Ray. They're holding guns and Uncle Ray's all bloody.'

Oh, sweet Jesus. Stanley realized now that the two little girls were using the window glass like a television – the drama unfolding a mile away appearing right in front of them like *NYPD Blue*.

'Come over here, girls.'

They did as requested, but their eyes remained focused on the middle distance. He guided them to sit down on one bed, then dropped to his knees in front of them. Taking their cold little hands in his own, he was aware they couldn't see him.

'What's happening now?' he asked gently, his heart racing.

'Sheriff Frank has stopped the car, but he's told mommy to stay down out of sight,' Kara answered.

Lorri piped up. 'Sheriff Frank's getting out now. There's a lot of smoke.'

Tasmin Jonacezk's leg was healing fine, just as her mother would have expected. However, Dr Morrow was yet again astonished at how swiftly his young patient was able to recover from any injury or illness.

'Could've sworn she'd need another fortnight.' He rose and followed Ellie out of the child's pink bedroom. 'She really must have the constitution of an ox.'

'Charming,' grumbled Tasmin from the bedroom – only eight but eloquent beyond her years. She shared her mother's dark looks.

'Would you like a coffee?' asked Ellie, blowing her nose. She insisted it was only a cold, but the doctor suspected something worse.

A widower in his late fifties, Dr James Morrow was still actively seeking a partner, so accepted her offer with customary enthusiasm. As she led the way downstairs, he admired the sway of her bejeaned hips. She might be a dozen years younger than himself, but he was never one to discriminate on the grounds of age.

'You really should lie down, yourself, Ellie,' he suggested, knowing this advice would be ignored.

'I'm fine. Just feeling a bit tired.'

Tasmin suddenly cried out in pain.

Dropping the percolator with a crash, Ellie beat Morrow up the staircase – and reached her daughter's bedroom just in time to catch Tasmin falling out of the bed.

'What is it, honey?' Ellie demanded.

'They're shooting at the sheriff,' mumbled Tasmin, her eyes looking distant.

'What does she mean?' asked Dr Morrow, helping Tasmin back on to her pillows. The girl seemed to be in a trance.

'They escaped from the cells. They've started shooting,' she intoned mechanically.

The doctor exchanged an anxious glance with her mother. He was aware of the girl's remarkable ability to heal herself, but this was something else.

But Ellie Jonaczek knew full well what was happening: her daughter was experiencing another psychic episode. She had kept quiet about these, hoping they might be a passing phase.

'They've got hold of Deputy Ray. They won't let him go. There's a black man and a fat man and' – she shivered – 'a tall man with horrible eyes.'

The scene confronting Sheriff Frank Cantrillo as he approached his office at the top of Main Street looked fairly normal except for two details.

Outside Baxter's Bakery a pair of vans, one belonging to Channel 8 NewsEye, had collided, and their occupants – together with some terrified bystanders – were now huddled inside the bakery itself. And beyond, in front of the single-storey Sheriff's Office, stood Ray Fischer's cruiser, two of its tyres shot out. It was wreathed in smoke pouring from the office entrance.

What the hell had happened here?

Suddenly four people burst out through the door.

Recognizing them instantly, Cantrillo brought his Explorer to a screeching halt side-on across the middle of the street. Ordering Cheryl to keep down, he slid out and leaned across the hood, training his revolver on the little group which had just emerged.

Huddling down in the back of the police car, Cheryl felt angry and frustrated. She was no heroine these days – her brave moments had ended in a Coast Guard Sea King helicopter in Seattle nine years before – but that didn't stop her from feeling the urge to participate. The only weapon at hand was a crow-bar.

'Stop right there!' Cantrillo ordered.

The three escapees all stared at him.

'Put down the gun, sheriff,' countered Lebrett, 'or you'll see your deputy here decorating the street! This ain't a nego-tiation: I got all the aces.'

'State troopers are already on their way,' countered Cantrillo.

'Got a good ten minutes yet – all the time in the world. So while I got your man here eating my gun, I want some information from you.'

'You signal surrender by raising your hands.'

'I want the name and address of that little bitch who put me in here.'

Cantrillo was astounded. 'What?'

'I want that little girl who fucked up my head. I want her name.'

'No way, Lebrett. You know I ain't gonna give you that.'

'Then your deputy's gonna die.'

Cantrillo didn't reply.

'What's this little girl shit?' Pinder hissed to Lebrett, aware how easily they could be picked off by a sniper. 'We should get outta here right away.'

'I'm with fat boy,' agreed Hilts, scanning the street nervously. 'We got the leverage, so let's beat it out of this ass-wipe town *now*.'

'Shut up, you. I want the girl.' Lebrett jabbed his revolver deeper into Fischer's mouth. 'You got three seconds to give me a name, sheriff!'

Cantrillo was confounded. What the hell was this maniac trying to do? 'You kill my deputy, you got no hostage.'

'One!'

'Hey, man,' whined Pinder. 'You shoot him, we're *all* fucking dead.'

'I want that fucking girl. Two!'

'Shit, man, this is crazy!' yelled Hilts in obvious panic.

'Three!'

'He's coming here! He wants to come here!' Kara squealed, her eyes wide.

'Who does, baby?' asked Stanley, stroking her hair.

'The bad man. He wants Sheriff Frank to tell him where I am.'

What the hell for? 'Don't worry, baby.'

'Why does he want *me*, daddy?'

'Now they've started shooting!'

Stanley could hear it, too. But why was Lebrett so obsessed with an eight-year-old girl?

On the count of 'Three', Ray Fischer let out a strangled cry – but no shot followed.

Lebrett had eased his finger off the trigger. He so wanted to get that girl, he had almost lost his senses. Of course, he needed the deputy for a hostage – what the hell had he been thinking of? Their first priority was getting away. *Then* he could figure out how to get hold of the little bitch.

Everyone breathed a sigh of relief – but it was short-lived. Lebrett yanked the gun from Fischer's mouth, and turned to fire at the sheriff himself. Pinder and Hilts followed his lead, their gunfire again shattering the calm.

As Cantrillo ducked behind his car, he remembered that Cheryl was stranded inside. He had to draw their fire away quickly from the Explorer.

Glancing to his right, he saw there was a good twenty feet of open blacktop before he could reach the cover of some cars parked at the side of the street. *Hell and damnation!* There was no time to waste. He pulled open the rear door.

'Get out, but keep down!' he hissed. 'I'll draw their fire!'

Then he charged over towards the parked vehicles – and almost made it.

Tasmin suddenly screamed and fell back, clutching the thigh of her unbroken leg.

'Baby, what is it?' asked her horrified mother.

'The sheriff's been shot! It really hurts.'

The pain on her face almost convinced Dr Morrow the child herself was wounded. He pulled the protective hand away from her thigh, expecting to see blood there. But there were only the smiling bunny-rabbits on her pyjama bottoms.

'He's fallen over. He can't get up,' Tasmin gasped.

'Have *you* any idea what's happening here, Ellie?' pleaded Dr Morrow.

Ellie Jonacezk knew full well what was happening, but was too upset by her daughter's terror to explain.

As Tasmin became increasingly hysterical, Dr Morrow rooted in his bag for a sedative, till the pale-faced mother restrained his arm.

'Jim, she'll be all right, trust me. But Frank Cantrillo really *is* hurt. *He's* the one who needs you. I'll look after Taz.'

Dr Morrow looked very uncertain. 'Okay, I'll talk to you about this later, Ellie,' he said, closing his bag. Then he hurried downstairs, confused and frightened in equal measure.

As Cantrillo's leg buckled he sprawled on to his front, bullets still pinging around him. Crawling frantically, he managed to reach the cover of the nearest parked vehicle without further injury. As he rolled on to his back, he saw blood rapidly staining his beige pants. He wasn't going anywhere further.

Cheryl dropped out of the cruiser and hugged the macadam. At least they had stopped firing at the cop car, but she could soon become a target again. Suddenly two men appeared from behind, crouching down on either side of her. Her initial panic subsided as she recognized temporary deputies Ed Spurrell and Nick Renzetti, both more used to dealing with summer tourist traffic than with gunfights.

'The three of us here could take those lot out,' muttered Spurrell, handing Cheryl a Colt .45, then cocking his Remington rifle.

'None of us is a good enough shot,' she cautioned. 'We might hit Ray – and we're pretty exposed here.'

They were trapped right in the middle of the broad highway running through the heart of Rhododendron. Colonial-style, pastel-painted stores and guest houses flanked the wide sidewalks on each side, and cars were parked nose-in to the kerbs. At intervals along the sidewalks stood large tubs carrying picturesque arrays of the town's famous rhododendrons: red Elizabeths, Britannias and Cynthias mingled with Pink Pearls, Purple Splendours and white Sapphos. They were looking tired now, their flowers bleached pale, but they still gave the street its distinctive appearance. A photogenic display that seemed unrelated to the bloody scene unfolding beside them.

Right ahead stood the Sheriff's Office and the town church, the latter fronting on to a small cobbled square used for street markets and live concerts. The three escaped prisoners had set the Sheriff's Office on fire, and the gates to neighbouring St Mark's were firmly locked, so Lebrett's only chance of escape was along the road behind him, which led to the town of Keene.

Cantrillo was slumped against the trunk of a silver Mitsubishi Carisma. 'You surrender now, no one gets hurt!' he croaked defiantly.

'No more fucking chit-chat!' Lebrett shouted. 'We're leaving town, sheriff, and there ain't a damn thing you can do about it!'

'We can nail 'em,' insisted Renzetti to Cheryl. 'I take the black guy, Ed gets the fat one, and you go for a head shot on Lebrett.'

It was tempting but there was still too much risk of them hitting Ray Fischer.

A billow of smoke suddenly belched from the doors of the Sheriff's Office, engulfing all four men in a dark, choking cloud. As it drifted further across the street, Cheryl decided to take her chance. Leaving the cover of the police car, she darted to one side, and dived down between the Carisma itself and an Escort. She then shuffled over on her knees to check out the wounded sheriff.

'I'm okay,' he gasped. 'Just keep your head down.'

As the smoke dissipated, Cheryl realized that only two of the fugitives remained guarding Ray Fischer. The black man, Hilts, was missing.

She edged round to the front of the Escort, then crept alongside two more parked vehicles until she had narrowed her angle of view towards the Sheriff's Office. They wouldn't have long, and this crisis was only going to be resolved with bullets, so the closer she got, the better her chances of getting in a good hit.

Looking backwards across the sidewalk to Agnathia Whipple's flower shop, she could see the terrified seventy-year-old kneeling just inside her open front door. Cheryl was about to move on to the cover of a Bravada pick-up, when she received a sharp dig in the back.

'Lose the cannon, bitch.'

She glanced over her shoulder to see Hilts right behind her, his dark face sheathed in sweat.

'Okay, okay.' She carefully placed the .45 on the hood of the Oldsmobile pick-up. Still crouching, she slowly turned to face him.

'Shoot me,' she suggested.

'What?'

'Shoot me, you little cocksucker,' she hissed. 'Show me how big your balls are, and shoot me in the face.'

The guy raised his .38 to aim at her head. 'My pleasure.'

If ever Cheryl needed proof she was losing her self-defence mechanism, she had it now. Her normal defence abilities invariably guaranteed surrender from even the most violent of assailants. Only yesterday, in the store, she had subdued this very man with a stare, but now that was no longer working, and the evidence was his finger squeezing the trigger two feet away from her face.

She couldn't run, couldn't duck, couldn't beg for mercy or plead that she'd made a mistake – all she could do now was die.

'Bye-bye, cunt,' he sneered.

'What would Lebrett do?' she suddenly blurted.

Hilts paused, his leader's name acting like some religious invocation, but this small delay was long enough for her to slap the gun away from her face, and launch a fist at his chin. Her knuckles made contact with his jaw just as the gun went off. Totally unprepared for her attack, he crumpled.

Picking up the weapon, she leaned over and whispered in his ear: 'He wouldn't hesitate, asshole.'

Satisfied her assailant was otherwise unarmed, she turned and glanced towards the Sheriff's Office – only to feel a punch on her right shoulder, and hear a loud report as she was powered back into a parked Geo Prizm.

Oh hell, I've been shot!

'How bad is the sheriff hurt?' demanded Stanley.

The twins were gripping Kong and King so tightly their knuckles were white.

'Hurts here bad,' said Lorri, tapping her thigh.

Stanley was beside himself with worry. Cheryl was probably still somewhere close to Cantrillo, yet he couldn't bring himself to ask his daughters what was happening to her. Suddenly both girls' eyes widened in horror.

'Mommy's shot! Mommy's shot, too!' gasped Lorri.

Ice gripped Stanley's heart as he watched the colour drain from their faces.

'Where was she hit?'

Each girl ran a shaking hand up to her right shoulder, eyes squinting as if in pain.

Oh Jesus, what should I do?

'She can't move her arm.' Kara was now clutching her sister's hand. 'Oh, daddy, daddy, mommy's hurt.'

With another gunshot, the car window beside Cheryl's face disintegrated, showering her with glass. Dropping down again, she tried raising her right arm but her shoulder wouldn't respond. She reached for the discarded .45 with her left hand, knowing she was a useless southpaw shot. Then she realized that Spurrell and Renzetti, still crouching behind the Sheriff's Explorer, might now take the situation into their own hands.

'Ed! Nick! Don't—'

Too late! There was a loud exchange of gunfire, a yelp of pain – then horrible silence followed. Cheryl forced herself further alongside the Prizm until she could observe the police vehicle more clearly. *Oh hell, no!* Spurrell and Renzetti were both lying on their backs in the road, rifles discarded next to their feet. Renzetti twitched once, then stilled.

In front of the Sheriff's Office, she saw all three men were still standing.

'Sheriff? You still talking to me?' shouted Lebrett.

Cheryl watched the group of men start to edge forward.

'Hilts, where the hell you gone?' Lebrett demanded. 'If you've gone and hurt my boy, sheriff . . .'

Cheryl glanced over to see Cantrillo lying on his side, clearly dazed and bleeding badly.

Lebrett and Pinder took another couple of steps forward, dragging Ray Fischer between them. Cheryl knew her only chance now was to use Hilts as her own hostage. Stuffing the Colt into her waistband, she crawled on her belly towards the spot where she had left him. Except Hilts was no longer there.

Scarcely able to believe her bad luck, Cheryl pulled the gun from her waistband. Then she heard a voice.

'Hey, Jacob, don't shoot! It's me! Oren!'

'Hilts, where's your gun?' shouted Lebrett.

'That storekeeper bitch decked me.'

'Well, I just blew a hole in her, so get yourself over here.'

Cheryl watched Hilts stumble back towards his accomplices.

Then, with Hilts and Pinder scanning the street, the four men quickly worked their way over to the sheriff's Explorer and climbed in.

'Drive, deputy,' were the last words Cheryl heard before they roared off.

Pinder leaned out of a rear side-window and took several potshots at the line of parked cars. The gas tank of a Mazda erupted, tossing it several feet into the air before it slammed back to earth, spewing flaming fuel over the adjacent vehicles.

Spotting a river of flaming fuel heading towards her, Cheryl threw herself at the terrified Mrs Whipple, forcing them both inside the flower shop. Seconds later, its large display window was shattered by another explosion, and fire was scorching its way inside. Cheryl was hurled on to her back, covered in loose flowers, but she quickly tipped over a couple of large vases, spilling water to extinguish the approaching flames.

By the time she got to her feet again, four other cars were alight, and people had come running out of other stores and houses to check on the fate of Spurrell and Renzetti.

Someone had dragged Sheriff Cantrillo into the middle of the road, where they ripped off his belt to apply a tourniquet to his leg.

'Call the Fire Department!' Cheryl yelled at the dazed Mrs Whipple – just then remembering that Spurrell, Renzetti and Fischer themselves comprised fifty per cent of the little town's volunteer fire service.

CHAPTER 12

General Ward and Dr Gaines reached Andrews Air Force base at 1.40 p.m., Eastern Time. Despite the near-empty bottle of Jack Daniels they'd abandoned on the plane, both were feeling very sober. They were given a police escort straight to the Pentagon, then rushed through security and ferried immediately to an elevator servicing one of the inner rings of the massive five-sided complex.

After a minute's descent they found themselves in a small, dazzling-white anteroom, furnished only with a video console and a second, handleless door with the single word CRUX stamped on it in red.

As the elevator doors clicked shut behind them, the video screen sprang to life, revealing the head of a Marine captain.

'Please step forward and look directly into the view-finder. Also identify yourself by name, rank and serial number, then place both thumbs onto the slots on either side of this screen.'

Ward did as requested, staring through the goggles fixed above the screen.

'Now you, Alberta.'

'What's this?'

Ward explained. 'Retinal scan, voice-print, fingerprints – so they know you're really who you say you are.'

'Yeah, but when do I get to know who *they* are?'

'Just do as asked, please,' said the face on the screen.

The soldier's facial expression remained so unchanging that she suspected he was computer-generated. Nonetheless she did as requested, identifying herself as 'Alberta Gaines PhD, Project Head, World Asteroid Trajectory Computation Scheme.'

'Okay, you're both clear,' announced the captain. 'Please step through the door to your right.'

As they made their way into a short passage beyond, Gaines muttered, 'How the hell did they get hold of my retina pattern?'

'You submitted to an eye-test when you joined WATCH, didn't you?'

'The bastards.'

'Oh, we're not so bad,' said a grey-haired, middle-aged man offering her his hand with a smile familiar from television.

'You're Douglas Compton,' she gasped in embarrassment.

'Well, that puts you into the mere twenty-three per cent who can recognize their own Vice President. Progress, maybe?'

'I'm sorry—'

He held up his hand. 'We only have time for the formalities of security. So let's get on with it, shall we?'

He stepped aside to reveal a long, darkened room dominated by a bank of monitors filling the entire far wall. There were at least thirty of them, all showing different images, mostly in colour. In front of them, a long mahogany table boasted twin rows of traditional green lamps running down the centre. Seated around the table were some two dozen men, half of them in uniform. The room itself was cold, the air conditioning audible. Gaines shivered.

'I apologize for the rush,' said the Vice-President, 'but we'll leave the introductions until later. Suffice to say the only absentee of note this morning is the President. He's grounded by Hurricane Billy in Cuba, but we have a secure telephone link with him, as well as to other interested parties, should the need arise.'

Ward followed Gaines and the Vice-President the length of the room. He recognized the different uniforms, and many of the wearers. There were the Joint Chiefs of Staff, Admiral Lawrence for the Navy, and Generals McKee, Clarens, and Shakespeare representing the Army, Air Force and Marines respectively. He also recognized the Secretaries of State and Defense, the White House Chief of Staff, the President's National Security Advisor, and his Deputy Press Secretary. Others could be identified by their security badges – the heads of the CIA, FBI, Secret Service; the Secretaries of the Army, Navy and Air Force, and their senior aides. There was also a handful of senators and congressmen. That Ward was the lowest-ranking military man present spoke volumes. Aside from the President himself, all the most important people in the nation appeared to be seated around this table.

'If you could sit here, General Ward, and you here, Doctor Gaines. We've already set up the equipment for you.'

Hiding both surprise and terror behind a fixed grin, Gaines seated herself between an admiral and a senator, and began linking up her laptop to the controls built into the table top before her.

General Clarens was speaking. 'And you insist your computations are accurate?'

Gaines cleared her throat. Her beaded braids rattled with a nervous flick of her head. Ward looked skyward.

'Yes, sir,' she said. 'We've checked the data on our own systems eight times, run diagnostics on all the gear, and uploaded the data to SQUAWK at MIT.'

'SQUAWK?'

'A super computer secured for military purposes. Unbreachable from the outside, its information is wiped as soon as any program is run. It's a super-checker.'

'And?'

'Three times it's come back with the same answer,' explained General Ward, aware that Gaines's air of schoolgirl enthusiasm, to say nothing of her appearance – like Oprah Winfrey on a cheap date – was already grating with several men in the room.

'Could someone explain this for the non-scientists?' asked Willard, the President's Deputy Press Secretary.

There was muttered agreement. General Ward wanted to explain things himself, but knew he wasn't anywhere as clued up as Gaines. As she had predicted, he was now regretting his ignorance.

'I think it would be easiest if Doctor Gaines told you about it, since she has been working with WATCH from the start.' He leaned down and whispered to her, 'Keep it short, keep it simple – and stop grinning.'

Gaines walked to the head of the table. 'If I could have

the lights down.' She keyed up the laptop with its PowerPoint visual display system. Now that she was in the dark, and talking about what she knew best, her confidence returned quickly.

'Okay. To keep it simple . . .' she began, a diagram of the solar system appearing on every screen behind her. She then proceeded to repeat almost verbatim the explanation she had given Ward earlier waiting for their flight.

No one else spoke during the next few minutes and, once she had finished, there seemed a general reluctance to ask the obvious question. Finally, Admiral Lawrence cleared his throat. Everyone knew he had seven daughters and that, despite a long career at sea, he was a devoted family man.

'Bottom line, Doctor Gaines, what are our chances?'

For a long time Gaines stared at the men around the table, only the lower halves of their faces illuminated in the light from the table lamps. Suddenly, her knees went weak and she had to clutch at the table for support. Only now was she able to grasp the full import of what she was about to say, so long had she spent living with theories and programs.

'Our chances are zero, I'm afraid.' She cleared her throat again, and sipped some water.

'Meaning?' asked the Vice-President.

'Meaning zero, sir. *Nil.* When that asteroid hits, it will spell the end of all life on earth. The only question is how quickly afterwards we will all die. As the asteroid enters our atmosphere, the air will become super-heated and will ignite, and anything immediately below it will be incinerated. Within a few hundred kilometres of the initial impact, there will be instant and total destruction of all life. Basic physics demands that for every action there must be an equal and opposite reaction: you hit the earth with the power of ten thousand megatons, that energy has got to be released either as movement or as heat.

'When all the material blasted upwards from the impact comes back down again because of gravity, as it re-enters the atmosphere it too will become heated due to friction. There would be so much heat then, it would reach the surface as infra-red rays. Anything exposed would fry. Forests would spontaneously ignite. All car gas-tanks would explode. It's not a matter of a fire starting and spreading. Literally *everywhere* would go up. Imagine California – the entire state – on fire, and everyone and everything in it.

'Fires require oxygen. From where do these giant fires draw their oxygen? From the atmosphere. Result: firestorms. In 1923 a firestorm consumed Tokyo, killing 120,000 people. It sucked in all the oxygen, then exploded, roaring back outwards at speeds in excess of two hundred k.p.h. Now, think not of a city but of a state, a region . . . of the whole country. And all these fires will generate soot: combusted material rising into the atmosphere. So the sun is blotted out, darkness covers the entire planet. You saw what happened in the Philippines when Mount Pinatubo erupted. Imagine the entire world plunged into night. And this night will last for weeks, probably months. No sun, no light, no heat. Then, of course, there'll be the rain.

'Water vapour from oceans and the melted ice caps will have been released into the atmosphere in unprecedented quantities. All this water will eventually fall back as precipitation, aided by all those particles in the atmosphere which will provide the raindrops with their core. However, the heat generated by the impact shockwave and the subsequent super-heating of the atmosphere will also have led to a breakdown of the natural oxygen-nitrogen balance. The result will be the release of devastating quantities of nitrous oxide, which will react with the remaining oxygen and the water vapour to produce acid rain. I mean nitric acid, in fact, which would burn anything it touched – animal, vegetable or mineral.'

The silence in the room was as chilling as Gaines's words.

'Meanwhile, carbon dioxide levels will now be so high as to become incapable of being processed by what is left of the planet. Remember, green vegetation, of which by then there will be none, is the normal processor of carbon dioxide. The result is the greenhouse effect we've all heard about, and a warming of the climate. The entire planet would indeed become a greenhouse, with temperatures as much as thirty degrees Celsius higher than at present. And *this* will remain the situation for thousands of years, because without veg-etation there's no mechanism to remove the carbon dioxide.

'To be frank, gentlemen, when we locate the impact site, I'll gladly volunteer to go there myself. I'll see Erebus as a rapidly brightening star, then as a moon, then – as it eclipses the sun's brilliance – I will cease to exist. It will all be so quick I won't even know it has happened.'

'Why the hell didn't you spot this thing sooner?'

'Because we didn't have the proper resources to do the job. Something this small takes a lot of finding. All that's up there is a lot of white lights and even more black spaces. It's luck we spotted it at all, in fact. Normally asteroids come from outside the earth's orbit, but we were looking towards the sun when . . .'

She paused for a moment, something nagging at her. *When, and why, had they actually decided to examine that part of the sky?* But she was jolted back to the present when one of the senators spoke up.

'Surely we could set up some safe havens underground? Sheltered areas, with greenhouses, artificial light . . .'

'With respect, sir, this isn't the movies. We have just four days left.'

'Four days?' gasped General Shakespeare, fumbling for a glass of water and spilling its contents.

'Oh God,' said the Vice-President.

Bob Nazir, White House Chief of Staff shook his head. 'I don't think God has anything to—'

'God has everything to do with it!' insisted the Vice-President. 'According to Doctor Gaines, He's our only hope.'

'Somehow, if God is involved in the equation,' offered Gaines, 'I think He might have sent this asteroid someplace else.'

'So what the hell can we do?' asked Aldred Hyatt, head of the CIA.

'Nothing,' piped up Ward. 'There's nowhere to run, nowhere to hide. Just a matter of dying sooner rather than later.'

'When will the public know about it?'

'As soon as someone with half a brain and a telescope sees it, and gets it checked out.'

'And then?'

'You need to reassure people.'

'Reassure them that they're going to die?' asked General Shakespeare.

'Might I make a suggestion?' offered Ward.

'Anything,' pleaded the Vice-President.

'What's the absolute earliest we can predict its point of impact?'

'We know it will impact in the north-eastern USA. In a few hours from now we'll know the whereabouts to within a few miles.'

'What if it hit the Atlantic instead? Couldn't water absorb the shock?' asked another senator, wiping his brow with a handkerchief.

'Initially, yes,' sighed Gaines, making no effort to hide her contempt. 'But then you get a three hundred-metre-high tsunami travelling at up to six hundred kilometres per hour. That'd be quite a spectacle in Boston Harbor, but even if I was on top of the John Hancock Tower I'd still be looking up at it.'

'Where's all this leading?' demanded Nazir.

'Deflection – and hope,' said General Ward, glad to offer practical advice. 'If we can provide an honest and accurate point of impact, we can start evacuating people from that area.'

'Pointless!'

'Impractical.'

'A waste of resources!'

'I know, I know!' Ward stood up and paced the length of the room. 'But at least we'd be able to retain an element of order among the rest of the country for those two days. Otherwise we'll have total anarchy. What would *you* do if you knew everything was about to be destroyed without any hope of a reprieve? Every man, woman and child wakes up tomorrow to find themselves on death row with only their faith left to them – if they have one. For those without any beliefs, anarchy would become their god. No repercussions, no fear of trial or incarceration – hell, who's going to care about law and order when there's only days left? So what I'm saying is this: give us an impact site, and we can give people hope, however small, that it won't be as bad as they think.'

'He's right,' admitted Gaines, impressed for once. 'Tell them it's going to get colder, they'll just think of Finland. Tell them it'll get dark, they'll think of Finland in winter. Give those in the impact area the *impression* of a fighting chance. I'm not as pessimistic as General Ward about how people will react. I think you'll find there are a lot of decent people out there who will pull together—'

'Until they realize there's nothing to pull together for,' muttered McKintyre, Secretary of State. 'Surely we couldn't keep the scale of the event under wraps?'

'You can if you institute martial law and censor the media.' Gaines could see several of the military men shifting at this suggestion; plainly she was now talking their language. She folded up her laptop computer. 'I was wondering if I could have my team here with me. WATCH protocol has us coordinating world sightings and information on SQUAWK.'

'Yes, of course,' said Vice-President Compton. 'I'll get your people up here right away. We have a team securing your facility already.'

'To keep people out?' she asked.

'No, to keep your team in,' said General Ward, amazed at the woman's naivety. 'This mustn't leak—'

- 98 -

'Jesus, what?' gasped Compton, who was on the telephone.

All heads turned. 'All of them? When? And the . . . Christ. Any idea? No, no, secure it. Then get Specials in, see if you can find any clues. Keep me informed.'

He put the telephone down, and ran his hand through his lank grey hair. He looked around the table, then at Gaines.

'There's no easy way to . . . Doctor, I'm afraid your team won't be . . . Your people are dead. Our Secure Team arrived there ten minutes ago, and found them all dead at their posts – gassed. Software is missing, and all other material detailing your work on this asteroid.'

Gaines was suddenly unable to speak.

General Ward, however, was able to articulate the obvious question. 'Who?'

Compton shrugged. 'No idea of who, unless Specials can turn up forensic evidence, but whoever it is, they now know everything we know.'

'They were *gassed*?' said Gaines in disbelief.

'Powerful agent, instantly effective, quick dispersal. Professional.'

It was this last word that had the most effect on the assembled minds. As Gaines rushed from the room, all eyes came to rest on the imposing figure of Declan Brodie, Chief of the Secret Service.

He picked up a phone. As he waited, he covered the receiver with his hand. 'WATCH is military. Not my jurisdiction.'

'Maybe not,' said the Vice-President. 'But I doubt those responsible for this were from the military, do you?'

'So what contingencies have we for an information leak?' asked the President's Deputy Press Secretary.

General Ward let out a bitter laugh. 'We don't have contingencies for the damn event itself, never mind a leak!'

CHAPTER 13

Stanley found Cheryl sitting in the passenger seat of Dr Morrow's green VW Rabbit. She grimaced as the doctor tended her wound through the open door.

'You okay, honey?' asked Stanley, taking hold of her good hand.

'Have a guess.' She offered him a sarcastic smile.

'Just a flesh wound. She'll be fine,' announced Dr Morrow.

Frank Cantrillo limped up, his right trouser leg caked with blood, the belt still tight around his thigh. For them, usually wounds even this serious would soon heal, but both suspected this was not the case today.

'Paramedics have taken away Ed and Nick. They predict they've both got a fighting chance. Brave but stupid men,' he concluded, wincing. 'Then they pulled Gino out of my office. Head wound and smoke inhalation: fifty-fifty. He must have made some small mistake in handling the prisoners, then Ray turned up and they got themselves a better hostage.'

'What will they do to Ray?' asked Cheryl.

'Keep him as long as they need him, then kill him. I just wish they'd taken me instead.'

'That's dumb talk, Frank,' said the doctor. He had now turned to Cantrillo's leg.

Bystanders were congregating, and the sheriff angrily shouted for them to move on. 'You know what happened in the Evergreen yesterday,' he said. 'If I had stayed close to those three in the cells, they wouldn't be on the loose now.'

'Not so sure about that,' countered Stanley, helping Cheryl to stand. 'Remember Lebrett realized our eyes are the key. And I don't think we've got even that facility as strong as before.'

'Eyes? What eyes?' interjected Alex Maslin, editor of the *Rhododendron Display*. Hot in his familiar tight, white suit, Maslin was also the local newspaper's proprietor, reporter, photographer and printer – with a corpulent frame large enough to accommodate all five roles.

'Nothing. We were saying Ray Fischer got a cut over his eye,' Cheryl lied. There were quite a few townsfolk who were in on their strange secret – were *part* of their secret – but Maslin wasn't one of them.

As Stanley followed Cheryl away, Cantrillo hobbled behind them towards Fischer's car. There he unhooked the radio microphone, and double-checked that his APB had been broadcast. Satisfied, he tossed the microphone back into the car and sagged against the door.

Just then, sirens filled the afternoon air and three state trooper cruisers screeched to a halt behind the pair already parked in the centre of the street. A couple of TV vans and a radio car followed in their wake.

A captain hurried up, and he and the sheriff engaged in a heated exchange before the man ran back to his car to issue orders over the radio.

A group of locals immediately surrounded Cheryl,

Stanley and the sheriff, like a delegation. A middle-aged teacher called Iris Bright snagged Cheryl's elbow.

'My son Petie "saw" all this,' she whispered.

'And my Bobby did, too,' added skeletal Carl Templeton, the local garage owner. 'Told me everything bit by bit while we were hiding out. He saw the sheriff and you and Ray . . .' he trailed off, plainly as baffled as Iris was.

Stanley and Cheryl had been aware of their own children's increasing telepathic ability for at least a year now. But were there other kids too?

'Is this the first time it's happened?' Cheryl asked quietly.

'Yes—' started Templeton.

But Iris Bright interrupted him. 'No,' she said. 'Petie's been seeing stuff for a few weeks now – but only involving people who have been "blessed".'

That would explain why the children had felt the physical and emotional pain of Frank Cantrillo's predicament but not Ray Fischer's. Frank was one of them, whilst Ray – and many others in town – was ignorant of the unusual psychic bond between forty-one of their fellow townspeople.

'Okay, keep this quiet,' advised Cheryl. 'I think we should call another meeting.'

'How about in my garage? Come round in an hour,' offered Templeton, desperate for an explanation for his son's odd behaviour. He pointed over Cheryl's shoulder towards a TV crew setting up their satellite relay outside the smouldering carcass of the Sheriff's Office. 'Most folks'll still be hanging round here, so we won't attract attention.'

They all agreed to pass the word round town to the other 'blessed'.

'I'll be tied up here with the troopers,' apologized Cantrillo. He suddenly gasped with pain. 'Or else in the hospital.'

'And what about Ray?' Cheryl began. 'Perhaps we should wait . . . '

'No,' insisted Cantrillo. 'Whatever you do isn't going to change what Lebrett's up to. Have your meeting, see what you can work out.' He clasped the padding Dr Morrow had strapped to his wound. 'Something strange is happening, and we need to know what it is.'

Stanley stared anxiously at Cheryl. If all the benefits of the mysterious gift they had both enjoyed over the last nine years were about to be taken away, they had better be prepared, because it would mean a strange and frightening new existence for the pair of them.

CHAPTER 14

The Sheriff's Explorer slewed from one side of the road to the other, Ray Fischer struggling to maintain control as the blood ran into his eyes. Trees bordered the road on either side as the two-lane highway twisted around on a hilly landscape.

'I can't see! I can't see!' he shouted in panic.

Lebrett nudged him in the side with his revolver. 'You can see all right, pig. Just fucking drive.'

They were ten miles out of Rhododendron when the helicopter appeared. Lebrett knew that a hick town like Rhododendron wouldn't have its own chopper, and it was highly unlikely that state troopers could have got one into the area so fast, so who the hell was it up there? He peered up through the trees to watch the machine's progress.

Pinder leaned out of the rear window, and got off two shots at the black MD-500E before Lebrett punched him on the back of the head.

'Leave it, asshole! You want that fucking thing dropping on top of us?'

Lebrett studied the helicopter for clues to its occupants but could see no markings. Suddenly the off-roader's radio crackled into life.

'Pull over immediately or we'll be forced to fire.'

Lebrett urged Fischer to drive even faster, then a spray of machine-gun fire peppered the road in front of them.

'Holy shit!' yelled Hilts. 'They mean it!'

Lebrett studied his options and realized he had no alternative.

'Pull over!' he ordered.

Fischer gratefully brought the Ford to a sliding halt beside an empty view-point overlooking a scenic gorge.

As they slowly got out of the car, the helicopter swung over a low wooded rise and landed in a nearby clearing. Two men climbed out, both tall and blond and dressed in expensive suits, one blue, the other brown. They approached down the middle of the road, each holding a Glock pistol.

'My name's Parvill Rodin; this is my brother Christie,' announced the one in blue. 'And you are the infamous Jacob Lebrett, murderer of at least seven people.'

'Nine,' boasted Hilts. 'And he don't give a shit.'

'Shut up,' Christie ordered Hilts. 'We only talk to the chief, not the squaws.'

Fischer piped up. 'Hey, you guys I—'

Lebrett elbowed him in the face. 'Shut up, cop.'

Eyeing the deputy, Parvill smiled. 'We've had a report, Jacob. Seems some very odd things happened prior to your capture yesterday.'

'What the fuck do you want?' asked Lebrett.

'We want you, Jacob,' explained Parvill.

'Well, you ain't having me. And we've got a hostage here—'

Christie raised his pistol and fired once at Ray Fischer. The bullet ripped out his throat, and he dropped like a stone.

'You were saying?' said Parvill.

The three startled men quickly turned their weapons on Christie.

Parvill smiled. 'Any one of you fires, I guarantee at least two of you will die. Now, I'm not a gambling man, but with those odds I'd think before I acted.'

'You'll *both* die,' growled Pinder.

'Maybe so, but the difference is we don't give a shit, and you're one very fat target.'

Pinder's hand started shaking as he looked straight into Christie's staring eyes. A voice spoke in his head.

Then Pinder turned and shot Hilts in the chest. The man peered down at his rapidly reddening shirt in amazement, then collapsed slowly.

Astonished, Lebrett looked up from the dying man – and immediately shot Pinder in the face.

'Oops,' said Christie. 'Look likes the odds have shortened.'

'So, Jacob,' Parvill continued, 'what's it to be?'

'It's the eyes,' said Lebrett, lowering his own gun. 'What the fuck is it with eyes round here?'

Parvill smiled. 'We've got a deal for you, Jacob. Work for us, you live. Refuse and you die.'

Lebrett pocketed his gun. 'Think I'll live, so what's the deal?' He pulled out a packet of Camels, ripping off the filter and lighting up the ragged stalk.

'No deal. You do exactly what we say, you get to breathe a little longer. Don't be under any illusions: when you've done what we want, you'll die anyway. But you know that. So, if you don't want to live those extra hours, just say so and we'll cap you now.'

Purposely avoiding Parvill's eyes, Lebrett eased out a lungful of smoke. 'I'll go with it.'

'Of course you will,' agreed Parvill. 'Okay, now for the collar.'

'What?' said Lebrett, puzzled.

Christie fired a shot at the wooden railing an inch from Lebrett's thigh, distracting him. Meanwhile Parvill stepped over Hilts's corpse, and deftly clipped a thin gold collar around Lebrett's neck. He then pulled out a pin from its rear, tossing it over his shoulder.

'Armed and ready,' he announced to Christie.

'Saw it in a movie once,' explained Christie. 'Some Schwarzenegger shit. Got our people to experiment. Be warned, there's explosive inside that collar. Try to run – and *kaboom*!'

'So what do you want from me?' asked Lebrett, unable to comprehend this rapid turn of events.

'Tell us about those two little girls in the tourist shop.'

As Lebrett explained what had happened, he was surprised that neither of the men derided his bizarre account.

'You were right about the eyes, Jacob. I don't suppose you know their names?'

Lebrett silently shook his head.

'Didn't think so,' said Parvill, smiling. 'But it's personal, right?'

A cellular phone rang, and Parvill pulled one from his pocket. 'They have? . . . They are? . . . And no witnesses? . . . Excellent.'

He folded up the phone, Christie eyeing him apprehensively.

'The observatory went just like we planned, little brother,' Parvill explained. 'Won't be long now before the big boys panic and do our job for us.' He turned back to face Lebrett. 'I suggest you get moving now, Jacob. It's a good few miles back to Rhododendron. But remember you're a wanted fugitive. We'll be in touch later.'

'How?'

Parvill indicated the collar. 'You're bugged, so we can hear you, and you'll be able to hear us. Plus, you're being tracked by satellite. We'll know where you are at all times to within a couple of feet. Just do what we say – and your neck bone'll stay connected to your head bone.'

The two brothers watched as he crossed the road, and hiked up into the cover of the trees. Christie was still a bit puzzled, so Parvill explained.

'We feel pretty sure Lebrett has a psychic link with this girl. Our local informant told us that much yesterday. So the chances are she's one of the children we're looking for.'

'Okay, fair enough. So why don't we just ask our own informant for the girl's name?'

Parvill stooped and ripped the name badge from Ray Fischer's bloody shirt.

'Because you just shot him.'

'Oh shit . . . So why not ask Lebrett, then?' He nodded after the man who had already disappeared into the trees.

'Because they made very sure he didn't find out.'

They walked back to the idling helicopter.

'Why not just ask the sheriff?' Christie persisted. 'It was his arrest.'

Parvill's patience was now exhausted. He cupped Christie's chin in one hand, and gently slapped his face with the other. 'You saw Drexill's decoded file. The name Rhododendron came up twenty-one times, implying there are twenty-one people in that town who could help us. But with that many of them, *anyone* there could be infected – including the sheriff himself.'

Shielding his eyes, he looked up at the bright afternoon sky. 'We're too close, and the clock's ticking too fast, for us to slip up now. So we swamp the town with agents – all that media interest gives our people plenty of cover – and then we wait. We find Drexill, we find the girl. We follow Lebrett, we find the girl. Either way, we can't lose.'

He gave Christie's face one last pat, then stalked back to their helicopter.

'I wish you wouldn't do that,' complained Christie, rubbing his face.

'It's what big brothers do.'

CHAPTER 15

Templeton's Autos was a modest affair. Two ageing Getty pumps stood out front, and inside there was space for three cars to be repaired and two hydraulic ramps. The only garage in town, it enjoyed steady if unspectacular trade – much like the community as a whole. The workshop was gloomy and smelled of oil but, with its double doors secured, it was a world away from the media circus under way at the other end of Main Street.

As soon as he was certain Cheryl would be all right, Stanley drove back home to pick up the girls and fetch them to the garage. There he found a dozen townspeople already gathered in the repair shop. Greetings were muted, the adults keeping to themselves while their children gathered in a corner, equally subdued.

Fifteen minutes later everyone had arrived, except Ellie Jonacezck and her daughter Tasmin – and, of course, Frank Cantrillo. Cheryl was the last to turn up, bringing news that both Spurrell and Renzetti would survive their wounds. As Stanley filled a paper cup for her from the water cooler, she surveyed those assembled.

There were several storekeepers, a librarian, two school-teachers, one lawyer, three farmers ... a cross-section of any New England community. Except for the one significant factor they all shared: each one – or their married partner – had witnessed a certain aerial event in 1977 in the small town of Didra in Washington State.

Draining her cup, Cheryl filled them in on Lebrett's escape.

She glanced over at the children and teenagers sitting attentively in one corner. There were sixteen in all, ranging in age from four to nineteen. Only later would she realize how they had all grouped themselves around her own twins – as if to protect them. Her two girls, dressed identically in knee-length dark-blue dresses with white lace piping, looked the picture of innocence.

'Something else has come up,' she continued. 'During the prisoners' escape, some of our children here received clear visions of all that was happening. Now, I think such experiences are increasing among them, so I would like you all to be honest, and tell us *anything* else you think is relevant. We live here in Rhododendron to protect ourselves and our children, so we need to be aware in advance of anything that's likely – well, I don't know, but . . .' She trailed off.

Stanley took over. 'Whatever infected us all those years ago, it has been passed on to our kids.' He glanced at Kara and Lorri. 'But maybe the children should tell us themselves. After all, it's *their* experiences.'

The twins came over to stand beside Cheryl.

'What should we say, mommy?' asked Kara, her face bright and innocent.

'Yeah, what should they say, Mrs Carter?' said a voice from the shadows.

All heads turned as Alex Maslin emerged from behind a tarpaulin-covered vehicle.

'What the hell are you doing here, you fat shit?' asked Cheryl.

The mood in the garage quickly turned ugly.

'Hey, people, all I want is the facts,' placated Maslin. 'I need to know what's going on here in my own town.'

'It's our town, too.'

'I was born and raised here! You lot all moved in over the last twenty years. Not one of you is a genuine Rhoder. Now, you're all in on something weird, and I want to know what it is.'

'And then?' demanded Templeton.

'Then I'll decide what. A guy's gotta make a living.'

Cheryl picked up a tyre-iron.

'Hey, there's no need for that,' said Maslin, eyeing her makeshift weapon.

'Oh, there's every need, Maslin,' she warned. 'You see, we're only trying to protect our kids from creeps like you.'

He was plainly nervous but stood his ground. 'So what makes them so special?'

'None of your business.'

'I'm making it my business,' he insisted.

Cheryl raised the iron but the twins yelled at her, 'Stop it, mommy! Tell the man.'

Cheryl turned to them, puzzled. 'You don't know what you're saying.'

'Yes, we do,' they chimed. 'Tell him the truth.'

She continued staring at Kara and Lorri, but they simply nodded.

'Tell him the whole story,' urged Kara.

Cheryl scanned the rest of the group. The adults looked confused or frightened, yet the children were all now nodding encouragement. For a moment Cheryl felt a new chill – there was a lot more to this than mere second sight. She slowly lowered her arm. 'Okay, the short version. You won't believe it, Maslin. And even if you do get any of it in print, it'll only be the *Enquirer*.'

Maslin leaned back against the shrouded car.

'Back in 1977 an alien spacecraft exploded over a small town in Washington State.'

He sniggered, but Cheryl continued.

'Three hundred people were there at the time, including at least half the adults in this room. Gradually, over the following months, we discovered we had all developed a strange talent: a sort of self-defence mechanism. Whenever we were threatened by anyone, they would rapidly turn scared and inexplicably back off. What's more, our immune systems became heightened to the point where we're virtually invulnerable to disease, and any degree of injury would heal abnormally quickly. Over the years some of us somehow gravitated here to Rhododendron, and settled down, and became friends. You see, whatever it was that infected us all, it craves peace and quiet – and no town comes much safer or calmer than Rhododendron. It also obstructs us from taking unnecessary or dangerous risks. You must have noticed how fit and well we always seem?'

Maslin, instead of laughing again, shifted uncomfortably.

'Well, something new has started to crop up among our children. They are showing strong signs of becoming telepathic. They can "see" things as if through the eyes of any of us adults who are exposed to harm or danger. My own children experienced the whole of this afternoon's shoot-out through *my* eyes, and also through those of Frank Cantrillo. We want to know why. Whether you believe this or not, everyone else here knows it's true, but we want it kept quiet.'

Maslin let out a long sigh. 'Why make up such a stupid story? You trying to cover up some kind of abuse here – a secret Satanist coven?'

Stanley grabbed the oaf by the hair, and pulled him to his feet. 'What my wife has just told you must never be repeated outside this room, understand?'

'If I repeated that shit, I'd be laughed out of town.'

Cheryl prodded the man's expansive gut with the tyre-iron, then raised it over her head.

'Hey, don't!' Maslin panicked.

He backed away, but skidded and fell heavily into a puddle of oily water.

'Look, I promise I won't . . .' he pleaded, alarmed now.

'You sure won't.' Cheryl raised the iron again.

Fumbling in his inside pocket, Maslin pulled out a small pistol. It looked like a toy in his hands. 'Get away from me! I'm not afraid to use this.'

'Oh, but you are, aren't you?' said Stanley, reaching for the tyre-iron. He stared hard into the eyes of the terrified man, expecting him to drop his weapon just as they usually did. But this time something wasn't right. Maslin cocked the pistol instead.

'Leave me alone! I swear I'll shoot!'

Stanley faltered. This wasn't working; the man wasn't backing down. He began to lower the tyre-iron in confusion.

Suddenly, Kara stepped up right beside Maslin. 'Mr Maslin, look at me.'

The fat man did as asked, swiftly dropping his weapon on the floor, and started babbling incoherently.

Kara let out a long-held breath. She walked over to Maslin and gently raised his tear-streaked face, peering into his eyes.

'Go home, Mr Maslin,' she said. 'Go home and sleep. You'll feel better afterwards.'

'Yes. I'm tired. Need sleep,' he mumbled. He slowly hauled his bulk upright, then pushed through the crowd of watchers as if they didn't exist.

As the side door slammed shut behind him, Kara turned to her mother and noticed a fresh spot of blood staining her shoulder dressing.

'That hurts?' she said.

Cheryl merely nodded.

As Kara reached out to touch it, Cheryl shied away, then relaxed. A warmth flowed through her wounded shoulder like a ray of heat.

'There, all done,' said Lorri nearby.

'What's she done?' asked Stanley, as Cheryl peeled some tape from her upper arm to lift up the padding.

There was now no blood, no wound, no scar. Her shoulder looked completely unmarked.

'Oh, holy shit,' he gasped.

Others crowded round to see this latest marvel.

'They're genuine healers?' suggested Iris Bright.

They all stared over at Kara and Lorri, who were back among the other children.

After a minute, Stanley began to explain his other fear: that the self-defence mechanism each adult had so long enjoyed was now failing. Other parents began acknowledging similar doubts. It all added up to a crisis they never expected.

The meeting eventually broke up in general despondence. Stanley and Cheryl drove home in silence.

'What's wrong?' Lorri finally asked from the back seat.

'Nothing's wrong, honey,' offered Stanley unconvincingly.

Cheryl turned to face them. 'We're just surprised at what you can do.' God, but they were bright little buttons. 'It just takes a little getting used to, that's all.'

'Sorry,' said a contrite Kara.

Stanley glanced in the rear-view mirror. 'Hey, don't be sorry. There's not anything wrong.'

Both twins smiled with relief.

On reaching home, Stanley parked up beside the house. It was 4.50 and none of them had eaten since lunchtime.

'I should phone to find out what's happened with Ray Fischer,' said Cheryl.

'Of course,' said Stanley. 'I'll cook us something.'

But as they reached the front door, he thrust out an arm to stop the twins.

'Door's open, and I'm sure I locked it,' he whispered.

Kara nodded. 'You did. I remember.'

Before Stanley could decide what next, a gun barrel emerged through the gap in the door, which slowly opened.

'You get in here now,' hissed a voice. 'Act like nothing's wrong.'

CHAPTER 16

Cheryl entered the house first, deliberately shielding the girls between herself and Stanley.

Once Stanley was inside the hall, the armed intruder slammed the door behind them, and ordered them into the living room. There, Cheryl turned, intending to launch an attack on Lebrett before he could harm her children.

'Don't you dare hurt my babies!' she screamed.

'Shut up!' shouted an unfamiliar voice. 'Just stop it now! I'm too damn tired for this!'

Cheryl gaped at a handsome but haggard man of about sixty with short grey hair, dressed all in black. He was holding a semi-automatic pistol.

'Who the hell?' she exclaimed.

'Drexill!' Stanley stepped back in surprise.

'Who?' repeated Cheryl, too confused to think straight. She had never seen this man before.

After almost a decade, Stanley still recognized him. 'It's Drexill – the guy who took over from Siemens at OCI. He's the guy who let us go.'

'And now you've changed your mind?' She eyed the gun.

Drexill slowly lowered the Glock 17, then suddenly collapsed. It was only as he rolled sideways on the sage-green carpet that they noticed the bloodstains on his black shirt and chinos.

Cheryl and Stanley lifted him from the floor and laid him gently on his front on their prized blue- and gold-striped couch. He moaned in pain as Cheryl pulled the shirt out of his trousers, then gently peeled it from his back.

'Get me some warm water and a sponge,' she ordered, fighting back nausea.

Stanley headed into the kitchen, while the twins watched silently.

'We can help him,' whispered Lorri at last.

After Stanley returned, Cheryl dipped the sponge into the bowl of steaming water, and began gently wiping it over Drexill's back. He shifted and winced, but she continued undeterred until all the dried blood had been cleaned away. He was a dreadful sight, punctured in a dozen places by shrapnel wounds, as well as several where metal and glass fragments were deeply embedded.

When Stanley suggested calling Dr Morrow, Drexill suddenly roused himself. 'No! Don't get anyone.' He tried to push himself up, but the pain was too great.

'Look, you're in really bad shape,' said Cheryl. 'What caused all this?'

'House exploded. Only got out in time . . .'

'You've obviously lost a lot of blood—' began Stanley.

'No time to . . . Got to get away, all of you . . .'

'Why?' said Cheryl, afraid he might be scaring her daughters.

However, the girls, far from being frightened, seemed fascinated by the man's ruptured skin. She was about to order them up to their room, when Kara stretched her hand out over Drexill's back – and lowered her thumb and forefinger to a large wound in his left shoulder.

'Kara, baby, don't . . .' started Stanley. But then something incredible happened.

'Oh my God,' was all Cheryl could manage, watching a two-inch-long sliver of metal slowly rise out of the wound. Nipping it between her fingers, Kara dropped it in the bloody water.

She then moved to another smaller wound. This time a shard of glass rose up, as if pushed out by some force inside the man's body. As it left his flesh, Cheryl could actually see the fragment suspended in mid-air before homing in on Kara's fingers. Drexill groaned, oblivious to what was happening.

'Kara, what are you doing?' Stanley crouched down beside her.

'Making him better,' she said simply.

She pulled another glass fragment out of his right shoulder.

'How do you do that?'

'By wishing.'

'What do you mean, honey?' asked Cheryl.

Lorri took over the explanation. 'We want him better, but first he has to have this bad stuff out of him.'

Kara's next extraction was a small metal bolt. Stanley began to feel sick.

'But how are you doing that?' he asked. 'You're not even touching him.'

Kara shrugged. 'It does what I want.'

Cheryl and Stanley could only watch in awe as their daughter continued to remove bits of debris from the wounded man's flesh.

Five minutes later, there were fourteen separate items submerged in the bowl of rosy water, and Drexill's back was now running with fresh blood. Cheryl went to the kitchen and tipped the bowl, fragments of glass and metal clattering, into the sink. She refilled the bowl with warm water and an antiseptic solution, and was halfway back to the living room when she heard Stanley's gasp of surprise.

She found Lorri leaning over Drexill's back, Stanley standing aside aghast. She noticed that half of Drexill's wounds were already healed, without even a scar.

'Oh fuck . . .' she muttered.

As Lorri ran her hands over one last deep wound at the base of Drexill's spine, it closed up as if zippered. Then she stepped back, giggling. 'That was fun.'

Drexill was already sitting up, tentatively feeling round behind him. 'What did you give me: some serious painkiller?'

Stanley nodded at his daughters. 'Just those two.'

Drexill looked puzzled, then whispered, 'Oh Lordy . . . '

Five minutes later they all sat drinking hot chocolate when Drexill spoke up. 'I don't want to cause alarm but we'd better get moving soon.'

'Why exactly?' said Stanley.

Drexill put down his mug. 'When I took over OCI, I made sure that every trace of your own encounter with Siemens was destroyed, as well as everything about his crazy plan to eliminate all those who'd been infected at Didra. For several years, everything proceeded okay. OCI got on with the good work, coordinating information on criminals and corruption, and Siemens's misdeeds were thankfully "lost". Until two years ago . . .

'I had a team cooperating with the Canadian authorities trying to track down a supermarket extortionist up there who had an MO identical to one previously used in Wichita and Fresno. I sent up a pair of computer whizzes, the Rodin brothers. The extortion demands were always sent by e-mail, and I needed to see if they could trace anything back from there. Everything went fine until they announced that the said extortionist's car had crashed into a lake. I thought nothing of authorizing its retrieval – except they weren't really after a car. And the place was called Upper Arrow Lake.'

Cheryl let out a gasp at this familiar name. In 1977, when the UFO had exploded over Washington State, four smaller craft had escaped, only to crash in different areas many miles away from the scene of the original explosion. One such crash site had been at Upper Arrow Lake, the remains there presumed to be lost in the icy waters. Another crash had been into deep snow near the ski resort of Ellert in Oregon where, by chance, just nine years ago she and Stanley had themselves been 'infected'.

'What happened at the lake?' asked Stanley.

'They never told me the truth of it, but since then their rise to power has been inexorable. I myself came to be seen as staid and old hat, while they represented the new wave. However much I tried to suppress them, they always found some powerful ally to help their cause. In only two years they were ready to take over.'

'So what do these two brothers want?'

'I really don't know. I don't even have evidence they actually found anything. But what I do know is they've been tracking down any survivors from Didra – and their children.'

'Do they know about Rhododendron and us?'

'Until recently, no. But since they've started trying to eliminate me, I suspect they're getting close to the truth.'

'So what are their plans?' asked Cheryl.

'I don't really know, but it does involve the children. I presumed the Rodins had acquired the same self-defence mechanism as you possess, so I made sure never to confront them in person. And when they finally cornered me, I just ran. You may have seen the news story about a massacre in that Boston hotel? That was Parvill and Christie Rodin's team trying to kill me. After failing, they traced me to a shack only forty miles from here. Realizing they were there, I did enough to make it seem I was still inside the place, then I hightailed it out – but not fast enough to avoid getting some of that shack blown into my backside.'

'So you think you were followed here?'

'I don't know. And you're the only people I can turn to.'

Stanley glanced at Kara and Lorri. 'So now the girls are in danger, and we need to do something about it.'

'What do you suggest?' Cheryl asked angrily.

'Run. Get away. Nothing else will work.'

'Go on the run with two eight-year-old girls?' spluttered Stanley. 'If they've also got OCI at their disposal . . . '

'Oh, they have. They've got the whole shebang behind them now. I'm *persona non grata*; been accused of selling vital information on the black market. But the excessiveness of their attempts to kill me up till now may be our one ray of hope.'

Cheryl nudged the remains of his bloody shirt with her shoe. '*This* is hope?'

'I think they're on a desperate schedule. They've got to get me – and your twins – within a time limit. God knows why, but that explains why they're willing to be so public about eliminating me.'

'But surely there'd have to be consequences, even for them. I mean, shooting up a five-star hotel . . .' Stanley remembered the recent news coverage: four dead, eight wounded.

'Yes. Even Siemens kept discreet about his assassinations – which makes me even more worried about them. It's as if, once their deadline's passed, it won't matter anyway. As if they're not going to be held accountable then.'

'And you can't turn to anyone else?' asked Cheryl.

'I've tried – and every single time I've been betrayed. I simply don't know who to trust any more, except you.'

Cheryl sat back. Too much was happening too quickly. 'Why are you so sure they're after Kara and Lorri?'

'They are the only children born to not one but *two* "infected" parents. Everyone else in Rhododendron who was infected was either single or alone at Didra; and no other two of these people have married each other.'

'How do you know this?'

'When I said I destroyed Siemens's files, I wasn't strictly truthful. I did keep an encrypted file containing the list of names taken from a laptop he had stashed in the headquarters basement before you killed him – and I've been quietly keeping tabs on those names ever since. I traced one hundred and ninety-six people nationwide, but over the last year some fifty of them have disappeared. I can't work out how, but it's obvious the Rodin brothers got to know about this file. As a last resort, I erased all my records before I fled, but they found a way to retrieve them. And once I'm dead those two will be safe to do what they want. Look, we'd better be leaving now.'

Kara called over from the TV, 'Better do as the man says, mommy. Those bad men he's talking about are getting close.'

'How do you know where they are now?' asked Cheryl, crouching beside her, but knowing the answer as she glanced at the screen.

Lorri scrunched up her face. 'I can see a big man with an axe.'

'They've got an axe?' blurted out Stanley.

Kara laughed. 'No, they're next to a big man with an axe.'

Stanley and Cheryl stared at each other. 'Cleaver!'

Drexill leapt up. 'You mean the town Cleaver with the axeman statue? But it's only five miles from here!'

Within minutes the four Carters were driving away from home in their Cherokee, following Drexill in a stolen Hyundai coupé. The house lights had been left on, the TV blaring.

Kara sat thoughtfully in the back of the Jeep, watching her home disappear. When she had announced that the bad men were coming, she had wanted to warn them that Lebrett was also close.

CHAPTER 17

The assault on the Carters' home took exactly seventy-five seconds.

The house was surrounded by a dozen armed men and, once the smoke from the stun grenades had cleared, Parvill and Christie Rodin themselves entered. They were dressed in the same dark-blue, bulletproof LAW gear as their men.

'Sense it?' said Christie, taking in the five unwashed mugs, the TV running an advert for Chevrolet, the bloodstains on the carpet.

His brother nodded.

The kitchen floor and sink were also dotted with evidence of bleeding.

'I want this blood-type checked.' Parvill summoned over their forensics man.

As the two Rodins headed back through the lounge, they noticed the TV was now running a news report about Jacob Lebrett's escape from custody. Both smiled as they retraced their steps into the hallway.

'I want to see the children's bedroom,' Parvill bellowed.

'Up here, sir,' called a voice from above.

Parvill led the way upstairs, then gestured the other OCI agents out of the room. He and his brother stepped inside and closed the door behind them.

Parvill ran his hand over the covers of each twin bed, stooping to sniff at each pillow in turn.

'It's them, all right,' he hissed, rolling on to Kara's bed and wrapping himself up in its monkey-patterned quilt. 'I can even *taste* them.'

As Christie sat down on the other bed, he immediately felt a vibration like that of a built-in electro-massager.

'Freaky,' he conceded.

Parvill pulled a pillow over his head, and hugged it to his face, inhaling deeply. 'Yeah, ain't it grand.'

'So what now?' asked Christie, just wanting to get out of that room, the strong residual presence of the twins making him increasingly nauseous.

Parvill tossed the pillow across the room, knocking over an array of multicoloured furry apes. He stared for a moment at a poster of the original King Kong. What was this ape obsession about?

'We're closer than we've ever been. We couldn't have missed them by more than half an hour. We'll get the sheriff to give us the make of their vehicle and its licence number, then we'll have them soon enough.'

Christie moved towards the door. 'But what if they go to ground? What if Drexill's already warned them—'

Parvill leaped from the bed and grabbed his brother in an arm lock, forcing his head down.

'How many times have I told you?' he intoned. 'Drexill knows *nothing* about what we're doing. He couldn't begin to dream why we're after those kids. But the fool thinks he led us here, doesn't he? Otherwise why run?' He let Christie go. 'Okay, *we* know we're here because of a tip-off, but Drexill isn't to know that. He's tired, wounded, old, and by now he'll be panicked. He'll screw up, count on it.' He checked his watch. 'And soon there'll be a whole lot more for him to worry about.'

Christie rubbed his neck, then opened the door. The forensics man came in, waving a microscope slide.

'Blood was O type, sir.'

'Drexill's, then – good,' said Parvill. He picked up a Mighty Joe Young doll from the chest of drawers, toying with it for a moment. Then he pulled its head off, stuffed it into Christie's waistband, and tossed the body aside. As they walked down to the hall, one of the men saluted, trying to avoid looking at the monkey's head peeking out above Christie's trousers.

'What should we do with the house, sir?' asked another agent.

Parvill looked around him, taking in the colourful rugs, the framed children's drawings, the folk art and the shelves crammed with books about helicopters.

'Burn it,' he muttered.

'What?' said the man.

Parvill stared back up at the open door of the children's bedroom. 'Burn it to the fucking ground.'

CHAPTER 18

'I think you'd better see this,' said Vice-President Compton to the hastily assembled group in the CRUX room. He flicked on every TV monitor, each channel presenting the same hysterical story.

Even the most seasoned newscasters on the screens seemed barely able to hide their terror. To report dispassionately on a tornado in Texas or a jet crash in Milwaukee was one thing, but to announce to the nation irrefutable evidence that a large part of the north-eastern United States was about to be obliterated by an asteroid was impossible to manage without emotion – not least when most of them were speaking from studios within the area of predicted impact.

The messages were very much all the same: stark, and barely likely to quell panic.

'... the incoming asteroid, code-named Erebus, will hit lower New York State at a speed in excess of fifty thousand kilometres per hour. The explosion resulting will be equivalent to eight million megatons ...'

'... millions of people are now in danger ...'

'... the government is evacuating ...'

'... all we can do is pray ...'

'... the devastation will be unimaginable ...'

'... world stock markets are already tumbling ...'

And on and on, no channel even pausing for the normal commercials. The graphics were crude and hurried. One reporter speaking from Manhattan suddenly bolted from the studio. A Fox affiliate went off the air, leaving just colour bars on a humming screen.

Compton turned down all the sound, and slumped in a chair. 'We've had to declare martial law, with Army troops and the National Guard already in New York City. We also had to announce this disaster before whoever stole that material from Escaledo Del Dios got to leak it anyway. This way, we keep a semblance of control. We've also lied about the size of the damn thing, to try to limit the panic to New York City alone. We've sealed off all commuter routes, and taken control of the railways and the subway. Now the hard work really begins. Of course, all this panicky news coverage doesn't help, but working alongside the Mayor's office, the County Commissioners and Borough captains, we're attempting to coordinate an orderly evacuation. We'll take people out by car, coach, truck, Amtrak, subway, boat, chopper. The airports will be working overtime. We'll have DABU, FEMA and NERA on the ground coordinating trouble spots.'

'Who are they?' asked Gaines.

'Disaster Assessment Bureau, Federal Emergency Management Team and National Economic Relief Agency. Each has already enacted scenarios involving city-wide evacuation: nuclear attack, chemical spill, earthquake, flood, tornadoes and hurricanes – even release of bacteria. They have drawn up emergency plans for the top fifty metropolitan areas in the country, and are ready to roll. Obviously there's no set protocol for impact by asteroid. And, given the timescale, we'll be operating a One Chance policy.'

'You've lost me again,' said Gaines.

Ward quickly explained. 'Normally, when you evacuate an area, you attempt to get everyone out first, then search every building for stragglers. And, whether people want to leave or not, they're forcibly removed. Troops then secure each sector and deal with the inevitable looters. But this operation needs to be so big and so fast, everyone has just one chance to leave. If they refuse, we leave them there, but they've voluntarily abrogated their right to receive any further help from us. So if they later change their minds, that's *their* problem.'

Just then, the pager clipped to Gaines's belt bleeped. She looked down to read its single word message: CONFIRMED.

She cleared her throat to get attention, looking ill and visibly shaking. 'It's pointless.'

'I thought you'd agreed with General Ward that evacuation—'

She ignored General McKee. 'That was then. This is now.'

Slamming a file down on the desk, she flipped it open and extracted a computer print-out. 'God, I'm sick of looking at these things. I didn't believe it when I checked it, but it's just been confirmed. I've already explained meteorites hit the earth at about sixty thousand kilometres per hour. That speed is dictated by gravity; it's a constant. Friction in the earth's atmosphere will slow them down some, destroy most, but when anything does get through, it will impact at a minimum of eleven kilometres per second. It seems Erebus is currently travelling at two hundred thousand k.p.h., so it's somehow speeded up. At that velocity, it will smash into the land surface like a bullet hitting a piece of fruit. It will bury itself seventy kilometres into the earth, penetrating the crust into the lithosphere, the upper layer of the mantle, scoring a borehole fifteen kilometres wide. Breaches of this covering are usually small pipes, only metres across; they're called volcanoes. This impact will not only annihilate the USA, it will rupture the earth itself. Consequent seismic activity will not only destroy everything on the globe – and I mean mountains, whole continents – it may actually fragment it, or knock it out of its orbit . . . But what it actually does do frankly doesn't matter because, ten seconds after Erebus hits, none of us will exist – wherever we are.'

She picked up a peach from a bowl of fruit on the table.

'Imagine that wall over there is the force now coming straight at us with Erebus, and this peach is the earth itself.'

She hurled it at the wall, where it splattered and fell to the carpet in several pieces. She went over towards the remains of the fruit, picked up the stone with the juicy pith still clinging to it, and held it aloft.

'Gentlemen, I give you our planet and its six billion inhabitants at 02.02 Eastern Time tomorrow morning.'

There followed gasps, oaths, muttered prayers from both those in the room and those listening in on speaker phones.

'Where exactly will it hit?' someone asked after a pause.

She slumped back in her chair, toying with the beads in her hair.

'That's the odd part. Impact is still due in the northeastern USA and, as near as damn it, New York City. It's increased its speed, yet altered its trajectory to ensure impact on exactly the same target. It's almost as if—'

'It's being deliberately aimed?' said General Clarens, Air Force Chief of Staff.

'Yes,' agreed Gaines.

The ensuing silence was broken only by Clarens' ringing telephone. He picked it up, listened intently, then nervously replaced the receiver, casting an eye at the speaker phone in front of him.

'But that's absurd, isn't it?' he continued.

'What, that it's being controlled?' said Vice-President Compton.

Clarens nodded, avoiding Gaines's gaze.

She cleared her throat again. *Why has he changed his tune?* 'There's a possibility its increase in speed is explicable, but not the change in trajectory.'

'But it *is* an asteroid,' the general insisted.

'Spectral readings confirm that it is, yes.'

'Photographs?' added Admiral Lawrence.

'Yes, from what we can make out.'

'Well, there you are.' Clarens slapped the desk, and walked over to the water-cooler.

'There you are *what*?' asked Gaines in exasperation. Just who had he spoken to on the telephone to thus kill his curiosity?

Ward touched her arm. He, too, was puzzled by Clarens's changed attitude, but didn't want to enter an altercation. Instead he asked if they should call off the evacuation.

After a good deal of discussion, Compton finally shook his head.

'Wasn't it your idea to give them hope? Bad enough knowing what's happening without exacerbating the situation.'

Gaines was about to speak again, but caught a look from Ward which stopped her.

'And there's nothing we can do?' asked a senator.

'No,' she said bluntly. 'I'll continue to study it for as long as possible, but . . .' She trailed off. Hours from now all of them would be dead, so there wasn't any more to say.

CHAPTER 19

Jacob Lebrett was tired, wet, frustrated and very angry. Angry at the two men who had collared him; at the little girl who had got him arrested; and at himself for being so stupid. If only he had acted quicker ... After all, when you've mixed with the general population in Perciville SCI you learn to hone your instincts, because there's always some motherfucker eager to earn a rep. Yet here he was, like some goddamn hound dog at the beck and call of those two assholes. Maybe there was nothing he could do about them, but before long he certainly meant to watch that souvenir store kid *die*.

On reaching the outskirts of Rhododendron, he needed a plan of action. Pausing in the persistent rain to study the town map displayed in a deserted rest area, he suddenly remembered that fat reporter who had been brought into the jail by the dead deputy. Before they had scared him off, he had slipped Lebrett a business card, complete with his home address. Pulling the soggy card from his back pocket, Lebrett quickly located the street it mentioned on the tourist map.

Maslin answered his front door fifteen minutes later, only to be punched unconscious. Another fifteen minutes, and Lebrett belched after taking another pull on a bottle of iced Miller's. He hadn't realized just how much he missed that taste when he was inside.

As he exited the small kitchen of Maslin's rundown home, he drained the bottle and smashed its neck against a door jamb. In the living room the TV was showing some disaster movie, and he switched it off. He didn't want any distractions.

Maslin was securely tied to a high-back chair amid a pool of piss. He was gagged with a wad of rolled-up Kleenex tissues. Crouching in front of him, Lebrett waved the broken bottle in his prisoner's face.

'I ain't got time to mess around, tubs, so I'm going to show you I mean business before I start. Clear?'

Sweating, Maslin eyed the bottle, nodding spastically, terrified and confused.

Lebrett placed the jagged edge of the bottle up against Maslin's cheek, and gave it a quick jab. The man's shriek could be heard through the tissues as blood began to course down his chin. Lebrett carefully dragged the broken bottle down the man's face to the corner of his mouth. He then pulled it away and laid it gently on Maslin's lap. Drops of blood rained down on it as Maslin thrashed furiously with eyes wild. But Lebrett merely raised an index finger, and pushed it deep into the man's wound. Scraping his nail along the outside edge of his exposed upper teeth he snagged some of the tissues, then pulled them out through the wound so they hung like slack musculature. Maslin fainted.

Lebrett sat back with a smile. He had made his point. He pulled out his pack of Camels and lit up. Then, wiping his hand on his thigh, he grabbed Maslin by the hair, pulled his head back and slapped him hard on his undamaged cheek.

'One nod for yes, two for no – understand?' He blew smoke into his victim's face.

Maslin squeezed his eyes shut, as if willing him away. But, on opening them again, it was only to see Lebrett holding up the bloodied bottle against his other cheek.

'Now, you going to cooperate? You know the people who run that store?'

A desperate nod.

'The two little girls?'

Another nod.

Lebrett pulled the bloody tissues out of Maslin's mouth, and watched as he retched blood, splattering them both.

'How do I get to their house from here?'

Maslin looked up at him. Their eyes met. 'Their house burned down a couple of hours ago, and nobody knows if they were still inside.' The words caught in his throat – at the same time as the jagged beer bottle.

Lebrett watched the man choke on blood gushing from his new wound.

For the first time, Lebrett spotted a notebook on the coffee table. The top page held the beginnings of a list of names under the heading WEIRD KIDS IN RHOD. The first two were both surnamed Carter, possibly the twins, but there was another name too. Clearly he had interrupted Maslin's attempt to compile this list.

Lebrett eventually deciphered the second surname from the blood-spattered scrawl.

Suddenly Maslin's chair tipped backwards, taking the man with it. While he writhed on the carpet, blood fountaining over his shredded face and neck, Lebrett went to look in the phone book for the other surname Maslin had provided.

There was only one match: *E. Jonaczk, 19 Squire Street.* Lordy lordy, they were even next-door neighbours.

Just then a police car cruised quietly by, its whirling flashers strobing the street like it was Christmas. Lebrett instinctively ducked, then cursed his reaction. Time to hunt out replacements for his blood-drenched clothing. Quickly dressing in baggy jeans, grey Boston University sweatshirt and a battered Patriots cap from the dead man's wardrobe, he made his way out of the house and slipped across the empty street to Number 19.

A two-storey house, it was painted a delicate yellow, like a woman's place – but Lebrett couldn't take any chances. Checking the street was still deserted, he strode up to the front porch and rang the doorbell. As a musical chime announced his presence, he scooped his hair back, hiding its length inside his sweatshirt. From inside, he could hear Frank Sinatra insisting he had done it his way, before the music was turned down. A dark shape appeared behind the small, stained-glass blue window set in the centre of the white-painted door.

'Yes?' It was a timid female voice.

'Mrs Jonaczk? It's Sergeant Carver, State Police. Is your husband home?'

'I'm not married, sergeant.' There came a chesty cough.

'I'm sorry, ma'am. Despatch fouled up again. We're checking security for all houses in this neighbourhood. You got locks on all your doors and windows?'

'Not all the windows, no.' Another cough.

Getting better, but don't push it. 'I suggest you nail them shut until this emergency is over.'

'I'm not sure I know how to—'

'I've got a hammer and nails with me, ma'am and' – *the sucker punch* – 'I could leave them on the porch.'

Ellie Jonaczek peered through the coloured glass. 'No need, sergeant. I'll take them now.'

People are just so damn gullible . . .

As soon as the door was open, Lebrett knocked it back into her, and had it closed again before she hit the floor.

He rolled the woman over and ripped open her blue silk dressing gown, pulling her white cotton nightgown over her face to cover her eyes – just in case she possessed the same freaky power.

'Do exactly as I say.' He slid a knife across her heaving stomach. 'Is there anyone else here in the house?'

She moaned a 'No' a fraction too quickly.

Clamping his hand over her cotton-covered mouth, he prodded the knife deeper into her side, feeling it slide an inch into her flesh. She screaming hotly into the material under his palm. He pulled the knife out slowly.

'I already said, is there anyone else here?'

'Yes!' came a voice from the top of the stairs.

Lebrett looked up to see a young girl about the same age as those two Carter brats, staring down at him wide-eyed. One of her legs was in a plaster cast.

'Leave mommy alone!' she screamed.

Lebrett sat back, but returned the knife to Ellie Jonaczek's throat – all the time avoiding the girl's eyes. He sliced off a broad ribbon from the woman's nightgown.

'I'll not hurt either of you as long as you come down here.'

'Run!' screeched Mrs Jonacezk.

Instead, the girl hobbled downstairs, and kneeled awkwardly beside her mother's head. Keeping his gaze away from hers, Lebrett handed her the cotton strip. 'Wrap this round your eyes. You and me are gonna take a little trip.'

CHAPTER 20

Cheryl was woken suddenly by Lorri tugging at her arm. She glanced at the Cherokee's dashboard clock. It was a little after 11.00 p.m.

'What is it?' She sat up, still half asleep.

'Tasmin needs help.'

'Tasmin Jonaczek? What do you mean?'

Just then Kara piped up. 'That bad man with the funny eyes, he's threatening her – and her mommy.'

'What's going on?' said a bleary-eyed Stanley, seated next to her.

Just an hour after they had abandoned their home, Drexill, in the lead, had driven his Hyundai Accent off the road and into woods, signalling for Stanley to follow. Once out of sight of the highway, he had walked over to the Jeep and suggested they bed down there for the night. With heavy rain pummelling the roof, no one had argued. With OCI after them, no roadside motel could be considered safe tonight.

Kara shifted on her father's lap. 'Tasmin's in danger,' she whispered.

Lorri continued. 'That bad man from the shop, he's in her house. He's got her eyes covered – her mommy, too.'

Jacob Lebrett had come back? Stanley thought. 'You must be dreaming, honey. It's been a tough day.'

'No, look!' urged Kara, pointing at the windshield.

Turning, both Stanley and Cheryl were staggered to see the interior of Ellie Jonaczek's house in front of them. The woman herself was lying on the floor, bound and blindfolded, blood on her nightgown. Scrawled on the wall in foot-high red letters was the single word: COME.

'Oh hell,' groaned Stanley. The entire windshield had become a wide-screen television – but what he had presumed to be a static picture suddenly sprang into life, and two more words appeared on the living room wall.

HERE NOW.

' "Come here now",' repeated Cheryl. 'Is this *real*?' She then noticed another blindfolded figure crouching to one side in shadow, hugging her knees. Tasmin?

'Oh God, do you see her?'

Despite the horror unfolding before them, Cheryl was puzzled. They could see both Ellie and her daughter – so who was the witness of what was happening there?

Kara sensed her surprise and explained, 'I can see what the bad man sees.'

'Lebrett? But how? He's not one of us?'

Kara began sobbing. 'I don't know, mommy, I don't know why, but I'm in his head –' she looked up at Cheryl – 'and he's in mine. Make him stop, mommy. Stop him from hurting Tasmin, and stop him wanting to hurt me.'

'Oh God, baby, baby . . .' She hugged Kara tight . . . as still the drama continued on the windshield.

'Tasmin needs help!' cried Kara suddenly, pulling herself away from her mother's embrace.

'What do we do? Call the police?' asked Stanley.

'No,' said Kara. 'Go and save her. Go help Tasmin now!' It was a direct order.

Stanley was halfway out of the car door before sense prevailed.

'Go and help Tasmin,' intoned Kara, her eyes turned to her mother.

'I don't think . . .' Cheryl trailed off. Never before had she seen such steely resolve in her child. 'We can't leave you,' was all she could offer.

'Mr Drexill will look after us,' said Lorri simply.

'You go too, daddy,' added Kara. 'Mr Drexill will stay with us.'

Stanley and Cheryl glanced at each other, then back at the windshield. Ellie Jonacezk's living room was still there, though the picture was darkening. Then Lebrett began moving about, and the scene grew dim.

The girls were already buttoning their cardigans and gathering up their blankets. It was decided to use Drexill's vehicle, which he had stolen off a used car lot. Their own Jeep would be known.

Two minutes later, Stanley was reversing the Accent towards the highway, Cheryl seated beside him, the car's head-lights picking out the small figures of Kara and Lorri peering out of the back window of the Jeep.

Drexill watched their rear lights disappear from his mirror. Their parents had explained what was happening and, quick to catch on, he soon noticed the girls again scrutinizing the black rectangle of the Cherokee's windshield.

'What are you seeing, girls?'

'Tasmin's gone,' said Kara. 'That man's taken her.'

'Any idea where?'

'Not yet,' said Kara. Then she shivered. 'But we will soon.'

'And then we'll go there,' added Lorri.

'Sorry, darlings, but we must wait for your parents to come back.'

'They'll be all right. It's Tasmin that matters now.'

'Tasmin's more important than your mom and dad?'

Lorri stared at him in surprise. 'Of course.'

'You don't understand, Mr Drexill. We have to go to Tasmin,' chorused Kara and Lorri.

'Well, I'm not moving,' he said, folding his arms.

Kara leaned over and touched his shoulder, her voice strangely monotone. 'We made you better. We can make you bad again.'

He spun round. 'What the hell are you saying?'

He saw two white faces, eyes wide, pupils big and black. Hell, they looked possessed!

'We'll go now, Mr Drexill.' It was an order.

He turned back round and switched on the ignition.

'Where to?' he asked flatly, selecting reverse.

'We'll tell you when we know.'

CHAPTER 21

'Why are we doing this?' demanded Stanley.

He was driving the unfamiliar Accent coupé towards Rhododendron as fast as he dared. In the space of one day, the cosy cocoon they had inhabited for nine years had been shattered, and the two small people they loved more than anything in the world had become strangers to them.

'I don't know why they're so insistent about protecting Tasmin,' Cheryl offered. 'But if Kara's become psychically linked to Lebrett, I want him stopped. While he's free, he remains a threat to her.'

'You don't know that.'

'Believe me, I do,' she insisted, then recounted Lebrett's demands earlier.

Her words served to increase their driving speed, as anger and fear multiplied within Stanley.

Once they reached town, Stanley took a roundabout route to Squire Street, and parked in the shadows. As Drexill had said earlier, they could no longer trust *anyone*.

They slipped out of the vehicle and ran along the grass verge until they stood outside the almost darkened Jonaczek house. After a careful pause, Stanley led the way up the garden path to the front door. He found it was unlocked, but the house seemed too quiet, as if shocked into silence by something terrible it had witnessed. He gave the door a gentle push, and they edged their way into the hallway.

On the beige carpet a large dark stain – showing black in the moonlight – confirmed their worst fears. It was Stanley who braved a peek into the dimly lit living room – and immediately vomited. Cheryl pushed past him to see for herself.

Their long-time friend Ellie was lying on the floor. Even in the gloom it was evident her wrists and throat had been slashed, leaving pools of fresh blood under head and arms. One leg was bent, with knee crooked upwards, as if she was stretched out in sleep. On the wall behind her, the bloody message COME HERE NOW was clear to read.

Of Tasmin, however, there was no sign.

Stanley stumbled back into the room to find Cheryl staring down at the butchered corpse.

'That sick bastard. Where is he now, do you think?'

He heard Cheryl gasp, and spun round to see what had caused it. There were two more words daubed in blood on the facing wall.

FOLLOW ME.

'Where to?' gasped Cheryl in frustration.

Just then, a siren screamed, and flashing blue and red lights were bouncing off the walls. Seconds later, an armed State trooper burst into the room. A neighbour must've heard a scream and rung the police.

'None of you move!' He was young and looked like he had just walked off a movie set – his tailored uniform looking more like a fashion accessory than a symbol of office. He pointed a shaking finger at the corpse: 'Jesus H Christ . . . who's she?'

'She's Ellie Jonaczek. This is her house,' said Cheryl.

'And who are you?'

'Just friends who came by,' said Stanley quickly.

'I want you both on your knees with your hands behind your heads.'

Stanley complied, too shocked to argue, but Cheryl held her ground. 'There's been a kidnapping here. We need to—'

'Shut the fuck up!' The trooper cocked his gun. 'Now get down on the fucking ground!'

Cheryl slid to her knees trying to avoid the blood.

'No, move back further, back to the chair.'

As she rose again, the cop moved his hand to a radio hooked to his lapel.

'Charlie One, Charlie One, this is Echo Eight. I've got a 187, repeat 187. Code twenty, Code twenty. Squire Street, Rhododendron. See the lights. Repeat, Code twenty for a 187.'

As the radio crackled an indistinct reply, Cheryl nudged Ellie's foot with her own. The woman's raised leg slumped to floor level. Cheryl then glanced over at Stanley who, despite his panic, realized what she was up to.

'She's alive! She's alive!' he yelled, startling the trooper. 'She just moved her leg. Come on, man, we've got to save her.'

The trooper froze.

'Okay, okay, but I need only one of you.' He nodded at Stanley. 'You, step away.'

He unhooked the handcuffs from his belt and tossed them over. 'Turn around first so I can see, and put these on, with your hands behind your back. Then lie face down on the ground. You, lady, don't move.'

He slowly kneeled down by Ellie Jonackezk's head, his eyes still flicking between Stanley and Cheryl.

'Put those damn cuffs on now!'

Stanley slowly turned his back. This was not working out. But, as the shocked trooper fumbled for a pulse on Ellie's neck, Cheryl leapt forward, catching him off balance and bowling him back against the couch. His gun fired once before she knocked it from his hand. It went flying over the couch.

Stanley jumped on to his chest to pin him down.

'Punch him out!' yelled Cheryl, clambering on to the couch and peering over the back for the man's weapon.

The cop squirming frantically underneath him, Stanley raised a bunched fist. *Christ, I haven't hit anyone in nearly ten years*, Stanley thought. *Well, here goes . . .*

'I can't find his damn gun,' Cheryl complained as another siren howled in the distance. She gave up hunting for it. Instead, after gazing for a moment at her friend Ellie's mutilated corpse, she picked up a discarded cardigan and gently placed it over the dead woman's face. *Poor, poor, innocent Ellie.*

'What now?' asked Stanley.

Cheryl shrugged. Plainly, Lebrett wanted them to follow him, but he hadn't left them any obvious clues.

Suddenly the television blinked into life. As they turned to the screen, both swore in unison. They were looking into the familiar interior of their own Cherokee, which Drexill was driving. Through the windshield a road sign loomed, the vehicle turning aside to follow one direction.

But Cheryl was already heading out the door.

'Where are you going?' Stanley asked, swiftly following.

'You saw,' she muttered grimly.

Across the sidewalk a State Police Chevrolet Caprice waited, its flashers colouring the night.

Cheryl had already reached the driver's door.

CHAPTER 22

By the time he reached his mystery destination, Lebrett felt like a rally driver. The Rodin brothers had been barking instructions into his ear for the last half hour. But he had finally been ordered to pull into an empty and unlit parking lot, his headlights revealing a sign:

THE GREENGAGE ELECTRIC RAILROAD.

FIVE MILES UP THE QUIET WAY.

THE MOST RELAXING RIDE IN MASSACHUSETTS.

Lebrett had long given up trying to second-guess his new masters' plans. Instead, he dragged the now unconscious Tasmin Jonaczk out of her mother's Pinto towards the ticket office, where he eased them both through the turnstile on to the small platform beyond.

There he found a single railway carriage, its interior lights providing the only illumination in the deserted station. Its old-fashioned wooden bodywork was painted red with a gold trim, and it reminded him of a San Francisco cable car. Parvill Rodin appeared at the front of the carriage, hanging out of the doorway.

'Our first guests. Welcome aboard, Jacob! I trust the child is still alive and well?'

Lebrett murmured a curse as he carried Tasmin along the platform.

Parvill stepped down, and ushered him aboard. Dressed all in black, with a brown leather holster prominent under his arm, he reminded Lebrett of Ilya Kuryakin in *The Man from UNCLE*.

Once they were all inside the carriage, Parvill punched a button to close the door. Christie Rodin was seated inside the cramped driver's cab at the far end. He ignored the newcomers, preferring to stare at the upward-sloping rail track ahead.

Parvill gestured to a slatted wood bench seat. 'Put your charge down here, then sit over there on the other side.'

Lebrett dropped the girl unceremoniously on the bench, the cast on her leg clunking against it loudly, then turned and slumped where he'd been instructed.

'What the fuck is all this?' He ran a finger around inside his collar and found it slick with sweat.

'Patience, Jacob. I trust you left those messages, as instructed?'

'Sure I did. So what now, asshole?'

Parvill cuffed him across the head. 'Better manners, for a start.'

Christie stepped out of the driver's compartment, holding what looked like a TV remote control. He said coldly, 'Remember, one button, one head.'

Lebrett was instantly subdued again.

A hundred yards from the railroad station, Drexill eased the Cherokee to a halt. He turned to the two girls seated next to him, both of them still hugging their toy gorillas. They looked really frightened now, which he hadn't expected.

'Do you know who's inside that carriage?' he asked.

'Not all of them, but they're still bad.'

All of them? This was getting worse.

He felt ridiculous asking two kids what he should do next, but he had no idea how to approach the problem. Kara and Lorri were staring fixedly at the windshield. Drexill followed their gaze but could still see only darkness there.

'There's a door at this end of the train,' explained Kara, seeing what Lebrett himself had seen a short while earlier. 'We climb up there.'

'We? Hey, girls, there's no *we* here – just me. I'll go try to save this Tasmin girl, but you'll be staying here, out of danger.'

'How will you stop us?' asked Lorri quite reasonably.

Shit.

A minute later the three of them were crouching by the station entrance.

'This is Tasmin's mom's car,' said Lorri, referring to the Pinto they were hiding behind.

Peering over the trunk, Drexill could see a single carriage through the station's wide entrance. Lebrett was seated midway along it, talking to someone out of sight.

'You sure you want to get on board?'

Both girls stared at him. *Oh hell*, Drexill thought, *they don't know. They're being used as much as I am!*

He checked his Glock pistol. He had no qualms about shooting Lebrett, but didn't want the children witnessing any more violence than they already had.

'We go *now*,' hissed Kara, stepping out into the open.

Drexill grabbed her arm to restrain her, but she whirled on him angrily. Seeing her tense little face, he instinctively let go and she relaxed.

Lorri moved up beside her sister. 'Pick one of us up to hold in front of you like a shield,' she ordered.

'What?'

'There are other bad men on board – but they won't hurt *us*.'

'How do you know?'

Lorri shrugged. 'We just do.'

'Now shut up, Mr Drexill,' ordered Kara impatiently. She held up her arms, Kong clutched in one hand. 'Just lift me up.'

As Drexill stared at her, he found himself slipping in and out of reality – the surrounding night becoming a dream as he drowned in her pale blue eyes. It seemed he was going to be carrying her, like it or not. So, with Kara's arms and legs wrapped round him, and his free hand holding on to Lorri's, he advanced along the platform and clambered up the steps.

Immediately a voice boomed out from the opposite end of the carriage interior. 'Well, if it isn't Drexill and the twins! You working for Fedex now?'

'What?'

'Well, you delivered them right to us!' explained a smiling Parvill. 'And just in time. We were beginning to worry.'

'I've come to collect the Jonaczek girl,' Drexill announced.

'*Au contraire*,' shouted Christie from the driver's cab.

'You've come here to die. Now, put the girl down, and let's get it over with.'

'You can't shoot me without hitting the child,' Drexill said, sickened by his very words.

Whipping out a pistol, Parvill strode the length of the vehicle until he was only a step away. He prodded the gun into the small of Kara's back.

'Drop her now, or I blow her spine out.'

Kara turned to stare at him. As their eyes held each other, there was a brief silence, and Parvill opened his eyes wide. Then he stuck his tongue out. Kara let out a little whimper.

'See, it doesn't work on me, kid. Now drop her, Drexill, or you'll be wearing her insides for a waistcoat.'

Drexill lowered Kara to the floor, then nudged her to move around his legs and join her sister standing behind him. They hugged each other fearfully.

Christie yelled, 'All aboard!' The doors closed, a bell clanged twice, and the carriage jerked into motion.

Parvill raised his pistol to Drexill's face. 'If you're carrying a weapon, drop it now.'

Drexill slowly eased one hand behind him to grasp hold of the Glock concealed in his waistband. Then he discarded it as commanded.

Parvill glanced down. 'One of you girls, kick Mr Gun through Mr Drexill's legs.'

When Lorri obliged, Parvill slid it behind him with one foot.

'What's this all about anyway?' asked Drexill suddenly.

Christie laughed from the driver's cab, as he drove the

carriage slowly up an incline. 'Appearances to the contrary, *boss*, this is about the future of the human race.'

'Or rather – ' corrected Parvill, with a malicious leer – 'the end of it.'

Cheryl braked too late to stop the cruiser slamming into the rear of Ellie Jonacezk's Pinto.

Stanley kicked open his door, and ran through on to the station's platform. By then the carriage was only a distant bright speck winding its way through tree-covered hillsides.

He hurried back to the car and jumped in. 'Better follow the road now. It goes all the way to the top. We may be able to catch them up at one of the stations further on.'

'And then what?' Cheryl asked, reversing into a fence.

He kicked at the lock securing the pump-action shotgun to the dashboard. 'Then we put a stop to this shit.'

'Now you're talking my language.'

But they were too slow in reaching the next station; the carriage was already a hundred yards farther along the track. The third stop lay at the end of a long access footpath, and Cheryl realized they couldn't negotiate it in time. As she continued up the winding road, Stanley finally freed the shotgun, then broke open the glove compartment in search of some 12-gauge shells.

As Parvill peered out through the carriage's rear windows, he spotted headlights farther down the hill.

'Looks like we've company,' he announced, then caught sight of the coloured flashers. 'Damn cops! How the hell . . . ?'

'This could complicate things,' fretted Christie.

'No, it just means more corpses.'

Drexill was trying to figure some way of escape, but knew any sudden movement could get him shot – leaving these little girls at the brothers' mercy. As long as he remained alive, there was just a chance he might resolve their predicament. What he needed now was an ally.

'Lebrett, what are you doing working for these shitheads?' he hissed.

'I ain't got a choice. Believe me, man, I'd be down there right now ripping heads off if I could.' Then he caught Kara's eye, and both of them experienced a frisson that went beyond simple fear or hatred; it was almost as if their souls had touched. Lebrett quickly looked away, cursing his vulnerability.

For her part, Kara squeezed Lorri's hand. That man seemed like an exposed electric socket waiting to give her a shock if she made one tiny mistake. She tried instead to concentrate on Tasmin, but the other child's mind was still dark and locked.

'He's all talk,' sneered Parvill at Lebrett's threat. 'Jacob here's one of our little experiments. You remember the prisoner collar? Show the man.'

Drexill was astounded. 'But we never got that contraption working properly. It's far too susceptible. It could be set off by a cellphone, even a microwave oven.'

'You bastards . . .' growled Lebrett.

Parvill merely smiled, his eyes fixed on Drexill. 'For

someone thinks he's so smart, Lebrett, you're one gullible sonofabitch.'

Furious at being duped, Lebrett dived for Drexill's discarded Glock, but Christie fired once, and the bullet slammed into Lebrett's shoulder, the pistol flying from his grasp. He rolled to one side as Christie took a second shot. This time the bullet hit his metal collar, whipping Lebrett's head to one side and smashing it against a wooden upright which knocked him cold.

Parvill glanced round. 'Nice work, bro—' he began.

Suddenly Drexill jumped him, bringing them both crashing to the floor. Parvill landed on his back, with Drexill on top of him. Covering the other man's eyes with one hand, Drexill scrabbled for the gun lying under the seat. But Christie stalked over to the writhing pair, and clipped Drexill neatly across the skull with the butt of his gun. Rolling his ex-boss's dead-weight away, Parvill staggered to his feet.

'Well, that was a touch intense . . . Okay, girls, time to party,' he announced.

Parvill seized Kara's hand, Christie grabbed Lorri's, and together they dragged the twins the length of the carriage. Christie leaned into the driver's cab, brought the carriage to a grinding halt, then opened the forward doors.

Parvill eyed the police car following them, and glanced uncertainly at the still form of Tasmin Jonaczek. 'She was only a lure; we've no need of her now, or them either,' he said. 'So let's get rid of all three of them, and also throw those cops off our tail.'

Having dragged the twins out into the cold night, Parvill circled the front of the carriage and, stooping, emptied his pistol into the hydraulics of the brake holding the carriage on the incline. As hot oil splashed over his trousers, there was a strange creaking noise and the tubing parted – then the carriage started lumbering back down the slope. It gathered speed as gravity took charge.

It was at that moment that Tasmin regained consciousness. Pulling off her blindfold, she opened her eyes to find herself on a passenger bench, with two men lying motionless on the floor nearby. She vaguely recalled something bad happening to her mother – and then all the bloody memories crashed back. She started pounding her fists against the window, screaming hysterically as the train gathered momentum.

As the carriage rounded a bend, disappearing down the hill, Parvill waved after it. 'Enjoy your trip, sweetie.'

Kara burst into tears.

'Now, let's go find Mr Chopper,' murmured Parvill.

'We've nearly caught up with it!' yelled Stanley, slapping the final cartridge into the Mossberg 590's chamber.

Cheryl stamped on the cruiser's brakes. 'It's catching up with *us*, you mean. Look, the damn thing's moving downhill again.'

As they peered through the trees, they caught a nightmare glimpse of the little girl hammering on the carriage window, her mouth open in a silent scream.

'It's Tasmin!'

'Oh God, the train's a runaway!'

'What about *our* girls?' demanded Cheryl.

Stanley shook his head, panic gripping him. 'That damn thing'll come off at the first tight bend!'

Cheryl spun the Caprice around, and roared off back down the hillside.

On the winding road, they occasionally lost sight of the carriage's lighted windows, but by the next station they found they were almost level.

'How the hell are we going to stop it?' Stanley asked.

'I'll get the car in front of it!'

'But it must weigh tons. We'll be crushed flat.'

Ignoring him, she crashed the car through the gates, speeding along the access walkway towards the station platform itself. The Caprice demolished the ticket office, lurched on to the narrow platform, then slammed itself down on the rails below. Cheryl whipped the steering wheel to the right to align the car with the rails. Flooring the gas pedal, she caught a brief glimpse in the rear-view mirror of the monstrous carriage bearing down on them . . . and then it struck their rear end.

Although the impact was lessened by the increasing forward momentum of the police cruiser itself, the sudden jolt threw Cheryl and Stanley against the dashboard. But then their car began to gather pace, its wheels straddling the narrow-gauge rails, juddering noisily over the ties, so as to jar their bones and blur their vision.

'We've got to get on board that thing and help them off!' Cheryl yelled, aware that should they stall on any obstruction, the carriage behind them would simply run over them like an M1 tank.

Both struggled desperately to open their doors, but the

initial impact had buckled the Caprice's chassis, and Stanley couldn't get into the back because of the security grille.

'Shoot out the damned windshield!' yelled Cheryl, covering her face with one hand.

He raised the shotgun and let off three shots, which were deafening inside that confined space. Pushing out the shattered remnants, they both slithered out on to the hood. They were now doing at least thirty miles an hour and, with all its tyres blown, the car was shaking furiously as the uncushioned metal wheel-rims mashed against wooden railway ties. Grabbing a side mirror, Cheryl hauled herself on to the roof, squirming over the rattling flashers. She turned to give Stanley a hand, but he waved her away.

'You go on! Do what you can!' he bellowed over the racket, his foot still caught in the rapidly vibrating steering wheel.

Cheryl wormed her way over the cruiser's roof and down on to its concertinaed trunk. Managing to stand upright, she found a handhold on the carriage's rear, and worked her way around one side till she reached the door. But it was firmly closed, with its OPEN button out of reach. Clinging on desperately by one hand, she looked back at Stanley, now out on the car roof.

The car's bonnet suddenly sprang loose, flying off into the night – barely missing Stanley as he jumped on to the carriage.

With the pump-action shotgun safely stuffed into his shirt, he gripped the rail running along the roof edge and, extracting the Mossberg, blasted at the carriage's rear window. Falling inside in a shower of glass, he lurched straight for the entrance door and banged the button to one side. The carriage door slid smoothly open, allowing Cheryl to haul herself inside. Meanwhile the carriage heaved and jerked, barely in contact with the rails beneath.

Cheryl shouted out for her girls, but could see only Tasmin, looking very frightened, and two dead or unconscious men. As she gently lifted Drexill's head, his eyes fluttered briefly. The other she recognized as Lebrett, and so ignored him.

Stanley meanwhile stepped over Lebrett's bloodied body to grab hold of the hysterical child. She clung to him tightly, sobbing and trembling.

'It's okay, Tasmin. It's okay now.'

Meanwhile the carriage was further gathering speed, the police car in front no longer doing anything to hold it back. Disaster seemed inevitable.

'Move up front!' Stanley yelled a warning to Cheryl.

She slapped Drexill's face. 'Come on, gotta move!'

He groaned, then looked up at her, trying to focus.

'Come on, move your ass!' She hauled him upright.

Stanley clambered on through the carriage, Tasmin clinging to him like glue, her plaster cast banging against every seat they passed. Entering the driver's cab, he tried every switch and lever to no avail. But at least Cheryl and Drexill had followed him, clutching at seat-backs for support. Then, beyond them, Stanley saw the police car rise up. Before he could react with a yell, it smashed broadside across the carriage's rear with a deafening crash, causing windows to explode along its length, before the cruiser fell out of sight again. The carriage teetered to one side just as a bend was looming. Surely they were going to topple over? Finally shouting a warning, Stanley hurled himself to the floor on top of the screaming Tasmin.

The carriage itself lurched off the track, ploughing into the fields on one side. Landing upright, its speed was undiminished till it eventually hit some obstruction and veered over to one side. Glass showered over them as their hands and feet scrabbled frantically for purchase.

There followed a succession of violent bumps and crashes, then a sudden eerie smoothness as if they were in flight. Finally another muscle-wrenching impact, then, slowly but surely, the carriage ground to a halt.

Stanley was the first to rise. Ignoring the pain lancing through his side and a serious clout to the back of his head, he managed to slide Tasmin carefully out through the broken driver's window on to some tarmac outside. It was only then he realized the carriage had ended up on some country road. Satisfied the child was undamaged, he made his way back for Cheryl and Drexill.

Although battered and dazed, both had made their way to the front end of the carriage. Then, scrambling out on to the road, they collapsed on the grass verge.

'What about Lebrett?' gasped Drexill, his mouth bloody.

Stanley peered back through one of the broken windows. 'Can't see him in there. He must have been thrown clear.'

'Hope the bastard's underneath it,' coughed Cheryl. She turned to Drexill. 'Where are my girls?'

'Those Rodin brothers have taken them, I don't know where. I'm sorry.'

Cheryl badly wanted to blame Drexill, but guessed it was the girls who had insisted on being brought here.

'So what do we do now?' asked Stanley.

'I've no idea,' said Drexill. 'But I do know we'd better get away from here. I left your Cherokee at the bottom of the hill.'

As they limped down the winding lane towards the Jeep, Stanley tried soothing the whimpering child. 'It's okay, Tasmin honey, it's all over now.'

CHAPTER 23

The MD-500E touched down in a whirlwind of spray just after heavy rain began to pummel the landing strip. The helicopter had been airborne for half an hour, Kara and Lorri ignorant of its destination. Huddled together in one corner of the cabin, they had tried to be brave, hugging Kong and King tightly. Meanwhile, Parvill Rodin had been seated across from them looking totally unconcerned, his brother riding shotgun with the pilot. The rotors were still whirring as Parvill stooped out of the craft, and offered them a hand down.

'Come on. It's raining. We'll need to run,' he urged.

When Kara and Lorri refused to budge, they were lifted bodily out of the machine and carried squirming and shrieking across a hundred yards of windswept tarmac to where a cluster of hangars, workshops and offices surrounded a small control tower.

The twins could see various planes and helicopters standing either in the open or inside hangars. Several of these aircraft were as big as those they had once seen at Logan Airport, but these ones all looked dark and dowdy, painted in shades of grey or dark-green and black, contrasted only by blue circles containing a single white star. Everywhere there were men in uniform loading up the machines with fuel or weaponry. Kara noticed the sign INCHMARK AIR NATIONAL GUARD

BASE and committed it to memory, although it meant nothing to her.

Once inside a warm building, they were released. Immediately, both bolted for the nearest door, only to find it locked. Behind them, the Rodin brothers were laughing.

'That's the spirit, kids,' announced Parvill. 'You're our kind, all right.'

As his cellular phone sounded, he pulled it from his jacket pocket and flicked it open. 'Yes . . . Okay, Clarens . . . Certainly . . . I'll have to get to my scrambler. Call back in two minutes.' He closed the phone and smiled. 'Business before pleasure, my little beauties.'

Unlocking a door stencilled with the letters REC, he stood aside and ushered them through. 'Don't worry. We're not going to hurt you, but you'll be our guests for a while. Then . . . well, we'll see. Do you want anything to eat or drink?'

Yellow walls, stained wooden furniture, brown-corduroy-covered easychairs and a threadbare carpet that might have once been blue. A worn pool table and large, old-fashioned television threatened sub-standard entertainment. The room also smelled of sweat, and of disinfectant failing to disguise vomit. The girls hated the place on sight.

'Hot chocolate, please,' said Kara politely, even though she wanted to scream. Lorri requested a Dr Pepper.

A fat woman suddenly appeared behind Parvill, black and middle-aged, wearing a tight blue uniform. Her voice was deliberately light, but both girls instinctively distrusted her.

'If you'll take a seat, ladies, I'll see what I can rustle up,' she promised.

As she and the Rodins left the room, locking the door,

the twins heard muted laughter receding along the corridor. They stood and surveyed the room to find it was windowless, with only the one exit, so they were effectively trapped.

'What should we do?' asked Lorri.

Kara merely shrugged as Lorri squeezed in next to her, the pair of them dwarfed by a deep, musty-smelling armchair.

'Let's think *hard*,' she persisted.

But before they could even start to concentrate, the door opened again, and the plump woman returned carrying a tray with drinks and cookies. As she crouched to set the tray in front of them, her knees cracked audibly.

'Here y'are, darlin's: hot chocolate and a Dr Pepper. My name's Bessie. What's yours?'

'Bessie what?' asked Kara, carefully lifting the hot chocolate.

'Just Bessie.'

'No one's got only one name.'

'Well, I do.'

Already they could sense the woman's patience wearing thin. This one would be an easy target.

'We want out of here, Bessie One-Name,' said Kara.

'Well, you ain't gittin' out.' The woman stood up again, wincing at the punishment to her overburdened joints.

Without warning, Kara hurled her mug at the wall, the hot liquid creating a spectacular stain. 'We want out *now*.'

Bessie sighed. 'Nothin' cussed you can do will—'

Lorri tossed the glass of Dr Pepper in her face. But the woman jumped back surprisingly quickly, the brown soda soaking the worn carpet at her feet.

'Now that was very foolish,' Bessie snarled.

'Then clean it up,' ordered Kara, determined to provoke her further. Both girls climbed out of the chair together to confront her.

'No, it can just stay there.' Bessie forced a smile.

But they could sense she was really angry – maybe wasn't keen on children in general. All they had to do now was make that dislike *particular*.

Lorri picked up a cookie, and lobbed it. 'Want a cookie now, Bessie One-Name?'

'Have a cookie,' taunted Kara, tossing another.

'You goddamn little brats!'

As she launched her elephantine bulk on Kara, Lorri finally caught her eye. Within seconds Bessie collapsed docilely into an empty chair.

'What do we do now?' asked Lorri breathlessly.

'At least I know where we are,' answered Kara. 'It's Inchmark Air Base. But we don't know where that is, so there's no point in running. We need mommy and daddy to come fetch us.'

'Yeah, if we can tell them where we are, they'll come and get us quick,' Lorri murmured.

'Of course, they will,' said Kara. 'So all we need to do is let them know.'

Both girls turned to the television screen.

'We'll need to write it down first, so they can read it.' Kara remembered they could only send images of something they were actually looking at.

Lorri eventually found a ballpoint and a scrap of paper, and together they inscribed their message as clearly as their eight-year-old hands would allow. Then, as Bessie One-Name continued in her motionless stupor, they seated themselves back in the armchair, joined hands, and stared together at the piece of paper on their knees.

CHAPTER 24

'We shouldn't have abandoned her.' Cheryl would not be placated.

'Tasmin's perfectly safe there,' argued Drexill. 'The police will have found her straight away. It's Kara and Lorri we need to worry about now.'

Drexill returned to fixing the radio – but it seemed as lifeless as their chances of ever seeing the twins again.

They were already half an hour and twenty miles away from the wrecked rail car, and parked in a track running off the main highway from Greenfield, Massachusetts. Twice they'd had to pull off the road to avoid encounters with approaching police cruisers but, with nowhere specific to aim for, Drexill had finally called a halt to their journey.

Despite Stanley's occasional attempts to comfort her, Cheryl remained sitting alone in the rear, steadfastly out of reach.

Finally Drexill admitted defeat over the recalcitrant radio, and tried to focus his mind instead.

'Let's consider what we know. Clearly the Rodins need your daughters for some special purpose – and it has to have something to do with them being "special". So, tell me a bit more about the twins. How does it manifest?'

Cheryl merely burst into tears, so it was left to Stanley to explain.

'After Siemens died, and with your connivance, we tried to disappear completely. We spent some months in Gudgen, until we found Cheryl was pregnant, so we got married. I'd already changed my name to Carter. It's then we settled in Rhododendron. I don't know why *there*, but it just felt right to us. With the bit of money we had, we bought the souvenir store.'

'Kara and Lorri were so perfect,' Cheryl finally chipped in. 'Identical twins, and always so healthy. We guessed early on that whatever had lodged itself in us had somehow been passed on to them; and for that we were grateful. It meant our girls would be safe from harm, could live decent lives. It was when they were only three, during a children's party, that we got talking to some other parents and the strange coincidences began to emerge. How so many of the other children in Rhododendron never got sick either. Inevitably the name Didra came up – and soon everyone had a tale to tell. There were as many as twenty other adults in the town who had been there in Didra when that UFO exploded. They had all been infected, and like us had ended up in Rhododendron. The only person uninfected there who knows anything about us is Doctor Morrow. He's seen too many miraculous healings and recoveries not to become suspicious, so we had to take him into our confidence.'

It was raining hard now, its splattering on the windows serenading the rasp of the Cherokee's faltering heater.

Drexill interrupted. 'What we really need to know is why they specifically targeted *your* daughters. They already had

Tasmin, but they only used her as bait. Obviously, Kara and Lorri are more important to them than anyone else – but why? What *exactly* can they do that's so special?'

Stanley started running through their abilities. 'Well, they can heal both themselves and others, they can hypnotize with their eyes—'

'They can read our minds,' Cheryl interrupted again. 'They can make objects move of their own accord; and now we realize they can even project mental images.'

'But what else is so important that the Rodins are pre-pared to kill to get hold of your kids?'

'Double strength?' suggested Stanley, looking thoughtful. 'Remember, when we two got infected at Didra, it was a much more concentrated dose than for the rest of them.'

'And the two of you *both* passed your extra power on to your kids, making them considerably stronger than the rest? That could be it, but still doesn't explain how the Rodins came to realize they were stronger. Unless . . . '

'Unless those two also have been infected to the same degree?' suggested Stanley. 'So now like is seeking out like? You said earlier that they recovered something strange from Upper Arrow Lake. If that was anything like the thing we found in Ellert, it could certainly have made them as strong as us two.'

'But why go to the trouble of *kidnapping* your girls?' mused Drexill. 'If they posed some kind of threat, why not just eliminate them immediately they had the chance?'

'No. The Rodins definitely want our girls alive, and they're operating on some sort of timetable.'

'Unfortunately it's one only they can read, so far.'

Suddenly Drexill felt pressure on his thigh as Stanley gripped it hard.

'What's wrong?' gasped Drexill, then saw Stanley's gaze was fixed on the windshield.

Behind them, Cheryl let out a cry of recognition and relief. It must be another of those freaky visions. To Drexill the windshield was still just a grimy, rain-spattered sheet of glass looking out on to dark woodland.

Stanley and Cheryl, however, could now see the interior of a room: chairs, a pool table, a dartboard – and then, mercifully, two pairs of small knees, on top of which rested a piece of paper inscribed with childish writing.

'Can you read that?' whispered Cheryl.

Stanley peered at the screen. 'I can make out "GUARD BASE", and "AIR", I think.'

'Air National Guard Base,' she interpreted.

Drexill piped up. 'Is there nothing else?'

'Doesn't make much sense, but looks like "ink mark"?'

'Inchmark! That's in Connecticut, about a hundred miles south-west of here.'

'Never heard of it.'

'They keep it very quiet, but the Rodins could easily have taken your girls there. It's fully secure, and they'd have the authority.'

'Well, let's get going.'

'Whoah, hold on. And just how do you intend to infiltrate an air base?'

'Kara and Lorri need us, damn it.'

Drexill was insistent. 'I'm just advising you to think this through.'

'There isn't time,' insisted Cheryl. The vision was already fading. 'We can think about that on the way.'

Drexill drove them back out on to the highway, and steadily accelerated the Cherokee to its limit. Inchmark Air National Guard Base was a good ninety minutes away.

'Hey, another thing,' said Drexill. 'You've told me you think you're losing your own powers, but your kids are acquiring stronger ones. A coincidence, you reckon?'

'You mean like they're draining us in some way?'

'Could be.'

As Stanley and Cheryl exchanged glances, she fumbled for his hand and squeezed.

'Welcome back to the real world,' Stanley murmured.

CHAPTER 25

General Ward sat in the front pew of the small chapel, staring up at the purple-shrouded altar. He seemed mesmerized by the twin flickering candles. The chapel itself must have seemed startlingly contemporary when built in the 1950s, but now seemed as outdated as God Himself, given current circumstances.

Alberta Gaines eased into the pew behind him. By no means a religious woman, she still retained respect for the faith of others. After all, her own belief in the immutable laws governing the physical universe was as much a religion as Ward's apparent belief in a Christian God. It was just a pity that the benevolence of the latter wouldn't be able to counter the ruthless machinations of the former.

She glanced at her analogue watch, which read eleven minutes past twelve. She was still so distressed by the death of her colleagues – and the deadly implications of her recent discovery – that she could no longer tell if this was day or night. But such distinctions would soon be irrelevant – a night was coming for which there would be no ensuing dawn.

As her pew creaked suddenly, Ward spun round, plainly annoyed.

'Wouldn't have taken you for a religious man,' she offered weakly.

'I was here looking for some peace and quiet. I wanted to be alone.'

But Gaines ignored the snub. She nodded at the altar. 'So all this means nothing to you?'

'I've never bothered Him: He's never bothered me.'

'Sounds kinda lonely.'

'Sometimes.' He let out a sigh and leaned back. 'You religious, Alberta?'

'I believe in God but I don't believe in religion. Leastways not in any religion that denies me what I am.'

'Gay, you mean?'

'You know?'

'Security files. Yeah, I know you're gay. Radinsky is . . . *was* bulimic. Costello smoked more grass than a Kansas prairie fire . . . '

'But you kept us all on.'

'You did the job. What do I care if you like to use strap-ons?'

She couldn't help laughing. 'You're *so* predictable. You think all us gals go at it like lapdancers on speed.'

'I . . . Sorry. Speaking of lonely, you got anyone special now?'

'How many dykes do you think live within a fifty-mile radius of Escaledo Del Dios?'

'You get time off.'

'With my track record, no one deserves me as their girlfriend.'

Ward knew the feeling. Two ex-wives and a couple of crazed steadies had convinced him that any relationship that lasted longer than a night, or cost more than fifty bucks, was a waste of time for everyone involved.

Likewise, Alberta Gaines had realized that her work would always get in the way of her love life. Accepting her position with WATCH – and its three-year tenure – had ended her relationship with Madeline in Chicago. Better a clean break than the inevitable winding down. It wasn't as if either could pretend a child psychologist would be able to run a successful practice in the New Mexico desert, any more than an astronomer could study the stars while riding the subway.

It surprised Gaines how little she really knew her boss, even though she had been working with him for almost a year. 'You ever thought of doing anything other than the Air Force?'

Ward was tempted to ignore her, but felt compelled to talk – almost as if he was in a confessional.

'The military life is in my genes. My old man was Navy. Dragged me and mom all around the world. He ended up in charge of a training facility in San Diego. At eighteen I joined the Air Force, just to piss him off. Went career: flew fighters in 'Nam, but it was late on, so no combat. Came back pissed off at not getting any action, and pissed off at being treated like a baby murderer by the population here. Vowed to marry the first girl who didn't look like she'd swallowed shit when I told her what I did. That was Mary.' He sighed at the memory. 'A psycho, heavy into the military in all the wrong ways. I divorced her after the incident with the pistol. Don't ask! I concentrated on my career again. I was going places, tracking all the right connections, but just prior to the Gulf War I married again. Janine. I seem to attract these women. I got out when she started stripping as a sideline. She was forty-one. I think that's when I lost it. Since then I've made do: lived for the present rather than aim for any goal. Even *that* was working, but then I stood on some toes. A hooker I'd provided on an Eastern tour turned out to have gonorrhoea – and two senators and a three-star general had to explain to their wives why they needed to get to the clinic for a shot. So here I am now, watching people watching rocks in outer space.'

'Bit of a wasted career.'

'That's the saddest part, Alberta. The career I'd stopped caring about; I just wanted to get to my pension. But now . . . What about you?'

'I was born with the proverbial silver spoon in my mouth. Hell, I had the whole goddamn canteen! Daddy got rich in the seventies with black magazines. As a teenager, we were so well off, the house help was white. I had two sisters, one older, one younger, but I was sort of neglected. Ray, she works on TV comedy shows as a writer. Earns more in a month than I earn in a year. Pris is head of a microbiology department at McGill. Me, I just look at the stars.'

'That takes qualifications.'

'Tell me about it: seven years, including my PhD. But unless I come up with an explanation for the origin of the universe, all I'll be doing for the next twenty-five years is numbering stars ten billion light years away. It's not exactly dynamic. That's why I took up this WATCH offer.'

'To protect the planet?'

'Yes – and because of the NASA affiliation. I might be able to move over to where the action is, after my three years is up.'

'You mean your high-minded ideals aren't so high-minded?'

'Depends on your ideals. One of my ideals is to do the job I'm paid to do – to the best of my ability. Seems we part company on that point.'

'You're all heart, Alberta.'

'And you're all self.'

'Hey, someone's gotta look out for me.'

Just then, Gaines's cellphone bleeped. As she pulled it out and answered, her expression revealed she was receiving bad news. She slapped the phone shut and slumped back in the pew.

'Do I have to hear it?' asked Ward, his heart already racing.

'You're the boss.'

'I'm afraid Erebus is the boss now. I *presume* it's bad news.'

'Bad *and* good, but good in a bad way.'

'Ah, the precision of the scientific mind . . . '

'I've had some new calculations confirmed. What's happened *shouldn't* be happening. Hell, it *can't* happen . . . but SQUAWK has double-checked the findings. Erebus has slowed down again.'

'What?'

'It's more than halved its speed. At its new rate it'll hit almost two hours later than last predicted.'

'Well, that's good, isn't it? All that shit of yours in CRUX, with the peach . . . '

She walked round to his pew end, and sat beside him.

He could smell her perfume – Giorgio, if he wasn't mistaken. Gaines, however, could only smell Ward's sweat.

'You're missing the point, general. Planetary bodies are governed by the laws of gravity, just like any other object. Hell, even light is affected by gravity near a black hole. Erebus should never have gained speed before – nor should it be losing speed now. That's impossible.'

'So your calculations are—'

'Absolutely on the nail. At its current speed, it'll impact at 03.58, Eastern Time in the same area.'

There was a long silence. Somewhere a boiler clicked on. Air trickled through vents.

'But what, Alberta? What aren't you telling me?'

For once, she managed to contain her natural enthusiasm. 'As I explained, Erebus's behaviour defies all the known laws of physics. It shouldn't be acting as it is, changing its speed and trajectory. Which leads to one conclusion . . . '

'What, for Chrissakes?'

'Erebus is being controlled.'

DOOMSDAY

WEDNESDAY
20 SEPTEMBER

CHAPTER 26

They were parked, feeling cold and damp, about a half-mile from Inchmark Air Base, staring intently at the fogged-up windshield. The rain was heavy, the wind shovelling it against the Jeep's front window like loose gravel. Both side windows were leaking, the heater long expired.

Cheryl and Stanley were still trying to interpret the scenes occasionally provided by Kara and Lorri on the same windshield, but these images had been as unclear as Channel 16 in a snowstorm. Over the last couple of hours the girls had apparently been moved from some sort of lounge to a room filled with green radar screens shining like cats' eyes – perhaps the control tower. There were people all around them, but the room itself was too dark, and the images too vague, to reveal anything other than the occasional glimpse of a uniform or a control panel. Both parents had willed their kids to reveal something more, but plainly this type of communication worked only one way.

'Radar screens, uniforms, lots of activity,' Stanley explained to Drexill, who had seated himself between them like the unwanted younger brother on a date at the drive-in.

Drexill wondered why the girls would be up in the control tower. He also asked if there was any sign of the Rodins, but neither parent could detect any men resembling two 'young

Robert Redfords'. And then, forty minutes ago, Cheryl and Stanley's privileged view of events had disappeared completely.

All three were now very tired, cold and depressed; it was an effort simply to stay awake.

'Okay, you're the professional.' Stanley turned to Drexill. 'How the hell do we get in there?'

'Through the front gate, I suppose.'

'Very funny,' snapped Cheryl.

But Drexill expanded on his apparently facile suggestion. 'The whole area will be surrounded by a ten-foot-high electrified fence topped with razor wire. The perimeter will be patrolled by armed men and dogs. It will also be rigged with silent alarms and infra-red video cameras. The gate, however, will be manned by just a few men, so it's probably the safest option.'

'Then what?'

'You only asked me how we get in.'

By the time they had edged through the undergrowth to within sight of Inchmark's main gate, all three were soaked to the skin. Drexill, in the lead, signalled the other two to duck while he checked out their objective.

'There are two barriers with a guard hut in between,' he whispered. 'There's one man outside checking vehicles, probably a couple of others inside the hut. The base itself lies in a small valley to the right.'

'How do you know?'

'I've used this place a couple of times on OCI business. Cheryl, you take over now. Go tell the first guard your car ran out of gas. They'll find a woman more plausible, less of a threat. We'll work our way over behind you.'

'Then what?'

'We'll wing it.'

'Wing it? Are you kidding?'

'If you still had that hypnotizing thing in your head, there'd be no problem. So you're left with two choices: wing it or let's leave straight away.'

Before Stanley could even argue for the second option, Cheryl was already crossing the road.

The bespectacled guard looked very young, perhaps not even twenty years old. He was plainly cold and miserable, and Cheryl's arrival caught him by total surprise.

'Halt! No further. Identify yourself.'

Cheryl swept her hair behind her ears. 'I need help. My car's out of gas about a mile up the road.'

'Sorry, can't help you, ma'am.' He sounded extremely tense.

'Can't I just use a phone, then?'

'No, ma'am. No one can be admitted under any circumstances.' He wiped raindrops from his glasses, and continued to stare at her.

She edged closer, thrusting her chest out, knowing full well that her nipples would be clearly visible through the soaked material of her blouse.

'Please. I'm not exactly a threat to national security.' She nodded towards the guard hut. 'At least get someone else in there to phone for me – just any garage prepared to come out.'

'Sorry, ma'am, I've got my orders—'

'You little cocksucker.'

'What?'

'You little faggot. Ain't got the guts to help a real woman. Rather play at soldiers with your buddies? They're probably in there jerking each other off right now. You been left out? Not *big* enough?' She knew this was pathetic, but it was the quickest way to upset almost any man.

'Hey, lady, I don't know who—'

She leaned right into him, her breath fogging his spectacles. 'Bet you can't wait to get home and slip your little dickie to your momma. Bet *she'll* tell you it's big enough.'

'You fucking bitch!' He brought the rifle up.

'Put that down,' ordered a voice from behind her.

The guard glanced over Cheryl's shoulder. 'Who the hell . . . ?'

'Put down the rifle, soldier, or I'll blow your freaking head off. Now!'

As the young man lowered his rifle, Cheryl grabbed for it, turning it on him. He meekly got down on his knees, hands clasped behind his head, without even being ordered. Drexill walked up into the light, holding a leafless branch.

'Hey, it worked,' he said.

Stanley dodged past them, ducking under the gate and peering inside the guard hut.

'It's empty,' he reported.

Drexill suddenly whacked the boy soldier across the head, then dragged him unconscious out of sight. He joined Stanley by the gatehouse.

'It's gone,' muttered Cheryl sadly. 'Our power's completely gone.'

'Which means you were really stupid to taunt him like that,' admonished Drexill.

'Hey, old habits die hard.'

'And *you'll* die hard too, if you don't take care. You're just like every other poor sucker on this planet now.' Drexill couldn't help wondering why there was just one lone guard manning the main entrance of a base of this size.

'So what now?' demanded Stanley, still surprised at the speed of Drexill's casual violence. 'There's a Jeep out back we can use to get us over to that tower.'

'How long before this one's missed?' asked Stanley, nodding towards the unconscious guard.

Drexill shrugged. 'He might be due to report in regularly, or someone else might decide to enter or leave the base. No way of telling for sure.' He took the rifle from Cheryl. 'We now got us a weapon here, but if we get into a serious shooting match, we've had it. So, if it comes to that, remember, we surrender, okay? That way we all remain alive.'

The rain was finally beginning to ease as they headed over to the covered Jeep, then drove off towards the airfield.

Ten minutes later found all three huddled behind a collection of oil drums inside the largest of the hangars, wary of the number of troops scattered elsewhere around the base. Though the smell of aviation fuel was almost overpowering, the temptation to move somewhere else was tempered by increasing activity nearby. Drexill was puzzled by such sudden commotion, which surely must indicate some kind of exercise in process, but why such disturbing lack of security?

They could hear orders barked, commands repeated. Small groups of personnel occasionally crossed the hangar floor, their footsteps echoing within its huge space. Drexill pulled the other two down as they heard the sudden sound of helicopters being fired up, the whirring of their rotors like giant angry insects. There followed simultaneous lift-offs, as two identical black machines floated out into the night. A semblance of calm descended again, save for a lone jet engine throttling up some distance away. Drexill took this lull in activity as their chance to move.

Crouching low, he gestured the other two to follow him behind the oil drums, then they broke for the nearest side door. Drexill wrenched it open, and all three tumbled out on to the wet tarmac, diving for cover in the shadow of a small lit-up office building. A fuel truck zoomed by, spraying them with rainwater. As they spat out grimy water, a voice called out.

'Hey, you, soldier!' A sergeant came stomping towards them.

Immediately Drexill ducked further out of sight, but the others were too slow to react in time.

Cheryl grabbed the initiative by stepping away from the office wall and into plain view.

'Yes, sergeant?'

'What you two doing?' he barked, eyeing the man behind her. 'This area's supposed to be kept clear.'

For want of anything else to do, she attempted a salute.

'Do I know you?' the sergeant continued, taking in her soaked civilian garb.

Stanley felt Drexill slip the M-16 into his hand from the shadows behind. He raised it to the sergeant's face. 'You do now.'

The soldier instinctively reached for his own pistol, then

wisely stopped. They hustled the man into the shadows, and forced him to the ground.

'My two daughters are somewhere on this base, and I want to know where the fuck they are,' Cheryl demanded.

'My name's Peter Radzill, sergeant, United States Air National Guard, number four-eight—'

Drexill lashed out with his foot.

'What are you doing, Drexill?' demanded Stanley, startled.

'You want answers or don't you?' Drexill snatched the rifle from Stanley, then rolled the soldier on to his back. 'Stick your hand out,' he ordered.

The sergeant stretched out his right arm on the wet cement.

Drexill smashed the butt of the M-16 into his fingers.

The man screamed in agony, till Drexill clamped a hand over his mouth.

'You've got another hand, too, son – and you've got knees and elbows – so answer the lady's question, understand?'

Wide-eyed, the man nodded desperately, and Drexill withdrew his hand from the sergeant's mouth. He was shaking, almost sobbing with pain.

'Okay, the girls?' repeated Drexill.

'One of them's been flown to New York City,' he gasped through clenched teeth.

'Whereabouts in the city?'

'Flight plan logged for Manhattan ... prepped the chopper myself an hour ago ... oh Jesus ...' Tears streaked down his agonized face.

'What about the other girl?'

'She'll be going to Erebus.' The man shivered convulsively.

'Erebus?' asked Cheryl, puzzled. 'Is that some place out of state?'

The sergeant shifted his stunned gaze towards her. 'Out of state?' he whimpered. In desperation, Cheryl took a lead from Drexill's example. She stomped her heel sharply on the sergeant's injured hand. Again he screamed.

'Where the fuck have they taken my other daughter?' she spat.

'To Er-Erebus!' he cried, then passed out cold.

'Smart move,' muttered Stanley.

'Shut up,' snarled Cheryl. 'Is that office in there empty?'

Drexill braved a glance through the window, and confirmed it was unoccupied.

Dragging the unconscious man inside, they stretched him out along one wall, well out of view of any window. As Drexill tried vainly to slap the man awake, Cheryl and Stanley's attention was drawn to a portable TV resting on top of a filing cabinet.

At first the images flashing on the screen made no sense to them, but then the significance of the news story slowly filtered through. Except for the familiar CNN logo in one corner, they might have believed they were watching some sci-fi movie on cable. The screen changed to reveal a map of the USA with a huge circle covering the north-east section of the country. Massachusetts – and therefore Inchmark Air Base – fell well within its circumference.

With a trembling hand Cheryl turned up the volume, and over the next few minutes they pieced together the looming nightmare, flicking through a couple of dozen other channels to encounter the same story. The asteroid's massive size, speed and destructive power were being spelled out again and again on almost every channel remaining on air. Some had resorted to filming communal prayer sessions instead, or church congregations pleading to the Lord for mercy and forgiveness.

Cheryl was lost for words as she stared open-mouthed at the horrors unfolding on that tiny screen. Occasional aerial photographs of New York City showed every road and highway out of the city jammed solid with vehicles. Countless thousands were also trying to flee Manhattan on foot, with the army and police trying in vain to facilitate their movement. She reached for Stanley's hand and squeezed it until her nails drew blood. After a few moments, he gently freed himself and edged towards the window, peering out.

The rain had now ceased and the clouds had parted. The night seemed suddenly exceptionally bright, the moonlight almost too intense to look at.

'That's some moon,' he muttered, blinking.

A hand suddenly tugged at his elbow. It was Drexill, pointing out another window. 'So what's *that* then?'

Stanley followed his quivering finger, to see another moon. The *real* moon.

He glanced back at the first dazzling orb he had spotted. Already it seemed to have grown larger. Erebus was there right in front of their eyes.

'Oh God, oh God,' was all Stanley could offer.

'It looks so damned close,' gasped Cheryl. She had just been hearing about it from all those news reports, but the reality of it was immeasurably more terrifying than she could have imagined.

Yet mesmerizing as was the sight of the approaching asteroid, Drexill noticed that troops were still moving busily about the base, as if unconcerned. Aircraft and helicopters were being prepped for take-off, apparently oblivious to everyone's impending extinction. *Where the hell do they think they're going? The damn thing can't be more than a matter of minutes away.* Every news report they had seen was predicting that the whole north-eastern coast of the USA was due to be destroyed in less than an hour. Even flying supersonic, no one could hope to escape this catastrophe at such a late stage.

'Why?' he muttered, watching a de Havilland Canadian jet trundle down a taxiway.

'Maybe God hates us?' offered Cheryl flatly, joining them at the window.

Drexill drummed his fingers on the window sill, as yet another helicopter lifted off. 'But where are they going? Why bother sending people off in planes when the whole world's about to end?'

Cheryl stared up at Erebus, dazzling in its evil luminosity, yet couldn't feel genuine fear. *Perhaps it's all too much to take in*, she reasoned.

'And why send your daughters away to separate destinations, anyway?' Drexill continued to speculate. 'One to New York, the other straight up *there*?'

Stanley and Cheryl glanced at each other.

'You said the Rodins were operating to some sort of timetable,' suggested Stanley, forcing himself to think things through. 'It's like they had to get hold of our girls by a definite time – so maybe they know something about this asteroid that the rest of us don't.'

'But even if they do, what the hell can they do to prevent it colliding?'

Cheryl suddenly dashed for the door. 'I want to find my children!'

Cursing, Stanley ran after her, but she was already well out in the open, charging across to the nearest hangar. As he rushed after her, Drexill snatched up the sergeant's pistol and followed him.

As Cheryl reached the hangar doors, a large unmarked Bell 222B helicopter came hovering into view. She skidded to a halt, amazed to see a child's face staring out of one of the side windows. But before Cheryl could react, the huge machine flew straight across the airfield, then lifted itself in a direct line towards the approaching asteroid.

Stanley, too, had caught a glimpse of his daughter. His cry of relief turned to anguish as the machine rose up towards the light above.

Cheryl shouted, 'Those bastards do know something! We've no chance of tracking them to New York, but that chopper's heading straight up there – so we're following!'

Shielding his eyes, Stanley tried to follow the helicopter's progress. Christ, they might as well be heading into the sun.

Cheryl meanwhile approached another helicopter, punched out a startled and unsuspecting crewman, and scrambled quickly on board. Two soldiers were visible, moving their way.

'Just get on board, man!' Drexill shouted as he ran past Stanley.

Drexill climbed in beside Cheryl, forcing Stanley into the rear. As the door slammed shut, he could hear Drexill snarling, 'What the hell *is* this freak?'

The control section was dominated by a daunting array of dials, switches and lights that covered every inch above and below the windshield – and yet Cheryl seemed to know her way around all these instruments. She gestured for them to put on their headsets. It was essential that they could communicate with each other. Like all the helicopters they had seen earlier it was black and anonymous, but this one was noticeably bigger, with the body of a pregnant twin-tailed executive aircraft; but instead of jets its short roof-mounted wings boasted two enormous upward-pointing, fat-bladed propellers.

'It's a V22 Osprey,' Cheryl explained, familiarizing herself with the controls. She had seen them before in videos, even read the manuals, but this was the first time she had taken control of such an advanced machine.

'It's really fantastic! It's a tilt-rotor counter plane,' she continued, firing up the twin rotors on either side of the cabin. 'We take off like a helicopter, then I tilt the rotors forwards, and from there on we fly like a plane.'

The engines roared and Stanley felt the machine rise unsteadily several feet off the ground, then it glided forwards. Airmen ran for cover as the big machine reeled drunkenly towards the hangar doors.

'If we're ever gonna catch up with that 222B, this thing'll do it,' she yelled in triumph.

Suddenly, they were out in the open. To Stanley's horror, the giant propellers on either side began to slowly angle forwards until they were positioned at ninety degrees to the wings.

'Their ship can only do one-sixty; this baby'll do three-sixty flat out. Work that out for yourself,' she gloated. And, with that, Cheryl began to throttle up.

'How the hell does she know all this stuff?' Drexill turned to Stanley.

'She's the Leonard Maltin of helicopters, believe me.'

Just then there was a burst of gunfire and, even above the roar of the engines, they could hear bullets thudding into the Osprey's bodywork.

Taking the craft upwards as fast as possible, Cheryl zoomed across the airfield and angled up towards Erebus itself.

CHAPTER 27

Ants! They looked like so many ants. On every street, every freeway, even in the open countryside, people were scurrying about like ants. *Thousands* of them. Kara stared out of the helicopter window, entranced by the terrible sight below. The street lights, the full moon and the blazing light of Erebus all conspired to show this mass hysteria in pitiful detail. Fires had already begun breaking out, and looting no doubt (though what pleasure a stolen TV could offer to the thieves in the few minutes left to them, was baffling even to an eight-year-old).

She had cried quietly for a few minutes, hugging Kong now all damp from her tears. She was so sad at being parted from Lorri, though each girl could sense the other was well.

Parvill Rodin crossed to take the seat next to her. 'You and your sister, myself and my brother, we are very special people. There's no one else like us in the whole wide world.' He brushed his lips across the top of her head, his next words muffled by her damp hair. 'It's inside here, kid. Inside this pretty little head lie all the secrets. And all we need is the key.'

He leaned back to look down at an exploding gas station. 'So much potential, so little achievement.'

'Pardon?' said Kara, curiosity outweighing her terror.

'The human race, just look at it,' he sneered. 'They've been warned there's no escape, so what do they do? They still desperately try to get away. They might as well try and dodge a giant bullet; but then' – he winked – 'it depends how fast that bullet's travelling, doesn't it?'

He returned his gaze to the pandemonium two thousand feet below.

Kara stared at her knees, trying to make contact with Lorri, but all she could picture was a blinding whiteness – a whiteness that blotted out all thought and hope. The light was becoming so painfully intense, she was forced to turn her gaze back to the city below.

She was only familiar with Manhattan from repeatedly watching the movie *King Kong*, so nothing had prepared her for just how *big* it all was.

Just below them lay a grid of low-rise buildings, but in the distance rose skyscrapers alive with lights. Entire walls of windows reflected Erebus's brilliance, giving the city the appearance of a shiny space-station. She could see other helicopters and jets dancing about elsewhere in the dark sky, like fragments from some long-past explosion. And as their own helicopter drew closer to them, the tall buildings grew ever larger, until the windshield seemed filled with metal, glass and stone. Then suddenly below them appeared an immense swathe of open ground, with the light dancing on several expanses of water. To her it seemed astonishing, like a large piece of countryside that had lost its way.

As they started to descend, Kara could pick out more details. Streets arrowed their way like luminous snakes through the canyons formed by towering buildings, and all of them were choked with stationary vehicles, headlights blazing, hazard lights blinking. Here and there, wrecked cars were smouldering. Looted goods were strewn across the sidewalks.

Again Parvill Rodin sneered. 'Doomsday is upon them, and still they steal their camcorders and designer dresses. God bless the human spirit.'

Kara didn't really understand what he meant, but she now caught sight of the dead bodies dotted everywhere. On every street corner there were groups of soldiers, one of whom took a stray shot at the helicopter overhead.

Parvill turned to the pilot. 'Get us down to the junction of Broadway and 34th. I don't give a shit what's in the way, you land this bird just there.'

The machine swooped lower to follow one wide avenue, its buildings now rising on either side, their windows looking like countless eyes following their progress. They continued on over a jammed intersection, garish advertisements flashing neon images in reds and greens and yellows. She stared at a sign that ran repeatedly around the top of one particular building:

++ NICE KNOWIN' YA, NEW YORK ++
++ SEE YOU IN THE NEXT WORLD ++

An open space below them was filled with a large crowd of people. Braziers lit up the sidewalks and there seemed to be dancing, while others were fighting and several were naked. And yet more bodies, bloody and broken.

As the helicopter arrived at the next intersection, it slowed down, then banked tightly and descended. With a final bump, it settled next to an overturned fire truck, which wore a dead fireman splayed over its cab.

Parvill pulled open the chopper's door. 'Out now,' he ordered.

Still clutching her toy, Kara let him lower her to the ground. He took hold of her hand as he surveyed their surroundings.

In all four directions the streets were clogged with stationary vehicles. All around them alarms sounded from cars or buildings, and in the distance could be heard shouting and screaming and the occasional snatch of gunfire. Immediately nearby nothing was moving however, and all was still like a photograph. Kara's wide-eyed gaze finally settled on one large, white stone building which dominated an entire corner. Its giant sign read:

WORLD'S LARGEST STORE. MACY'S.

'Spooky, eh, kid?' said Parvill, squeezing her hand, as he too marvelled at the stillness amongst chaos.

Kara raised her head to the sky. The surrounding tall buildings hid Erebus from view, but their upper-storey windows still reflected its eerie light, and the sky to one side seemed as bright as midday, even though night had fallen hours ago.

'How long?' she asked.

'How long till what?' Parvill taunted.

'Till the end.'

Their eyes locked. 'It depends on what you mean by the end.'

'The asteroid, of course.'

'Kid, listen, that's just the beginning.'

Suddenly the helicopter's engine roared, and it began to

rise off the ground behind them. Parvill let go her hand, and dashed forward waving.

'Put down! Put down!' he raged, but his voice was lost in the screaming downdraught.

Kara huddled away as litter and grit swirled about her.

Parvill drew a pistol from his shoulder holster, but the pilot continued with his take-off.

When the helicopter was thirty feet above him, Rodin coolly took aim and fired at its tail rotor. Before he had emptied the ten-shot magazine, the small blades had begun to disintegrate. The helicopter began revolving wildly, its main rotors spinning it uncontrollably. The terrifying clatter of its engine now drowned out all else.

On its third wild revolution, its tail clipped a nearby building and, tipping over, the machine whipped across the street and slammed into the second floor of Macy's. Debris and flaming fuel showered the street, as a horrifying explosion boomed across the city. As the façade of the department store became drowned in flames, Parvill turned again to Kara.

'Pretty, isn't it?'

Several flaming Stars and Stripes flags fluttered to the ground like lazy fireworks.

'You killed that man,' Kara gasped, shielding her face from the heat.

There was another explosion inside the big store, and burning mannequins were catapulted over the roofs of vehicles like suicidal acrobats.

'He killed himself,' was the simple answer. 'Learn that lesson, kid. Now, let's get to work.'

A car suddenly exploded, leaping into the air.

Grabbing her hand, Rodin started heading west along 34th Street, but he found progress impeded by Kara dragging her heels.

Parvill's angry response was to grab Kong and toss him across the street right into the flames.

'Now can we stop playing?'

Kara watched in horror as her cherished furry friend was consumed, then she burst into floods of tears.

Their mournful continuing journey was to be a short one. Within just two minutes, they turned into a side alley. It was very dark, not even the light from Erebus intruding.

He dragged aside a dumpster which had previously been hiding a scruffy-looking door. Right to one side of it stood a black motorcycle half hidden by a dark sheet. Ignoring the machine, Parvill extracted a loose brick from beside the door frame to uncover a digital key-pad. He punched in several numbers and the door swung inwards.

Quickly he hauled Kara inside after him and, as the door closed behind them, he pushed her through a second door, made of steel, which had opened automatically to reveal an elevator. Again he keyed in numbers, and they started to descend.

As the steel door glided open again, Kara gasped at the scene before them.

'Yes, impressive, isn't it?' Parvill said proudly. 'Now you and I have a job to do.'

They were standing in a huge semicircular vault, fifty yards across and at least twice as deep, before it disappeared into the darkness. The only feature on its blackened, brick-lined surface were eight continuous strips of yellow neon lighting running the length of the tunnel in equidistant rows, the lowest of them right down where its sides met the bare cement floor.

'This once used to be part of Penn Station,' explained Parvill, his voice echoing. 'It was closed down in the early nineteen hundreds, when the railway company that then owned it went bust after water seepage caused a tunnel collapse about half a mile further along. No one had any further use for it, so the city authorities sealed off this end. We now own the only access, so all this is ours.'

Kara now felt more scared than at any time since Rodin had kidnapped her. But it wasn't her own plight, or the scale of this underground world that scared her, as much as what lay there in the tunnel itself. Further along, in the centre, was a strange yellow glow, too dim to determine its precise source.

Infinitely worse, however, were the other people.

There seemed to be about forty of them – men, women and children – lying in what resembled the hammocks her parents would string up in the back yard in summer. All these figures were face down, totally immobile as if dead. They hung there in four long parallel rows, of ten hammocks each, two rows down either side of the vault's central aisle, towards which all their heads were pointed. Each hammock was suspended about four feet off the ground, supported by thin cables attached to bolts fixed into the tunnel ceiling. The face of each body or corpse could be seen poking through a hole in the underside of its hammock. Worst of all, wires connected to their heads trailed across the floor to disappear into the murky glow at the vault's very centre.

'It took us a year to assemble all this. And do you know

what? It isn't even worth a tenth of you, kid. Hell, not even a *thousandth*.'

But Kara wasn't really listening to him any more. She could now hear other voices.

Just as she often picked up what mommy and daddy were thinking, here too she could 'hear' these people's thoughts. And every one of them seemed to be a cry for help, a scream of pain. Kara tried to hide her panic, but even more frightening than the horror of it was realizing that not all these voices were human.

'Who are they?' she managed to whisper at last.

Parvill took her hand again, and led her along between one pair of rows, just as if they were visiting a museum.

'These are people like you, kid, special people. I don't know if your momma ever explained to you why you're so special. Okay, long before you were born, some aliens came to visit this planet . . .'

He had pushed her along until she found herself standing right next to the body of a boy who looked about twelve. His down-turned face was completely blank and deathly pale. He could just as easily have been dead, but Kara knew for certain he wasn't. For she could feel his pain. The wires leading away towards the yellow glow had actually been *stapled* into his head, and the resulting wounds looked raw and unclean. He also smelled rank, and she could see dark stains on the hammock's underside where he had soiled himself.

'This one here is Jonathon Rondor from New Jackson, Arkansas. He's been with us now for three and a half months. His family assume he was murdered by bikers, then his body dumped in a swamp. The police suggested that, because I instructed them.' He ran his hand over the boy's filthy hair, and insects stirred. 'Many years ago, Jonathon's mother took a vacation in a small town called Didra, at precisely the time those aliens arrived. Since then she herself has been "special", and she passed her specialness on to Jonathan here. Just like *your* parents passed theirs on to you. Except the difference is your mommy and daddy received an extra big dose, and when they had you two kids, you inherited an even extra, extra big dose. Much more than any of these ones here.'

Wiping her eyes, Kara sniffed. 'What are they all doing here?'

Rodin walked them a bit further along, to pause in front of a middle-aged woman whose face was all purple, her tongue poking out. The wounds around the wires inserted into her forehead were green and stinking. Yellow pus ran into her eyes, which were closed and swollen.

'This is Mrs Schultz, a pharmacy assistant from Independence, Missouri. One of our first real successes. She's been here just over a year. She herself was at Didra.' He pointed out several others nearby. 'Dick Jervis, Pittsburgh, tool salesman. Sheena Halifax, Flagstaff, comptroller. Greg Heeney, Wenatchee in Washington State, baker. Erica Creek, Everett, also Washington State, schoolgirl. Enrico Elms, Fort Wayne, carpenter . . .' He continued to recite names and occupations as if introducing favourite friends and relatives.

Sobbing openly now, Kara meekly followed him, her distress caused as much by his gloating pride in destroying these strangers' humanity, as by the sensations inside herself of the endless torture they were enduring. She turned her gaze to the central yellow glow, but that frightened her, too. That light was the reason all these people were here – but that still didn't explain why *she* was here. Or did it? She shuddered massively. He mistook it for a yawn.

'Bored already?' she heard Parvill say. 'While I'm kindly introducing you to others of your own kind . . .'

'My kind?' she said weakly.

He stepped in front of her, blocking her view of the yellow glow. 'My brother and I discovered yet another of these alien craft up in Canada. We managed to salvage it intact, then brought it here—'

He suddenly checked his watch, then grabbed her hand. 'Anyway, you're particularly special, Kara. And now you've got a very special job to do for us.'

She slipped her hand from his, and edged towards the glow.

As its warmth enveloped her, drowning her vision, she closed her eyes . . . and saw dozens of voices and heard hundreds of minds . . . and all of them were her friends, and all were suddenly happy, fulfilled, ecstatic.

Then came the colours, bright and vivid beyond imagining: the warmest blues, and the most delicate greens, golds, reds, lilacs and yellows; sun-bright, night-dark . . . They went on and on, bathing her, caressing her . . .

And at that moment, finally Kara understood.

Despite her tender age, her ignorance, her dread, she at last knew why she was here in this evil place with this evil man – knew what she was meant to do, what she had already done, by simply acknowledging what that glow represented – and simultaneously she realized this man's true purpose. Could she herself have done wrong by doing so much right? But already it seemed too late. What would be, would be.

She heard groaning all about her, and saw the bodies in the hammocks begin to writhe and jerk, the wires loosening and coming adrift from their skulls. And, once disconnected, each one of them died, but their faces now looked beatific. Their suffering was over – but it had served a purpose, there had been a point.

Kara staggered away from the glow as if pushed back by a gust of wind, collapsing on her backside. Although only eight years old, she now knew everything that every other person in that room had known – *except for this one man standing in front of her.*

He knelt down beside her, massaging her shoulders.

'Good girl. I told Christie you would come good. Now all that remains for us is step two.'

Then she felt his hands slip round her throat, and begin to squeeze.

CHAPTER 28

Dr James Morrow and Sheriff Frank Cantrillo were standing by the window of Tasmin Jonacezk's room in the Rhododendron Clinic. The girl had been driven to the small hospital by Cantrillo himself, since the town's emergency services were now all but non-existent. There she had been examined and sedated, and Morrow – with no family of his own to care for – had decided to keep vigil over her for the past hour.

For his part, the sheriff had been forced to remain in the clinic to have his thigh wound re-dressed. Dr Morrow had taken care of it himself. Cantrillo had tried calling his sister May in Philadelphia, but got no reply. He only hoped his worthless brother-in-law was comforting her and holding her hand, but he doubted that.

Both men glanced up at Erebus simultaneously – now too bright to look at directly.

'Hell of a thing,' said Morrow.

'Yeah, hell of a thing,' agreed Cantrillo.

The men regarded each other, and smiled. For several years now they had been rivals for the Ellie Jonacezk's affections.

Dr Morrow nodded towards the sleeping girl, a surrogate daughter to them both. 'It's her and every other youngster I feel sorry for. I don't want to die, but at least I've already done some living.'

'Never thought I could get philosophical about death, but you're right,' agreed Cantrillo. 'Now that it's inevitable, well, it kinda puts things in perspective.'

Someone, elsewhere, screamed in despair.

'Nothing we can do,' sighed Morrow. 'Everyone will react in their own way. If you're a panicker, you'll panic; a drinker, you'll drink . . . '

'Tired old assholes on their lonesome – '

'Like us?'

' – will be staring out the window.'

'Leastways, it'll be quick.'

'Some consolation. But on the whole, I'd rather it wasn't happening.'

Morrow snorted. 'That's just about the dumbest thing I ever heard you say, Frank.'

'No, Jim, the dumbest thing you've ever heard me say was "Is this going to hurt?" '

Again they laughed, but with a hollow ring.

Cantrillo looked at his watch. 'Shit, got about four minutes.'

'Think I'll sit with Tasmin.' Ellie Jonaczk's death angered him. 'Only wish we could have got to that bastard Lebrett.'

'At least he's going to hell.'

'You believe that?'

Cantrillo considered this. After all, when would there be a better time to think about the afterlife than three minutes before entering it?

'Yes. I believe there's a hell – and a heaven, too,' he said.

'Well, I don't,' said Morrow bluntly, 'but I want to believe there is. If only for Tasmin's sake.' He turned away and stroked the pale child's hair.

The whole room was ablaze with light, Erebus now bigger and brighter than any full moon. Cantrillo stepped back from the window.

'I don't want to see it happen.'

He sat down on the opposite side of the bed. 'Sweet little thing – just hope she's dreaming nice thoughts right now.' He checked his watch again. 'Only another minute.'

'Oh God . . .' gasped Morrow.

'Thought you didn't believe in Him?'

Just then a wailing arose from various parts of the clinic. Apparently others were clock-watching, too.

'Maybe I do, now.'

'Funny,' said Cantrillo, a churchgoer all his life, 'I'm now having doubts.'

On an impulse, he reached across the recumbent girl and took hold of Morrow's hand, a gesture that at any other time both would have considered distinctly unmanly.

A tear welled in Morrow's eye as he squeezed both Tasmin's and Cantrillo's hands together.

Suddenly the room dimmed, so the only light was a small lamp on the bedside table. Both men cried out in surprise. Then Cantrillo broke for the window and stared out into the darkness.

Erebus had vanished.

It was several long moments before he found the strength to speak. 'I think I just found my faith again, Jim.'

'Yeah – you and a few billion others.'

CHAPTER 29

'This, as they say, is a whole new ball game,' admitted General Ward.

The number of personnel in the CRUX room had fallen by a third. Most of the absentees had returned home, there to await the end with their families. Bradford Billings, Secretary of the Navy, however, had chosen not to wait at all. Instead, he had ended his life in his office with a single gunshot. No one had yet bothered to remove his corpse.

Alberta Gaines, who until the last few moments prior to impact had seemed to be shouldering some sort of blame for Erebus, had changed her mood completely.

'And what a game!' she exclaimed.

'You goddamn maniac!' muttered Ward, blatantly swigging from a hip flask.

Gaines had previously been intimidated by all the high-ranking politicians and military in the room but, as Erebus had come closer, she had witnessed the same fear appear on these men's faces as on those who served them. As a result, she had found new confidence.

'Hey, ten minutes ago we were doomed; now we've got a mystery,' she explained, pointedly taking a pull from a bottle of Perrier. 'I'd rather play detective than play dead.'

'Good attitude,' applauded Vice-President Compton.

'And when the President gets here, I'll expect you to have some answers.'

Air Force One had braved a take-off from Havana and was expected within two hours.

'But I don't think I can give you any answers, sir.'

'Try. We've got other experts on line from the Jet Propulsion Lab, NASA, Arizona, Berkeley, Stanford . . . None of them agrees, and none has any practical answers.'

'So what makes you think I can do any better?'

'Because you're here, and they're not.'

'That's not very logical, sir.'

A voice came over the speaker phone positioned in front of General Clarens. 'Everyone in this room is here because they're important, because they have a say in what we do in the event of a crisis. If you really cannot offer any answers, Dr Gaines, then your presence in the CRUX is no longer deemed essential.'

There was a coldness in his speech that underlined her unpopularity with some there, but she didn't know who the speaker was, so wasn't sure how to respond. The men gathered around the table stared at her expectantly, several taking the comment as a cue to become openly hostile or dismissive.

'There's now no way around the obvious conclusion that Erebus is not only being controlled by an extraterrestrial force, but that it may itself be some kind of spacecraft. Yet it has the appearance and the physical make-up of a Type-M asteroid.'

'Spacecraft? It's nearly six miles across!'

Gaines shook her head, trying to remain patient. 'And it accelerated from sixty thousand k.p.h. to two hundred thousand k.p.h. within moments, then twice slowed to ten thousand k.p.h. for entry into the earth's atmosphere, and now it's gone down from that to its current speed of fifty kilometres per hour in just thirty seconds.'

'Well, nothing could have survived that,' Clarens said dismissively. A light winked on the speaker phone before him, and he picked up the receiver. 'Where are you? New York? But—' He suddenly shut up, and turned from the table.

'Nothing *human* could have survived such changes.' Gaines laughed. *Why do they have such limited vision?* She glanced at Ward, but he seemed distracted. 'But Erebus itself survived. True, it might be remote-controlled but, with that technology . . . Just look at the thing.' She pointed at all the screens carrying different TV stations still on air. 'It's a *mountain.* Whoever controls that place, we can assume we are powerless to do anything about them.'

'I wouldn't be so sure about that.' General Clarens rejoined the argument.

Ward was about to speak, but stopped himself. He had just recognized the voice on Clarens's phone. What he didn't now understand was why Parvill Rodin should be involved in this business.

Gaines let her contempt for General Clarens show. 'We estimate its mass at seventy billion tonnes, yet it's managing to fly steady at—'

'What kind of damage will it inflict if it hits at its current speed?' interrupted Compton.

'At that speed it would obliterate an area approximately twice its own size. There would be neighbouring seismic destruction equivalent to seven point five on the Richter scale.

There will be no global threat, however. It would be like a fat man sitting on a toy.'

'So where's it heading now?'

She relayed her calculations via the monitors. 'If it continues on its current course . . .' She called up a map, and zoomed to show an area ten kilometres square. 'It will impact just here in four hours.'

Everyone stared at the screen.

White House Chief of Staff Nazir spoke up. 'I thought you said it wouldn't represent a global threat?'

'Not if it maintains its current speed. There are no nuclear facilities in that area, and it's already being evacuated. Granted, it'll be expensive—'

'Expensive?' General Clarens rose and walked over to the screens. He tapped one of the thirty identical images of the impact zone's epicentre.

New York City.

'Lady, you drop that rock on Manhattan, you can kiss goodbye to the USA *and* the world economy. That rock will cause a bigger crash than '29 – and then we've got to pay for the mess! Even Albania's economy will be healthier than ours.'

'So what are you proposing?' asked Ward.

'What we didn't have time to do before,' he replied. 'I mean Operation Jackhammer, phase three. At that time we didn't have the delivery system; and now we've got both the time and the transport.'

'You're kidding,' said an astonished Ward.

'What?' said Gaines. 'What could knock that— Oh shit.'

'I can have a F-17 stealth deliver a hot arrow within two hours.'

'But, even if you can fragment it, all that rock's still got to fall out of the sky,' Ward pointed out, equally appalled by the general's suggestion.

'Better it falls on Maine than Manhattan. So we lose a few trees, a few farms – at least the world's leading financial centre will be saved.'

'Whose bright idea was that?' protested Gaines.

CIA head Hyatt indulged her. 'An hour ago the world was going to end, and now we lose part of New England. That's a trade-off I'm more than happy to live with.'

Ward was astonished. 'And the nuclear fallout?'

General Clarens sighed, pulled out a file, and threw it on the desk.

'We recently studied every possible nuclear fallout scenario: nuclear-transport accident, broken arrows, meltdowns, missiles, terrorist attacks – even the need to nuke incoming space debris. The risks are acceptable.'

'To whom?'

'To everyone who lives in New York for a start! To the banks, to the government, to the people who will make the decision in this room.'

Gaines was livid. 'And just who worked out this would be safe?'

'Not that it matters to you, doctor' – Clarens used her title as if it was a rank lower than private '– but the study was completed less than a year ago by OCI: the Office of Central Intelligence.'

'The same OCI who financed the WATCH programme?' asked Ward, eyeing Clarens's speaker phone.

'Yes.'

CARL HUBERMAN

'What the hell has it got to do with them?' demanded Gaines.

Clarens's telephone winked yet again. He picked it up, muttered an oath, then covered the receiver with his hand. 'Enough. I really don't see—'

'You don't, do you, you moron?' exploded Gaines.

Ward could see she was losing control – and also the room's sympathy. 'I don't think you—'

'That's your fucking problem, Roland. You *don't* think,' she harangued. 'Work it out, man. For once in your life, look further than your dick or your pension.'

There were snorts and gasps at her insults.

'Alberta, there's no need for this.' He held her elbow, aware she was going too far; and that there was more going on here than either of them understood.

'Let go – and don't Alberta me, you prick! OCI pay us to look for asteroids, and we find one. OCI run programs to check the feasibility of downing an asteroid, and they approve. What are the chances?'

'Chances of *what*?' asked the Vice-President, with surprising patience.

There was muttered agreement at his question.

'Chances?' What *was* she trying to say? 'You've seen from the way it behaves that Erebus is being controlled—'

'Unlike you,' sneered Bob Nazir.

She tossed a glass of water at him. There was a chorus of protests; several men rose from their seats. Clarens smiled, but she was undeterred.

'Haven't any of you got the brains you were born with?' demanded Gaines.

'On the contrary, doctor,' suggested the Vice-President, 'it appears you're the one who has lost her mind.'

Ward made one last attempt to defuse the situation. 'Alberta, gentlemen, we're all stressed. Perhaps a break?'

Again he grabbed her elbow, intent on steering her to the exit. But she whirled on him, picked up a ballpoint pen – and stabbed him in the back of the hand.

'I told you to get your goddamn hands off me!' she shrieked, silencing the room with her fury.

Senator McMullen stepped forward. 'Doctor Gaines, might I suggest you leave us now, compose your thoughts, then return when you have something constructive to say.'

'I don't need—'

He raised his hands in surrender. 'Doctor, no one is going to listen to you in your present state. We need cool heads, calm voices, cold logic. Please?'

She stared at him, breathing hard, feeling the heat of her flushed face, then offered a curt nod and strode swiftly out of the room, her beaded braids clicking a furious farewell.

Again General Clarens conferred on his phone, then immediately demanded she and Ward be barred from the CRUX.

'I don't think there's any need to—'

'Ward,' demanded Clarens, astonished that he should still be siding with the mad woman, 'what the hell is it you want?'

He stopped sucking at the puncture in his hand. 'A Band-Aid?'

CHAPTER 30

'Down! Get down!' yelled Drexill.

At the moment the brightness of Erebus was suddenly extinguished he had been sure they were already dead, but the sound of the helicopter's twin rotors quickly roused him again. Heart hammering, he had opened his eyes, and found himself staring up at a continuing blackness. At first he had assumed this must be the night sky, but then he failed to detect any stars and he realized this meant something else.

'*Down!*' he screamed again.

Cheryl finally reacted to his warning. The Osprey dropped with stomach-churning speed as something awesomely large and dark slid over the top of the helicopter. All three occupants shrank back in their seats as a gigantic shape seemed to weigh down on them.

'Jesus! Left! Turn left!'

Cheryl had also seen the object of his terror, and kicked the Osprey to port, watching wide-eyed as the right rotor came within inches of hitting a large black shape that hung from the base of the asteroid like a mammoth stalactite. Once turned, she continued her descent, the chopper buffeted by the huge volume of air displaced by the asteroid.

'What the hell happened?' gasped Stanley, staring at the island of rock that seemed to rear endlessly over them.

Drexill was stunned. 'That thing stopped – just *stopped*. From moving at thousands of miles an hour, it's gone to this. That's incredible.'

Suddenly the Osprey slipped out from under the massive shadow and once again they could see stars glittering above them like grateful tears. She checked the altimeter: 14,000 feet.

Slowing the helicopter, she turned it until they could now see Erebus below them, its black mass like a vast hole in the electric quilt of New England spread out in all directions three miles below.

'You know what this means, don't you?' she yelled into her head microphone, adrenalin pumping furiously. 'That thing is being controlled.'

'What do you mean?' asked Stanley, still too shocked to think clearly.

'She means the earth should be dead right now, except that hunk of interstellar rock slammed on its brakes.'

'You mean it's not an asteroid at all?' Stanley could feel his bladder loosening.

'Ten out of ten, Stanley,' acknowledged Cheryl with almost childish glee. 'What's more, I think the Rodin brothers knew that all along. Look!'

Even as the two men tried to grasp the enormity of her conclusion, they spotted the flashing lights of another helicopter. It was a mile ahead, but a thousand feet below them – and chasing the mass of rock that was now dropping very slowly to earth.

'What the hell are *they* doing?' asked Drexill, as they watched the other helicopter fly over the top of the five-mile-wide object.

'Proves my point,' Cheryl said. 'Those bastards are going to land on it – and they wouldn't do that unless they had good reason.'

'So why did they take your daughter along?'

'Let's find out, shall we?'

The Osprey's altimeter now showed 13,500 feet, with an air speed of forty m.p.h. Cheryl was keeping level with the rear end of Erebus, holding 150 feet above its jagged black surface. They had lost sight of the other helicopter as they drifted through cloud, but she guessed they too were seeking a suitable landing place.

Drexill, however, was not keen on the idea. 'It might have slowed down,' he warned, 'but it's still descending.'

'Yeah, but at this rate it'll take a few hours. Check it out: we've dropped only a hundred feet in five minutes. At that speed it'll take six hours to hit the ground.'

'What if it speeds up again?' he pleaded.

'And what if it doesn't?'

'Okay, but you saw how hot it looked earlier. It'll be like landing on a volcano.'

'It doesn't look too hot to me now,' she said.

In fact the asteroid now looked like a vast chunk of age-old rock: dark, cold and uninviting.

Drexill could see he was losing the argument. 'Then what about that jagged surface?'

This did start to worry Cheryl. Fighting to hold the helicopter steady in the wind, she kept glancing at the landscape below her. It did look forbidding, displaying sharp edges ranged at every conceivable angle; that would be like landing on a bundle of giant razors. Any one of a hundred spikes could easily pierce the underside of the helicopter. There was simply no way they would be able to land safely.

Stanley just stared in horror at the black mass, praying his wife would see sense in time. Much as he wanted to recover his child, he didn't want to die in the process. He leaned forward between the two front seats.

'You're not really going to land on there?'

'No, I think we'll just try and locate the— Oh shit.'

'What?' Stanley panicked.

'Fuel.' Cheryl tapped a gauge in the centre console.

She let out a bitter laugh. 'It looks like we don't have much choice. Either they didn't fuel up, or some of those shots hit the tanks.'

'I hate to point out the obvious,' said Drexill, 'but if you do land us on that thing, we won't be able to get off again.'

There was an ominous stutter from one of the engines. She shook her head. 'The amount of fuel we got left' – another brief cut-out – 'we won't make it back to earth, anyway. Our only chance would be to auto-rotate down.'

'What?'

'I kill the engine, let the wind spin the rotors, we float down.'

'You can do that?'

'In theory, but I've never tried it – and I've never heard it done from this height. And, in this big machine, it's a helluva long way down.'

The engine coughed again.

'Well, do it, then!' urged Stanley. 'We get stuck on this thing, we're totally fucked.'

Cheryl reluctantly agreed . . . but to have come this close to recovering one of her kids . . .

She pulled the helicopter up again, angling the rotors to give her enough downthrust to gain height before she was forced to cut the engines. She didn't reckon their chances, having no idea how powerful the wake caused by Erebus would prove, nor what the general atmospheric conditions were. She had risen 300 feet above the surface of the asteroid when a flash of silver caught her eye.

'What's that over there?'

Both men stared out of the cockpit.

'It's that other chopper,' gasped Stanley.

It had crashed on its side, smoke trailing behind it, its shape clearly outlined by the moonlight. Cheryl pulled the Osprey round until she was able to hover over the wrecked craft. The 222B looked as if one of the needle peaks had clipped it while it was attempting to land.

'Can you see anyone?' yelled Cheryl.

Yes, they could: a body.

'That's an adult – a soldier,' Drexill reassured her.

The engine coughed again.

'Time to go,' Stanley urged. 'That just proves you can't land here.'

'But my baby's down there,' Cheryl countered calmly. 'Hold on.'

Stanley stared at the broken Bell helicopter. Now more than ever, he needed logic to convince Cheryl that this was a *very* bad idea.

'Where in hell *are* you going to land?' shouted Drexill. 'The terrain's like a junkyard!'

'There's one flat surface over there,' Cheryl pointed.

'Where? Oh God, no.' Stanley realized she was planning to land right on top of the already fallen machine.

Cheryl checked her controls, knowing she was about to enter what helicopter pilots call the Dead Man's Curve. If a helicopter's engine fails, it is possible to auto-rotate down to earth, the rotors spinning sufficiently to provide some lift as the craft descends. However, this only works if the helicopter is at least thirty feet in the air, and travelling at more than thirty miles per hour, and, as the coughing engines kept reminding her, she only had seconds of power left to play with. It was now or never.

She eased the craft between two stark spikes, watching the rotor tips come within feet of impact. Luckily, the wind-shear from the asteroid's momentum was reduced by its own primeval landscape, but there remained eddies that ripped round the mini-mountains to jog the helicopter, straining her every muscle to keep it steady.

She slowly descended, judging herself fifty feet from landing. She had no idea if the crashed ship would take their weight, or if she was set to crush anyone still inside it. But there was no other practical landing place.

Now thirty feet. One of the engines finally cut out, the ship tilting to drop ten feet, then it picked up power again.

Stanley and Drexill erupted with obscenities.

She checked upwards. It would be touch and go what made contact first: the undercarriage or the rotors.

The undercarriage!

She punched the wheel release, lost control of the ship, and it slipped sideways. The left rotor clipped one of the peaks, the blades smashing instantly. The helicopter rose to the right and slammed into the unyielding rock, then slid down, tumbling on to the crashed 222B. There was a moment of stillness and silence, then a loud metallic groan – and the other helicopter collapsed beneath them. Their own craft rolled sideways, its lights went out and everything went dark. All three clung to their safety belts, tensed in readiness for a fiery blast, convinced they were about to die.

But no explosion followed.

Stanley opened his eyes, discerning nothing that made sense. Instead, he concentrated on working out whether he was still the right way up or upside down.

Drexill was surprised to find himself still upright in his seat. The Osprey must have rolled over in a complete circle.

'Cheryl, Stanley – you okay?'

Cheryl coughed. 'Yes, I hope. Anyone see anything to worry about?'

'No,' gasped Stanley. 'But I can smell leaking fuel.'

'And smoke,' added Drexill. 'We'd better get out of here.'

Only the door beside Cheryl was operable, and it was several frantic seconds before all of them had struggled free of their seats and clambered out on to the asteroid itself.

When they had got a dozen paces away, Drexill stopped, puzzled. 'This stuff should be burning us alive,' he said, indicating the black surface.

Cheryl coughed and hugged herself. 'It's damn cold is what it is.' It could not have been much above freezing point.

'Air seems okay to breathe, though,' said Stanley, also shivering.

Cheryl patted him on the head. 'This is not another

planet. We're only ten thousand feet up. It's like being on a mountain. The air is thin, that's all.'

'This isn't a mountain,' Stanley muttered.

'Before you two start bickering, I think we'd better get away from these choppers.'

This they had to agree with, but any movement was a lot less simple than it might appear. For one thing, the black surface was slippery, as if soaking wet, even though it was in fact totally dry. Secondly, progress appeared lethal: every jagged point looked sharp enough to puncture their skin, every edge fine enough to cut deep into flesh. They needed to be very careful not to slip and grab instinctively at some razor-sharp obtrusion for support. Cheryl stopped to examine the terrain more closely.

At Evergreen Souvenirs they sold ornaments made out of compressed coal dust, and this rock-like substance exhibited much the same intense blackness and a similar shiny surface but without the smoothness. It didn't seem to be striated or to have any natural order to it. And everywhere it all looked exactly the same. She shivered as she imagined either of her daughters trying to negotiate a path through such evil terrain. She next ran her fingers over a small, even patch, barely six inches long by two inches wide. It felt cold and rough, as if stroking sandpaper. But when she tested its resilience, pressing hard, it became suddenly smooth like black marble. Puzzled, she picked another spot and rapped it with her knuckles. At once the ragged edges vanished, leaving her a hard but level area under her hand. *Shit, it knows when I'm about to touch it.*

She drew the others' attention to her discovery, though no one could explain it.

Something else had attracted Drexill's attention, meanwhile. Over one of the peaks beyond the wrecked helicopter, there had appeared a light – and it was growing. Gingerly he edged up a nearby incline to get a better view of it – and then saw other, smaller lights rapidly closing in on them.

'Incoming!' he yelled.

The first thing any of them felt was the pain, then heat from the blast as a missile exploded somewhere above them. There followed more explosions, and all three hugged the unyielding surface as light and flame scorched above them. After four explosions, their strange new world fell silent again, the only sound being a whistling around the shallow peaks surrounding them. When they peered up again, they couldn't see anything – not even smoke.

'Those *were* missiles, right?' said Cheryl.

'Yes,' confirmed Drexill. 'I recognized a couple of attack helicopters. They must have been firing at *us* – or at least at the asteroid.'

'But why?' gasped Stanley. 'Whatever they could fire would be too small to even scratch this bastard.'

'I doubt they were firing at us. Why should they? They may be testing to see what hurts it.'

Then they heard the helicopters again, and saw twin Apaches hovering a hundred yards away, cockpits tilted down as the pilots took aim.

Stanley waved. 'They could take us off this thing! Hey! Hey! Don't shoot.'

Too late. Each helicopter had released two missiles from its underwing pods. All the helpless three could do was watch as destruction raced towards them.

Suddenly one of the nearby peaks soared up directly into the missiles' path. They impacted, exploded, and totally vanished without any debris from the missiles themselves, or even from fragmented rock.

Then, as a couple more missiles bore down on them, another two peaks silently telescoped into the air, instantly expanding laterally until they formed a single wall about seventy feet high. Again the missiles slammed home without aftermath, all three peaks slowly sinking back to their former level, leaving the landscape exactly as it had looked before the attack commenced.

Undeterred, the helicopters circled to a new position, then fired a fourth round.

This time a series of six peaks suddenly lurched into the air, absorbing the missiles as if they were snowballs.

For another minute the Apaches hovered menacingly, then peeled away and out of sight.

'What were *they*?' gasped Stanley, staring at where the peaks had been.

'Some sort of defence,' suggested Drexill.

'Yes, but for who?' groaned Cheryl.

'What do you mean?' said Stanley, limping back towards the wrecked helicopters, and finding a flat sheet of metal to sit down on.

'Well, those rocks changed shape either to protect the asteroid itself or to save *us*,' she hazarded.

Drexill expanded. 'It was done for *us*. Those rocks shot up between us and the Apaches. They could have risen behind us, or even under us, with just the same result.'

The meaning of his words hit home. 'Oh God, this whole place is alive, then.'

Cheryl tried to calm their anxiety. 'Look, let's deal with what we know. Maybe we'd better check that other helicopter.'

As the men scouted the wreckage under the Osprey, they found two more corpses. As Drexill silently pointed out to Stanley, both airmen had been shot once in the back of the head.

However, the empty cockpit itself looked relatively intact, and there was no sign of anyone else about.

'So where the hell did they go?' asked Stanley, scanning their limited horizon.

'Where the hell could *we* go?'

'Whatever those Apache pilots report back to base, I guarantee they'll come back armed with something bigger,' warned Drexill. 'They may have taken the wreckage to be the result of aggression, or mistaken it for a weapon. Either way we're still in the firing line.'

Cheryl forced herself to rise. 'Okay, we've got three options. We sit here and wait for their next attack; we wait for this goddamn rock to land on earth; or we try to find the missing passengers from the helicopter.' She then made her own preference clear by walking away from them.

Stanley and Drexill reluctantly followed.

Looming peaks regularly blocked out the available moonlight, throwing most of their surroundings into inky blackness, and making their stumbling progress all the more draining.

'Where are we heading?' asked Stanley gloomily, but nobody answered.

'The right way!' Cheryl suddenly shouted.

She stooped to pick up what looked like a ragged lump of fur – either from Kong or King. She hugged it to her. It felt damp as she ran her fingers through its matted pile, then licked it.

'Blood.' She spat out, her mind filled with terrible images.

'So they went this way, then?' Stanley quickly said, thinking the same dark thoughts.

It looked no different to any other route they could have chosen, except it also looked like becoming a dead end, the hitherto separate peaks converging about fifty yards ahead like a wall.

'They might have turned round,' he suggested.

'Or gone ahead and found a way through,' offered Cheryl. 'Let's carry on.'

But it was indeed a dead end, all the shiny black peaks closing in to block their way, like a stockade. They also found another corpse, this time some unfortunate soldier shot in the chest.

'So where the hell are they?' Stanley yelled angrily.

He was feeling as frustrated as Cheryl about his daughter's whereabouts, but it would have been a damn sight easier staying near the helicopter than coming out here on such a wild-goose chase. He was just about to say as much when they heard a noise: a roaring that came closer by the second.

'The Apaches again?' suggested Cheryl.

'No,' concluded Drexill. 'Worse.'

His words were drowned as four jet fighters zoomed in low overhead.

'Bloody F-16s! And I bet those boys are armed with more than Sidewinders. They'll never blow this rock up, but they'll manage to bloody dent it.'

'And kill us all, too!'

They heard the jets approach again, their exhaust trails scarring the sky above. They broke formation, two of them heading straight towards the asteroid, the others looping back for a follow-up run. All around the rock was stirring, as if getting ready to leap up and catch the missiles once fired. It was only a matter of seconds now.

'Look here!' Cheryl shouted.

Stanley and Drexill whipped round to see her indicating a black space behind her.

'It's a door,' she explained. 'It just opened.'

To Stanley it looked more like a threatening mouth.

The F-16s screamed overhead, their missiles released.

Drexill leaped at his two companions, hurling them through into the black maw.

They heard explosions behind them, everything flared brilliant white, a hot wind blasted them – and all three lost consciousness.

CHAPTER 31

'The captain would like to know when we should be leaving.'

Parvill Rodin laughed at this. Switching off the black Harley-Davidson Super Glide he had taken from the alley above the secret vault, he trotted up the tugboat's gangway. A young and jittery Coast Guard lieutenant was staring up towards Erebus. As the asteroid had slowed down, it had lost its fiery brilliance and darkened, but it was still just visible in the distance, black on black like an ever-growing rip in the sky.

Parvill stepped past him and into the wheelhouse. The tugboat captain was an overweight expatriate Russian with a complexion that spoke more of seasoned drinking than of seafaring. He looked at Parvill expectantly.

Rodin ordered the man out of the wheelhouse.

'But that thing out there is—'

'You've been paid to wait until I'm ready to sail,' barked Parvill. 'I don't want to sail yet, so you just wait. Now, get out of here!'

'But as captain—'

'You're a hired fucking hand now. It's my boat and you're just the one who drives it.'

Scowling, the Russian stomped out of the wheelhouse.

'You, too,' Parvill told the lieutenant. 'But stick around.'

As soon as he was alone, Parvill knelt down and opened the small briefcase he had brought along with him. Inside was a transmitter complete with scrambler and decoder. He switched it on, then lifted the cellular phone. Seating himself in the captain's high seat, he dialled a number.

'Hi, Clarens, how's everything in the safety zone?'

'You still on the *Leanora*?'

Parvill leaned forward and peered up at the sky. 'Front-row seat.'

'Don't you think you'd better move? Latest figures give impact in just three hours.'

'Don't you worry about me. I presume phase one of Jackhammer is being mooted.'

'Mooted and done. Phase two as well.'

'*What?*'

'Phase three's just waiting the Presidential okay.'

Parvill was astonished. This meant that they had already fired on the asteroid. He had no guarantee that Christie was safe. And now they wanted to go with phase three?

'Why the hell didn't you tell me?' Parvill demanded.

'Pilots saw something on the surface, tried to take it out. We need something bigger.'

'Jackhammer wasn't meant to be taken seriously. Christ, Clarens, just look at the figures. Millions dead, fallout contaminating—'

'The way Erebus is behaving, they now think it's controlled.'

'No shit. Has it actually done anything hostile yet?'

'Hostile? An hour ago we thought the goddamn world was going to end!'

'Who's the senior man there now?'

'The Vice-President.'

'Senior *military* man.'

'Admiral Lawrence.'

'Put him on.'

Parvill let out a huge sigh, running his fingers through his hair. Democracy!

'Hello, Mr Rodin, Admiral Lawrence here.'

'I understand phase three of Jackhammer is a go.'

'Yes, it seems the only way to prevent it hitting New York.'

'But the devastation if you bring it down?'

'Your own figures suggest it's the best chance we have.'

'For what size of asteroid are our figures computed? Just ask that dickweed Clarens.'

'There's no need—'

'There's every fucking need! Now, ask him.'

There was muted conversation, then the admiral came back on.

'A mile wide.'

'A mile. And how big is Erebus? Christ, admiral, you nuke that fucker, you'll lose New York City to the radiation! How's Wall Street gonna look glowing in the dark for a thousand years? All that gold and those bonds untouchable, worthless ... I understand you're retiring next summer? Got yourself a yacht out at San Diego, nice beach-front property, too?'

'How the hell—'

'Kiss them goodbye, admiral. Kiss it all goodbye. You nuke Erebus, you'll irradiate New York and half the eastern seaboard – and send America right back fifty years. And the Japs, fucked up though their own economy is, will win after all. You want to watch some nip bastard waving at you from your own yacht, while you're sitting on the dock trying to fish for a free supper?'

'Who the hell are you, Mr Rodin?'

'Someone who's trying to save a major city.'

The admiral tried to reassert his authority. 'We have a simple choice: destroy it now and continue to hope, or watch it crush New York anyway. Add the fact that it's being controlled, and I think – we *all* think – it presents a threat that has to be dealt with sooner rather than later.'

'Admiral, you're making—'

'Rodin, you are merely an adviser. You've given your advice, so thank you and good day.'

As the line went dead, Parvill resisted the temptation to hurl the phone through the cabin window. Instead, he took several deep breaths and paused to consider his options.

Phases one and two involved firing on the asteroid to test its defences. But, on his way across gridlocked Manhattan, he had received news that the parents of the Carter twins – along with that damned Drexill – had gone flying off to Erebus in pursuit of Christie and one of the little girls. Well, if they succeeded in landing, the missiles would fry them also, but to hit it with nukes, when everything was so close to fruition? That had to be stopped.

He dialled another number, and a woman answered.

'Hello, Mrs Tegrey, this is Parvill Rodin, OCI. May I speak to the President, please?'

'I'm afraid he's tied up at the moment.'

'Obviously, Mrs Tegrey, but this is a matter of extreme urgency.'

'He's not to be—'

'I need you to say just one thing to him. Then he'll speak to me.' He typed her name with the keyboard, and her personal details appeared on screen, including the photograph from her DC driver's licence, and the fingerprints from her Secret Service file. No one, but no one, had access to wider information than OCI.

The indomitable Estelle Tegrey was not the President's personal secretary for nothing, and could be as effective as any Secret Service agent in protecting her employer.

'I said I'm sorry, I have strict—'

He punched his thigh, studying the screen. 'Mrs Tegrey, I understand your mother lives in New York on the east side.'

'Yes, but she's already left—'

'I'm afraid she hasn't,' he lied. 'There was a breakdown. Now, I can get her out on the next chopper, or treat her like any other civilian and ignore her. So, can you proceed to get my message through to the President?'

There was a long pause, then, 'What do I ask?'

'Ask him what the capital of Bulgaria is.'

'What?'

'Do it, or mamma gets left behind.'

He waited as the doughty woman called up Air Force One, now on its return flight from Havana. Twenty seconds later, President Golding was on the line.

'What is it, Rodin? This is neither the time nor—'

'It wasn't the right time or place for Sophia either, but we all got over it.'

He could almost smell the man's panic. 'Is this line secure?' His voice rose in pitch. *Ah, guilty memories.*

'Securest there is. Okay, Tom, this is the deal. Operation Jackhammer phase three? Cancel it now.'

'But I was just—'

'Well, don't – or that little nightmare of yours from way back gets to see the light of day.'

Both men knew the undisclosed scandal the name Sophia implied.

'Now, you're going to do exactly what I say,' continued Parvill. 'Jackhammer is *over*, right? You can mutter about balance and responsibility all you like, but you'll refuse to ratify it.'

Minutes later, General Clarens rang to confirm the 'goddamnedest most stupidest chickenshit decision this asshole President has ever made'.

CHAPTER 32

Kara awoke in impenetrable dark: a darkness as near solid black as the oil that occasionally leaked from her daddy's old Cherokee. Blinking made no difference, so she listened hard instead. But no sounds now disturbed the blackness. She had never known such quiet. Even in the depth of night in her bedroom, she could always hear her sister's breathing or the cicadas' chorus outside the house. But here there was nothing, as if the darkness, not content with stealing the light, had taken all sound as well.

So she listened next with her mind, seeking some reassuring voice, the warmth of physical communion, but again there was only icy silence – the quiet of the grave.

She felt a coolness against her face, as if she was lying sideways on bare cement. Maybe she was still down in that underground vault with all those dead people. Her wrists were tied together behind her, and forcing herself to her knees, she made several attempts before successfully getting herself upright. But, without any light, she found it difficult to keep her balance.

When she had touched that strange yellow glow, she had suddenly known all the answers, but now her memory was receding. She was just a little girl again, alone in the blackness with forty corpses, and perhaps with the man who had tried to strangle her.

Although clearly recalling the layout of the tunnel – four rows of ten hammocks each running the length of the tunnel, two of them on either side of that strange glow, their occupants heads towards the centre aisle – she didn't know her current position in this layout. Her first task was to establish that. She shuffled forwards carefully, pausing after each heel-to-toe step. After a dozen steps she paused again to listen. There were no new sounds. The all-encompassing darkness suddenly felt like hundreds of hands pressing in on her. She wanted to scream, but knew she must persevere in finding her way back to the elevator door.

She stumbled and almost fell but somehow kept her balance, trying to wrench her hands apart, but the bonds wouldn't give. Then she collided against something solid with her shoulder, which sent her spinning – only to cannon into something else. Taut material dug into her throat – it was the edge of a hammock – but at least it kept her upright. Finally forcing herself to calm down, she edged back until her jaw was free. She stepped sideways, trying to judge the hammock's length, but on walking forward she mashed her nose straight into a corpse's face in the total darkness. Its flesh was soft and pliable, but also cold – so cold.

Recalling the layout once more, she took a deep breath, then ran her chin along the hammock's edge until it rose up out of her reach. Then she took two steps back, turned at a right angle and carefully proceeded in a straight line. She realized that, as she was walking away from the corpse's head, she would be heading towards one of the side walls. And sure enough, after a dozen or so measured steps, she bumped into solid brick. By stooping slightly, she was able to keep her shoulder in regular contact with the wall's surface, but she had no idea how far she would need to go to reach the tunnel's end containing the elevator. But what if she was heading in the completely opposite direction? She set off, cautious step following cautious step.

She had never felt so alone or so frightened in her life. Always before there had been her parents or Lorri, but here she truly was cut off from the rest of the world. If there still *was* a world out there . . .

Suddenly there wasn't even a wall. Catching her breath, she braved two more steps, but still contacted no wall. Now she began to panic. She must have walked deeper *into* the tunnel – and she didn't even know how far it continued.

She shuffled to her right three times, then stepped backwards, terrified of losing her direction again. But when her foot encountered nothing, she pulled it back quickly. Completely disoriented, she suddenly fell heavily, knocking the breath out of herself.

Kara immediately dissolved into tears while, all around, the darkness suffocated like a blanket. She realized she was losing the will to keep trying, with no idea where she was nor which direction she should take – just that there was a large hole in the floor close by, waiting to swallow her up. So she pulled her legs up tight and huddled into a ball, shivering in terror, desperate for her parents, her sister, her favourite Kong.

But what she got instead was Jacob Lebrett.

*

He had been following a back road, unimpeded by increased activity on all the main highways. And suddenly there she was, standing at the roadside, staring at him.

At first, Lebrett had dismissed the small figure as just another kid; some child waiting for her parents to come by and pick her up. But then he noticed the same figure again. And again.

She was waiting around every bend; it was like goddamn clones: the same wet and ratted blonde hair, that identical torn and muddied blue dress, the same fearful white face. But each time he roared past her and glanced back, she was no longer there.

Finally, on her sixth or seventh appearance, he slowed down and let the electric blue BMW R1100 motorcycle come to a stop, its idling engine grumbling in the damp air. She now stood barely twenty feet from him, on the other side of the road under dense tree cover which hid the stars and the moon. And yet she seemed to glow, as if lit by a spotlight.

'I'm scared.' Her voice sounded fractured with fear.

It was that same kid, wasn't it?

'I'm frightened. No one will help me . . . '

Lebrett killed the BMW's engine, and dismounted.

'I'll help you, little girl.' He stepped towards her.

Her expression remained unchanged, her face unearthly pale as if somehow floating above her thin body.

He was within five feet of her now, his hands fairly itching to close round her scrawny neck. But then she glanced straight up at him – and shrieked in terror.

He jumped back, genuinely startled by this outburst.

For the first time their eyes met full on. He immediately averted his, wary of her power..

'How the hell did you get here?'

Her gaze was still fixed on him. '*You're* the bad man.'

He smiled. 'Too right, honey, I'm the bad man.'

'You must help me.'

'How?'

'Help me escape. I've got to get out.'

He looked around. Cold, dark woods surrounded them, the damp stretch of road curving out of sight in both directions, its presence an irrelevance in this centuries-old landscape.

'Escape from where?'

'I'm underground. I need to get out. Mommy and daddy can't help me now, and Lorri's gone. You're the only one left that I can reach.'

'Yeah, I'll do you a favour, kid. I'll end all your worries right here, right now.'

He lunged towards her, but she wasn't there – and instead he found himself on his knees in the mud. Swinging round, he realized she wasn't anywhere to be seen. How the hell could she slip away so fast?

All he could see were the trees hissing mockingly in the steady drizzle. He stood up, wiping muck from his clothes. *Damn bitch*. He was completely alone again.

'You there, little girl?'

Nothing but his own raspy breathing, and himself standing looking foolish on a no-account road near Durham, NY.

What the fuck was going on?

- 241 -

And then he started laughing, and tapped his head.

The old booger upstairs was kicking in, wasn't it? Charlie C – the Black Spot. The doctor had warned him that the first symptom of his developing tumour might be hallucinations, and that they would seem as real as any acid trip. Well, that little girl at the roadside sure as hell had seemed real.

He strode back to the bike, and ran his hand over its rain-spotted chrome. 'You ain't gonna turn into an elephant or a bookcase on me, are you?' he asked the stolen machine.

He started the motorcycle, and set off again. After a quarter mile, he turned for I-91, aiming again towards New York City. Common sense dictated otherwise – you don't ride straight into a place about to be obliterated by a giant rock from outer space – but now something was leading him on. Something, or someone . . .

He was hitting sixty when he spotted her again, standing there in the road ahead of him, silhouetted against an illuminated billboard advertising some local diner. Easy meat!

Mind-fuck or not, the bitch was going under his wheels this time. He accelerated, leaning over the handlebars. *Byebye, baby.*

But just as he anticipated feeling her bones crunching beneath him, she vanished yet again. He pulled hard on the brakes, howling in outrage. The bike slewed into the verge, throwing him off. Slamming across gravel, he found himself tumbling over before landing on his back in a ditch.

It was several moments before he could cough activity back into his lungs. Gasping, he thrashed around, trying to regain self-control, then slumped back exhausted. Eventually he opened his eyes to stare up at the black sky, the grey clouds scudding stealthily across it. It would be so easy just to lie here, to let those silent clouds calm his frenzied mind; for once to just give up fighting the world.

But then, as if somebody had pressed a switch, the strange movie began in his head.

Dark city streets, with buildings looming in on either side like cliff faces. Ahead, a white building ablaze with light. The sign: MACY'S. Burning flags ringing its upper floors. Crashed vehicles littering the street. On a broken fire truck, a dead fireman, his hand outstretched, pointing. Lebrett's view following the line of the bloody finger towards a dark space between two buildings. This darkness was growing in size, swallowing the buildings around it, and advancing towards him until he found himself also enveloped in total darkness – and falling, falling, falling . . .

Kara tried to imagine a long shaft leading up to the surface, and at the end of it, her parents or sister. But all she could see was blackness. There was *nothing*.

And so Kara realized she was truly alone, lost somewhere underground, at the mercy of Mr Rodin.

But then she had made another contact instead. Been right into his mind.

The bad man, Lebrett.

At first she had felt so terrified, she had tried to close the tunnel linking them. But it remained defiantly open; binding them together. Though acutely aware he would take great joy in killing her, something else told her he might be of help to her as well.

CARL HUBERMAN

He'll want to kill you, yes, but you can stop him. You can control him.

Even in her terror, Kara could see an advantage.

Call him here. Make him come. He can save you against his will. He's your only hope.

And so Kara began to lure him towards her, through her mind. While lying on the floor in pitch blackness, unable to move, unable to see, she envisaged Lebrett – moving towards New York, the person in the world who wished her most harm.

She began to weep. However logical the strange voice in her head, she was feeling petrified at the thought of it. Soon her sobbing filled the vault . . . But then she heard another sound that instantly put a stop to her wailing.

Mocking laughter, then a voice, close by. 'Scared, little girl? So you should be.'

Kara screamed and screamed.

CHAPTER 33

'Stanley, are you there?' It was Cheryl's voice.

'Yes.'

'Mr Drexill?'

'Yes.'

'Where?'

'Here.'

'Where's here?'

'I have no idea.'

All was black, a total all-consuming darkness – no fragment of light penetrating. Only sound could give them any sense of direction, but even this was distorted by a faint echo which might prove deceptive.

Cheryl reached out her hand. She felt nothing but cool emptiness, so remained still rather than stumble about blindly.

'We need to determine exactly where each of us is,' hissed Stanley.

'Can either of you locate me just from my voice?' said Cheryl.

Stanley thought she was somewhere to his left.

'Keep talking,' he suggested. 'I'll move towards you.'

He took three steps over ground that felt hard like rock, yet smooth. Then he made contact with cloth, and reached his arms wide to hug her.

'Thank God,' he said. 'I've never wanted to hold you so much.'

'That's a comfort,' replied Drexill, 'but I do believe you're looking for your wife.'

Stanley instinctively withdrew but Drexill grabbed him by his upper arms. 'Don't take this the wrong way, Stanley, but I'm not letting you go. Cheryl, come find us now.'

Suddenly Stanley felt new contact from behind, and soon all three were hugging tightly in sheer relief.

'Okay, enough already,' said Drexill. 'I suggest we keep our hands linked, though.'

'At least we're safe here from whatever's happening outside,' Cheryl commented.

'I have my doubts,' muttered Drexill. 'They're probably planning to use tactical nukes.'

'Would they really do that?'

'Depends who's got the President's ear.'

Cheryl sighed. 'Why do I suspect the Rodins are involved?'

'OCI's a big organization now. Much bigger than when Stanley left it. The Rodins are also considered neutrals; whereas the CIA, the FBI and the NSA are seen as having their own agendas. But the Rodins obviously *do* have an agenda, too – Washington doesn't know it, that's all.'

'We're more than safe,' argued Stanley, thinking out loud.

'Meaning?'

'We were *invited* in here to shelter from attack. And those peaks springing up everywhere, they were shielding us.

Whatever this place is, it knows we're here.' He stared into the blackness.

'So what is "it"?' asked Drexill.

'Let's be logical, and work this through,' started Cheryl. 'It's pitch black in here, so we can't see anything in any direction. But we know we're *inside* the asteroid, and wherever we are, it must have sides and a top and a bottom.'

'So we could try walking?'

'Until we find there's a too sudden way down,' cautioned Drexill.

'Now who's being negative?' said Cheryl. 'I say we all start walking together carefully in one direction. Any of us finds the floor suddenly missing, they yell out quickly.'

'I don't think we need telling that,' said Stanley.

'Let's form a ring,' suggested Drexill.

Stanley took Drexill's hand in his right, Cheryl's in his left. 'We all together now? Right, which way?'

'I'll move backwards,' Cheryl said. 'I'm the lightest, so it'll be easier for you two to haul me up if I go over the edge.'

They started a shuffling progress, which was understandably slow, the only sound their nervous breathing.

'I just wish I could *picture* what kind of space we're in,' said Cheryl eventually. 'To give it some kind of dimension at least. Let's concentrate on that, shall we.'

There was a pause. 'I'm imagining a tunnel. High, wide, flat-bottomed,' said Stanley, suddenly inspired.

'So am I,' agreed Cheryl, pleased to have come up with the same mental image.

Then the darkness suddenly vanished and their world was revealed.

They were indeed in what appeared to be a massive tunnel: a perfect semicircular vault rising out of a smooth flat floor. It was like a rail tunnel wide enough to accommodate half a dozen tracks. They could see they were at one extreme end of it, a half-circle of blank wall right behind them, the tunnel disappearing away into the distance ahead. Even though they could see now, they didn't let go of each others' hands.

Drexill was carefully studying the section of wall nearest to him. At first it seemed to be made of brick, but as he ran his fingers along the joins, they disappeared at his touch to leave a uniformly flat surface like polished slate. Once he removed his hand, the brick work pattern returned. The wall was like a giant chameleon altering its appearance at will.

'I really don't like this place,' he concluded. 'And where is that light coming from?'

Cheryl realized for the first time that there was no visible source of illumination. She swept her eyes around the massive curve of the ceiling. 'Right, I'm going to try an experiment, but I need your cooperation. Remember how the light appeared when we tried to visualize this place? Perhaps if the three of us together could visualize—'

'A way out of here?' offered Stanley.

'That would be nice,' agreed Drexill.

The rear wall of the tunnel suddenly opened like an iris lens to reveal the flaming surface of the asteroid. Heat rushed in and scorched their faces.

'No, we don't want an exit!' she yelled.

The two men nodded, then all three willed the opening closed again.

'See, we're in here for a good reason. The exterior's no longer safe.'

'What the hell was going on outside?' asked Stanley.

'Looked like wreckage,' answered Drexill. 'Missiles maybe, or one of the fighters got too close.'

Cheryl had visions of one of those black peaks suddenly shooting hundreds of feet into the sky to skewer a passing aircraft and drag it down, like a giant frog snatching insects from the air.

'So what next?' asked Stanley, catching her eye.

'If one of the twins is in here somewhere, we need to find her. Let's get moving.'

They peered along the seemingly infinite tunnel.

'This asteroid thing's five miles across,' reminded Drexill. 'This tunnel could run the full length of it.'

'Maybe so,' said Cheryl. 'But I don't fucking care.' She strode away from them.

CHAPTER 34

Kara was too terrified by the voice even to run. She emptied her bladder, shrieking herself hoarse. Finally out of breath, she paused – only for the voice to return, just as close as before.

'I expected better of you. Now, shut up.'

Between her sniffles, Kara asked who was there, all the time glancing about, but all she could see was never-ending blackness.

'It's your friend, Parvill,' he answered, so close she expected to feel his breath on her face.

'Why are there no lights? Why are you doing this?'

There was silence.

'Where are you?' she wailed.

'Tiresome. All that talent, and you're behaving like a silly little girlie.'

'I'm eight!' she protested.

'Yeah, eight going on eight hundred . . .'

'Where are you?'

'Remember on the train Lebrett was wearing a metal collar?'

'Yes.'

'Well, now you're wearing one, too. It keeps us in touch, tells me exactly where you are.'

'Where's Lorri? What have you done with her?'

'If you don't know by now, your value to me could be less than I hoped.'

Kara did not know what he meant. She had no idea what was happening down here. As for Lorri, whilst each usually knew exactly how the other was feeling even when apart, down here she was cut off and literally in the dark.

'I'm . . .' she started, then hushed. The man's tone of voice told her not to say anything more about Lorri.

'Look, I've got things to do now. I'll get back to you. Don't be going anywhere, honey lamb.' And he was gone.

She called after him several times, until she was certain he had abandoned her. Then she allowed herself to cry. Far worse than her own predicament was not knowing if Lorri was even alive.

Her sobbing lasted a long time, but when it eventually died away so did her fear. In its place came resolve. Now she knew she was alone again, she could work unhindered. And, with Lebrett on his way, she needed to be ready for him.

First, she must see if she could free her hands. She rolled on to her front, then carefully eased her knees up under her stomach, all hunched up. Taking a deep breath, she pushed her shoulders back, and slid her bound hands around her buttocks until they were down behind her knees. Next, she rolled on to one side, then on to her back, pulling her knees to her chest as tight as she could, then, despite the agony, pushed her wrists down to her ankles. In seconds her hands were in front of her, and she was able to breathe a sigh of relief.

At all costs she must avoid that hole. So, crawling on her front, she felt around in the pitch darkness with her bound hands until she could discern the edge of the pit. Now certain of its location, she squirmed through 180 degrees, and on aching knees crawled for a full minute in that new direction, until she felt sure she was far away from the hazard.

Finally, she tackled the bonds themselves, first testing them with her teeth. They seemed surprisingly thin, but wrapped around her wrists many times. She recognized the material as plastic-covered electric flex. She ran her tongue over the wires until she located a single knot, but rather than attack the knot itself, she bit into a strand of flex adjacent, biting at the soft plastic with her canine teeth. Once she had exposed the wire inside, the task became considerably more unpleasant as her teeth ground into the thin strands of copper. She had to stop regularly to spit the bitter taste of it out of her mouth, the loose ends stabbing her tongue painfully.

Every time she felt a strand of wire part she would tug experimentally at her bonds. Only when the fifth wire had been severed, and her jaw was aching almost intolerably, did the bonds shift as she tried to tug her wrists apart. One more wire, and she was able to wriggle one hand free, then discard her bonds completely. Her next problem was to produce some light.

Again, her mind ran through all the possibilities until finally a solution occurred: she must search through the corpses for some matches. She remembered they were dressed in ordinary street clothes, presumably the same ones in which they had been abducted. Maybe their pockets had not been emptied – and with forty corpses to choose from, surely one might be carrying matches. Reluctantly she started feeling her way forward in the dark until she encountered the cold, taut canvas containing the first body.

Reaching up on tiptoe, she ran her hand along the length of the recumbent figure's side until she located a trouser pocket. But that pocket being empty, she scooted underneath the hammock and tried the next one along that same row. Although there were no matches there either, she was at least encouraged to find some small change; so clearly their pockets had not been emptied.

She moved on until her outstretched hand found the next corpse. Again, just some coins, and a handkerchief.

After investigating six of the bodies, she now knew exactly how far she must proceed to make contact with the next one.

She had counted off eight of them in all when she at last found what she was looking for. Pulling out the slim package, she raised it to her nose and sniffed triumphantly.

Fumbling the matchbook open, she located just four remaining cardboard stalks. Excited, she ripped one off and ran it across the scratch board – squealing with delight as it flared into life.

Just inches away, a face with bloodshot, bulging eyes stared back at her, open-mouthed with its tongue protruding like a purple slug. Terrified, Kara screamed and dropped the burning match. Its weak flame sputtered out at her feet. Turning away from where the gruesome sight had been, she struck a second match, eager for its comforting light. Mesmerized, she stared at it like it was a long-lost friend. Finally the flame reached her fingers, forcing her to drop it quickly. Like a starving child at a banquet, she ripped off a third match.

No! her mind screamed. *You've only two left!*

But how could she ensure more light than the two remaining matches could offer? To her disgust, the voice in her mind quickly provided the answer. But it was also utterly horrible. She felt herself rising, puppet-like, and walking back to the same hammock. She felt the material and found the canvas was dry, so she carefully struck the third match and held its weak flame against the hammock's edge. But, too soon, the match flickered and died.

Only one match left. This wasn't going to work.

Then again, inspiration. Holding the matchbook between her teeth, she reached up to the hideous corpse. She grabbed his waistband, looping her fingers under the leather belt, then pulled herself up. After a struggle, she kicked her legs up too, then climbed on top of the body. Fighting nausea, she pulled the dead man's trouser pocket inside out until it made a bunny tuft. Then, taking the matchbook from her mouth, she leaned close and lit the final match. As the material caught alight, she watched in fascination as the flame began to spread.

As, slowly but surely, the grey trousers ignited, soon she had to back away. Losing her balance, she toppled off, staring up from the floor at the fire spreading along the man's legs and buttocks.

Soon the hammock itself was alight. Glancing about, she could now see clearly a good half of the vault, the other bodies shimmering in the dancing fire glow.

Just then, the hammock bottom disintegrated and the

burning corpse slumped to the floor. The stench of burning flesh drove her backwards towards the elevator doors. Now able to see them in detail, she tried in vain to prise them open with her fingers.

Smoke suddenly enveloped her, and as she knelt down, coughing, she could hear another sound. A buzzing noise from far away, but definitely a new sound nonetheless. She stood up and began hammering on the elevator doors.

But then she heard a high metallic screech. Such an ugly sound could not mean good news. She peered behind her through the flickering gloom. The burning hammock was giving off less light now, but the corpse continued to emit a weak lambent glow, almost like a giant candle.

For several minutes, the high-pitched whining continued. Moments after it stopped there was a clatter at the bottom of the elevator shaft. Surely rescuers would identify themselves or Rodin would talk to her again via her collar? But now there was only silence from above.

She stared around the hazy vault, but there was nowhere to hide. And at the far end lay that frightening hole in the floor.

For a long while she stared at the elevator doors, the light from the listless flames dancing weakly on their metallic surface. But there were no further sounds. Perhaps the mystery intruder had gone. Then a thud just the other side of the doors made her start. Something heavy had landed at the bottom of the shaft.

Then she heard a voice. 'Sonofabitch. Son of a fucking bitch!'

It was him – Lebrett! She tried to reach through to his

mind again, to calm him. But that was like hitting a brick wall; he was out of control. As if she could ever hope to control the raging bull of his rage and vengeance.

Lebrett was not here to rescue her but to kill her. And, unless he made some stupid mistake, she would never be given the chance to overcome him again. All she could do now was hide. But *where*?

By the time Lebrett's feet touched solid ground again, the shaft was filled with a foul-smelling fog. Just what had he let himself in for here? He found the crowbar he had dropped and forced it into the gap between the elevator doors. He eased them apart – and stepped into hell.

Never in his wildest imaginings could he have foreseen what confronted him. Bodies dangling from the ceiling like some goddamn science-fiction mortuary. *Dozens* of them! And one of them lying burning on the floor. Then there was the thick acrid smoke, the stink, and the darkness at the far end of the tunnel. His eyes began to water as he edged along one wall. What the fuck *was* this place? And where was that damn girl?

He waited until his eyes had become accustomed to the wavering light, then stepped forward. Her presence hit him like a searchlight beam, and he faltered as that knowledge stamped itself on his mind. *She's here!*

'Beep-beep, girl. Gonna kill you, bitch. Gonna kill you *so* much. Come and get what you deserve. Give me some screaming, give me some blood, give me some . . . peace.'

There was no response save a muted spitting from the

burning corpse, its weak flame fuelled by the flammable body fat under its crisped skin.

'You done that?' he continued. 'You got you some barbecue?'

Reaching the first row of bodies, he looked closer. *Goddamn, what is happening here?* Some of the bodies looked half decayed, covered in sores, their hammocks stained. It was disgusting.

'What the fuck is this place, girl?'

He walked along the row, until he came across a girl in her twenties. He pulled her head up by her long red hair. She had once been attractive; now she was rat meat.

He dropped her head, and addressed the vault.

'Look, girl, I got limited patience. Longer you make me wait, the worse it's gonna be. So, come on, show yourself.'

Where the fuck is the little bitch? Maybe she's run off into the dark down there at the end.

The light from the corpse wasn't strong, and he himself only had a lighter. He cursed himself for not bringing a flash-light from the fire truck. Before he ventured further, he needed to check out all these bodies just in case one of them was the little girl herself. At the centre of the vault he paused. There were corpses strung from the ceiling in twin rows of ten on either side of him, making forty in all, but in this dim light he could distinguish neither age nor sex.

He pulled the fire axe from his waistband and turned to the nearest one, then swung the blade down as hard as he could, feeling it slice inches into flesh. Perceiving no reaction, he moved on to his next victim.

*

Kara knew her only chance of survival was to look straight into Lebrett's eyes, but that would mean coming within feet of him. She had clambered up on to the slender corpse of a teenage girl – lying flat on top of her. She could see Lebrett across the vault, hacking at each corpse in turn. His downward strokes were lethal. She was trapped in the presence of the beast.

Lebrett had completed the first of the two rows on one side of the vault and was working his way back up the second. He was becoming angrier at his lack of success, until soon he was screaming incoherently, hacking at each new body more viciously. The attack on one corpse was so ferocious, a dismembered arm fell at his feet. He ignored it, moving on to his next victim. He then dashed across the vault to the remaining two rows, where he vented his fury on a middle-aged man. A dozen blows lopped off both hands, the head, and then the rest of his arms.

Kara hugged the dead girl's cold body, watching with one eye as Lebrett assaulted another hammock. Now there was only one between her and the madman.

Then the hammock next to her own crashed to the ground. Its occupant, a boy barely older than herself, was decimated in a flurry of blows. Lebrett paused for a moment, drawing in breath, then stepped towards her, arms raised ready to strike. Suddenly, she pushed herself up from the hammock and screamed.

Lebrett froze, startled, and their eyes met. With a howl, he averted his gaze and charged with axe high. Kara threw herself backwards off the hammock.

The axe missed her by inches, burying itself in the corpse's spine.

'Got you, you fucking bitch! Got you good!' He hacked again and again, laughing maniacally.

Kara crabbed backwards, trying to keep herself from Lebrett's sight. As the hammock split, tumbling the remains of the girl on to the floor, he caught sight of Kara seated on her backside.

'Don't!' she shouted, her voice pathetically small.

Lebrett stepped over the body, his eyes trained on Kara's feet. At all costs he must avoid her eyes – until his axe split her skull in two.

'Not this time, bitch. Whatever the fuck you got, it's not gonna save you this time.'

He was only two steps away.

'Please, stop,' she begged. 'I haven't done anything wrong—'

'Keep talking, girl. Gonna cut those words right out of your throat.'

Kara quieted. All she could do was stare up, still hoping to catch his eye, but Lebrett was too wise for that even in his fury. He raised the axe, still staring at her socks. 'I win, baby. I win.'

'Lebrett?' said a male voice. 'Is that you, Jacob?'

'Help me!' shrieked Kara.

Lebrett faltered. 'Who the . . . ?'

Kara rolled sideways. Lebrett followed her movement –

then noticed her gold collar for the first time. He grabbed it, pulled her up, choking her.

Parvill Rodin spoke again. 'You hurt that girl, Lebrett, and I'll finish you.'

'And how will you do that, cocksucker?' he yelled, saliva flecking Kara's cheek. 'Beam down like fucking Captain Kirk? There's just me and the girl here!'

Kara's collar had become a noose. She could no longer breathe, and knew she only had seconds left.

Lebrett hissed into her ear, 'Gonna watch you choke, baby – let your friend hear you die. Then I'm gonna cut you up into iddy-biddy pieces.'

'Let her go, Lebrett,' ordered Parvill.

Lebrett laughed, and yanked harder on the collar.

Kara flailed her arms, tugging at her throat. Her vision started to turn red. Then that small voice spoke to her again. *Go limp*, it said. *Pretend you're dead.*

It wasn't difficult to obey.

Lebrett stared for a moment, then he dropped her. She lay unmoving. He nudged her with his boot. No response. He laughed.

'Now for some carving . . .'

When he rolled her over, her face was purple. Her eyes were shut and she wasn't breathing. This had been quicker than he wanted – another disappointment.

'Lebrett?' came Parvill's angry voice. He ignored it. *So, what comes off first?* He raised the axe. *Let's start with the arms.*

Suddenly, Kara sat upright, grabbing his ears, and pulled his face forward till it was inches away.

As their eyes locked, he screamed.

Kara waited until she felt him go slack. 'Put it down,' she said hoarsely.

He meekly lowered the axe.

CHAPTER 35

Jacob Lebrett was now sitting slumped against the wall, head in hands, looking confused and sorrowful. Kara Carter stood in front of him, small hands on hips.

'Mr Lebrett, we need to get out of here.'

He stared up at her, his face an amalgam of grief and hatred. For, now she was in control, he was afraid of her.

'Leave me alone,' he rasped.

'You said we can't go back up the elevator shaft,' she persisted. 'So we have to find another way out.'

'Why? We're doomed anyway.' He sounded like a petulant child.

'Not if we can get out of here.'

Puzzlement crossed his face. 'What do you mean? That thing's going to hit soon.'

She stamped her foot. 'Not if you can get us out of here!'

He rose as if to attack her, but an inexplicable horror again grabbed his mind, and he slumped back trembling.

Kara walked over to the second burning corpse – which Lebrett had ignited on her instructions. The smell of burning flesh was appalling, a yellow fug lying across the floor like a sickly mist.

She realized that Lebrett was currently in her power, but

he was a creature of cunning, and his mind would be fighting against hers all the time.

She was beginning to gag at the foul stink, so moved away towards the darkness at the collapsed end of the tunnel.

Lebrett peered after her, hugging his knees. Whenever he began to feel hatred towards her, his stomach would flip over, his heart start to race – and he knew that to harm her was to harm himself. She had planted something inside his head.

After Christie Rodin had shot him, Lebrett had been certain he was dead. Thrown out of the bucking carriage, he had lain semi-conscious in a field. Only the sound of police sirens had roused him. Moving into the shadows, he had headed for the lights of a nearby farmhouse. There he had persuaded the owner to dress his wounds – before killing him and stealing his car. He had headed south, ignorant of the threat posed by the approaching asteroid. At a solitary roadblock near Waterbury, Connecticut, he had killed a National Guardsman and stolen his uniform, his M-16 rifle, and a BMW motorcycle. But still he continued heading for New York City, at first ignorant of its fate. He figured that once there he would have a better chance of avoiding detection by the authorities.

But even after he had learned the truth of the city's impending doom, and had been summoned by the girl, he knew deep down it wasn't just her who was calling him; it was also the lure and excitement of the impending catastrophe. Instead of terror, he felt exhilaration. This Erebus, it was the most *beautiful* thing he had ever seen – and that's why he knew he must go to New York, to be there when it happened.

As he had travelled through a panic-stricken New York City, the stolen motorcycle enabling him to outrun any challenges, he had found his strange dream coming true. Instinctively, irresistibly, like following a beacon, he had been drawn to the alley outside, and to the elevator shaft – and the certain knowledge that the bitch was there under his feet.

Using gear taken from an abandoned fire truck on 34th Street, he had first cut through the elevator floor. Then, arming himself with an axe, he had tied several fire hoses together to lower himself down the deep shaft.

He realized now that, all the time, the girl had been giving him directions. Trapped as she was, she needed a saviour, and he was the only one she was able to communicate with, thanks to their damned psychic link. He wondered if it was all her doing, or if his tumour was playing a part. Either way, he was like a puppy dog and she was his mistress – until he worked out a way to outwit her . . .

He could hear the bitch calling him now.

'Mr Lebrett, there's a big hole over here. It might be an escape route, so come and help me.'

Kara's collar was becoming uncomfortable, so she decided to risk enlisting his help.

'This collar, Mr Lebrett, could you take it off me?' Parvill Rodin hadn't come through recently.

The prospect of getting his hands near her throat excited him, but the thought vanished as quickly as it formed. He found her collar was much looser than his own, and with his eyes held steady by her powerful gaze, he eased fingers inside the rim to lever its lock-joint. It parted surprisingly easily, and he tossed it aside, then turned his attention to the gap in the floor.

It wasn't wide, about three feet only. In the weak light there was no way of telling how deep it ran. Maybe a crack caused by subsidence.

'You want to go down there?' he asked.

'You go first, and take a look.'

'Can't, not with my shoulder. Got shot, remember?' It did hurt like a sonofabitch, although it hadn't hindered his descent down the elevator shaft.

'Let me see it,' she said warily.

He removed his jacket to show his bloody bandage. She extended a couple of fingers and touched it.

'There,' she said. '*Now* will you get down the hole.'

He flexed his shoulder. The pain had vanished! He edged away from her. What the hell was she?

'The hole,' she insisted, and he lowered himself over the edge.

The stench from the two burnt corpses was almost over-powering, but a rising breeze was strong enough to dispel it from the gap. He soon discovered the source of the air current, for his lighter revealed another tunnel, perfectly circular and sloping downwards, the hole itself clearly caused by the collapse of a section of this new tunnel's roof. He was tempted to head off down it and leave the girl behind, but doubted he would be able to escape her mental control.

'Found another tunnel,' he announced instead.

With Kara clinging to his neck, he worked his way back down into the dark cleft till they drew level with the second tunnel's entrance. There Lebrett told her to jump down. She studied the entrance in the flickering glow from his lighter.

It was a circle of brick, eight feet in diameter. Though the floor seemed dry, the walls were covered in dark lichen. It smelled musty, as if succumbing to mould.

'What do you think this is?'

'Probably a sewer,' he sniffed, 'though not used recently. Maybe for draining off flood water. But we're very deep here.' He did some mental arithmetic. 'Maybe two hundred feet below street level.'

'And we really need to go up.'

They walked in silence for ten minutes, the tunnel continuing to slope gently downwards, its shape unchanging. Several smaller tunnels joined it, entering at steeper angles. There was no sound except the distant rush of water, but from which direction it was impossible to tell.

'So what are you going to do when we get out of here?' Lebrett asked.

'I don't know. I just know I must get out.'

She realized she had spoken the truth: it *was* imperative she get above ground – and not just to escape the impact of Erebus. There was something else she *had* to do; she only wished she knew exactly what.

The flame from his lighter had grown steadily weaker, reducing their world to a couple of feet in all directions, and then it died altogether. Unable to spark it back into life, Lebrett tossed the lighter away. As pitch darkness enveloped them Kara felt him grab her hand. For a split-second she gained comfort from his presence, but then his grip tightened, ragged nails digging into her flesh.

Suddenly he sniggered in the returning blackness. 'Dark, ain't it, babe?'

'If we keep—'

'If you keep your trap shut.'

She sensed him leaning down towards her, and felt his tongue on her ear.

'Can't see your eyes now, girl. Your witchcraft ain't got no juice.'

Kara began to tremble with fear. She tried to pull her hand free, and began to scream.

'That's it, girl. Let me hear you.'

There was a rushing noise, distant but growing.

'What the fuck's that?'

Kara was too frightened to think, but used the distraction to squirm free of his grasp.

'Not so fast, bitch,' he yelled, but he didn't follow her.

The roaring sound was growing, air rushing past them strong enough to ruffle their clothes. And then it was on them, their ears popping with the pressure as a wall of water smashed into them, tumbling them end over end down the pipe.

Now and again they managed to draw breath, but the disorientating shock of their immersion in numbing cold water contrived to defeat every effort made to right themselves. And then, as the tunnel turned a bend, they were scraped along its wall, heads and limbs thudding against brick.

How long they were carried along neither could tell. All they knew was pain and a terrible coldness. Lebrett gulped desperately for air only to swallow more water. As he began to give up the struggle, something gripped his wrist and he felt himself being wrenched against the flow of water. Then there were more hands, and suddenly he was being hauled out of the water. He was thrown face down, coughing up water and bile; and then he was clubbed across the head.

Kara's mind was screaming for Lorri, for mommy and daddy, no longer able to feel sensation in her arms and legs. Pain seared through her head as she was pulled out of the water by her hair and tossed on top of the unconscious Lebrett. As she began to pass out, a dark shape loomed over her and she heard a voice above the roar of water.

'Pork bellies on the rise! Trading good, trading good!'

CHAPTER 36

'Couldn't we move faster?' suggested Cheryl.

'Yeah, but why tire ourselves out?'

For an hour, they had been walking along the same unchanging tunnel. Stanley glanced back again.

'Still there,' he announced wearily.

Cheryl looked back too – to see that the rear wall of the tunnel continued to keep pace with them. Yet the tunnel ahead of them seemed as long and straight and endless as ever.

'The floor could be moving backwards under us,' she said wearily. 'We might not even have moved an inch.'

Drexill decided to add to their gloom. 'Might I also point out that this rock we're in is about the size of lower Manhattan. Think of all the tunnels in that city. And think how long it would take to walk them. *Especially when you don't even know where you're going.*' He rubbed the bridge of his nose. 'It's useless.'

Cheryl stamped on the floor in frustration. 'We came here to find our baby. I'm not stopping now.'

'Neither am I,' agreed Stanley.

Drexill suddenly crouched down and rubbed his hand across the tunnel floor. 'I think this is some kind of metal,' he said. 'And I bet all that stuff outside is metal too. Not rock as we thought.'

'Knowing that doesn't help us though, does it?' complained Cheryl.

Drexill tried to calm her. 'We're only in a tunnel because you two *thought* of a tunnel. Maybe you should have thought of something else.'

'You're saying that if we'd thought of an elevator, that's what we'd be on instead?'

'Yes. Seems to me we've only got two choices,' he concluded. 'Either sit and do nothing, because we don't know where we're going . . .'

'Or go *somewhere*, for the sake of doing *something*?' added Stanley with a long sigh.

'There is a third possibility,' offered Cheryl. 'Stanley and I could together try and contact one of the twins. They can read our thoughts perfectly, so maybe they could pick up on us, and let us know where they are.'

'Worth a try,' agreed Stanley. 'But I think we need something like a TV screen.'

An area of the black metal at their feet suddenly smoothed over.

Cheryl took Stanley's hand. 'So what should we think of?'

'A distinctive image,' suggested Drexill. 'Something that's simple and clear and *safe*.'

'The two girls, playing out in the yard in their yellow dresses,' said Stanley. Why the image had sprung to mind he didn't know, but it seemed to fit ideally Drexill's suggestion.

Cheryl squeezed his hand as she too fixed on this familiar image. They elaborated the details, in each other's mind building up a perfect family day. It was a June afternoon, a

Sunday, and a small rubber paddling pool had been filled with water. The girls were making daisy chains. There was the smell of barbecue: tofu burgers and skinned chicken drumsticks sizzling. It made both their hearts ache to think of simple pleasures that they might never experience again. One of the girls turned and smiled at Stanley. She said something but he couldn't understand her.

Cheryl, too, watched one of her daughters talking, but the words weren't clear to her either. She couldn't even tell for sure if it was Kara or Lorri, as they were dressed identically.

'What is it, honey?' she pleaded. 'Tell momma what it is.'

But her answer remained indistinct.

'Please,' begged Stanley. 'Please let us know where you are.'

But the little girl merely pointed at the paddling pool.

'What about the pool?' Cheryl wondered.

Drexill found himself stepping away from the pair, both of them now addressing what to him was still a blank surface.

As Stanley and Cheryl stared intently at the pool, bright blue decorated with a yellow fish pattern, it seemed to fill to the brim. The little girl was standing to one side of the pool, pointing down, and mouthing over and over a single word. 'Water.'

Stanley was about to give up trying to understand – the scene had become static, like a paused videotape – then the water started to bubble, almost immediately overflowing the rim of the pool. It flowed towards them, lapping at their feet, and they both stepped back. Suddenly, Drexill grabbed Cheryl's arm.

'Hey, pay attention!' His voice sounded curiously distant.

Stanley heard the man's voice, too, but was also too absorbed by the phantom tide of water welling from the paddling pool. Soon it was gushing ten feet into the air before splashing down into the grass at their feet.

'Will you two wake up!' yelled Drexill.

Cheryl was the first to lose sight of the vision and to refocus on the man's frantic face.

'What? What is it?'

Drexill stepped aside, and pointed beyond.

'Oh, my God . . .' gasped Cheryl, nudging Stanley in the side.

All three stared along the tunnel at a dark wall of water racing towards them. Already chest high, it was rising all the time – and travelling much too fast for them to outrun.

'And we were thinking of water just then . . .' said Cheryl.

Stanley started to edge backwards as the wave rose to fill the entire height of the tunnel, pushing a wall of air in front of it.

'We were being *made* to think of water,' he shouted back.

'By who?' yelled Drexill, mesmerized by the sight.

'By our daughter. But *why*?' Cheryl gasped before she was engulfed.

All three were slammed backwards by the force of the surge, then dragged down into its icy blackness, rolling over and over until they found themselves tumbled together to the ground, spluttering like stranded fish. The water wall then continued along the tunnel until it dashed itself against the end wall – and vanished.

Stanley was the first to sit up, desperate to get air back into his lungs. As he finally caught his breath he saw Cheryl on her knees, vomiting, while Drexill lay on his front, hacking on to the tunnel floor.

'You ... you okay?' he demanded, hugging her shoulders.

'I ... I've felt better,' she managed.

'Did you see that?' Drexill gasped. 'It was a bore.'

'A what?'

'A single wave,' explained Drexill. 'There's no water behind it. Look.'

Stanley peered along the length of the tunnel. It was totally dry. He spun round and looked back towards the end wall. There, too, there wasn't a drop of water to be seen. And then he realized none of them was wet either. Astonished, he helped Drexill to sit up.

'Another illusion,' said Cheryl. 'We were thinking of water ... '

'Wrong,' countered Stanley. 'We were *made* to think of water. We may have pictured the paddling pool – but *I* didn't imagine the damn thing exploding like that ... '

'There's another thing I don't understand,' said Drexill. 'If I can't see your visions, why do I see what's happening in here, like this tunnel and all that water?'

Cheryl considered this. 'Our visions usually come through Kara or Lorri, but something else is making them stronger; strong enough for even you to experience.'

'And that something else also protected us outside,' added Stanley.

'Something else?' muttered Drexill.

All three looked around, as if they were being watched.

'Which means they could think up anything else, too,' Drexill concluded.

Cheryl took Stanley's hand and they walked on side by side, her tight grip asking the question *What next?* Suddenly she stopped short, jerking him to a halt.

'Do you hear that?' she hissed.

'What?' he whispered back.

A few steps in front of them, Drexill halted and turned, puzzled.

'Can you hear the voices?' Cheryl asked him.

She slowly turned her head to locate the sound. It seemed to be coming from the side wall to her right, and she pressed her ear up against its cold surface. There was a distinct whispering, like a crowd of people taunting her from the other side of wall. None of the words were clear – just a generalized hubbub.

Stanley moved over to the opposite side, and he too could hear hundreds of voices whispering behind the rock's surface.

'What the hell are you two doing?' demanded Drexill, hearing only silence.

Startled, Stanley and Cheryl exchanged looks, then shrugged.

'What is it?' Stanley asked her.

'Family,' said Cheryl quietly before continuing to move on, leaving the two men to stare after her, eyebrows raised.

CHAPTER 37

Kara smelled smoke and for a terrible moment feared she was back in the vault with the burning bodies. Then she heard the crackle of wood, and found the smoke pleasantly familiar. Its embracing heat reassured her: she had been rescued and the fire was there to warm her.

She opened her eyes, and through stinging smoke she studied her new surroundings. Beyond the light cast by the fire everything was in darkness, and even the vague shadows thrown on a nearby wall failed to provide any further clues. She sat up noticing her blue dress was still partially damp. She looked around for Lebrett but could see no one else near. She got to her feet a little unsteadily, then began to circle the blazing fire.

It was fuelled by large planks of wood, possibly railroad ties, and above it was erected an eight-foot-high metal tripod with a large hook hanging down, as if to attach pots to.

'Pork belly futures looking good,' a voice hissed from the shadows.

She spun round, but still could see no one.

'Hello?' she said, her voice echoing.

'Sit down, girl. Gold on the rise.'

She continued moving away from the fire.

Suddenly, a snarling figure leaped in front of her, baring

yellow teeth in a blackened face. 'Sit down before I buy you out!' a shrill male voice cut through the darkness.

The scarecrow figure was tall, emaciated, filthy, and dressed in a lumpy profusion of grey rags. He stank.

'Where am I?' she asked, as calmly as she could.

'On the floor,' he mumbled, his face betraying confusion. He had obviously expected a stronger reaction.

'What floor?'

'The floor, the floor. Zinc looks good.'

Another figure loomed up behind her, grabbing her shoulder. 'He said sit down.'

She wheeled on him, eyes blazing. He immediately let go, as if electrified, and sloped back into the shadows.

'How many of you are there?' she asked.

There were assorted mutterings.

She turned back to the wreck before her and stared into his eyes. 'How many?'

'Six. Was seven before, but Clancy was bought out. Steel was good.'

'And where's the man who was with me before?' she demanded.

'I'm here,' Lebrett spoke from the shadows.

Kara pushed past the cowed scarecrow man to find Lebrett lying on the ground, his hands and ankles trussed up behind him.

'Tell these fuckers to untie me.'

'Maybe,' she said.

'Hey, I saved your life,' he reminded her.

She knelt down and caught his eye. 'And what will you do if I don't tell them to untie you?'

He stared at her, trying to articulate threats, but eventually he tore his gaze away.

Kara rose. 'I want to see you all clearly,' she ordered.

'You can go fuck . . .'

Despite a lot of other threats, soon the other five of the strange group were standing in line alongside Scarecrow, near the fire. Their clothes were so ragged and filthy that the only thing distinguishing one sorry specimen from another was height or girth. Scary though they looked, they trembled as they stared back at this eight-year-old intruder, each now frightened beyond reason.

'Make them untie me!'

'Hush, Mr Lebrett.' Kara did not take her eyes off the ragged assembly. 'Now, tell me what you're all doing here.'

'Pork belly futures down,' muttered Scarecrow. 'Bad investment, bad investment.'

A teenage boy, the smallest of the group, stepped forward.

'We live here.'

Kara stared around her. They seemed to be in yet another abandoned tunnel, garbage strewn everywhere.

'You *live* here?' She shuddered.

'We're undergrounders. Molers,' he explained. 'Got tired of all that up there, so we moved down here.'

'Chrome bad, chrome bad,' Scarecrow mumbled.

'But it's horrible here,' Kara protested.

The stench from the six of them – like a mix of excrement, vomit and rot – was beginning to make her feel sick.

'We get by,' muttered another, distinguishable only by a long, matted beard.

Kara thought she saw insects running through his hair. 'But it's filthy here.'

There was a sudden scuttling at the base of a wall.

'Rats!' she exclaimed.

'We got lots of company.'

'Pork bellies, pork bellies.' Scarecrow's chanting voice bounced around the tunnel. 'Need to invest in steel. Steel good prospect, good prospect.'

Kara shivered, but it wasn't from the cold.

'I need to get out of here,' she explained. 'Up into the city. Can you help me?'

None of them replied. Even Scarecrow just stared at his feet.

'What's wrong?' she asked, puzzled.

'Clancy went up there last night,' offered another of the ragged bunch. 'Told us he saw on TV that some big rock was going to mash everything up there. Said we'd be safe down here.'

'I can help stop it,' she said without thinking. Then realized that was the truth, even if she didn't understand it.

There was fractured laughter.

'Bad speculation. Rumours. No substance. Ignore...' said the Scarecrow; but when he caught Kara's eye he stopped burbling.

The youngest spoke for them all. 'You're just a girl.'

'If I don't get up there, everything down here will get mashed, too,' she tried to explain.

'Clancy said we'd be okay.'

'Well, Clancy was fucking wrong!' screamed Lebrett. 'Listen to the little bitch. She's telling the truth, you ass-wipes.'

'Don't like your mouth, mister,' said the beard.

'I don't like any part of you, fuckhead. Now untie me, and I'll get the girl up there where she belongs.'

'New issue. Very risky,' muttered Scarecrow.

'You hold your tongue, mister, or I'll cut it out.'

'Gotta buy steel, gotta buy steel!'

'Stop it,' insisted Kara. 'One of you has to guide me out, *now*.'

Beard stepped forward. 'Only if *he* stays.'

'Pork belly futures good!'

Kara glanced at Lebrett. Whatever he might have done for her, it was only because she had forced him to.

'All right,' she murmured.

Lebrett started yelling. 'You goddamn fucking bitch! If I get outta here . . . ' Then he turned his venom on his captors. 'You fucking freaks! You're dead, all of you. I'll carve up everyone of you, feed you to your rat friends!'

One of the men stomped over and kicked him in the face.

'How long does it take to get up there?' Kara asked them calmly.

'Street level?' said Beard. 'Half an hour.'

'That's a long time.'

'That's why we're left alone here.'

'Who are you?' she asked.

A boy explained. 'Just people. We didn't fit in. On the street it's hard. Got weather, got hassle. Down here we got each other.'

'But it's *horrible* down here,' she repeated.

The boy edged towards her, held out a hand with two

fingers missing. 'There's worse, much worse up there,' he confided darkly.

There was muttered agreement.

'I'll take you up,' the boy continued.

'Don't leave me here!' shouted Lebrett in panic.

'You'll be all right,' said Kara uncertainly.

'Index on the rise,' cried Scarecrow. 'Good trading today.'

The boy stooped down by the fire and pulled out a blazing brand, dipped it into a pot, then relit it so it gave off a long, lazy flame. He then led the way to a small archway and gestured for Kara to follow, leaving Lebrett to scream his abuse.

As they wormed their way along a dark, narrow passage, their world became reduced to the small circle of light the boy held aloft.

'Where do you find food?' she asked, hoping he might have something to offer.

'We steal things,' he said, 'from garbage bins. And there's always the rats.'

Kara shivered. Suddenly she wasn't so hungry any more. She changed the subject.

'What happened to Clancy?'

'Soldiers got him. Killed him in the subway.'

'Why?'

'You ask a lot of questions . . . He wouldn't stop for them. None of us do.'

A rat ran in front of them, making her start. Her curiosity eventually got the better of her. 'How can you eat rats?'

'Not so bad if you cook them on the fire.'

Somewhere in the distance, Scarecrow could be heard

shouting, 'Pork bellies, pork bellies! Steel paying off. Sell now, sell now!'

A terrible thought occurred to her. 'What are they going to do to Mr Lebrett?'

The boy didn't answer, just stared off into the darkness.

'Look at me!' she shouted. 'Look at me now!'

The boy glanced up. He was terrified, shaking.

'What are they going to do to him?'

'Why are you here?' he blustered.

Just then, there was a terrible scream. Lebrett!

'Take me back there, now!'

The frightened boy bustled past her and began loping back down the tunnel. Kara was barely able to keep up.

There were more screams and incoherent oaths. Something terrible was happening. They arrived back at the fire to find Lebrett on his knees. His shirt was slashed open, two men prodding him closer to the flames.

'Stop that!' shouted Kara.

They turned to her defiantly, then both fell back.

'Untie him!' she ordered, trembling.

'Pork futures down. No profit, no profit!'

Lebrett was yelling uncontrollably, spittle flying everywhere. 'The fuckers were gonna *cook* me!' he screamed. 'Gonna fucking *eat* me!'

Kara, shocked, turned to the boy.

But before he could say anything Beard had stepped forward and cut Lebrett's bonds with a knife ... and Lebrett had whirled round and punched him in the face. As the limp body hit the floor, Lebrett grabbed the knife and slammed it into the man's forehead up to the hilt.

'No!' shrieked Kara.

He turned on her. 'I ain't threatening *you* this time, girl. It's *them* who are gonna pay.'

And pay they did.

Within minutes, every one of the remaining five had been stabbed fatally through heart or throat. Lebrett's animal howls of revenge resounded around their underground lair, which had now also proved their tomb.

Kara screamed in horror as, one by one, each sorry human bundle of rags fell dead or dying at Lebrett's feet. Finally he paused, panting hard with blood splattered all over him, his eyes crazy behind the curtain of lank hair: a nightmare incarnate.

For a long while he and Kara stared at each other. There was no sound now but the crackling from the fire. He was pointing the bloodied knife towards her, his gaze unwavering.

'Beep-beep, baby . . .' he hissed.

CHAPTER 38

'Cantrillo, I think you'd better come see this,' urged Dr Morrow.

He had roused the sheriff from an exhausted sleep in the chair by Tasmin Jonacezk's bed in Rhododendron Clinic. A long day and night, combined with a heavy dose of pain-killers for his wounded thigh, had made the cop really drowsy. Coughing himself awake, the sheriff was grateful to be woken from a nightmare too confusing to recall.

'What's up?' he asked wiping his brow, then setting his cap on his head. He checked his watch. 2.05 a.m. Outside, it was still dark – and the world still existed.

'We've got visitors.' The doctor went back to the door and held it open to reveal a group of adults and children standing in the dim hallway.

Cantrillo limped past the doctor, grimacing at the stiff-ness of his thigh. He was amazed to find at least thirty people crammed into the narrow confines of the corridor. 'What's all this? And what's wrong with the lights?'

'Brown out,' explained Dr Morrow. 'We got an emergency generator going.'

Tasmin crept up behind Cantrillo and grabbed his hand.

'Holy shit!' he gasped, startled at her touch. 'You should be in bed.'

She stared up at him, her face very white, eyes red-rimmed from crying. 'That man who killed momma is now trying to kill Kara.'

When she had been found at the scene of the Greengage Railroad crash, she'd had a note in her pocket reading: JACOB LEBRETT MURDERED MY MOTHER.

'Lebrett? Where are they?'

'New York City,' answered half a dozen other children.

Cantrillo whipped his head round towards them. This was getting spooky.

They disengaged themselves from their parents' hands, and moved as one towards him, young faces with wide eyes appearing in the light cast from Tasmin's doorway.

'Kara needs our help,' confirmed Richard Viffer, a bright lad of twelve. 'Or it's all over,' he added mysteriously.

'Kara Carter?' Cantrillo realized with a shock he had forgotten all about the little girl's parents. After the Carters' house was burned down, and the family disappeared, he had issued an APB, but hadn't expected any further information on their whereabouts.

'What will be all over?' Cantrillo looked to the boy's parents for an answer, but they, like others, merely shook their heads.

'We must go to New York,' urged Tasmin, leaning against the door frame to relieve the weight of her cast on her injured leg.

Dr Morrow nodded towards the TV. Though the sound was turned down, the image of the ominous black shape slowly approaching Manhattan from the north was still plain to see.

'But the whole city's in danger,' he pointed out.

'Not yet,' said Tasmin.

Karl Gance, a ten-year-old redhead with freckles, explained. 'If that man gets Kara, then it's over.'

Cantrillo was lost. 'Kara has something to do with that thing? That thing over New York City?'

From a dozen children's voices an emphatic 'Yes.'

Cantrillo exchanged glances with their anxious parents. 'So what do you want *me* to do?'

'Take all of us to New York,' Tasmin answered simply.

Again, young voices echoed her demand.

'But I can't. What do your parents . . . ?'

There was muttered consternation from the adults.

'We'll go there anyway,' insisted Tasmin, her voice shrill. 'It would be safer if *you* took us, but if you won't . . .' She hobbled on into the corridor.

'That's enough,' insisted Dr Morrow. 'Tasmin isn't fit to travel, and you kids can't go on your own.'

Several parents took this as a cue to step forward to retrieve their children, but the youngsters shied away from them, advancing past Cantrillo and the doctor into Tasmin's room, where a solid group of them filled half the room's available space. All then proceeded to stare unblinkingly at Frank Cantrillo. Unnerved, he tried to speak, but Tasmin interrupted him.

'Sheriff, you'll take us to New York *now*. Kara is in danger and only we can help her.'

'Everyone remaining in the city is in extreme danger,' Dr Morrow pointed out. 'And how do you even know she's there?'

Tasmin turned towards the television screen. All adult eyes followed her gaze.

'Holy hell . . .' muttered Cantrillo.

There were gasps from all round.

They saw Jacob Lebrett staring at them from the screen, his face curled into a snarl, lank hair hanging over it, a blood-stained knife held out in front of him. The fanatical hatred in his face was plain to see.

'This is real?' gasped Dr Morrow, stunned.

'Yes,' said Tasmin. 'It's happening right now. So, you see, we must go.'

She pushed past Cantrillo, and the fifteen other children trooped out after her, ten girls and five boys, their ages ranging from six to seventeen. Some were still dressed in their pyjamas. Several parents attempted to restrain them, but at one look they stepped back as if their sons and daughters were contagious.

As the children marched down the corridor towards the reception area, Mrs Singerman begged Cantrillo to stop them.

'You know I can't, Martha. They're special, and special for a reason – and it looks like, after all these years, they've got that reason. All I do know is we can't stop them now, so we'd best go with them.'

'How are we going to get there?' asked Bill Monkman, a local farmer. 'You'll need a bus to carry all of us.'

Cantrillo brightened. 'That's exactly what we'll use.' He pushed his way through the hesitating crowd of parents. 'Anyone wants to come along with us, follow me.'

But then the questions began.

'What about the roadblocks?'

'What about the National Guard?'

'Will you come with us, doc?' begged Angela Arnold, the only black woman in the group. 'They may need you.'

Dr Morrow agreed, and not too reluctantly. Truth to tell, he was intrigued by this turn of events and anxious to witness the outcome of it all.

Outside, he found Frank Cantrillo leaning in pain against a parked ambulance. He was clasping his thigh with fresh blood staining his trouser leg. A grey-haired nurse was trying to tug him back inside the clinic.

'You're in no fit state to go anywhere, sheriff,' she chided.

'Leave me alone, woman,' he gasped. 'For Chrissakes, Jim, just give me an injection.'

'Frank, no medication I can give you will help that wound. Best give this up.'

'No!' cried Tasmin, shoving her way through the crowd.

'What are you doing?' asked Cantrillo, as Tasmin kneeled in front of him.

Three other children quickly joined her forming a semi-circle around him. Before he could object, all four of them had placed their hands on his injured thigh. He let out a yelp of pain raising one hand instinctively to swipe them away, but suddenly the agony vanished.

'There,' Tasmin announced. 'All better. Can we go now?'

Cantrillo's face was a picture as he tested his thigh, first by pressing down gently with his foot, then stamping on the ground. Finally, he thumped the location of the wound with his fist. It was as if it had never happened.

'How the hell do you *do* that?' he asked in awe.

But all he received were bemused stares.

Iris Bright suddenly became hysterical. 'I've never seen them do that before. *Never.*'

Her husband put an arm around her shoulder. 'S'okay, s'okay. Come on, calm down.'

'Kara?' reminded Tasmin grimly, her pale face seeming to glow in the dark.

Cantrillo pointed down the sweeping driveway of the clinic and, like the Pied Piper, led his motley band into the darkness.

Twenty minutes later they were all aboard Rhododendron's yellow school bus, Cantrillo in the driver's seat, and behind him were fifteen determined children, twenty-three concerned parents, and one increasingly frightened doctor. Ahead of them was a four-hour drive to a mighty, doomed city in search of a single eight-year-old girl.

CHAPTER 39

'You can't kill me,' Kara gasped, more from hope now than conviction.

'I know,' said Lebrett breathlessly, slipping the knife into his waistband. 'Pity, ain't it?'

Kara sat down with a bump, and began crying again, while Lebrett stood laughing at her, hands on hips.

The persistent adult voice in Kara's mind was urging her to get up and get on with her task, but the child in her was too terrified, too confused to listen. She was lost in a world of darkness, with madmen everywhere, and had just witnessed cold-blooded execution. It didn't matter that they had posed a threat to her also: six living, breathing people had just had their lives ended right in front of her. Their *blood* was on her! All she wanted to do was curl up and sleep – hoping that when she woke up mommy would be there to tell her it was all a bad dream. But Lebrett's laughter forced her back to the present – and to the ugly truth he represented.

'See you around, kid.' He began walking away.

Kara stared after him in disbelief. 'You can't just *leave* me!'

'Oh, and like you weren't gonna leave me here to become their pot roast.'

'I came back, didn't I?'

'Tell it to the rats.' And he was gone.

Kara stared into the blackness, suddenly very afraid.

'Please!' she shouted, knowing it would only provoke more laughter.

Go after him, Kara's voice told her. *Annoy him. Make him angry.*

Kara eyed the pile of corpses scattered around the fire. Somehow, that didn't seem such a good idea.

Go after him!

She felt her body jerk as if her mind had sent an electric shock to her limbs. She rose to her feet and started to obey.

Lebrett had taken a burning brand from the fire to use as a torch, so she was able to track him easily. *Just keep him in sight. That way, at least you know you're on your way out.*

But then she saw the light heading downward.

'No! No!' she shouted.

The light stopped moving.

'You have to go up if you want to get out of here,' she yelled.

'But this passage slopes down.'

'So it's the wrong passage.'

'You gotta map, little girl?'

'No.'

'Well, shut the fuck up.'

His light then descended even further, before disappearing completely. Kara raced after him, remembering just in time to look out for steps. Sliding to a halt, she felt around with her foot, located the edge of the first step, then carefully she worked her way down. The passage turned to the right, where she again saw Lebrett's brand flaring a couple of dozen paces ahead. Again it had stopped moving.

'Dead end,' he announced wearily. 'You'd better not be in my way when I get back there, babe.'

As he began working his way towards her, Kara's first instinct was to turn and run up the steps. But her mind refused to let her move. *Stand your ground*, it said. *He can't hurt you.*

'No!' cried Kara, unable to suppress her inner conflict. What was left of her own mind raced with images of mutilation.

'Oh, yes,' sneered Lebrett. 'Runaway truck coming, runaway truck. You don't want to get caught under the wheels!'

Stand still, her voice urged. *Once he gets close . . .*

Lebrett's face loomed closer, the flaming brand held above his head.

God, he so wanted to mess her up.

He thrust his face towards her. 'See ya!' Then he pushed past her, turned the corner and mounted the steps.

Kara rushed after him.

Hit him, the voice urged.

As they reached the top of the staircase together, she started kicking at his ankles.

He whirled on her, knife in hand. 'Gonna end this now . . . Oh shit . . . '

'You can't hurt me, Mr Lebrett.' She held his gaze. 'Do what I say, and we'll both get out of here.'

'How?' he said wearily.

'We have to get back up to the city. Do you hear that noise?'

'What noise?'

'Listen. Just listen for a minute.'

They stood in silence; no sound except for the occasional scuttling of rats. But then a faint roar, getting louder, then receding.

'Okay, I hear it. So what?'

Kara looked at him disdainfully.

'A train!' he suddenly whooped. 'And where there's trains, there's other tunnels.'

'And stations!'

Progress was slow locating passages that sloped upwards, but the intermittent roar of subway trains gave them continued hope of escape.

But Lebrett still had another form of escape on his mind: escape from this little girl's control.

He knew he couldn't attack her directly. If he imagined choking her, his own breathing became restricted; if he thought of stabbing her, he felt cramps in the stomach. It was confusing, it was weird and it was painful. But what if he could *distract* her; make her drop her mental control over him for the couple of seconds it would take to punch her unconscious. Then he could do whatever he wanted with her. But how to distract her? It seemed her mind could encompass half a dozen things at once, and one of these was keeping his rage at bay. Maybe if he could scare her, tell her things that would upset her . . . So, how do you scare an eight-year-old without physically threatening her?

He'd tell her of his childhood as they stumbled along the dark passages; of what it was like to be Jacob Lebrett at her age, and how his father would regularly take him and his older brother out into the woods at night. And how they would walk down the same dog-legged trail, until the Reverend Nathaniel Lebrett would reach the little cave hidden by brushwood. And then the torture would begin.

Jacob would be stripped naked – 'for God is not ashamed of His creation' – and first his father, then his fourteen-year-old brother, would abuse him mercilessly. He was there merely as a receptacle for their perverted lust. Presumably, Noah had been subjected to the same torments in his turn. Whatever, he had become every bit as brutal as his father. And not just sex, there was also the torture. The Reverend Nathaniel was an inventive bastard.

So Jacob started to tell his story, his voice echoing chillingly in the surrounding darkness, his face dancing dementedly in the flames from the burning brand. But whenever he went into the worst details, his mind would shut down and he would lose the thread; and he would find himself locked into that terrible scene as if it was happening all over again. Struggling free of this terrible illusion, he would try again and again, but as soon as he began the scene would crash back into his head – his mouth dry, his father advancing towards him, his brother leering in the background – and then he would be crying and begging, like he himself was just eight years old.

In the flickering light Kara watched the man's performance, knowing that he was trying to relate something awful, but having no way of imagining what it might be. Apparently, he went into the woods with his daddy and brother. What happened there remained a mystery to her. She couldn't help feeling sorry for that little boy lost in his terror, having never known terror herself until now.

After he had recovered from his latest fit of trembling,

she urged him on. They had to find a way out before what little light they had left was extinguished.

But again they reached another dead end.

'What now, Supergirl?' demanded Lebrett, frustrated almost beyond reason.

'Check the whole wall in front of you, in case there's a door.'

Lebrett felt around it and located a handle, but it was coarse with rust and wouldn't move. He kicked at it angrily, then charged it repeatedly until there was a loud crack and the wooden door broke in half.

Lebrett stepped through on to a narrow cement platform. There were red and white lights spaced evenly along each of the tunnel walls. They weren't very bright, but strong enough for them both to make out the tunnel's shape, and how it curved. They had emerged at the inside of a subway bend – and something was approaching fast.

Kara edged herself out on to the walkway and stood beside Lebrett, entranced as a blaze of light moved towards them, a delicious rush of warm air blowing on her face.

Lebrett let out a yell which was drowned as the subway train screamed towards them, carriage lights blazing. Kara clapped her hands over her ears and pressed back against the wall, convinced they would both be scraped away.

Then it was on them, like a screaming snake of noise and light; and, just as quickly, it was gone, rattling away down the tunnel, its animal roar trailing in its wake. Thirty seconds later, silence surrounded them again.

Lebrett let out a high-pitched whoop. 'See that? Goddamn train was packed with soldiers!'

Kara too had noticed the uniformed men seated and standing in the train.

Lebrett was excited. 'Makes sense. You got gridlock up there, you commandeer the subway. That way you can move troops anywhere you want. Which means every station'll be crawling with the military.'

'They'll help us get out of here.'

Lebrett's laugh echoed harshly in the tunnel. As he sat himself down on the walkway, he continued. 'Oh yeah, they'll help us. Me, a convicted killer on the run, and you a kid on a mission to save the city. Think they're gonna listen to your big mysterious plan for stopping that damn rock? And whether it ever hits or not, I'm dead meat anyway. All I got left is deciding how I die; and it sure ain't gonna be in front of a firing squad. They take one look at my Guard threads, they'll know I looted one of their own – and the only way you manage that is if one of their guys is dead.'

'So you're just going to sit here?'

'Seems like a good idea to me.'

'Well, I'm going on.'

And with that she set off along the narrow ledge, not waiting to see if he would follow; it didn't matter now. All she had to do was keep walking until she reached a subway station. There she would decide what to do next, but she must get there first. Unfortunately, the ledge in front of her ended abruptly. By the row of dim lights along the wall, she saw the walkway had partially collapsed, so that she would be forced to climb down right beside the twin tracks. She eased herself over the edge, landing on oily cement three feet below. The entire floor of the tunnel seemed solid, fortunately.

'Watch out for that third rail!' his voice taunted.

'Third rail?' she asked nervously, noticing that each track did indeed have three rails.

'It carries the electricity to power the trains. Touch that, and you'll end up one big French fry.'

'Which is the third rail?'

'Your guess is as good as mine.' He snickered again.

Logic told her that the rail not used for supporting the train's wheels would have to be the electric one, otherwise why was it there? She visualized the train that had recently passed them – and decided it was the outer one of the two running close together. Armed with this knowledge, she walked on.

Since the tunnel curved in front and behind, she could see no lights that might indicate a station. All she had to hope was another train wouldn't come rushing by meanwhile. But then that roaring began again, and the warm wind, and then the blazing light. One train was approaching from the same direction as the first – *and along the track next to her.*

She stared down at the line, eyeing the third rail, then across the divide to the other track. It had a third rail, too, another chance of death. But she certainly couldn't stay where she was.

Above the howl of the train, she heard Lebrett's laughter. 'Choo-choo coming, babe!'

She glanced back as it approached, bright and deadly. She had only seconds in which to act.

She hopped towards the divider but slipped, fought to steady herself. Realizing she might fall, she hurled herself towards the opposite track, grabbing at the rail to stop herself rolling into danger, then screamed as the train bore down on her.

The noise was ear-splitting, the vibration bone-jarring. Her shriek was lost to the hot wind and noise, and flashing lights, and sparks – and then the beast was gone, rattling round the bend and out of sight.

Get up! Get up! her mind now screamed, but her body refused to obey. She had been seconds away from death and could no longer cope with the trauma. So instead she lay still, gripping the rail as tightly as ever she had gripped her mommy's hand.

Lebrett was suddenly there, nudging her foot. 'That was a close one, kid. I thought you were a goner.'

'Shut up! Shut up! Shut up!' she screamed.

Anger now overwhelmed her and she knew how to control him further. She lunged for his leg and sank her teeth into his ankle.

'You little fucker!'

She rolled on to her back and glared up at him.

Lebrett stumbled back, both hands clutching his head. 'You . . . you . . .' he gasped.

'And watch that third rail,' she warned suddenly.

Lebrett froze and slowly looked down. He was just a fraction of an inch from treading on it.

'Now we walk together to the next station,' commanded Kara.

She carefully rose, and began to move away.

For a moment, Lebrett remained rooted to the spot. But

then, as he too began to move, there was a heavy metallic click, followed by a shriek.

Kara was staring down at one foot. The rails had shifted, trapping her shoe.

'Help me, help me!' she shouted in pain.

Lebrett followed her, then knelt down to look.

'Yep, you got it stuck. They must have flipped the junction. Next train along must be switching tracks.'

'*Next train?*'

Suddenly, that roaring again, but this time from the other direction.

'Oh dear,' mocked Lebrett. With her panic, her renewed hold on him had vanished.

'Help me!' cried Kara, tears welling up.

'Now why should I do that?'

'Because you have to.'

'Uh-huh.' Lebrett stepped over the rails and mounted the walkway again.

'The train's coming!' yelled Kara.

Already the tunnel was brightening, the air stirring.

'Don't I know it,' said Lebrett gleefully. 'And I got a front-row seat.'

'Please, Mr Lebrett. Please!' she shrieked.

'Hey, kid, I'm not the one who's threatening you. You know you're my best friend. That train, however, it ain't so discriminating.'

It was visible now, two hundred yards away – and bearing down at full speed.

Kara and Lebrett's eyes locked.

He grinned. 'Too late now. Seems there is a God after all.'

The train was only seconds away, her foot refusing to come loose. And then, even above its all-enveloping roar, she could hear Lebrett chanting.

'Beep-beep, baby! Beep-beep!'

CHAPTER 40

The tunnel just stretched on and on. How long the three of them had been walking Cheryl couldn't tell, but the ache in her calves told her it had been for quite some while. The lack of any measurable perspective was also taking a psychological toll.

Stanley called a halt at last. 'We need to rest,' he said.

'We haven't time,' Cheryl insisted. 'This thing's going to hit soon.'

Drexill was torn between them; he was tired but knew they only had so much time before the asteroid did reach its ultimate destination. So he was reluctantly about to agree with Cheryl, when he heard an unexpected noise.

'What the hell is that?'

It was a distant howl, growing in volume. Something was approaching – something big.

All three stared into the blackness ahead of them. Stanley glanced back over his shoulder to see that the tunnel's end wall was as close to them and as solid-looking as ever.

'Nowhere to go,' he said, raising his voice above the approaching roar.

What the hell is it? three minds chorused.

Hot wind buffeted their faces; a familiar smell assaulted them. All three instinctively stepped backwards, unable to tear their eyes away from whatever was charging towards them over the vibrating ground.

Finally, a shape could be discerned, black against black, growing dramatically in size.

'Oh, my God . . .' was all Stanley could offer.

A subway train was coming fast.

'What the hell do we do?'

'But there's no rails here!' yelled Drexill. 'How the—'

As if to complete their vision of hell, tracks suddenly appeared right under their feet. All three gazes flicked down, then immediately back up at the train.

They tried to throw themselves away from the rails but the train was filling the tunnel, and was now upon them. There was a blinding flash and they felt themselves falling down yet another long dark tunnel, towards a million lights.

CHAPTER 41

Lebrett wouldn't have believed it if he hadn't seen it with his own eyes.

That train was seconds from slamming the little bitch into the next world when there came a blue flash and damned if she didn't *fly* straight out of its path, slap up against the wall just above his head, then crash down on to the walkway next to him.

As he tried to grasp what had happened he heard the train start to brake, the tunnel filling with an ear-splitting shriek as steel ground against steel.

He peered down at the girl in the light from the receding carriages. Her short hair was sticking straight out, her clothes smouldering, and the foot that had been trapped looked twisted and bloody, its shoe and sock both missing. Her eyes were wide open, however, and staring straight up at him. He flinched instinctively but then realized there was no power behind them now. They saw nothing: they were dead eyes.

He noticed her other foot: how the shoe strap was melted, the sock frizzled and scorched. Whether by luck or judgement, she had obviously touched the live rail and the shock of contact had blown her out of the train's path. But it had also killed her – *hallelujah!* Inside his brain, Lebrett had outlived the little bitch.

Kingdom Come

The carriages slid to a stop a hundred yards along the tunnel. Men began immediately jumping out, heading back up the tracks, mounting the walkway.

Gotta get yourself outta here, Jacob.

He leaped up and started running in the opposite direction.

Then two shots rang out. 'Halt! Halt or I'll shoot!'

Lebrett continued a couple more steps – till a shot ricocheted off the tunnel wall beside him, fragments of brick grazing his cheek.

'Okay, okay!' he shouted, raising his arms.

He turned slowly to face a couple of National Guardsmen, their faces already betraying curiosity.

'Who the fuck are you? What unit?'

Lebrett decided to say nothing. He glanced over at Kara, and saw soldiers bending over her. If the bitch stayed dead, then he would be satisfied.

'Face the wall,' ordered a lieutenant. 'Hands behind your back.'

Lebrett pressed his face against the dirty brickwork.

Kara could see and hear the men trying to revive her but she was unable to react. It was as if she was watching a movie; and she could only lie there and stare – just as she could only stare as the train had borne down on her. But then that same voice in her brain had taken over, forcing her to kick out at the live rail. The shock had thrown her out of the train's path, but it had also frozen her nervous system, stopping her heart and her breathing. And soon her brain would also shut down.

- 303 -

In some ways she was glad of that: it would mean an end to all the fear and struggle. All the time she had been trying to escape back up into the open, she'd had no real idea of what she would do out there – just the vaguest notion of her own importance in somehow saving the city. But, as Lebrett had pointed out, what could one little girl do to stop an asteroid? And now what could a little *dead* girl do?

From the corner of his eye, Lebrett watched the men trying to thump life back into the little bitch's corpse, every passing second taking her closer to the grave.

'Take that fucking grin off your face. That girl dies, you're gonna join her.'

'As long as she does die, I don't give a shit.'

This remark was rewarded with several blows to the backs of his legs, forcing him eventually to his knees.

Kara felt numb. No pain, no worries; it was peaceful now. If this was what death was like, she wasn't worried. She only wished her parents and Lorri could be here. But the mere thought of Lorri induced a stabbing pain.

Lorri! Lorri! she heard herself screaming, even though her mouth didn't work.

All that time underground up until now she hadn't known if her sister was alive. But now she was convinced of it. Not only alive, but somewhere close.

You can, you can, said a voice.

Lorri? Are you there?

There was no reply. Maybe she was wrong. Maybe Lorri was already dead.

She felt so tired.

There's no time to be tired. No time to die.

Please, leave me alone.

The pain in her chest returned.

'Got a pulse!' she heard.

Who said that?

The blurred figures over her had been swimming like ghosts, but now they suddenly came into focus. Men in green pressing in on her, almost choking her, thumping her. Pain lanced through her again, till she cried out ... Blinked ... Jerked awake.

There was a shout of triumph. 'We got her! She's back!'

Pain continued to race through her body: her feet, her legs, her back, her head, her chest ... *everywhere.*

She began to cry, sobbing with the hurt. Then she was coughing, desperate for breath. She tried to speak but her throat had seized up; all she could do was weep and tremble. Then she was lifted and carried along the dark tunnel towards the light, while, behind her, she heard someone yelling and cursing.

As Lebrett watched the girl revive, he lost control. Screaming incoherently, he collapsed under a rain of rifle blows. In seconds he had been kicked unconscious, still cursing the girl through bloody, broken teeth.

CHAPTER 42

Ward was drunk and had been for quite a while. He had commandeered both an office and its liquor cabinet, and was making every effort to beat Erebus into oblivion. For some reason he had put up a vigorous defence of Alberta Gaines after she was barred from CRUX. The result of this had been his own ejection from the room: his demonstrable ignorance and low rank seeming of little value to those remaining, and particularly to the man at the other end of General Clarens's phoneline: Parvill Rodin. What Ward couldn't understand was why he had felt motivated to defend Gaines.

All that woman had ever done was annoy him, so seeing her brought down and shown the door should have filled him with satisfaction. But instead he felt bitter towards the members of CRUX. As he downed another shot of bourbon, he stared at a framed poster of the Grand Canyon on the wall. That seemed a fair representation of what New York would look like soon, though the scale of the impending destruction was impossible to comprehend.

Fuck it, he thought, concentrate on why you want to save Alberta's ass. As he poured yet another shot, the door opened and she stormed in.

'I guess they're not going to let me back in there,' she

complained angrily, placing her bulky briefcase on the floor beside her.

'If it's any consolation, they've kicked me out, too.'

'It's not. And at least I was of some use to them. They *need* me in there. I've been with this thing since it was first detected.'

'Drop it, Alberta,' he urged. 'So you spotted some big rock that was heading our way. Big deal.'

She swept the glass from his hand and it smashed against the wall. 'A rock on course to destroy our entire planet!'

'*Was* on course.' He opened a drawer and took out another glass. 'And it isn't like you stopped it yourself, is it?' On impulse, he extracted a second crystal tumbler, placing it on the desk in front of him. He then filled both glasses and held one out to her.

Again she smacked the glass from his hand.

'That's a waste of good liquor, woman.'

She leaned forward, her face inches away from his own. 'And you're a waste of space.'

He pushed his chair back from the desk, adjusting his uniform jacket. Then he pointed a shaky finger at the furious woman looming over him.

'We had a dog once, Alberta. A poodle called Jingo. Mom's little treasure. It used to yap all the time: yap at the postman, yap at the neighbours, yap at cats and dogs and kids, at any fucking thing. The only reason it survived so long was because we all loved momma, and she was ill and she loved that dog. Well, momma died and that dog kept yapping. After the funeral, we got everyone back to the house for food and drink, and that damn dog was out in the kitchen, yapping for scraps. Dad took it out back and put a bullet in its brain. That ended its yapping, and everyone applauded. You remind me of that poodle, Gaines. You may be bright, but you never know when to shut up. Yap, yap, yap.'

'The feeling's mutual, but at least I care. You've just been working your way to your pension, not giving a shit about anything but keeping your shiny boots clean.'

Ward laughed. 'That's *exactly* what I'm doing, but it ain't as simple as you think. Yes, I'm an asshole, but there was a time I was a dedicated asshole, a career asshole. Then I got railroaded. Okay, I was dirty, but I wasn't the dirtiest. So I took what they offered – and I let *you* get on with your work. You've got to admit I never got in your way, so long as the budgets permitted.'

Gaines surprised him by pondering this then admitting, 'You *did* leave us to get on with the job.'

'Damn right. And you may be as irritating as that damn Jingo, but at least you did get the job done. My only problem about that is: who for?'

'OCI, of course. Their name on the pay cheques.'

'Ever wondered why?' he whispered conspiratorially. 'All they're supposed to do is compile data for law-enforcement agencies. Damned if I know what interest outer space could be to the FBI or Immigration.'

'Illegal aliens?'

They stared at each for a moment, then burst out laughing. Ward motioned her closer. 'The way that goddamn asteroid's been behaving, it *could* be some sort of UFO.'

Gaines took his glass and drained it, letting out a long sigh as the warm spirit coursed its way to her stomach. 'Of course, it's a UFO. Asteroids don't stop and start like that. Erebus is being controlled; it's obvious.'

'So what are we doing sitting here?'

'Getting drunk, apparently.' It was an unfamiliar experience but she could well get used to it.

Ward, however, was sobering rapidly. 'Get serious, woman. You're suggesting this really is a UFO? You mean an alien spacecraft?'

Gaines pulled a face. 'I wouldn't go that far, but it's controlled in some way. How? No idea. Who? Haven't a clue. Why? God knows.'

'But we know it's headed right for New York City – and according to you it's always been headed there. Now it's due to collide in three hours; and right from the start that little rat Rodin's been working Clarens in CRUX like Kermit the Frog.'

'Rodin from OCI Rodin? *Our* Rodin?'

'Yes, that Rodin. He was the guy phoning Clarens all those times. I recognized his voice. And he was obviously controlling him: telling him what to say, what not to say. What I want to know is why? And why they called off the nuke attack. Everyone else in that room voted for it.'

'The President saw sense maybe?'

'Golding wouldn't see sense if you tattooed it on the back of his hand. If Rodin already knew Erebus was appearing and where it was heading, then more than likely he knew it would slow down – and *why* it's here anyway. So he wouldn't want it blown up by nuclear missiles.'

'Coincidence? Besides, we never reported to him directly.'

'But someone killed the research team. Someone forced CRUX into letting the world know about Erebus.'

Gaines was astonished. 'But why would Rodin do that?'

'Good question.' Ward drained another glass of bourbon. 'Suppose the research information hadn't been stolen?'

'The news wouldn't have got out so quick. As you say, it made CRUX evacuate the city early.'

'Leaving NYC pretty well empty and controlled by the military. But then Erebus doesn't impact, it comes in at a stroll. And where's Rodin all this time? You heard Clarens talking: Rodin's in New York! Any sane person would be out of there, but strangely not Rodin. And, as head of OCI, those left on the ground would be obliged to follow his orders, so he'd have the run of the city. Rodin's there for a reason; and it ain't to get tickets for Letterman.'

'So what do we do?'

Ward considered this. 'You're the computer whizz, and I think it's time to find out more about Mr Parvill Rodin.'

Finding an office with a computer was easy. Ward may have been excluded from the CRUX meeting but his security clearance hadn't yet been revoked. However, accessing information about Parvill Rodin would prove more difficult.

They spent a frustrating hour side by side as Gaines raided numerous databanks, but she could uncover little beyond his Social Security records and his educational and employment histories. Rodin and his brother Christie had been headhunted at college by OCI because of their outstanding computer expertise. They had risen swiftly through the ranks, almost too swiftly perhaps, but there was no indication of anything underhand. Evidently the Rodins had got to know a lot of useful people, but that seemed to be it. They were thirty-something whizz-kids running a successful and profitable agency handling time-consuming data correlation for other government agencies. Initially, it had involved police and legal data, but then they had moved into other areas, including their current involvement in WATCH. That was number-crunching again, their experience apparently used as a money-saving ploy by NASA.

Eventually, Ward called a halt. 'Whatever he's up to, we're not going to find it here.' He sat back wearily. God, he felt tired.

Gaines flexed her overworked fingers. 'If only we knew what exactly he was saying to Clarens during the CRUX meeting.'

Ward sat bolt upright.

'What is it?' she asked.

'I've been involved with CRUX once before,' he explained. 'During Operation Desert Shield, I acted as an aide to General Stamford. He explained that they recorded everything said there, just as they record everything in the Oval Office and in cabinet meetings. His nickname there was Paws, which everyone thought referred to his big, hairy hands. But it really stood for *Pause* as in taking his time answering, so he would always say exactly the right thing for the record.'

'Very interesting . . .' she began impatiently.

'Don't you see?' Ward grabbed her thigh. 'If everything in CRUX goes on tape, we might still be able to decipher some of the stuff Clarens said to Rodin.'

'So how do we get to it?' she asked, pointedly removing his hand.

Ward shrugged, having visions of gloomy storerooms chockful of racks of tape reels, each bearing an indecipherable coding.

'Is there anyone present in the room who might trust you enough to let you review those tapes?' she asked.

'No. But Senator McMullen owes me a favour. I got him out of a fix with a girl once.'

'Now there's a surprise. Call him and tell him . . .' She thought for a moment. 'Tell him I'm now too drunk to talk, but you need to hear something I said at the meeting – and are there any recordings?'

He picked up a phone. 'Worth a try.'

Twenty minutes later, a Marine corporal arrived to deliver a mini-CD.

As the man eyed the apparently comatose woman slumped on the couch, he explained to Ward that his instructions were to return for the disk in one hour's time.

Once he was gone, Gaines 'woke up' from her drunken stupor, slotted the disc in the machine and together they checked its contents.

'Hell, it's time coded,' she announced.

'That should help.'

'And it covers seven hours of meetings.'

She called up a window to indicate the time periods during which the recordings were made. Ward paced back and forth, trying to recall the sessions in which Rodin came on-line.

'Okay. I would guess the best time to pick is the last

session when we two were there and we know for sure he talked to Clarens. That'd be number five. How long did it last?'

'Sixty-eight minutes.'

He checked the clock on the wall. 'And we've got fifty-five. Okay, rewind forty minutes from the end, and play it.'

The recorded discussion in the CRUX meeting was much as Ward remembered.

'There's Rodin talking on the speaker now ... He's asking General Clarens for a word in private ... then he's patched through to a phone. See if you can pick up Clarens talking on the phone.'

'We won't be able to hear what Rodin says.'

'Maybe Clarens will say something useful.'

It was another fifteen minutes before they caught the name Rodin in the background again, spoken in Clarens's Texan drawl. 'That's the bit we need to hear. But the damn microphones are meant to pick up only whoever's speaking at the table, not on phones to the side. If we only had a filter ... '

Gaines looked gloomy for a moment. Then, inspiration. 'Pass me my briefcase.'

Ward watched as she extracted her laptop and connected it to the desktop PC.

'I've got our isolation software here with me,' she explained, opening a flap in the briefcase lid to remove a single red disk. 'When we request radio telescope confirmation of a visual finding, we use this to isolate single signals from all the background noise. I think I can adapt it to amplify Clarens's conversation with Rodin, filtering out the main speakers.'

'Well, you've got twenty-six minutes.'

After twelve minutes she had to admit defeat. Replaying

CARL HUBERMAN

what little of the conversation they had cleaned up, they strained to make more sense of the general's final words.

'*Time enough. I'll complete . . . then make contact on Leanora.*'

'Leanora or Leonora. A street?'

Gaines called up on screen a street map of New York from the Pentagon's almost limitless databanks. There were two Leonard Streets, but no Leanoras or Leonoras.

'He definitely said *on* Leanora,' Gaines pointed out. 'What else could you be on? A boat?'

'He's on a damn boat! Can you access the port authority and see what craft they've got in at present?'

It took Gaines six minutes to download the files. 'No ship called *Leanora* or *Leonora* has entered or left New York Harbour in the last six months.'

Only seven minutes left.

'Okay. Try vessels paying berthing tolls.'

'Yes! *Leanora*, a tugboat at Pier 65. Suffered from a fire a couple of years back. The insurers sold it as scrap to a company called Hacienda Salvage.'

'Can you check?'

'Already doing it.'

Ward watched as Gaines worked her way around an incomprehensible succession of menus and windows, trying to trace ultimate ownership of the salvage company. With barely two minutes remaining before the corporal's return, she stopped when she found a parent company registered in the Cayman Islands.

'You buy scrap iron, you don't need to be as mysterious as that,' he said. 'It's obviously a cover. I'm willing to bet this is the *Leanora* Rodin was talking about. Good place to hang out, a derelict tugboat moored off a pier. He may even have made it seaworthy again, to escape from the city when the time comes.'

'So what now?' she asked. Then, catching sight of Ward's grim expression, horror dawned. 'Oh no, count me out.'

'Think of our team, Alberta. That bastard had them slaughtered. Don't you want revenge?'

'That's not fair.'

'Yeah, I know. So, do you just want to yap, or do you want to bark.'

Gaines thought back on the good times she had spent with Janice, Costello and Gil at the observatory. Good people, dedicated scientists . . . 'If that bastard really did have them killed, I'll want to do a lot more than bark,' she said.

Ward tapped his pistol. 'I think I might be able to make a contribution on that score.'

CHAPTER 43

They had now been on the road for over three hours. The main highways were crammed with fleeing traffic so Cantrillo had stuck to emptier secondary roads, with some success. Fortunately, most of the traffic coming their way was keeping dutifully to the correct lanes. However, nearing Bridgeport, NY, on Highway 8, they came across their first roadblock. Cantrillo slowed the bus as soon as the barbed-wire barrier, running across the entire road, came into view. He had anticipated something like this, but not so far out of the city. They still had a good eighty miles to go.

As the bus jolted to a halt, Cantrillo opened the driver's window.

'Hello, sergeant.' He addressed a muscular National Guard.

'Please step outta the vehicle,' ordered a thick Bronx accent.

'We need to get to New York,' explained Cantrillo, leaning out to display his own badge of office.

'New York is strictly off-limits, sir.' The soldier stepped aside to point out the black mass of Erebus suspended in the early morning sky, the dawn light haloing it with orange. 'That thing could come crashing down any minute, and, with respect, I don't think it's any place to be taking a bunch of kids, do you?'

Dr Morrow stepped off the bus, and walked round to join Cantrillo and the sergeant. Vehicles were strung out along the road beyond, which led back towards the coast and, ulti-mately, to New York itself. People sat on their car roofs or lay on the grass verges. It was a great free show, and they somehow deemed themselves safe here.

'Look, sergeant, it's urgent medical business,' implored Dr Morrow, showing his credentials. 'These kids need special treatment at a clinic in the city. And if we don't get them there—'

The sergeant, a tough man in his thirties, appeared understanding but resolute. 'You need authorization, sir. Any-one entering the city limits now must have written authorization from FEMA, NERA, the mayor, the police, the FBI.'

'Who the hell is FEMA?' asked Cantrillo, getting out of the bus.

'Federal Emergency Management ... The fact you haven't heard of them leads me to believe you—'

Cantrillo was insistent. 'Sergeant, we need to take these kids into the city. Now please let us through.'

The sergeant waved over three of his men.

'Step back, sheriff. This isn't your jurisdiction. Just turn the bus round and go back home to' – he examined Cantrillo's shoulder badge – 'to Rhododendron, and pick some flowers.'

By now, several of the adult passengers had disembarked, as well as most of the children.

'You some goddamn cult?' asked the sergeant, slipping a rifle off his shoulder. His men anxiously followed his lead.

'No. We just have a job to do.'

Bystanders started to edge away, some taking cover behind vehicles.

'Sheriff, I'll give you one last warning.'

'Okay, okay,' he offered, trying to calm him.

'Looks like we got ourselves a whole heap of shit here,' the sergeant warned.

Cantrillo tried to soothe things further. 'Hey, kids, get back on the bus!'

But the children paid no attention to him. Within moments, ten of them were ranged in a line, looking plaintively up at the soldiers.

Obviously unnerved, the men looked at each other, hands fretting on their weapons.

'Look, you kids, get back on the bus like the head gardener here says.' The sergeant was clearly getting angry now, and turned his venom on Cantrillo. 'I don't know what the fuck you were aiming for, Mr Policeman, but I want you to undo your belt and drop that gun on the ground. And I want all you other motherfuckers to raise your hands, so my men can search you.'

All the parents had raised their arms, a couple of the women crying.

Sol Bright stepped forward. 'There's no need to talk like—'

His sentence remained unfinished as the sergeant's rifle butt cracked him across the face.

Cantrillo stepped forward, but another rifle prodded his belly.

Just then, Tasmin tugged at the sergeant's arm.

'Get away, darling. This is your folks' mess, not yours.'

When she wouldn't be deterred, he glanced down at her. And she quickly spat in his face.

Instinctively he swung the rifle towards her then stopped, dazed under Tasmin's stare.

'Tell them to put down their guns,' she said quietly.

'I . . . What . . . ?'

'Tell them to put down their guns.'

'Okay, men . . . Lower your weapons.'

Most of them had already succumbed to the other children's stares. Within a minute all the Guards were lying face down on the road.

'Okay, everyone, back on the bus!' ordered Cantrillo, as he began to dismantle the barrier with Morrow's assistance.

A young man ran up to them from the line of parked cars. He wore a black T-shirt reading 'I'M WITH STUPID', an arrow pointing upwards.

Cantrillo spun round, extracting his revolver. 'Stop right there!'

The man froze to a halt. 'Hey, hey, keep cool. Just wanna warn you. You'll never get that bus to NY.'

'The roads all blocked?' said Dr Morrow.

'Right, there are barriers everywhere. You wouldn't get half a mile. But if you need something else . . .' He nodded over at a couple of Hummers hunched to one side. 'Those mothers'll get you there okay. Get you off the road and round all the traffic. Even over it, if you want!'

'Makes sense,' agreed Cantrillo. 'But there's thirty of us.'

'You only need to take fifteen, sheriff,' explained Tasmin, poking her head through the bus window.

'You mean just you children?' said Dr Morrow.

'Yes. *We're* the ones who are needed. Kara needs *us*. And we'll be safe with you – but we must hurry.'

Cantrillo looked up at the bus, and the anxious parental faces.

'Did you hear that?'

There was nodding, and the occasional sob.

'I don't see that there's much point in arguing.' He sighed. 'These kids'll get their way whatever. Okay, all of you get into the Humvees. Doc, you go fetch the keys.'

Despite their capacity, the slab-shaped Hummers felt cramped inside. Cantrillo himself took the lead vehicle, with Dr Morrow in the second. Both vehicles had radios, so they could keep in contact.

None of the children even waved goodbye to their silent parents. Instead, sitting hunched together their gaze was fixed on the asteroid they could see through the narrow windows.

'How long before we get there?' asked Tasmin, squashed up against Cantrillo's right hip.

'Hard to say, with the highways blocked. Could be a couple of hours – maybe longer.'

'We don't have any longer,' she said quietly. 'Kara doesn't have any longer.'

Unfortunately, their swift progress early on soon became a tedious exercise in circumventing car wrecks and abandoned vehicles. A mere fifteen minutes after setting off, Cantrillo found himself stymied by another school bus. This one had overturned after ramming a semi hauling sheep. The animals' incessant bleating only added to the general misery as they were forced to retrace part of their route.

Pausing, Cantrillo clambered on to the Hummer roof and surveyed the horizon. Even if they got past the bus, there were numerous potential hold-ups further on. It seemed as if half the damn state had tried to escape via the same highway.

Morrow joined him, puffing heavily. 'Getting too damn old for this,' he gasped.

'Can't see any easy way, Humvees or no damn Humvees. Christ, a tank couldn't clear us a path through that lot.'

Their journey was over. Cantrillo was about to announce this sad fact to the children, when Morrow grabbed his arm.

'Over there, Frank. It's clearer over that way, so long as these Humvees can manage rough country?'

'That's what they're designed for.'

'All right, then. You get us over there, maybe we got us a way into the city.'

Cantrillo squinted at the direction Morrow was indicating. 'You kidding?'

'Well, it's either that or you tell them all that Kara's going to have to fend for herself.'

Cantrillo looked down at the fifteen expectant faces. There wasn't any option. 'Right, kids, Uncle Jim here's got us a plan!'

CHAPTER 44

'How is she?'

'Much as you'd expect. She's a fighter – no doubt of that – but I'm not hopeful.'

'Stats?'

'BP, pulse, respiration are all surprisingly normal. We've hooked her up to saline, given her morphine. There's massive bruisin' to her back, third-degree burns on her right foot, second-degree on her calf, possible fracture of her right ankle, crush injuries to her foot. We need X-rays to be sure. Short term, she's stable. Long term, don't know for sure what that shock could have done. We need intensive care, constant monitorin'. Regular blood counts, urine catheterization, kidney function, leg checks. Then there's the myoglobin—'

'I'm well aware of what we *need* to do, but what you have is what you've got. This is front-line—'

'What's the point?'

Kara had been listening for several moments but didn't understand what the men were talking about. She hurt all over and her head was muzzy, but she could detect a note of criticism in the man making the report. He had a strong accent, like those people in *The Dukes of Hazard*. She peered up at the plastic bag of liquid hanging from its stand, and at the tube running down into her arm. Ugh!

'The point? She's a young—'

'I know what she is – and you know exactly what I mean. This city is going to be pulverized by that thing up there in about an hour. Unless we get her out of here, along with the rest of us, her stability will be irrelevant. She was lucky our men found her when they did, but she's still here.'

'You've got your orders, captain. We control the tracks, the stations. We'll get everyone out that we need to when the time is right – and not before. Then we wait for a while, come back in afterwards, see what we can do.'

'Sir, if I gave the wrong impression—'

'Bill, you *always* give the wrong impression. Why do you think you've only made captain? Just do your best for her, and for anyone else brought in. We'll be leaving here soon enough.'

And with that the bald man left. The other man – about the same age as her father but thinner, and nervous-looking, with short-cropped white hair – picked up Kara's free hand and checked her pulse.

'Can I have a drink?' Kara asked, startling him.

'Oh, sure, sure.'

He poured a glass of water, then held up her head and let her sip it.

'Thank you,' she said. 'What happened to me?'

'You got yourself electrocuted on the subway track. Touched the live rail.'

'Shouldn't I be dead, then?'

He smiled. Despite what he had been saying earlier, Kara instinctively liked him. She read his name badge: W. COCTEAU.

'Yes, darlin', you should be dead. But you'll be okay now.'

'Even with my myoglobin?'

'What?' He looked shocked.

Kara forced herself to sit up, though aching all over. 'I heard what you were saying. Am I still in danger?'

The doctor, plainly flummoxed, took a while to phrase his answer. 'Electric shocks cause your muscles to contract, and they produce a substance called myoglobin. Sometimes it can get into your bloodstream and upset your metabolism.'

'Can it kill?'

'Oh, Lord . . .' He sat down and held her hand. 'Yes, but I'm sure you're—'

'No, you're not. But don't worry, I'll be okay. I always am.'

'Well, that's good to know,' he said, his smile as false as his hope.

'No, really,' she said. 'But I have to leave now.'

'What?'

She pushed off the sheet that covered her body. 'I've got to get outside.' She had guessed they were somewhere underground, maybe in a subway station. They appeared to be in a storeroom, just big enough for three beds and smelling strongly of disinfectant.

He replaced the sheet. 'I'm sorry, darlin', but that's out of the question. You can't be moved yet.'

'But you'll move me when we need to catch the train.'

Again, embarrassment. 'Yes, but that won't be – '

' – for about thirty minutes. Am I going to be better by then?'

The doctor was at a loss how to talk to her. She seemed much older than her years. 'No, probably . . . Look, you need rest, and lots of it.'

'I must go now,' she repeated.

'No,' he insisted.

'But my burns are much better. Look if you don't believe me.'

They had covered her leg with an improvised cage made from doubled-over chicken wire.

Dr Cocteau sighed, then eased back the sheets to the foot of the bed. He gently removed the cage and studied her ankle.

'Oh, my God . . .' he managed, stepping away from her. 'What the hell's goin' on?'

Kara stared down at her injured foot, which looked rather red as if she had just stepped out of a hot bath, but otherwise seemed unmarked. Even she was surprised at how healthy it looked, considering the pain earlier.

'I heal very quickly. Now will you let me out?'

'No, of course not!' he said, studying her foot more closely.

'Well, I'm sorry,' she said.

'Sorry for—' But before he could finish his sentence, she had kicked him in the face. And as he stepped back rubbing his lip, she kicked him in the abdomen, then in the balls. His doctoral reserve was rapidly exhausted.

'You little mare,' he bellowed, raising his fists. But as their eyes met, his anger turned to a glazed bemusement.

'I want you to take me out of here,' she instructed. 'I need to get outside in the open.'

'I don't understand,' he mumbled.

'Don't worry, Captain Cocteau. You just have to trust me.'

He was too confused to think clearly. 'But how do I get you out?'

'You carry me. You say it's an emergency.'

'I don't know . . . '

'Do it, Captain Cocteau.' She surprised herself with the firmness of her tone.

He meekly unhooked the IV drip, then wrapped her forearm in a bandage and lifted her out of the bed. After slipping her into her soiled blue dress, he carried her to the door.

Outside, a guard jumped to attention as the door was kicked open. Although tall and shaven-headed, he was barely out of his teens.

'Private, I need to get his girl topside, stat. So you come with me.'

'Yes, sir!' The private led the way, rifle at the ready.

Gunshots sounded some distance away, but in the acoustics of a subway station they couldn't be sure how far. They entered a wide concourse crammed with people all huddled together, their eyes turned in one direction – towards the foot of a crowded staircase. The gunfire seemed to be coming from there.

Every inch of floorspace was occupied by frightened civilians who had not managed to escape the city and were obviously sheltering down here from the impending impact. There must have been three hundred at least, some of them even clad in their nightwear. Babies were wailing, women sobbing. There were quiet prayers and an overwhelming air of hopelessness – but mostly silence.

The fact that they would be no safer here than up on

the street revealed just how bewildered they were; and the sporadic gunfire was now making them very nervous.

As Kara studied the crowd, they reminded her of people she had seen in TV documentaries about war: frightened people fleeing from bombing or invading armies, wide-eyed and fearful. And there was a sickly mixture of body odours: the smell of fear. She felt herself being jostled as someone grabbed Cocteau's arm.

'Where you going, mister?' said the woman. 'You gitting outta here?'

Cocteau tried to ignore her, but others grabbed for his legs. The human tide at their feet was rising menacingly.

'Get us outta here, too,' said the woman.

'We're not goin' anywhere,' he barked unconvincingly.

'No, you sure ain't,' said a young Puerto Rican, pulling out a flick knife. 'You're takin' us to a train, man.'

Cocteau looked at the private, who nodded and took aim with his rifle at the armed youth.

'Everyone stay calm,' ordered Cocteau. 'This girl is sick. She badly needs help.'

The Puerto Rican lunged at the private who fired, hitting him in the arm.

There was a shocked silence as the boy yelped in pain, then pandemonium erupted.

Kicking out at random, Cocteau forced his way towards the stairs, the young soldier following, holding his rifle to the face of anyone else who approached.

Clutching his wounded wrist, the injured youth was screaming for revenge. Several of his friends were already up and scrambling over the human carpet, in hot pursuit of Cocteau and Kara.

The captain had reached the foot of the steps where the crowd seemed older and frailer, made up of those unable to fight their way into the securer depths of the station concourse. They cowered back, offering a clear path up the stairs. Cocteau hurried on up, holding Kara tightly to his chest.

Behind them there was more gunfire, some screams, then a cry of terror from the young private. Cocteau didn't care to look back. The unfortunate boy soldier had been overwhelmed and was doubtless now being torn to pieces, but pausing to help him would invite certain disaster for himself and the little girl. He could only hope the terror that had driven these people down below would be sufficient to deter pursuit.

Two more flights of stairs presented themselves, their only occupants drunks just happy to be spared the sight of the approaching asteroid – out of sight, out of mind. As a result Cocteau was able to make quick progress.

At the top of the stairs, two guards turned their M-16s on him, but relaxed when they recognized his uniform and rank.

Again gunfire sounded from the concourse below. Someone had taken possession of the private's rifle.

'Sir, what should we do?' asked one of the soldiers nervously.

'Do nothin'. It's not our people,' ordered Cocteau. 'Just don't get into a shootin' war.'

'Yes, sir,' they both acknowledged with evident relief.

Cocteau carried Kara out on to the sidewalk, where he

gently lowered the barefoot girl to the ground. She tested her damaged ankle and found it bearable, so let go his hand. Only then did she take in her new surroundings.

The whole street was empty of people, but jammed tight with abandoned cars. Half of them were in darkness, the rest sparkled in crisp dawn sunlight. Looking up, she saw the reason – and gasped.

But then something else caught her attention.

'There! There!' she cried. 'I need to get up there!'

CHAPTER 45

Lebrett had been conscious again for several minutes before he let his guards know the fact. His body ached and his head throbbed but pain mattered little: he had a mission, more than ever now.

He squinted at his surroundings, carefully moving his head one way then the other until he had an idea of his location. Of course he couldn't see what lay behind him, but he guessed it was just a wall. He was lying on a cot, a standard army-issue collapsible bed, his hands tied or cuffed behind his back. There were a dozen other beds in the room, all of them empty except for one containing a naked man hooked up to an IV drip, his head swathed in bandages. He could smell ether. This was a makeshift hospital. There were two soldiers on duty by the door, sitting in chairs, rifles laid across their laps. The black man, a lieutenant, was dozing; the other, a ginger-headed kid, was staring into space and mumbling to himself. Lebrett guessed he was praying. He glanced about for a clock but couldn't spot one, so had no idea how long he had been out. But then he had no concern for time limits, did he? The moment was all that counted now.

Slowly he tested his legs. They hurt like hell, but he was able to move them and rotate his ankles. He would be mobile. *Okay, Jacob, let's get outta here.*

'Medic, medic,' he gasped, surprised at how weak his voice actually was.

The praying soldier switched his gaze to Lebrett, then looked away and resumed his muttering.

'Hey, medic! I'm gonna puke here.'

'Go ahead.'

'If I puke, I choke. I choke, I die.'

'I care?'

'You may not, but what about your lieutenant?'

The redhead leaned over and nudged his partner. 'He says he's gonna puke.'

The black soldier shrugged.

'But he might choke to death; and then we'll be in shit.'

'Okay, go roll him over. Let him puke on the floor.' The man picked up his rifle, and aimed it towards Lebrett. 'No funny business, fucker.'

'Oh, like I'm gonna dance outta here. Come on, come on . . . '

He started to cough dramatically, then stopped. His chest hurt too. God, these fuckers were going to pay . . .

The younger soldier walked over, laid his rifle on the next bed, and leaned over.

'Hey,' said Lebrett. 'Listen . . . '

'What?'

Lebrett mumbled something incoherent.

The soldier had to lean closer. 'What?'

Lebrett stared up at him. 'I said, if you don't get my hands untied, your nose is coming off.'

But before the soldier could react, Lebrett had lunged up and sunk his teeth into his nose, toppling the boy on top of him. As he shrieked in agony, Lebrett bit in harder, feeling skin break as his teeth sank into the cartilage.

The other soldier bounded over and rammed his rifle barrel against Lebrett's temple.

'Let go of him!'

Lebrett stared up at him and ground his teeth even harder on either side of the boy's septum. The redhead was screaming, beating at Lebrett with his fists, but he wouldn't let go.

Lebrett then rolled over, forcing his captive with him, till they both landed on the floor, Lebrett on top, all the time maintaining a steely grip with his teeth.

'Untie him!' the boy screamed through his intense pain.

Panicking, the lieutenant jabbed Lebrett in the back with his rifle. If he fired now, it would all be over but the redhead would also die. Then Lebrett felt his arms pulled back, the plastic cuffs tightening then slipping free as a knife slashed through them. But before the black lieutenant could retrieve his rifle, Lebrett had released the boy, rolled right under the bed and grabbed the lieutenant's ankles, toppling him on to the neighbouring bed.

While the boy thrashed about trying to stem the gush of blood from his mutilated nose and his lieutenant tried to heave himself upright, Lebrett squirmed back to the adjoining bed and snatched up the redhead's discarded rifle. Spinning round, he lunged at the lieutenant, jabbed the rifle into his open mouth and fired, blowing out the back of his skull. Then whipping round to the boy writhing on the floor he shot him in the forehead. Lebrett then sat back to catch his breath, letting the rifle slowly slide to the blood-soaked floor.

Okay, Jacob, two shots fired. Bound to attract attention, so get ready.

He grabbed the lieutenant's rifle, then dashed towards the double doors. He reached them just in time, and banged himself up against the wall to one side as the doors themselves burst open.

As three soldiers entered, he shot the first then the second, both in the spine, and as the third one turned towards him, Lebrett shot him in the hand, forcing him to drop his rifle. Quickly clubbing him across the head, he jumped on top of the fallen soldier and, grabbing him by his ears, spat into his face.

'Where the fuck are we?'

The soldier was still too shocked to answer.

'You wanna live? You wanna fucking live?'

The soldier nodded, in terror and pain.

'Where the fuck are we then?'

'Twenty-eighth Street subway.'

'Where's the little girl?'

'What girl?'

'The girl they brought in the same time as me.'

The soldier's face showed new confusion.

Realizing he didn't know anything, Lebrett pulled the soldier's head up then slammed it down hard again and again, until he heard bone crack and deep red blood splashed over his fingers. He watched the man's life leaving his eyes – always a good moment.

Then Lebrett was up again, grabbing a fresh rifle and edging to the door. He could hear boots running across tile and caught a glimpse of more men charging down the narrow corridor towards him.

Gotta think fast, Jacob.

'Whoever's in there, identify yourself!' came an order from outside.

Lebrett looked about him.

All the men were dead, so no chance of a hostage. But then he had an idea. He stripped the combat jacket from one of the privates, slipped it on, then donned a helmet, scooping up his long hair inside. Smearing blood from a pool on the floor over his face, he lay down on his front, his belly concealing the rifle.

'Identify yourself!' came the voice again.

'Help me! I'm wounded!' he called out. 'He shot us all.'

'Identify yourself.'

He glanced at the nearest corpse, a dead Chicano, then checked the man's jacket and grabbed his revolver.

'Alphonse. Private Alphonse. Help me. We're all shot.'

'We'll get you, buddy. Don't worry.'

Lebrett smiled as he hunkered down. *Beep-beep, suckers.*

Three minutes later four more soldiers lay dead after Lebrett had rolled over to reveal a rifle set on automatic fire. Now he was safely out on the station platform which resembled a war zone. People were fighting with each other everywhere, as if the heat generated by the failed ventilation was driving them truly mad. Many were clutching any item they could use as a weapon, and there was sporadic gunfire in the background. There was no way he would be able to make his way through this chaos to the street, so he ducked behind a pillar to keep out of sight.

Then, above the screaming and shouting, he heard a train approach. Peering round the column, he felt a rush of air. He suspected the train would be packed with soldiers, and if it stopped here he would be trapped again.

He stepped out in full view of the driver. Then, as the train slowed to a halt at the platform, he waved at him to move on. The driver ignored Lebrett until he noticed the fighting on the platform, then glanced at him again.

'Come on, come on, you turkey. Ain't no stopping here,' Lebrett hissed.

But the train continued to slow. Then a gasping woman slammed against a nearby pillar, shot in the stomach by a teenage girl. On witnessing this example of the mayhem consuming the entire station, the driver accelerated instead, and the train began to gather momentum.

As it drew level with Lebrett, he began to run alongside it, keeping pace, then jumped on to a narrow platform beneath the motorman's door. Even as he reached up to grab the roof, his M-16 slipped off his shoulder, tumbling out of sight. The train swept out of the lighted station and into the dark tunnel.

The alarmed driver gestured at Lebrett to get off, but he instead indicated for the man to open his window. Lebrett could see he was just a draftee Transit driver, too terrified to respond. As the train speeded up, he continued banging on the window.

'Open up, you fucker! Open the fucking window!'

Shaking his head, the man stared straight ahead.

They were soon approaching another station. Lebrett knew he was in trouble if he was spotted by any National

Guards there, but he couldn't jump now and this bastard driver wouldn't let him into the cab.

Pulling out his pistol, he pushed its muzzle up against the glass. He fired four times, each shot ripping into the motorman's side. The driver slumped backwards and, as Lebrett had predicted, the train's dead man's handle responded instantly, automatically slamming on the brakes. As the three carriages screeched to a halt in the tunnel, Lebrett swung himself round to the front of the car, then leaped off on to the walkway. He had covered a hundred yards before he heard the shouting of troops behind him, forcing open the carriage doors.

He crept as fast as he could along the narrow walkway until he reached the waist-high barrier separating it from the end of the platform. The 33rd Street station looked totally deserted: no troops, no civilians. That was odd.

Behind him there was more shouting, then bullets thudded into the brickwork above his head, zinged off the rails below him. Not troubling to return fire, he scrambled over the barrier diving for cover against the platform wall, then righted himself and ran for the stairs through a jumble of construction equipment.

At the top of the flight he discovered why the platform was deserted: the whole station had been closed for repairs, its gates locked securely.

He rattled them, cursing. Although they were of the metal trellis variety that could be folded back to the wall, they were currently as impenetrable as a brick wall. As his loud rattling ceased, he heard yelling from below and the sound of the train being slowly driven into the station. He couldn't retreat now and here he was a sitting target. He checked his weaponry: one .45 semi-automatic with six shots; a penknife; and, in the top pocket of his stolen jacket, a Zippo lighter featuring a *Meet The Beatles* album cover. Not much of an arsenal.

Noticing the gate was held fast by two padlocks, he placed the pistol against the lower one and fired twice till it sprang open. Next he turned to the upper padlock, but this time his two shots only dented it. Wiping sweat from his brow, he took careful aim for a third shot. As its report hammered around the station, he heard feet running along the platform below. He checked his handiwork. Fuck! The shot had fused the lock – and now he had only one bullet left.

There was a shout behind him and he turned to see a soldier taking aim with his rifle.

Instinctively, Lebrett raised his own weapon and fired, hitting the man in the upper thigh. The soldier screamed and collapsed, but another slid into view next to him. He glanced up, saw Lebrett with the pistol and threw himself out of sight, shouting a warning to his colleagues following.

Lebrett spun back to the gate. He had gained maybe ten seconds' grace but had used his last bullet doing so. Dropping the pistol, he stepped back as far as he could, then hurled himself at the lower corner of the gate.

The impetus took him half under the gate, enough to haul himself all the way through and in time to avoid a first fusillade of shots.

As bullets peppered the tiled walls above him dusting his back with ceramic chips, he squirmed along the floor on his front until he was out of sight. Then he jumped up and bolted along a passage leading to the next set of stairs. Behind him there was yet more commotion as soldiers began battering at the gate.

Round a corner and up another dozen steps brought him up to the passenger barrier. Scrambling over one of four turnstiles he headed straight for the street exit – to find escape again blocked by a set of gates.

Glancing around, he saw no alternative route. He was in a foyer filled with posters, official notices, ticket machines, a ticket booth, and a couple of doors marked PRIVATE; but no viable exit.

Behind him things had gone quiet, order having obviously been restored downstairs.

Running to one of the doors he kicked it open on a small control room which contained a lightboard to indicate train movements and couple of battered computer terminals. He didn't waste time checking the desk drawers but ran out to try the second door, shoulder-charged it open and fell inside.

A store room full of buckets, mops, brooms, cleaning solutions, toilet rolls. He tossed the stuff aside, desperate for anything resembling a weapon. And then, in one corner, he spotted two yellow five-gallon cans with the magic words HIGHLY FLAMMABLE stencilled on them. He didn't recognize the contents – something called AXCHEM 8 – and he certainly didn't care.

Grabbing both containers by their handles, he heaved them back out to the foyer. Quickly unscrewing the lid from one of them, he spilled a trail of pink fluid all the way across the floor to the top of the stairs, then lay it on its side to continue emptying down the steps.

Running back for the second container, he pulled out his penknife and stabbed its lid several times, then heaved it as hard as he could at the first one. As they impacted, both disappeared over the edge, producing a shout of alarm below as the cans went clattering downwards.

Lebrett pulled out the Zippo lighter, flipped the cap and spun the wheel. Its flame was big and lazy – but then he paused. What the hell was he himself going to do next?

Glancing back towards the ticket office, he remembered seeing briefly another door inside it. That would have to be his last hope.

Hearing scuffling beyond the rim of the steps, he simultaneously lobbed the flaming Zippo at the stairwell and hurled himself at the ticket booth. Slamming the door, he rolled to the floor – as the stairwell first ignited, then exploded, spewing flames towards the station entrance. There were screams amid the roar of flames, and Lebrett could feel heat blasting over him.

Lunging for the inner door, he found it unlocked. Pursued by black smoke, he darted inside and slammed the door.

The room was small – barely larger than a toilet stall – but he noticed a ladder fixed to one wall. At the top was a trapdoor and, fumbling with the bolt, he shrugged it open and found himself peering along a narrow passage lit by red emergency lights. At the end of this he could discern another ladder.

Stumbling along the passage, coughing from the smoke,

- 339 -

he lurched into the ladder and blindly hauled himself upwards until his head hit something metal. Bracing himself, he heaved at it with his shoulder to find it rising surprisingly easily, his world suddenly flooding with fresh air and daylight.

Seconds later he was lying on a dusty sidewalk, the counterweighted manhole cover slamming down next to him. Down the street the subway entrance was obscured by belching black smoke which had started drifting across the traffic-clogged street.

Hacking to clear his lungs, he clambered on to the hood of a Sierra pick-up and gazed up and down East 33rd Street. The only movement was the odd individual scurrying for cover. Lebrett glanced upwards and instinctively ducked.

Erebus blocked out half the sky.

For a while he sat on the Sierra leaning back against the windshield, just staring up at the massive black shape. It was fantastic. God, would he ever like to be watching when that thing made impact. But then he remembered he could *never* be master of his own destiny until he had eliminated that little bitch.

He hopped up on to the cab roof. He had no doubt she was alive, and would be out there somewhere. Whatever link she had forced on him, it hadn't yet been broken. So he closed his eyes, blotting out the smoke, and let his mind dwell on the child.

After a minute, a familiar image formed in his mind: one that connected with that damn toy monkey she had been carrying on the train.

Yes!

But his excitement was interrupted by a female voice. 'What you doing up there?'

He glanced down to see a young white woman with long, unnaturally black hair brandishing a revolver at him. Her face was streaked with make-up, her eyes clown-like, and she was wearing a short, gold lurex halter-top and a shorter black dress. Her red pantihose were laddered and she had no shoes.

'Just looking,' he answered.

'Looking for what?' the hooker slurred, either drunk or high, or both.

He gestured down at her shaking hand. 'Looking for a gun.'

'I gotta gun.' She smiled evilly.

'No, honey' – he hurled his penknife into her right eye – 'you ain't.'

He had jumped off the pick-up almost before she hit the ground. He pulled the knife from her eye socket, then the revolver from her frozen fingers prodding her too-firm breast with the gun barrel.

'Beep-beep, baby.'

Then he headed off west, towards the Empire State Building.

CHAPTER 46

Revealed to them was such a vast space, it was impossible to take in; it overwhelmed their senses. Seemingly moments before – but it could have been hours, weeks – all of them had been convinced they were about to die, smashed into oblivion by a phantom train, but now they were standing, awake and alert, in the middle of a construction that defied analysis.

This space could have held a hundred, even a thousand, Houston Astrodomes. In fact, it was so huge it was almost inconceivable they were actually *inside* anything at all. At least a mile high, five miles across, its ultimate shape indeterminate, they seemed to be somewhere near its centre – and faced with a brisk half-hour walk in any direction to reach the perimeter wall. But to add to their wonder – and their terror – they were not alone.

Stanley and Drexill struggled to their feet, joining Cheryl who was already standing awestruck. Running in parallel rows in front, behind and to either side, as well as in similarly equidistant rows upwards, were millions of tiny glowing lights, each about the size of an acorn, the rows separated from each other by a regular ten yards on each side, above – and below, for the rows of lights appeared mirrored beneath them. They didn't wink or flash, yet their colours seemed to change constantly. They were beautiful, fantastic and also strangely calming, despite the awesome scale of the place. It was like being caught in a frozen, geometrically ordered snowstorm.

'Stanley?' Cheryl spoke in a quiet voice.

'Yes,' came his muffled reply, then, 'Are we still alive?'

Studying the lights all round him, he found no frame of reference with which to compare them.

Drexill had not yet managed to speak.

Cheryl crouched down to touch the ground. Then she pulled her fingers back quickly, as if burned.

'This floor . . . It isn't there.'

'What?' said Stanley and scuffed the floor with his foot. It seemed solid enough. He had already convinced himself it was just a mirrored surface, the lights beneath simply a reflection of those above. But then he realized that he himself wasn't reflected, nor did he even block out the lights shining above him.

Drexill knelt down, fascinated. 'It's like rubber glass.'

Cheryl again crouched, pushing at the invisible surface with her fingers. Stanley held on to her shoulder, as if the pressure of her hand might weaken whatever they were standing on.

The floor, though seeming solid, yielded slightly at her touch and felt neither cold nor hot – almost as if it really wasn't there. Suddenly, she rose to her feet and started jumping up and down.

'It's not bouncy either,' she announced, a smile in her voice.

Stanley uncovered his eyes only when she had stopped. 'Happy, now?'

Drexill had edged towards one of the lights nearby, sliding his hand around its rear as if to cup it.

'No heat,' he said.

He then moved his hand towards him and the light slipped through it like a laser beam. Startled, he swiftly checked his palm.

'No marks and no pain,' he announced.

'No shit,' muttered Stanley.

Cheryl approached another of the lights, ten yards away. She pushed her outstretched hand towards it, and through it, watching it emerge through the back of her hand. She repeated this action several times.

'Happy,' she said.

'Not really,' suggested Stanley.

'No. I mean, I feel happy whenever it passes through my hand.'

Drexill was disappointed to admit he had felt nothing. He walked another ten yards to the next light and imitated Cheryl's manoeuvre, experiencing absolutely nothing this time either.

'Stanley, you try,' urged Cheryl, still passing her hand back and forth through the same light, each pass giving her a tingling feeling inside.

'All right, all right,' he agreed reluctantly.

He walked over to Drexill's light and, after a moment's hesitation, cupped the glow in one hand and drew his clenched fist towards him.

He smiled suddenly – couldn't help himself. He tried once more – and again his face muscles were forced into a grin. His anxiety also lifted, if only for the second he held the light within his grasp.

'See?' said Cheryl. It was a delightful and pleasurable experience.

Stanley found himself repeating the pleasing experience, all worry about their predicament temporarily banished.

'What the hell is this?' asked Stanley.

Drexill felt oddly jealous of their obvious enjoyment. To him it was just another mystery.

Cheryl slowly revolved, taking in their wondrous new environment. 'Do you notice something, Mr Drexill?'

'Just a vast space with millions of lights set in a regular pattern.'

'I love the colours,' Cheryl commented.

'There aren't any colours. They're all white.'

'No they're not,' countered Stanley. 'There's lots of colours.'

'Blues and reds and greens and golds . . .' agreed Cheryl.

Drexill stared about him. No colours could he see, just millions of small white lights like electric candles on a Christmas tree. To his companions, however, they apparently looked like multi-coloured fairy lights.

'And I don't feel anything the way you do,' Drexill pondered. 'What to you seems colourful and exciting to me looks just like a lot of plain dots. But what now? Lights and space, lots of both, but none of it getting us any nearer to finding your daughter – if she's here at all.'

Cheryl walked forward a dozen paces, then paused. 'Oh, she's here all right.'

She grabbed at another light, and held it in her fist. 'I can *feel* her.'

For the first time, Stanley too was convinced this was the case. He scooped his own fingers around another light, watching its glow leak between his fingers.

'Feel her?' Cheryl asked him.

'Yes,' he confessed. 'She's here, isn't she. Lorri?'

Cheryl nodded. 'It's Lorri.'

'So where's Kara?' asked Drexill, then realized his error in pointing out the obvious fact that Cheryl's other daughter was still missing.

Cheryl withdrew her hand from the light, her smile slipping. 'We don't know, do we, Mr Drexill?'

'So where *is* Lorri?' Stanley wondered, spinning round and round, scanning the horizon, till streaks of light surrounded him like neon tubes.

'Here,' said a small voice.

Stanley stopped turning as he and Cheryl faced the same direction. Drexill, who hadn't heard the voice, followed their gaze but saw nothing new.

Stanley and Cheryl, however, could see something else: far away, a light glowing gold, larger than the others, and next to it a deep-green spectre, even bigger and somehow threatening. They broke into a trot, heading towards these new apparitions, Drexill trailing behind. He still couldn't see what had excited them.

As Cheryl and Stanley got nearer to the gold and the green, they began to realize what they were.

'No!' cried Cheryl.

Stanley couldn't speak, the sight was so appalling. All he could do was stand and gape upwards.

Their daughter Lorri was floating thirty feet above them, a golden glow all around her. Her hands were outstretched, cruciform, her feet apart. And she looked as if she was dead.

Cheryl screamed and ran forward, grasping futilely at the empty air beneath her daughter's body.

'My baby! My baby!' she shrieked.

Stanley grabbed Cheryl by the shoulders to calm her.

There was another figure too, this obscured by a greenish aura but in the same trance-like state as Lorri.

'It's Christie Rodin,' rasped Drexill in awe at the strange sight, though he still could not detect the auras.

Neither Stanley nor Cheryl had yet encountered the infamous brothers. Christie Rodin looked to be in his thirties with medium-length hair and wearing a smart suit. His open eyes were fixed on Lorri's gaze.

'Are they . . . alive?' Cheryl forced herself to ask.

'I think so,' said Drexill. 'They're locked into some kind of eye contact.'

'What?'

'They're staring into each other's eyes like they're hypnotizing each other.'

'You said the Rodins possessed the same powers as our girls,' recalled Stanley. 'Maybe they're somehow cancelling each other out.'

'Or they've lost themselves in each other's heads.'

As Drexill stood looking up at each in turn, floating thirty feet above him, he noticed how they were the same distance apart as all the other lights filling the vast chamber.

Looking around him confirmed his suspicion: their heads were positioned exactly where two such lights should be. He could only assume they had absorbed them into their heads.

'I might have an idea,' he began. 'If one of you is willing to try . . .'

'Anything,' said Cheryl, her desperation obvious.

As soon as Drexill explained his theory, she rushed towards the nearest light. It hovered at chest height, so she dipped her head and slowly shuffled forward, making sure it touched the centre of her forehead.

Light exploded in her mind, blinding white and electrifying. Her body juddered, then she felt herself go rigid. She briefly heard Stanley's shout of concern, but another voice immediately caught her attention.

'*Mommy, help me, help me.*'

'*I will, I will,*' she heard herself reply.

Then a deeper voice boomed in her head.

'*Stay out of this. No place for you here.*'

Keeping her head in position, she spun on her heel and looked up to see Christie Rodin's gaze still fixed on Lorri; but his teeth were bared and his head tilted slightly forward as if in concentration. Again she heard him speak in her head.

'*Keep out of this!*' he ordered.

'*Leave my daughter alone!*' Cheryl's mind screamed.

She was about to try again when she saw his eyes flaring black.

'*FUCK YOU BITCH!*' his mind exploded at her.

She felt herself being propelled backwards, landing on

her rump. Her head pounded like the worst migraine imaginable, her vision all colours and flashing lights.

Seeing Cheryl's distress, Stanley charged over to put his own head around one of the lights. Feeling the same infusion of energy, he too screamed at Rodin to stop.

But something dark entered his mind, swamping his determination. Then the blackness seemed to leak into the rest of his body, until every limb felt controlled and Stanley had become a mere puppet. He tried to fight but his mind had been invaded so rapidly and completely, he wasn't able to muster any resistance.

And then he felt his feet whip up into the air, his entire body pivoting about his head, his neck supporting his entire weight. There was a terrible crack, and pain lanced its way through his body. Then he crashed forward to the ground and felt the darkness slipping out of him, leaving his body feeling strangely distant as if it was just a memory.

Catching sight of Stanley's suicidal ballet, Cheryl rolled over and crawled towards him.

Stanley could hear her screams but could not see her. He then felt hands brushing at his face, but no feeling elsewhere.

Then he heard Cheryl's terrible howl.

And then Drexill's grim conclusion: 'I think his neck is broken.'

CHAPTER 47

Captain Cocteau's boots clomped and Kara's bare feet slapped almost equally loudly as they walked the length of the Empire State Building's huge empty lobby. The immaculate art deco design in Hauteville and Rocheron marble seemed as unreal as the threatened city outside. A lone uniformed guard approached them warily.

Kara said, 'We need to go up.'

The guard – old, tired, fat, ex-military – ignored her and addressed the captain. 'All elevators are out of operation, sir. I told the last people who went up there they wouldn't be able to get down again – and that was around midnight.'

'Well, get one of them workin' again,' said Cocteau impatiently.

'Can't do that, sir. Strict orders.'

At any other time the captain would have admired the man's dedication, but there were now more pressing matters than duty. 'This city is under martial law, and that means *I* am the law. Now I'm orderin' you to re-start the elevators.'

'Why do you want to go up anyway?'

Cocteau could feel Kara's impatient stare like a boil tingling on his neck. He pulled his side arm from its holster. 'Get the damn thing workin' or I'll shoot you right now.'

Cocteau couldn't believe what he was saying. All his

fears seemed channelled into helping the little girl, even if that meant delivering her to the observation platform of the Empire State Building. All he had left now was what this child told him. He couldn't understand it, didn't want to understand it; he just wanted to get it over with.

'I can't do it,' the guard protested.

Cocteau aimed the pistol at the man's knee.

'You've got three seconds. One.'

'Look, I got my orders—'

'Two.'

'I need written authorization—'

'Three.'

The two men stared at each other, disbelieving. Then a sharp report, and the man fell clasping his knee.

Cocteau stared down at his smoking gun and dropped it in disgust.

Kara ventured out from behind the captain and knelt by the writhing guard. She placed her hands over his own, blood squishing out between her small fingers.

'It doesn't hurt,' she soothed.

Suddenly the man stopped groaning.

'There, it doesn't hurt,' she soothed. 'And it'll heal up real soon.'

She pulled her hands away and wiped his blood off on her dress. The guard removed his own hands and stared. Although his trousers were saturated the wound itself had ceased oozing blood.

'Goddamn,' he managed, then burst into tears.

'Now, can you start the elevator?' She stared at him intently.

'Sure, sure,' he said docilely. 'Just give me a moment.'

After a minute he got up and hobbled across the foyer to a control panel. Opening it with the key attached by a chain to his belt, he flipped several switches in succession.

'Where're you going?' the guard asked.

'That place outside, where you can look from.'

'The Observatory you mean. Take the tourist elevator to eight-six.' He flipped more switches. There was a metallic click followed by a hum, and then the unmistakable sound of an elevator car descending.

'Thank you,' offered Kara with a shy smile.

Cocteau, still dazed, followed her into the elevator. As they entered Kara turned back to the guard.

'Can you make sure no one else follows us up?'

The guard nodded obediently. 'I will, honey, I will.'

He glanced down at his knee. It was as if nothing had happened to it.

'Who are you two?' he asked, his porcine face oddly childlike.

'I wish I knew,' said Cocteau. 'I wish I knew.'

The ride up was uneventful, and eventually the car slowed to a rest. They exited on to the 86th floor.

'Can you jam the doors open?' suggested Kara as they stepped out. 'That way we can get down when we want to – but no one else can get up.'

'Unless they take the stairs,' he muttered.

He reached in, turned off the power switch, then placed a trash bin between the two doors. A second elevator was already wedged open. Checking the stairwell doors, he secured the handles as best he could. The first he jammed with a janitor's broom; the other he bound using his own tie, the simple knot having to suffice.

Meanwhile, Kara had gone out on to the observation deck. When he followed her round he nearly fainted at what he found.

The girl stood surrounded by a dozen bodies: all dressed in yellow robes, they lay beside and even on top of each other, fingers curled grotesquely, faces contorted in agony. One only had his throat slashed, his front stained a deep crimson. He was also the only one smiling, his dead eyes staring up at Erebus.

The captain's medical training prompted him to spend two minutes checking the corpses. All were dead, and all but the smiling man had been poisoned, the bitter almonds odour indicating cyanide. Some also had small glass fragments in their lips. Clearly they were members of some brainwashed cult, all dying to order.

'Who are they?' asked Kara, staring around.

'Just some lunatics,' sighed Cocteau.

Fortunately, Kara seemed satisfied with that; she wandered off along one side of the deck until she could look out over 34th Street and at the dark mass hovering overhead. Cocteau wasn't sure if he should move the bodies, but decided against it. What was the point? Erebus was close enough, and large enough, to fill most of his field of vision. The massive object in the sky was awesome, terrifying, *unholy*. For a brief moment he envied the dead at his feet; for them it was already all over. As he walked, zombie-like, after the girl, his eyes fixed on the gigantic black sphere hanging in the sky. It was impossible to judge how close it was, its size was so staggering.

- 353 -

But one thought had stamped itself firmly on his mind: *everyone is going to die.*

He had always believed in his religion, trusted in it, lived for it. But now he didn't feel so sure. Now all he believed was that he was simply going to die, crushed to pulp by a giant rock from outer space – along with every other being left in this city. The sheer unfairness of his fate proved to him that God wasn't to be trusted.

He lowered his gaze to the magnificent man-made vista of Manhattan. It was strangely quiet without the hum of traffic, but they were a quarter of a mile up in the air now and he supposed a lot of the city's sounds were lost to the circling wind. He wondered how many others out there had committed suicide too, either through despair or conviction. His own faith, battered and bruised though it might now be, would still never allow him such a solution. While there's life there's hope – but what hope was there now? Something the size of the city itself was about to fall on top of Manhattan and for some reason he was investing all his hopes in this little girl. He turned to check what she was up to.

She was standing clutching at the protective bars, staring up at Erebus and crying silently.

'What are you goin' to do now?' he asked.

'I don't know,' she sobbed.

Kara realized that some powerful force had been leading her here all along. From that fateful evening when Stanley had casually brought home a rental video of the black-and-white classic *King Kong*, she and Lorri had become increasingly obsessed. Over and over they had demanded to watch it until they had been bought their own copy to keep. They were particularly keen on the dramatic ending, with King Kong scaling the side of this same building.

In the movie, Kong had come all the way up here to escape, though ultimately he had died instead. For Kara, escape was impractical given the proximity of Erebus. Which seemed to now leave her only one possible outcome . . .

CHAPTER 48

Barely a minute after their elevator had started upwards another visitor appeared in the lobby, but this time the guard didn't get time to argue. Two slugs slammed him back against the wall, and he slid to the floor with his lifeblood tracing two wide smears down the beige marble.

Noticing that two of the elevators were stationary at floor 86, Lebrett dashed over and stabbed each call button but both failed to heed his summons. All the other elevators were clearly unpowered.

Returning to the guard, he rolled him over, unhooking the ring of keys from his waistband. Surely one of these must operate the elevators. After pocketing the man's revolver he tried each of the keys on the express elevator. Its panel lit up on the seventh attempt and he stabbed the button for floor 85. The elevator began to rise.

Pacing the car impatiently, he checked his two weapons. This time there could be no mistake: as soon as she was within range, she was dead. Ten beautiful .38 bullets' worth dead.

'This is it!' he screamed at the elevator car's ceiling. 'This is it, baby!'

Once his elevator reached the 85th floor, he shot out of it and ran up the emergency stairwell – to find the doors to the Observatory jammed shut.

Hurrying back down to 85, he dashed across the width of the building and then up the other staircase, but it was the same story. He pounded at the door until his arms were weary. He was so close to the bitch, just one damn door between them, yet he might as well still be out down the street.

Finally, he slumped to the floor, his knuckles bloody, his only company some coiled ropes and a window-cleaning cradle with a ragged sticker proclaiming WINDOW CLEANERS DO IT WHEN THEY'RE HIGH.

'The bitch, the bitch . . .' was all he could utter. His entire obsession had become the little girl, and how he must get her out of his brain – and now he was lost. From the moment he had stepped into that goddamn store in New Hampshire she had blighted his life. He had to destroy her before she reduced him to a robot.

Slowly he got up and entered one of the nearby offices. The view it offered of New York from one thousand feet was breathtaking, but the sight of Erebus hovering above was even more fantastic. Its size was such that he could feel he was looking at the world upside down; that the asteroid was really the earth and the city below him a mirage in the clouds. He leaned against the glass, feeling its coolness, and squinted upwards seeing only an expanse of slate-black rock. From this angle it filled every inch of his vision.

He glanced down again. Heights had never been a problem for him. Buildings that were monuments in their own right – like the Chrysler Building, the Citicorp Building, the old PanAm building – now looked as insignificant as souvenir statuettes. The whole city looked like a child's scattered construction kit cowering under the dark shadow cast by Erebus.

Anger suddenly overwhelmed him; he grabbed a high-back metal chair and smashed it into the window again and again. Eventually, the inner pane fractured and, pleased with the damage, he swung the chair several times more. Finally, he heaved it fully at the remaining outer pane. As it exploded out into the open air, the chair started plummeting eighty-five storeys.

Cold air gushed in to embrace him, sending loose papers fluttering across the office. Edging back to the open window, he peered out. Then, gripping the steel window frame, he leant his head out and looked upwards.

There were no handholds to give him access to the Observatory but, suddenly, he realized there was another way.

He scuttled back through the paper-strewn office to the staircase, and there inspected the dismantled window-cleaner's cradle. Picking up two lengths of nylon rope, he headed back to the shattered window. Securing the end of one rope to a column, he tied the other end around his waist and adjusted the knot.

Next, he looked round for something to act as a weight for the second rope. What he spotted was the heavy star-shaped metal base of another chair. Upturning it, he kicked the base free of the seat. Securing one end of the spare rope to it, he moved back to the window. Tying the rope's other end also to the column, he put his plan into action.

He climbed carefully on to the window ledge, buffeted by the wind whistling into the office, and carefully turned around until he was facing into the room itself. Ensuring his feet were firm lodged on the sill, he slowly played out the rope tied to his waist, an inch at a time, so he could gradually lean outwards. After eighteen inches of rope took the strain, he was leaning out of the window at an angle of forty-five degrees, able to look straight up at the rim of the Observatory on the floor just above.

Checking his footing, he then hauled out the second rope with its load, and began swinging the chair-base back and forth by his side. But as soon as the metal connected with the stonework, he knew his plan wasn't going to work.

Keeping a tight hold of the second rope, he looked down over his shoulder. The street below was entirely in shadow now, the asteroid pressing down over the city like a blanket. *Not much time!*

He pulled himself back inside the office, then turned around to face outwards. He leaned out gingerly until the rope held him steady, his entire life dependent on the two knots he had tied. But, staring straight down one thousand feet, far from being frightened he was exhilarated.

Reaching back, he took the strain of the heavy metal chair-base. Then, using both hands, he lowered the rope until the star-shaped object was dangling twenty feet below him. He began to swing it back and forth.

The momentum took a while to build, but finally it was swinging from side to side, level with his waist, then with his shoulders, then higher still. He knew he might have only one chance because, if he missed, the metal weight could fall back, smash him on the head and topple him off the window ledge.

Swinging back and forth, back and forth, he readied himself for one last crucial effort. Finally, he leaned over to the right and threw himself after the rope as it swung upwards to his left. Then he let go of it.

Suddenly, he lost his footing and slipped. Grabbing frantically at the window edge, he took a few moments to find what little purchase he could for his feet on the building's sheer granite wall, before hauling himself up on to the sill. Swinging a leg over he hugged the narrow shelf, then reached out to the dangling rope and tugged. It held firm, so his improvised grappling hook had worked!

He had remembered, from a visit made during his last spell of freedom, that the 86th floor Observatory had a protective cage to prevent suicide attempts. A fence was mounted atop the waist-high parapet that ran around the four sides of the viewing platform, its links large enough not to obscure the view, but small enough to prevent anyone climbing through. This wire fence was topped by a continuous row of metal prongs spaced about nine inches apart, that curved inwards to point down over the platform a few feet above the heads of the spectators. Climbing over these spikes was practically impossible from the deck itself, but it was this very cage top that he hoped the metal chair-base had snagged on.

He untied the rope around his middle. Making sure the two revolvers were secure in his waistband he grabbed the trailing rope with both hands and pushed himself out into space, wrapping his legs around the nylon fibre. Below him hung ten feet of flapping rope – then a fifth of a mile down to the sidewalk. All that lay between them was the strength in his arms, so better get climbing.

Pulling himself up hand over hand, he trapped the rope with crossed feet every time he moved upwards. He quickly found himself level with the Observatory, all those bench-presses in the pen paying off. He could see through the crisscross wire on to the deck, and higher, the metal star shape of the chair-base lodged between two of the curved metal prongs.

His only option was to keep climbing until he could slide over on to the top of the fence, so he hauled himself up another couple of feet. The rope juddered once as the chair-base shifted, and he cursed through clenched teeth. Glancing along the deck there was no sign of the little girl, but she must be somewhere on one of the other sides.

The chair-base shifted again and he slipped six inches. He strained every muscle to keep a grip on the rope, but now he was growing tired. The surging wind was chilling his body, and already his hands were getting numb. He didn't have much energy left.

He heaved himself up another foot, then another. As soon as his fingers curled round one of the spikes, he let go of the rope and grabbed out with his other hand. Just as his body slammed into the cage, the chair-base came free and plummeted out of sight.

He lifted one foot and rested his toe on the parapet of the Observatory. Then, using the diamond-shaped spaces in the protective wire as footholds, he worked his way up on to the rounded top of the cage, where he slumped on his front, exhausted.

Cocteau rounded a corner of the Observatory and was stunned to see a long-haired man climbing the fence. Where the hell had *he* come from? Then he spotted the guns in the man's waistband and realized they were in trouble.

Looking wildly about him, he could see nothing with

which to defend himself. For he instinctively knew this man had come to harm the girl. And no way could that be allowed to happen.

In front of him lay an empty expanse of observation deck, to his rear around the corner were the corpses of the cultists. The leader's knife! He ran back and pulled it out of the man's clawed fingers.

When he returned, the intruder was lying exhausted on top of the fence's thick curved tines, nine feet above the deck. But how to get to him without getting shot first?

Mr Lebrett was here to kill her. What should she do?

Hope, said her voice. *Mr Cocteau is your champion now. He may defeat him.*

But what if he didn't? She hadn't the strength to fight him as well as finish her task.

Lebrett felt drained, with barely the energy to lift his head. What strength he had left was concentrated in gripping tightly on the narrow prongs. Now he had got here, he wanted to be sure he was ready to take her out.

Suddenly pain lanced through his leg. Yelping, he looked back to see a uniformed officer kneeling on top of the narrow cage, stabbing at his legs. He tried to pull himself hand over hand out of range – but again the blade pierced his ankle.

'Motherfucker!' he screamed, grabbing at one of his revolvers; but it clattered on to the platform below.

Another stab, his right calf this time. He kicked out blindly, connecting with flesh and bone.

Cocteau had pulled himself up on to the narrow roof of the cage by standing on top of one of the telescopes, and immediately had started jabbing at the man's legs. But now the man had kicked him, hitting his shoulder and knocking him towards the outer edge of the cage – and he could feel himself losing his balance.

Mr Cocteau! Mr Cocteau! He's in danger!

But Kara continued to concentrate on the mass above her, terror and concern eating away at her mind like acid.

Concentrate! urged the voice in her head.

Lebrett rolled on to his side, lashing out again and again with his foot. 'Gonna die, motherfucker!' he yelled.

Cocteau took the blow full in the face. Momentarily stunned, he dropped his knife and slammed down full-length on the curved metal bars.

Now they were even, Lebrett saw his chance. Sitting up he eased himself forward, uncaring about his own precarious position. This bastard was all that remained between him and the bitch – so he was going to die.

Cocteau's teeth were smashed, his lips split, his mind reeling. He tried to raise himself, but lacked the energy to push himself fully upright. Lebrett forced home his advantage.

Another kick, another brutal contact.

As his head snapped back, Cocteau felt himself slipping sideways towards the edge of the building.

'Fly, boy, fly!' whooped Lebrett, kicking him twice more, then watching with glee as the other man toppled.

Cocteau could feel himself falling and he grabbed blindly at one of the prongs, but his legs were already over the edge, thrashing desperately for a foothold he knew he would never find. He tried to maintain a grip with his right hand, but the long-haired man stomped it with his heel. As Cocteau felt himself accelerating towards the ground, he screamed in terror, flailing his arms and legs. His eyes registered only rushing granite and flashes of glass. For thirty floors, forty floors, fifty floors he continued screaming. He tried to think of God and his wife and children, but his mind could only focus on the impending impact. Sixty floors, seventy floors – and still he screamed. For twelve seconds in all he screamed – until he hit the hood of a yellow cab at 120 m.p.h., smashing its suspension and driving its engine-block six inches into the road surface, his remains exploding over the street like a shattered box of red wine.

Lebrett didn't even watch him fall. Instead, he rolled himself over the cage top to drop ten feet on to the Observatory platform. Pain blasted through his legs and he groaned in agony. As he lay there on his back, he pulled out the second revolver. Above him, Erebus filled the sky like night made solid. But that no longer concerned Lebrett – he had urgent work to do.

*

Kara's mind faltered. She could feel Cocteau's descent, the ground rushing up to him, the inevitability of death . . . She screamed but no sound left her lips. She began to shake, her mind wandering, conjuring up images of Lebrett's murderous intentions.

CONCENTRATE! the inner voice insisted.

But Kara knew Lebrett would soon be coming after her, his mind fixed on one thing and one purpose alone.

Please, please, let me go.

No, do this! Do this! There's no time left.

Lebrett stood up, testing his manoeuvrability, but couldn't stop his damned ankles aching. *Pain's all in the mind,* he admonished himself. *Just electrical impulses telling your body something's wrong.* The girl was all that mattered now.

He made his way unsteadily to the nearest corner, pausing to pick up his other revolver, then edged along one side of the building. It was as dark as night now, no sound save for wind humming through the safety cage. He listened in vain for clues to the little girl's whereabouts.

He peered around the next corner to see sprawled bodies dressed in yellow robes. Stepping between them, he worked his way onward.

He was halfway along when he finally spotted her, and the sight of her left him weak at the knees. There she was, clinging to the protective wire and staring directly up at the asteroid itself. This would be so easy.

*

He's here, he's here! Her own thoughts screamed in panic.

Keep concentrating. Only a few seconds more.

But he's got a gun!

Then suddenly, her body stiffened, her eyes widened, as she stared directly up at the black mass in the sky. And then she saw it was *alive*.

And Lebrett was now forgotten. Compared to her task and to the consequences should she fail, Lebrett was an irrelevance.

For Kara was a beacon . . . and she needed to burn with all her brightness.

Lebrett moved forward within ten feet of her. She still hadn't seemed to notice his approach. Raising both revolvers, he took careful aim. His arms were still trembling as he sighted on her head. Oh, to watch that blonde bubble burst . . .

No, he admonished himself, *that would be too quick, too easy.*

He lowered his arms to target her knees. From this distance, a .38 slug would pass through both. He grinned. *What a treat!* But he wanted to witness her face when it happened.

He knew she would control him once they made eye contact so he cocked the hammer and squeezed the trigger as far as he dared, intending to fire the moment she turned – a split second before she could fuck up his head.

'Hey, kid, guess who's back?' he taunted.

But no response.

'Beep-beep, blondie! Look who's here!'

She continued staring upwards.

'Well, fuck you, bitch.'

Suddenly, there was a roar to his left and he glimpsed a shape moving across the skyline. A helicopter. What the hell?

He turned to stare at it, following its flight. It was small, without identifying marks. Soon it swung out of sight round the massive building. He waited for it to fly back into view. But, although he could hear its motor, it didn't reappear.

Fuck the distraction. He looked back to the little girl; and his cry of anguish echoed across the city.

She was gone!

He hobbled to the next corner but could see no sign of her. Should he turn back to meet her coming the other way? But what if she had already headed for an exit?

The helicopter suddenly hove into view again, but this time he ignored it. A few more cautious steps . . . and there she was! She had climbed the ladder on to the flat roof of the souvenir shop and was standing looking as distracted as before, her arms and legs starkly white against the black underbelly of the asteroid covering the sky.

This time, no mistakes. This time just do it.

He raised his gun towards her back and fired.

CHAPTER 49

Ward and Gaines were now flying along the eastern edge of the Hudson River on one side of Manhattan. Ward had requested a helicopter to ferry them to Baltimore, Jane Radinsky's home-town, to pay their respects to her grieving family. As they were no longer needed in Washington, his request had been eventually granted. Ward had taken control of the ancient McDonnell-Douglas Cayuse himself.

'This must have been the last damn chopper left in DC,' he complained, familiarizing himself with the controls of the juddering machine.

'You sure it's safe?' asked a worried Gaines.

'Where we're heading, we'd probably be better off if the damn thing crashed first.'

They had flown north-east and, to their dismay, were soon able to make out the shape of Erebus hovering ever closer.

Now, peering down out of the helicopter windows, they could see the numbers of the piers painted on the warehouse roofs, so it was easy enough to find their target, Pier 65.

'Don't want to get too close,' warned Gaines. 'With so little air traffic, we'll soon be noticed.'

Ward banked the Cayuse inland till they passed over a truck park and he spotted a large enough space to land –

which they did with a spine-jarring thump. As intended, the surrounding trailers shielded them from view. As the rotors idled to a stop, he handed Gaines a pistol.

'You know how to use one of these?'

Gaines took the Berretta, checking it over. 'I may seem a nerd, but I'm an American nerd.'

Looping a pair of field glasses around his neck, Ward clambered down from the helicopter and led the way through the maze of trucks and trailers to the street.

They paused by an abandoned and looted diner, scanning the wide expanse of pot-holed road between them and the water's edge. Pier 65 was a good half-mile farther on. There were a lot of stationary vehicles, most of them trucks and pick-ups: as a route to the Lincoln Tunnel, it must have locked up pretty quickly.

'Do you have any kind of plan?' asked Gaines at last.

Ward stared up at the giant rock above them which looked like the moon come visiting.

'Survival,' he said simply, then dashed across the pitted road.

Fifteen minutes later they were hunkered down behind a rusting pick-up truck, halfway along the pier itself. To their rear rose the vast length of a disused warehouse, its broken windows like sores along the black-painted wall.

'That's the *Leanora*, all right,' Ward hissed, passing the field glasses to Gaines.

She was one of four boats tied up to the dock, and the only one that looked ready for the junkyard. Her off-white hull was corroded with rust, the name barely legible on the stern.

'I can't see any activity,' muttered Gaines.

'He's probably below deck. Now, let's have a look.'

Ward studied the boat carefully again. He was no seaman but certain things didn't ring true about this vessel. For one, the radio antennae on the wheelhouse roof looked big, shiny and new. A second discrepancy was the video cameras: one positioned high up on the funnel pointing to shore, the other fixed above the wheelhouse focused up at Erebus.

A stiff breeze blew across the river bringing with it the tang of sewage. Seagulls wheeled overhead, as if squawking warnings. Waves slapped against the dock pilings and everything seemed normal, except for the silence inland behind them. Even at night, cities are noisy places, but now, apart from the occasional crack of gunfire or a siren wailing in the distance, they might as well have been the last two souls left in New York.

Ward suddenly stiffened. Someone had come up on deck. It was clearly an OCI man, the yellow LAW logo on the back of his flak jacket impossible to ignore. A second man joined him, also armed with a machine-gun.

'Shit. No way we're getting on that boat unseen,' muttered Ward.

He scanned the pier. There was a semi-trailer carrying a large white cargo container. It bore the legend CARRAS, PHILADELPHIA, and a large black motorcycle was parked nearby.

He motioned to Gaines. 'We have to make it to that trailer. It'll get us a lot closer.'

Waiting until the two armed men had walked forward to the bow, Ward and Gaines crouched low as they sped alongside the warehouse. Using assorted dumpsters, stacks of crates and abandoned equipment as cover, they were able to work their way up the rest of the pier until the Carras container loomed between them and the *Leanora*.

Although the container looked old and rusty, the trailer and its white flat-fronted Peterbilt cab looked new, chrome sparkling. Ward knelt down to peer underneath it at the tugboat.

'Three men on deck now, one in a suit. I think it's Rodin,' he added. 'He's heading this way.'

Grabbing Gaines, he dragged her well out of sight behind the rear wheels, then ducked down again to check where the three men were headed.

Damn, they were coming straight towards him. He looked about desperately for some means of escape.

But the three men halted halfway from the tugboat's gangway. He could no longer see their faces, but watched as Rodin pulled out something like a remote control which he then pointed at the trailer. From above Ward came a series of small popping noises followed by a strange creaking sound. Glancing up, Ward dragged Gaines right under the trailer, just in time as the two sides of the trailer swung down to the ground, the metallic clang of them hitting the concrete hammering around the harbour.

Luckily, the lowered sides now shielded them from view completely. Ward's ears were ringing so it was some time before he could distinguish a new sound: as the roar of a motor increased in pitch, he realized it was right above them, on the trailer bed – a helicopter was being prepped for take-off. Presumably it would ferry Rodin to some other location. *Damn and blast!*

Ward motioned Gaines to stay put, then crawled towards the front of the trailer where he could peer between the tyres of the Peterbilt cab.

Only one man was visible on the pier, walking back to the tugboat. That must mean Rodin and the pilot were now on board the helicopter. Just then the roar increased as the machine took off.

For a while it hovered overhead, the noise of it deafening, grit and dust blinding them. But eventually its clattering receded and, rolling over to peer in the opposite direction, Ward watched the two-man Robinson R22 slowly bank away along the line of the pier.

By now the third man had disappeared inside the *Leanora*, so Ward decided it was time to leave. He eyed the Harley-Davidson for a moment, but having never driven a motorcycle decided that attempting to use it could invite disaster. Instead, he quietly opened the truck's passenger door and climbed up. After searching for a minute he flipped down the sun visor and some keys fell on to the seat. He turned to lean out of the cab and gestured to Gaines to unhook the trailer.

Understanding his mimed instructions, Gaines pulled the release lever and unplugged the three hydraulic and electrical couplings. Then she herself climbed up into the cab.

'Right,' said Ward, gunning the engine. 'Keep that helicopter in sight and expect some fireworks.'

Feeling the cab jerk loose of its trailer, he wheeled it

round in as tight an arc as he could, carefully keeping the length of the trailer between themselves and the *Leanora*.

Sure enough, two men burst out of the tugboat's wheelhouse, leapt on to the dock and opened fire with machineguns.

Ward crunched up through the gears as he put distance between himself and their attackers. Bullets ricocheted off the cab rear, but their threat faded as he crashed the truck through the locked iron gates, partially fracturing the windshield.

'Where's the chopper now?' Ward shouted, steering adroitly between abandoned vehicles.

'It's hovering a couple of blocks north.'

Ward wheeled to the left and headed after it.

'It's moving into mid-town,' announced Gaines. 'Shit. I've lost sight of it.'

Ward accelerated but misjudged the gap between a Greyhound bus and a Safeway refrigerated trailer and the Peterbilt smashed to a sudden halt, throwing them both against the dashboard.

Dazed, Ward found the engine had stalled and refused to restart.

'Fuck! What now?' he yelled.

Gaines tried to speak, but bent over in pain.

He glanced around to establish their position, then got ready to jump out of the cab.

'You stay here,' he said. 'You're hurt.'

But Gaines was already clambering down. 'No way. I want to know what's happening. Not going to get any answers sitting in here.'

'Okay, but I got to hurry.'

She waved him on then stumbled after him, but he soon disappeared out of sight. By the time she reached the Cayuse, she was almost doubled over with pain.

Ward reached down an arm from the passenger door. 'Come on, come on! We don't want to lose the bastard!'

Gaines managed to buckle up, then sat back giving in to her pain. The Cayuse took off immediately, circled noisily over the congregated trailers, then rose higher again before easing along Twelfth Avenue.

'Can you see it?' he croaked.

But Gaines peered around through the grimy canopy in silence.

Eventually he wheeled the chopper over West 34th. Five hundred feet below, the cross-streets looked like parking lots.

'There! There! He's heading into the centre of town.'

Ward spotted it too, a dark speck against the larger shadow cast by Erebus, its navigation lights flashing its progress.

'He's going up!' warned Gaines. 'Maybe leaving the city?'

'No, he'd fly straight across to Jersey. He's going somewhere specific now – and I want to know where and why.'

'Looks like he's heading for the Empire State,' she yelled.

Ward slowed a bit to keep the distant craft in view as it became increasingly dwarfed by the buildings around it.

As it hovered above the top of the Empire State Building, he raised the field glasses. Though it was a long way off, he was almost certain he could see its door open and, bizarrely, someone leaping out.

'I think he just got off . . . '

The other helicopter turned round and started losing height.

'Jesus, will you look what happened to Macy's,' said Gaines, gaping at the chaos beneath them.

But Ward had no time for sight-seeing. 'The chopper's heading back our way. Those guys on the pier must have radioed Rodin.'

'You think it's armed?' she asked.

'Does Roseanne eat burgers?'

The Cayuse was lazy at the best of times, as if reluctant to do any work, and it would never be as agile or as quick as the perky R22, so flying through the canyons of skyscrapers would tax even a professional. Ward knew he would be asking for trouble if he did anything but land the machine.

'Hang on! We're going down!'

He dropped the Cayuse quickly, managing to halt its descent barely thirty feet from the street.

'What are you doing?' screamed Gaines.

'We gotta get out of this chopper! Otherwise Rodin's men will kill us easy!' He looked down frantically for a space to land but the street below was an endless river of cars.

Gaines watched as the other helicopter swooped low over the gridlocked traffic, charging straight towards them. There was no doubt who it had in its sights – and even from a distance she could see the weapons hanging from its underside.

Ward swung the Cayuse through 360 degrees, dust and litter swirling beneath them, the clatter from its rotors filling the deserted street. Finally, he spotted somewhere to land and eased the chopper backwards. Keeping his eye on the fast-approaching R22, he could see the machine-gun pods on either side of its slender cockpit.

They kept backing up, the ship shaking fit to bust, until a flat white slab of metal appeared underneath them.

'Hang on!' he bellowed, dropping the Cayuse as fast as he dared.

As it slammed on to the roof of the tour bus with a resounding bang, the suspension bouncing under the impact, windows along the coach's length exploding on to the cars on either side, Ward killed the engine and undid his seat belt.

'Out! Out! Out!' he screamed as the other helicopter came in for the kill.

Gaines kicked open her door and slid out on to the slick metal of the tour bus's roof. Following Ward, she edged towards the rear of the Cayuse, ducking to avoid its spinning rotors. At the rear of the coach, they were faced with a twelve-foot drop onto the taxicab that had rear-ended it.

Ward didn't hesitate, landing on the cab roof on his backside. Ignoring any damage to his lower back, he picked himself up and turned back for Gaines. Suddenly, there was gunfire – bullets smacking into cars on either side, fracturing glass, ripping metal and shredding interiors. He grabbed Gaines's ankles and tugged hard, cushioning her impact with the roof.

He had just dragged the weeping woman under the taxicab when the R22 turned to renew its attack.

Bullets ploughed through the vehicle above them, spitting debris, then the gunfire ceased. There was a dull explosion and heat roiled over them as a car nearby burst into flames.

'Gotta move,' he said, clutching her hand and leading the way.

They were just one lane from the sidewalk when the helicopter roared in to attack again, bullets pummelling cars and vans to one side before thudding into the sidewalk then on through a showroom window which disintegrated and erupted on to the sidewalk showering millions of glass shards like evil confetti. Another car exploded.

'Stay here,' Ward hissed. Heaving Gaines up against a pick-up truck, he spun round to watch the helicopter. It turned at the corner of Eighth Avenue, then angled towards him in a direct line. He knew he only had seconds to act.

Withdrawing the pistol from his holster, he climbed onto the hood of a black GMC, then leaped from there on to the roof of a Stratos, then to the Volvo in the adjacent lane, then up over its roof to the hood of a battered Mercury. There he paused as the pilot altered course to line up again. *At least Alberta's safe*, he thought – then he took careful aim.

Smoke drifted across the street as the machine-guns started up. The line of fire was only one car away when Ward finally squeezed the trigger. Fixing his aim on the windshield in front of the pilot's head, he fired off all six rounds before diving to one side as bullets scythed neatly through the Mercury behind him.

As the machine-guns ceased their chatter, Ward was hugging the hood of a Continental.

He turned to watch the helicopter begin climbing again, and then it continued straight up. *Oh shit* . . .

He jumped back off the Lincoln on to a cab, then on to the GMC, before leaping down in front of Gaines. He could hear the desperate clamour of the chopper's engine as it tried to follow its pilot's desperate commands, but no R22 had ever looped the loop. Pulling Gaines to her feet, he shoved her on to the sidewalk and through the shattered window of the automobile showroom.

Outside, the dying pilot continued to pull at his controls, the helicopter now vertical and rotating into a backward loop, until its protesting rotors were underneath. Losing its flying ability, it dropped like a stone, plunging into a gaggle of yellow cabs.

The resulting explosion bowled Ward and Gaines twenty feet back into the body of the showroom, showering them with a deadly, sparkling hail.

CHAPTER 50

As the R22 lifted off from Pier 65 the pilot asked Parvill for their destination, even though he was already directing the two-man machine towards the New Jersey shoreline and away from the metropolis. But Parvill motioned him to swing back towards Manhattan. Then as they hovered, Rodin pondered where the little girl Kara would be.

Up till the moment Lebrett had removed her collar he'd known exactly where she was, but since then nothing. He had no doubt she was still alive – hell, if she wasn't, Manhattan would have been flattened by now. She might not yet know her full purpose but she soon would, and he had to be there first. He hadn't counted on the crazy determination of Lebrett or the strength of the psychic link that had developed between those two. He had to give the girl credit for choosing her potential assassin as her rescuer, but where the hell was she now?

Last word he'd received, she had escaped from a riot in the 28th Street subway station with a National Guard captain. No doubt the officer would have had as much say in this escape as Lebrett had been allowed in her previous escape from the vault. So now she was out on the streets where would she go? Undoubtedly, she would want to go up high, driven by her need to get as close to Erebus as possible, and mid-town Manhattan boasted a plethora of skyscrapers, any of which would serve her purpose. No, not just any – one building was spectacularly taller than all the others.

'Empire State Building. Now!'

As the pilot flew reluctantly towards their target, Parvill continued, 'Slow and easy. Get half way up the side, then take it slow.'

Soon they were hovering over 34th Street, about midway up the side of the landmark building and rising carefully.

'Easy, easy,' whispered Parvill. 'Let's keep it a surprise.'

By then the helicopter had reached the eightieth floor.

'Move round the building, but keep it level.'

They slowly circled the skyscraper until Parvill spotted something that made him grab a pair of field glasses from the floor. One of the windows had been smashed and a rope waggled in the breeze.

He smiled. 'Okay. Take us up now, but *real* slow.'

The helicopter ascended thirty more feet until the Observatory itself was visible, and then continued to circle the massive building. The deck on one side was littered with bodies dressed in yellow, but then, swinging around another side of the building, he spotted two other figures. One was the girl herself, standing right at the corner of the souvenir shop roof two floors above the deck itself, hands raised upwards. *The beacon!* She seemed totally unaware of another figure twenty feet below her, aiming a weapon.

'What the—'

There was a puff of smoke. The girl remained standing.

The next gunshot was also drowned by the roar of the helicopter.

The girl didn't even flinch, just kept staring upwards. From the man's long hair he recognized the shooter.

'Get us down there,' Parvill shouted.

'Nowhere to land, sir.'

'You'll have to drop me. Get as low as you can.'

He could see that the observation deck was enclosed by a protective cage which curled inwards over the top. If he could only get on to that . . . Parvill pushed open the helicopter door.

Jesus. His first view was a thousand feet straight down as the helicopter hovered ten feet above the protective fence and its rounded top. Then he spotted another helicopter approaching.

'Once you've dropped me, head back down 34th – and shoot the shit out of that other chopper!'

The pilot grinned, happy for some action.

Parvill didn't want to waste any more time. As soon as he judged the distance acceptable, he launched himself straight out of the helicopter, slamming on to the top of the cage. Grabbing desperately with both hands he clung on to the metal struts for dear life.

I missed her. Lebrett couldn't believe it.

He fired again. Again the bullet went astray. *What the fuck's going on?*

He took aim a fourth time but saw his hand was now shaking so much he had no alternative but to get up closer to her.

After climbing the ladder, his ankles gave way and he

stumbled forward on to the shop roof. His vision was also blurring and he could feel his socks squishy with blood. It was now or never. He had to get the little bitch out of his brain.

She was still standing on one corner of the roof, seemingly oblivious to his presence. He dropped one of his guns and cocked the other with fingers that felt like they were made of Styrofoam. Finally, he sighted on her body as she stood, hands upraised, as if about to hold up the weight of the asteroid, like Atlas supporting the heavens. It was a bizarre sight. *All gonna come crashing down when I whack her*, he thought. *I kill her and splat, NYC gets flattened. Fucking perfect.*

'Beep-beep, got you now, girl,' he heard himself spluttering. 'Got you at last.'

Suddenly, she turned and glared down at him.

'No!' he shouted, expecting his hatred to be frustrated again. But the girl's intense gaze had no effect on him. He was startled.

'Stop,' she said simply, 'before it's too late.'

'You fucking bitch, fucking me up. You're gonna die.'

But she merely returned her attention to the rock-filled sky. Up there was what mattered, not down here. Lebrett would have to find his chance; for Kara there was no going back now. Erebus had become everything.

Blinking away the sweat of panic, Lebrett centred the gun on her back. He made one last effort to steady his aim. He concentrated all his remaining energy into squeezing his index finger on the trigger. Of all the destructive things he had done in his life, this was going to be the sweetest, most righteous of them all.

*

Parvill Rodin opened his eyes again to find himself spread-eagled over the Observatory cage. Slowly, he eased one leg after the other over the edge, until he felt confident enough to drop down to the platform. Checking his bearings, he moved along the deck to the next corner, reaching the ladder which led up to the girl. There was blood on the rungs and he suspected Lebrett was injured.

As he reached the flat roof, he felt for his automatic. It was gone. He must have dropped it when he jumped. Never mind, he still had the upper hand. He could now clearly see the child, staring up at the massive rock filling the sky above them. Between himself and the girl was Jacob Lebrett, in a National Guard jacket, pointing a gun at her with wavering arms.

'Wrong move, Jacob,' Parvill shouted.

Startled, Lebrett spun round. 'Well, if it ain't Blondini. Where's your fucking brother?'

Parvill glanced upwards. 'Oh, he's close by, but now I want you to put that gun down.'

'Course, you do, 'cept I ain't obliging.' Sweat ran into Lebrett's eyes. Why was everyone so intent on screwing up his plans? 'I want the girl that's all. Hell, you had the little bitch locked up underground. Just let me finish her.'

'No can do, Jacob.'

'You fuck!' Lebrett tried to fire but Parvill had locked his gaze. 'Oh, you bastard,' he whimpered.

Parvill advanced, his hand held out for the pistol.

With an animal howl Lebrett turned on his heels, trying to re-focus on the little girl. Her defences were down – and *she* was going down.

'Fuck you both,' he yelled.

But before he could squeeze the trigger, he heard a noise so strange and unexpected, he had to glance upwards through his stringy hair – to see a thin black spike plummeting towards him from the underside of the hovering asteroid.

He managed a single cry of uncomprehending horror before its needle-sharp point slammed into the top of his skull and continued without resistance through his brain, down through the roof of his mouth, his throat, lungs, stomach, groin, exiting in a split second through his inner right thigh, before continuing to penetrate several feet into the roof, skewering him in place as if he had been nailed there by God.

He stared at his feet, his senses dulling. *I'm dead*, he thought. *I'm fucking . . .*

As his hands fell limp and his eyes filled with blood, the gun clattered on to the deck between his feet. Then the black stiletto began to expand, pressing outwards from inside his skull and ribcage until his whole body was forced apart and it exploded, falling away in pieces which splattered like paint down on to the Observatory below. Then the bloody spike shrank back to its original thickness, and shot up silently into the blackness of Erebus.

'Now, that's what I call a defence mechanism,' Parvill Rodin marvelled, hunching expectantly.

Kara was surprised to hear his voice. She sensed what had happened to Lebrett even though she hadn't watched his demise. Just as she was able to defend herself, so the asteroid had defended itself. Or was it to save her? She didn't know; she was confused. She tore her gaze from the asteroid and looked round.

'What do you want, Mr Rodin?'

'It's not what *I* want. It's what our people want; or rather what they *need*.' He took a couple of steps towards her, avoiding the remnants of Lebrett's dismembered legs.

'Our people?'

'You really don't know, do you? You're so innocent; I *hate* that. That thing up there contains our people.' Parvill tapped his skull. 'The ones we have in our heads. They're here because they know we can offer them a safe haven.'

'Who can?'

He held out his hand, indicating the vast city beneath them. 'Everyone out there! Our alien brothers and sisters will invade them, take up residence and settle down to live a symbiotic existence. In return they make sure we stay fit and healthy, risk nothing dangerous, stop others from threatening us – while they enjoy a nice, comfortable retirement inside our heads. They drive us like fucking Volvos, kid. And there are *millions* of them up there, just waiting to disembark. Except there's one little flaw in their plan: they need a guide, someone to show them the way. You and your sister are supposed to be playing that role. You're both pure and innocent, and more perfectly infected than anyone. Because of your parents *both* being contaminated, you're actually more them than us! You're Miss Goody Two-Shoes, all set to help them make the world a nicer, safer place to live in. Well, I loathe all that shit. That's why I have *other* plans.'

He took another step towards her. 'My brother Christie and I have known for two years that this ship was coming. We got people constantly looking out for it with telescopes. Once it was spotted, we got the news leaked out so this city would be vacated and I could do what I wanted. And, meanwhile, you were supposed to stay down in that vault and finish off *your* part of the job there.'

'What was *my* part of the job?' she asked.

'This thing needs a beacon to guide it down. That's why we assembled all those people in the vault and tapped into their heads. They sent out the original homing signal, but that wasn't strong enough. It pointed our visitors in the right direction but it didn't provide either brakes or control. That's where you and your sister come in. You're the goddamn parking valets! Your job's to guide this thing on its final leg – you down here, your sister up there. Well, thanks for getting it here, honey, but I'll be taking care of the programming from now on. We'll be their guides, my brother Christie and I. Whoever gets to release them also gets to program them about the ways of the new world they're in. *You* do it, everything's daisies and fluffy bunnies. *I* do it, it's all thorns and wolves – just the way *I* like it. All that remains now is to snuff out your beacon and they'll have to turn to the nearest shining light.' He held his arms aloft. '*And I'm blazing!*'

'You're mad,' she whimpered.

He stared at her with a twisted smile. 'And what if I am? I like being me and I think the world needs a lot more like me.'

'I can stop you, Mr Rodin,' Kara said calmly, her inner voice prompting her again. She suddenly realized that this voice was actually Lorri who, although trapped inside the asteroid, had all the time been doing her best to help her sister survive.

'No, you can't,' Parvill Rodin explained. 'You see, our defence mechanisms cancel each other out, which right now makes us just like every other hapless fucker on this planet. But, hey, look at me: I'm one big mean mother and you're only eight fucking years old, with bones like twigs and a spine made of cardboard. And there's nothing you can do about it.' He advanced to within ten feet of her.

Kara glared at him. 'Oh yes there is. Not even a big man like you could survive having a giant rock fall on him.'

He stared back at her, then looked upwards.

'You wouldn't. It'd be suicide.'

'It's better than being murdered.' Kara said, switching off her mind.

And Erebus plunged to earth.

CHAPTER 51

Inside the showroom of Gillespie's Classic Autos, Ward was the first to find his bearings. He was gashed in several places, but the fact he had survived gave him the strength to deal with any pain. He scanned the surrounding chaos for Gaines, finding her sitting up against a ruined midnight blue Rolls-Royce Silver Spur, nursing a bloody forehead.

Pulling her hand away from her scalp, he examined the wound. It was nasty but not life-threatening. He slipped off his uniform jacket and ripped out its lining, winding this makeshift bandage around her head.

'What now?' She coughed.

The smoke from the burning cars outside had drifted all across the street. Ward gingerly peeled back his shirt sleeve to examine a cut on his elbow.

'Fuck it.' He settled back against the hood of a car. 'We did our best.'

'But he's getting away.'

Ward surveyed the wreckage. At his feet was a small black price tag: $135,000. It meant nothing to him. Nothing meant anything any more.

'We don't even know where he is now,' Ward reasoned. 'Even if he's on the Empire State, how in hell are we going to get ourselves up there?'

Gaines forced herself up and limped across a sea of broken glass towards the window. Looking up the street over several burning vehicles and past the smoking shell of Macy's, she concentrated on the Empire State Building. Having come this far, how could he give up now? Then she noticed something odd.

'Ward, have we still got those field glasses?'

They were still around his neck and he yanked them off. One lens was fractured.

'Oh God . . .' was all she could say before handing them back.

Ward trained them on the top of the skyscraper. Its familiar radio mast had vanished. Erebus was finally coming down.

'What the hell do we do now?' he gasped.

'Die, I suppose,' was her simple answer.

'Whatever's controlling that damn thing, it's descending . . . a floor every . . . five seconds. At that rate we've got only . . . six, seven minutes.'

'Not enough time for us to get away. We can't run . . . Hell, I can hardly walk!'

Ward clapped her on the back – and both dissolved into laughter.

'Screw it,' Ward finally said. 'If we're going to go now, let's go in style.'

He was pointing to the far end of the showroom where a gold-painted, open-top Bentley Azure gleamed under the remaining display lights. With its top down, the luxurious white leather interior was dazzling in its luxury. As they made their way across the shattered glass, Ward took comfort in one fact. 'At least we know Rodin's already dead.'

'There is that,' agreed Gaines, holding open the driver's door for him. 'But, on the whole, I'd rather be in Philadelphia.'

Then she walked around the front and settled herself in the passenger seat. It felt like sitting on a cloud. 'We could always try and get underground,' she offered lamely.

Ward shook his head. 'Somehow, I don't think even the subway was meant to withstand a small planet dropping on it.'

They both leaned forward to peer out at the black ceiling descending over the city.

'This is it, then,' said Gaines.

Ward gestured a CD rack between them. 'Play something appropriate, ma'am.'

Gaines inspected a few discs, then slipped one into the player.

'One Fine Day' from Puccini's *Madam Butterfly*.

'Recognize it?' asked Gaines.

'I'm a Country and Western man myself.'

'Cio-Cio San's married Lieutenant Pinkerton and she's had his child, but he's gone back to the States. She's singing to her maid that he'll return "One Fine Day".'

'Does he?'

'Yes, but only to take the baby away. So she kills herself.'

'Stupid.'

'Oh, and like *we* aren't?'

'You've got a point . . . You know, over the years I've pictured a dozen ways of dying, but I never thought it'd be in a Bentley Azure.'

'You thought maybe a Pontiac?'

Ward smiled as he listened to the music, but it provided no distraction. Erebus had lowered itself to the fortieth floor.

He stroked her thigh. 'I don't suppose there's any chance of . . . you know?'

She removed his hand. 'You know I'm gay.'

'Hey, I'm not particular.'

She shook her head. 'You're one prize asshole, Ward.'

'That I am,' he sighed. 'It's a curse, Alberta. You say you're a lesbian, one hundred per cent? Well, there's about as much chance of you going down on me now as there is of me ever becoming decent, loyal or caring.'

'So what's all this chasing Rodin shit?'

'Oh, that's *personal.* I want to get the man who played me for a sucker; he obviously ensured I was put in charge of WATCH because he thought I wouldn't create waves – and damned if the bastard wasn't right.'

'So this isn't all about saving the planet?'

'Good Lord, no; this is revenge, pure and simple.'

She patted his knee. 'Looks like you fucked that up, too.'

'Story of my life . . . '

The thirtieth floor had now disappeared.

'It's been nice working with you, Alberta,' he offered. 'I'm sorry I got you into this mess.'

'And I'm sorry if I yapped too much.'

'That you did, but you sure as hell had something to yap about!'

There was nothing more to say. Instead they stared in awe at Erebus; it was as if night was slowly pouring down into the city streets.

Swirling smoke suddenly obstructed their view, and it

was several moments before it cleared sufficiently for them to see the asteroid's progress. As it descended to tenth-floor level, suddenly the terrible inevitability of their demise struck home. But instead of cowering back like Ward, Gaines rose from her seat and leaned across the windshield, staring upwards.

It had now consumed the eighth floor.

'There's something odd about this,' she said.

'No kidding,' muttered Ward, crouching lower.

Fifth floor.

'What the hell is it?' puzzled Gaines.

'The fucking end, woman!'

The blackness outside had reached the fourth floor, just forty feet above them.

All the sunlight was extinguished now but the showroom lights remained ablaze.

'No, there's something *really* odd,' Gaines hissed.

But Ward couldn't speak. He could only watch as the unstoppable black mass descended until it finally touched street level – and Manhattan was gone.

KINGDOM COME

CHAPTER 52

Ward was weeping, and wasn't ashamed of the fact. He had imagined his death a hundred times – what military man hasn't? – but to die in such a helpless manner was too horrible, even for him. He sat up warily, as if any movement would precipitate the obliteration he expected. But it was, in fact, as if nothing had changed: he and Alberta Gaines still sat in the Bentley convertible, facing 34th Street.

'What the hell?'

Gaines was beside herself. 'I told you something was wrong. There's no debris! A thing that size comes down, it's going to crush hundreds of buildings. But there's no rubble out there. And there's lights, so many lights.'

Ward didn't reply as he climbed out of the car. At first, his legs refused to cooperate and he had to rest for a minute against the wing. Then he walked stiffly to the shattered front display window, glass crunching underfoot.

'Oh no . . .' he managed, before his knees finally gave way.

Gaines rushed over, but instead of helping him to his feet gaped at the scene before them.

The entire surface of the street was black. Buildings, cars, buses, garbage, lighting, telephones, trash cans, fire hydrants, mail boxes – all sat on top of what looked like a giant black paint spill. Then her gaze rose higher to the lights, thousands of them rising in regular lines in every direction to disappear into the sky. She edged outside the shattered window but her knees also weakened; she fell on her backside and found herself laughing.

'I don't see anything funny,' Ward muttered.

Gaines continued staring up at the jet-black covering that wrapped around them in all directions. 'We're inside the asteroid,' she explained. 'The damn thing just slid down and swallowed everything.'

'So now what?' he asked, surprised at how calm he was.

'Looks like we got only two choices: we keep going after Rodin, or we see if we can get out of here.'

Ward stepped gingerly on to the sidewalk. It felt solid enough, and when he knelt down and ran his fingers over its black surface, it felt smooth like metal.

Above them, the asteroid formed a canopy enshrouding the city. They might as well be in a huge cave, cut off from the rest of the world.

'What is it?' he asked, catching the puzzled look on her face.

'The power's still on,' she pointed out.

That was true. The city's lights were still functioning everywhere he looked.

'Electrical power is supplied underground,' she expanded. 'We have to presume this stuff' – she tapped at the sidewalk with her foot – 'has formed a kind of skin over the ground-level surface of the city. But everything else is working underneath.'

'Do you reckon Rodin's still on top of the Empire State?'

He looked over at the abandoned Cayuse, perched on top of the coach. Why hadn't everything been squashed flat? 'I say we get over there, and find him.'

'And then?'

Ward pulled out his pistol. 'We ask him some probing questions.'

'Sounds good to me. At least that bastard knows what all this means.'

'So we'd better hurry.'

He went back across the showroom floor to the sales office and smashed a glass cabinet on the wall, seeking the labelled ignition key for the Bentley Azure.

'Get in!' he yelled, jumping back into the car.

As Gaines slammed her door, Ward drove it right out through the smashed display window, turned right and carefully wove the vehicle along the broad and relatively empty sidewalk, heading for the Empire State Building.

CHAPTER 53

Parvill Rodin screamed, despite himself, as he detected the asteroid's descent. The black ceiling was creeping down in every direction. He ran for the ladder but his feet became tangled and he sprawled face down, mashing his nose in some of Lebrett's bloody remains. Rolling over, he watched the rock close in like a giant coffin lid.

That damn girl! 'All right,' he shouted. 'Stop it. Stop it!'

Kara stared at him blankly. 'Too late now,' she said.

She glanced up at the giant surface barely inches from her face and panic set in. The sky was falling on her.

'Stop it!' screamed Parvill.

She cowered, no longer daring to look up. '*I can't, I can't.*'

Parvill covered his eyes, a childish reaction he realized, but he could think of no practical alternative.

Then it was as if he was suffocating, his body being pressed into the roof itself. He opened his eyes to find everything was black. Blackness entered his nose, his mouth, and filled his eyes. For a minute his body felt as if it was being steamrollered into the cement surface . . . But suddenly, wonderfully, there was release; no more weight, no more pressure. He assumed he must have died, but, braving another peek, he saw the lights. Raising his head he gradually sat upright.

There were millions of lights, stretching row upon row in every direction. Their number seemed incalculable. He glanced across at Kara who was also staring about her in wonder. Instinctively, both knew what these lights signified.

'They're here.' He smiled.

He stood up and slowly turned, drinking in the beautiful sight. He hurried to one side of the roof, leaning over the balustrade.

The base of Erebus had now reached the fiftieth floor. As it descended, the city slowly emerged like a primeval forest from a newly drained swamp; except that the buildings now looked glistening and bright and new, as if Manhattan was being born again. And that was exactly what was about to happen, not just to this city, but to hundreds of others. And everywhere there were the lights in the sky at regular intervals, vertically and horizontally; they infested the city, like a 3-D portrait smothered in white noise.

Then a familiar voice sounded in his head. *Christie!*

He spun round but could only see the girl and the lights. She was staring straight up, her head craned back. He followed her gaze to a sight as bizarre as any he had ever witnessed.

Almost directly above them hovered two glowing figures; the smaller one gold, the larger one a luminous green: Lorri and Christie still both silently playing their part in controlling Erebus. But, to his surprise, there were other figures beyond: a man and a woman both standing, and a man lying on his front, staring down. The two girls' parents and Drexill. Incredible.

Where was Lebrett's gun? Pacing the small roof, he soon found it and, snatching it up, wiped off the gore on his trouser leg. Four bullets still, one of which would be enough for Drexill.

He watched the three newcomers slowly settle on to the roof next to Kara, as if lowered by an invisible elevator.

His brother Christie and Kara had also halted their descent, but were not on the roof but off to one side in mid-air.

Cheryl had barely comprehended Drexill's diagnosis of Stanley's injury before the floor all around them had begun to distort. Hugging her stricken husband, she had screamed for him to remain still.

Quite close by, a spike rose up in the air. It slowly continued to soar above them – ten feet, fifty feet, a hundred feet – while Cheryl clutched Stanley's limp hand tightly. Totally unable to move, he lay on his belly with the vibrations resounding in his head. Something huge was happening now, and terror began to consume what reason was left to him.

Too frightened to speak, Cheryl could only lean back and gape at the strange tower thrusting its way into the asteroid, barely yards away from where they were sprawled. Up and up it rose like a rocket, beginning to widen into a strangely familiar shape.

Then a parapet wall rose around them and the asteroid floor began to drop away, leaving them on a platform which surrounded the black tower.

Then the tower began to lose its blackness and slowly resolved itself into a grey stone needle with elongated corners and metal facings. Reluctantly, she let go of Stanley's hand and edged towards the parapet.

The gloomy, encapsulated city below was now host to millions of lights gridding the sky, like all the stars come inside for shelter. Then, at last, she caught sight of Kara.

She let out of yell of joy and was about to run towards her daughter, but then noticed the man with a gun.

'What the hell's happening?' she demanded angrily.

'Don't let it worry you. It's not your problem.' Parvill cocked the pistol.

'You can't shoot me.'

'Oh, but I can.' Keeping his pistol trained on Cheryl, he stepped across to one of the lights hovering at head height. Opening his mouth, he swallowed the light. For a second his eyes widened, then he smiled.

'Two against one,' he said.

'Who *are* you?'

'God.'

What Parvill Rodin understood, but Christie had not, was that once he and the girl entered the asteroid, they would become inextricably linked. What one did, the other would echo. Locked into each other's minds, they neutralized each other, but together also formed one half of the ship's landing system. Acting like a harbour pilot, their task was to guide the ship safely to its final resting place, while Kara acted as the lighthouse. But now the ship was safely docked, all he need do was eliminate the two girls and the craft was all his. He realized he couldn't harm either child directly, but by absorbing one of the lights he had made himself stronger – still not strong enough to cope with both girls at once, but certainly enough to overcome their mother's defences – and if her imminent death didn't distract her daughters, nothing else would.

'Thanks for all your help, Drexill,' he continued. 'You did good.'

'I didn't help you, you bastard,' Drexill growled.

'Oh, but you did, don't you see? Because it was your files that DECRYPT cracked,' replied Parvill. 'And in turn that information led us to the beacon.'

'What's he talking about?' demanded Cheryl.

Parvill enlightened them. 'Once we located that UFO which had crashed in Canada and had ourselves our very own close encounter, then we knew that more were arriving.' He held up his hands to indicate the lights. 'Hell, millions were coming. And we also realized their one tiny flaw: they assume the characteristics of their guide, their beacon. Now, *I'm* going to be that beacon.'

'So then there'll be millions just like you?'

His smile said it all.

'And then they invade any humans they can find as hosts?'

'Precisely. So everywhere becomes my kinda neighbourhood.'

'But what about the girls?'

'They were the alternative beacon, the brightest of all the bright things that could be detected. Thanks to Drexill's efforts, we tracked down fifty others of your kind and holed them up here in New York City, fed their clean little minds into what remained of that craft from Upper Arrow Lake and used *them* as the beacon. But I needed the girls themselves to control this ship once it reached here.'

'Control *this* thing? But it's huge. Just two little girls?'

'An aircraft carrier's steered by a control no bigger than a Sony Playstation. You can light a whole city with just a few ounces of uranium. Size isn't the issue here: power is. These two kids are the most powerful things on earth, more powerful even than Christie or me, because they come from you, and *you* came from the purest source. If only you two knew what you'd been creating during that hump you had ten years ago ... Hell of a responsibility that, fucking for the entire future of the earth – especially when you're gonna lose anyway. Now, where were we? Oh yeah, distracting attention ...'

He suddenly fired at Cheryl, hitting her in the arm.

She collapsed, crying out in pain.

Parvill smiled and glanced at Stanley, who was lying face down helpless as a motorless vehicle. He was about to fire again when Drexill toppled him over.

'Bastard!' He began flailing at Parvill's face.

Drexill's mind was still confused, but he had to act as best he could. Unfortunately, he was old, weak and un-armed.

Parvill forced his gun hand down under the man on top of him and pulled the trigger. Blood exploded above them both, spattering the roof nearby like scarlet rain. Drexill's frantic movements stopped instantly.

Parvill sat up, the smoking weapon warm against his crotch. He laughed as he surveyed the human chaos about him.

Cheryl Carter was staggering back against the parapet, looking vainly for some escape. Her husband lay on his front, burbling, his lips pressed to the cement. Drexill was on his side, his life leaking away. As for Lorri and his brother Christie, they were both still floating in the void, seemingly transfixed by each other's gaze. In a world gone weird, this was the strangest sight. He had sensed distraction in Lorri when he had aimed at her mother, but Drexill had then diverted his own attention. Time to test her reactions again.

'Lorri, I know you can hear *me*. Now let's see if you can hear your mother die.'

Cheryl tried to forget the pain drilling into her arm, focusing her energies on the man with the gun. If ever she had needed her self-defence system to work, it was now. But Parvill Rodin already realized she had no defence against him.

'Looks like momma's lost her powers.'

Cheryl glanced about her frantically. If she, too, could absorb one of those lights, she might become empowered again. There was one about fifteen feet to her left, just over the edge of the parapet. Parvill caught her gaze and shook his head.

'You'd never make it.'

He took careful aim again and Cheryl shrank back.

Parvill pulled the trigger.

Stanley uttered a hoarse scream.

Parvill looked up at Lorri, desperate to detect a reaction.

Her eyes finally flickered away from the rigid path running directly to Christie's eyes.

'Watch this, kid,' Parvill crowed. 'This time mommy *really* gets it.'

Cheryl had cringed as she heard the shot, then cement fragments peppered her face. But, even as she realized Parvill had missed her deliberately, she could now see his new aim was true. Nonetheless, she glanced up at Lorri floating above her. Why was Parvill so intent on getting her attention? Then she realized.

'Lorri, no!' she screamed.

As soon as her attention was drawn away from Christie Rodin, Lorri's appearance dramatically altered. From being like a statue nailed to an invisible cross, she suddenly became a limp little girl. The golden glow around her waned as if by dimmer switch and her arms lowered slowly. Cheryl could see her struggling, too late, to rectify her mistake.

Parvill laughed, relishing the sight.

'Bye-bye, baby,' he sniggered.

'Lorri!' screamed Cheryl, running along the roof towards her.

But the glow had vanished from Lorri's fragile flesh, and she began to drop, screaming. Without thinking, Cheryl plunged after her daughter – right over the edge of the Empire State Building.

As Stanley howled at Cheryl's suicidal lunge, Parvill laughed again with delight. But his amusement subsided as he noticed Christie's rigid stance also begin to crumple, the green light surrounding him dispersing.

'Christie, concentrate! Keep a grip!'

But his brother had been fixed too long in his unholy conflict with the girl and the sudden break in their connection was too big a shock. His face showed surprise, then turned to horror.

'Concentrate, Christie! Just get over here.'

Christie's chilling scream cut through the air. He looked

desperately to his brother for help but Parvill was powerless to frustrate gravity's grasp. Christie reached out towards him, then fell out of sight.

Parvill fell to his knees as his brother's scream of terror was swallowed up by the city below. But then, as Parvill imagined his brother's 120 m.p.h. impact with the street far, far below, he found that he didn't really care. One second, grief had engulfed him like an inferno and then it was gone, as if Christie had never existed. Parvill stared up at the lights studding the sky: the matrix of a race, the future of humanity. *His own future.*

All his life, other people had served simply to further his own ends. If a smile won him support, he would wrinkle up the sides of his mouth; if a kick ensured compliance, he would lash out without hesitation. And, through all his travels, Christie had been his constant companion, the shadow to his darkest deeds, inseparable. But now he was rent from him, Parvill could see for the first time how he had always been *singular* in his pursuit of power. Christie was merely a sounding board, a confidant, a tool. Now he was gone, it didn't really matter. Now all that stood between him and his ultimate goal was an eight-year-old girl. All he must do now was remove Kara from the asteroid's protection then he could kill her – and the world would be his.

He walked towards the cowering child. She was frantically stroking her inert father's hair, lost in anguish, unable to comprehend her sister's fate.

'Seems we've got something in common, kid.'

Kara looked up at him. She was too confused, too

frightened. Lorri and mommy and daddy, all dead or dying . . .

He grabbed her by one hand and yanked her towards the roof edge, and the ladder leading down to the Observatory deck.

CHAPTER 54

The dark-green Range Rover came out of nowhere, forcing Ward's Bentley Azure into the canopy jutting out over the sidewalk from the front of the Empire State Building. After a couple of minutes grappling with collapsed canvas, he and Gaines fought their way free.

'Who the hell was that?' Ward wondered, watching the off-roader continue down 34th, battering its way through the stalled traffic.

'Let's hope it wasn't Rodin taking off again,' said Gaines.

Ward stared up the sky-high slab of building, and nodded. It would be a long way up for a wasted journey.

They found a dead security guard in the lobby and boarded the empty tourist elevator beyond him. As they neared the top, Ward explained the layout.

'Out on the Observatory, there's no real cover. You walk straight out on to the platform, with a shop on your right. If someone's waiting there, you're a sitting duck. So I want us down on the floor to give us some advantage.'

Gaines didn't argue, despite the stabbing pain in her chest.

When the elevator doors finally slid open they were lying down side by side, their two guns extended upwards.

Realizing there was no one there both heaved a sigh of relief, struggling painfully to their feet.

'Keep alert. God knows what we'll find up here,' muttered Ward.

He glanced around at the rows of strange lights which dotted their new indoor-city world.

Unimaginable pain stabbed into Lorri's crotch. She tried to cry out but could only emit hoarse gasps. She had no real idea of what had happened, but then there was a cry beside her and she felt herself sliding backwards. Lorri opened her eyes to see her mother reaching towards her. She first grasped her mother's fingers, then clutched frantically at her sleeve.

'Keep hold, Lorri. Just keep hold . . .' she heard her mother urging.

When Cheryl had hurled herself after her daughter it had been an act of sheer desperation. She had no idea what lay beyond the parapet surrounding their perch atop the Empire State Building, nor that there was another deck thirty feet below surrounded by this safety fence. And it was on the thin prongs that curled in over the deck at the top of the fence that she and Lorri had landed – and nearly bounced straight off again. Luckily for Cheryl, the sleeve on her wounded arm had snagged one of these prongs, halting her fall to certain death. She glimpsed Lorri sitting upright facing towards the building on the prongs, and reached out to her just as the girl began to slip backwards towards the street far, far below.

Although she had prevented Lorri from falling, Cheryl found she had no room for manoeuvre. Worse, she felt she might be losing consciousness, only pain and terror keeping her awake. Lorri herself was struggling to hold on, her little hands gripping the sleeve, her legs flailing in mid-air.

'Climb up,' Cheryl gasped.

Lorri's eyes showed she understood but her feet were unable to find a foothold. Cheryl glanced down at the wire mesh beneath them. If only Lorri could get her toes into one of those diamond-shaped spaces . . .

'Lorri, listen to me carefully but don't look down. You must *lower* yourself a bit.'

The child began blubbering, terrified.

'Lorri, look at me. Look at me.'

She stared up at Cheryl, eyes red-rimmed.

'Good. That's it, honey. Now listen: try to get a bit lower, then poke your feet into the fencing.'

As a former helicopter pilot Cheryl had never been afraid of heights, but Christ they were hanging on by just their fingertips to one of the world's tallest buildings, where even hardened steeplejacks would get the jitters.

'A bit lower, Lorri. Get a foothold. Feel around with your feet, honey. *Feel with your feet.*'

Lorri released the grip of one hand and reached quickly past her mother to grasp one of the metal prongs. Then, certain she had achieved a firm hold, she lowered herself six inches and finally made contact with the fence. Soon both her feet were firmly planted, her hands clinging tight to a pair of prong uprights. With Lorri safe for the moment, Cheryl was able to consider her own predicament.

One of the metal prongs had speared her sleeve just above the cuff, but her efforts with Lorri had worked the spike twelve inches through the material. She was literally hooked on to the cage and, although now also able to lower herself to establish footholds on the outside of the fence, she couldn't climb back over the top. So both of them were stuck there, with only their tired legs to prevent them plummeting nearly ninety floors.

For Ward the first inkling of something strange was the crying. Although the wind had ceased within the confines of the asteroid, there were still distant sounds from the streets below: shouting, screams, the occasional horn blast. But much nearer to them was a sobbing child.

'What the hell . . .' Words failed Ward as he rounded the second corner.

Corpses dressed in yellow littered the floor grotesquely. But even more disturbing was the source of the weeping. A woman was hanging over the top of the safety cage, her feet barely clinging to the outside of the safety fence above the parapet. To one side of her, a young girl was holding on grimly, her tiny body shaking from cold and terror. Ward quickly holstered his gun.

'Alberta,' he ordered, 'can you give me a boost up.'

With Gaines's assistance, Ward too climbed on to the hooped top of the cage and lay himself flat along its narrow length.

'Okay, the girl first . . . Holy shit!' He was gaping straight down into the street. It was one thing to look down through the window of a helicopter, but altogether another to be supported by only a couple of strands of wire, feeling the chill air rustle his shirt sleeves. Taking a deep breath, he eased himself along until he could reach down and touch the girl's cold hand.

He pulled himself back and whispered to the mother, 'I don't want her to risk letting go of the wire.'

Cheryl nodded. 'But she can't hold on much longer.'

The girl stared up at him, a pretty kid . . . Behind her head, the sheer-sided canyon that was 34th Street. He would never have the leverage to pull her up towards him. She would have to climb up, but how?

'Alberta,' he yelled, 'give me your jacket.'

Gaines quickly removed her dark blue jacket. Ward then took off his trouser belt, threaded it through the garment's arms and secured the buckle. Tugging hard, he tested the stitching in the arms. His improvised breeches-buoy seemed reliable so he leaned over the side of the cage, dangling it above the girl.

'Listen carefully. I want you to slip this under your arms so it's looped round your back. But you'll have to be very, very careful.'

Lorri nodded. Despite her terror, a small voice in her mind told her this was for the best.

Holding on to the buckle, he gently lowered the jacket until it slipped over the child's head and shoulders.

'Now,' he said, 'take your right hand off the wire and push it up through the loop. But be *real* careful.'

She did as instructed, quickly grabbing back at the wire.

'Good girl. Now shift your shoulder until the jacket feels tight underneath.'

As if reading his mind, she completed the same

manoeuvre with her other arm, the jacket soon positioned safely under her armpits.

Now, for the worst part. 'You've got to climb up towards me. One hand at a time, then each foot.'

Reassured by the voice in her head and the jacket supporting her weight, Lorri was able to climb up bit by bit using the diamond shapes in the wire as footholds. Her head was now only eighteen inches away from Ward.

'Okay, honey. Now the last part.' He reached down and hooked his hand over her little arm. *Please, God, stick with us.* He pulled her up and over himself and the curved top of the fence until he could finally let the girl slide head first into Gaines's waiting arms.

Tears erupted as Gaines and Lorri hugged each other tightly. Ward next turned his attention to Cheryl.

Aware that his luck might start running out, Ward crawled along towards the woman. The rough and ready way was easiest, so he grabbed the waistband of her jeans and hauled, next grabbing her thigh and pulling her legs up and over the prongs until she was hanging right over the deck.

'You're going to have to drop,' he urged.

Cheryl didn't have much choice in the matter. With a yelp she fell backwards, landing at Gaines's feet. Ward then lowered himself as carefully as possible.

Cheryl hugged Lorri, and both were visibly trembling. 'Thank you, thank you,' she sobbed. 'But we need to find the others.'

'What others?' asked Ward, hobbling towards them.

'They're up there.' Cheryl pointed, then led the way to

a ladder running up the central structure. 'My other daughter's still up there with my husband.'

'What about a guy called Rodin?'

Cheryl was astonished. 'The Rodin brothers were up there, yes.'

Lorri suddenly pushed in front of them and started climbing the ladder.

'Alberta, stop her! We don't know what's up there!'

'Lorri, no!' shouted Cheryl, but it was too late.

Once on the upper level, Lorri was blind to all but her stricken father. She dashed over to him, wrapped her arms around his neck and began weeping uncontrollably.

'My baby, my baby,' he soothed. 'Where's mommy?'

'Mommy's okay. Oh, daddy, daddy . . .'

At the sound of voices, Drexill raised his head. Finding it hard to focus, he realized he was dying.

'Lorri . . .' He coughed blood. 'Lorri . . . Listen to me.'

He reached out his hand, but it fell back limply. *So weak, so goddamn weak.* He could envisage major organs leaking, his chest cavity filling with blood.

'Lorri!' he croaked again.

The girl peered over her shoulder. 'Mr Drexill, you look bad.'

'I feel worse . . . than that, honey. Your daddy needs help. His neck's bad . . . Do you think you could help him . . . like you did for me that time?'

Her face scrunched up in misery. She felt drained, empty. She shook her head, tears springing anew.

'Just try, honey. See if you can make him better.' Blood

was now dribbling from the corner of his mouth. He could no longer keep his eyes open. *Oh God, no. Not now – not until it's all resolved.* He blinked but saw nothing but a grey smudge. The world was rapidly leaving him.

Was all this my fault? he thought. *All my fault?*

'Mr Drexill?' beseeched Lorri. 'Mr Drexill?'

But the man remained unmoving, his eyes staring, unfocused.

'Daddy, I think Mr Drexill's dead.'

Stanley let out a bitter hiss. 'Don't worry, honey. Help'll come.'

'Help's here,' said Cheryl, kneeling down beside him.

Stanley wanted to reach out and touch them both, but he was as motionless as Drexill.

'He said I could make you better,' sobbed Lorri. 'But I can't – not any more . . . '

'Nothing can make me better, honey. We'll just have to wait for the doctors.'

'The doctors aren't coming,' she whispered. 'Only the dark.'

'What do you mean?' asked Cheryl.

'If Mr Rodin wins, everything will be dark. Everybody will be bad.'

Cheryl hugged Lorri tight, stroking her hair.

'Where's Kara?' she asked.

'Rodin took her,' murmured Stanley.

Gaines leaned down to look into his face. 'We'll get that bastard,' she promised, 'but first we must—'

'No. Forget me, go after Rodin,' Stanley urged.

'We don't even know where he's gone,' she insisted.

'You've got to find Rodin and Kara' Stanley beseeched. 'Or we're *all* screwed.'

CHAPTER 55

Now that Erebus had encompassed the entire lower half of Manhattan, up as far as 116th Street, those who had stubbornly remained on the island began to exit their apartments, offices and stores to view their strange new world.

As a result, Parvill was occasionally forced to swerve the stolen Range Rover to avoid gawping pedestrians stepping out in front of him as he drove it along the sidewalks of 34th Street. But even these near-collisions couldn't distract New Yorkers from getting their first sight of the mighty shell that now contained their city.

They were dazed, confused, terrified – but elated to have survived. Although they couldn't comprehend what all those damn lights meant, many began to celebrate: cheering, whooping and hollering in the streets like it was VJ Day all over again. Inexplicably blessed with continued existence, they shared their joy with one another, turning to sex, drink or drugs to celebrate their survival.

To the west it was as if a wall soared up from the New Jersey shoreline, cutting off Hoboken and Union City from sight and effectively turning lower Manhattan into a giant planetarium with its light show full on. It was this north-western perimeter that was Parvill's ultimate destination.

He could sense the little girl drawing power from within

Erebus, making her too powerful for him to destroy. But outside its range of protection he would have the upper hand. If he didn't know better, he would swear she was still deriving power from her sister. But that was impossible. Lorri Carter was as dead as Christie was; he had watched her fall.

Kara, however, did not see the perimeter wall, nor was she paying attention to anything they rode past. She sat beside Parvill, staring at him constantly. For the most part, he avoided her eyes, but when he did glance at her, they reinforced his inability to harm her. Taking her away with him was as much as he could do.

Bearing right off Tenth Avenue and on to West 26th Street, Parvill could see the Hudson River glinting as the millions of lights reflected on its dark and gently undulating surface. Traffic was as snarled here as anywhere else, but he was able to weave safely between abandoned vehicles until he reached the shoreline just beyond Twelfth Avenue.

Bouncing along a cobbled roadway they passed a pair of wrecked gates, then roared down the length of the pier, skidding to a halt beside a rusty tugboat. Two men emerged on the gangway to greet them, both carrying machine-guns.

'Any word from outside?' he barked, lifting Kara out of the car and holding her close.

Though plainly puzzled by the arrival of the child, one of them stuttered a response.

'Out. All c-communications down. C-can't receive, can't transmit.'

'Good. That means they won't know what's happened.'

'Th-that's good?'

Parvill clattered up the gangway. 'Cast off!' he ordered, as he stepped on to the deck.

'You w-want us here on board?'

'Couldn't give a f-fuck,' he mocked, heading towards the wheelhouse.

The two men eyed each other, then made their way over to the Harley-Davidson and climbed on. The tugboat began to chug away from the pier. As no one had unhooked the gangway, it fell into the water with a loud splash.

Inside the wheelhouse, the whisky-sodden skipper soon realized Parvill was in no mood for argument so immediately complied with his demand to sail upriver. He stared ahead at the black cliff which seemed to cut across the river several hundred yards ahead of them.

'We sail right through it? There's a door?'

Parvill placed Kara on a seat, laughing. 'Yes, of course there's a door. A boat-shaped door. Moron.'

'Where are we going?' asked Kara suddenly.

Parvill ignored her.

'They'll stop you,' she continued.

'Who will?'

'My mommy and daddy.'

Parvill whirled on her, pleased to inform her. 'Don't count on it, kid. Mommy's just a red smudge on the sidewalk now, like your sister, and your pathetic father's got a broken neck.'

'You're wrong.' Kara leaned forward, eyes widening. 'I *know* they're alive. And they're coming after you.'

He held her gaze for a long time, determined to catch

her bluff. But there was no sign of wavering; she was totally sure. He stepped back against the window.

He glanced across the city to where, even through the haze of lights, he could spot the familiar spire of the Empire State Building. For the first time in two years the icy fingers of fear touched his heart. There wasn't much time.

CHAPTER 56

'We need another car. This one's screwed,' cried Ward, after failing to get the Bentley started again.

'There must be dozens out there we could use.' Cheryl clung tightly to Lorri's hand.

'Yeah, but you'd need a bulldozer to make any headway through that tangle. It took us an age just to cover a couple of blocks.'

The street was jammed with vehicles, but, more ominously, they could see people moving around between them, and hear the sound of breaking glass.

'Looters already,' said Cheryl. 'Who was it said the cockroaches would inherit the earth? If we're going to get to the river, we need something big and safe.'

Since Gaines's ribs were continuing to cause her problems, it had been agreed she should stay on the roof and watch over Stanley, using her cellphone to call for medical assistance if and when it could be raised.

As Ward, Cheryl and Lorri had descended in the elevator, it was also quickly agreed that they first had to rescue Kara from Parvill's clutches before he could complete the final phase of his plan. Lorri had explained that Kara was somewhere on the river, and Ward already knew the vessel they would be using. The problem was how to reach them in time.

'There!' Lorri pointed across the street. 'See that green truck.'

It was a scruffy lime-coloured garbage truck carrying a SWIFT REFUSE SERVICES logo, and incongruous white racing stripes along most of its length. But it was as big as they come, a 32-tonne Ford lift-and-tip garbage-eating monster, its cab doors wide open and its hydraulic forks half-raised in front of it as if in surrender.

'Hell, it's exactly what we need,' said Cheryl. 'You're a clever girl.'

Ward led them across the street and climbed up into the cab. Fortunately, the keys were still in the ignition.

'I want to sit up there.' Lorri indicated the cab roof.

'No, honey,' said Cheryl. 'You must ride inside with us.'

'No, I have to ride up there – as high as the lights.'

'What do you mean?' Cheryl asked.

'The lights will help me,' explained Lorri.

'You mean make you more powerful?'

She nodded at Cheryl's suggestion.

'How many lights do you need?'

'As many as I can get.'

'There's certainly enough of them,' said Ward, leaning out of the cab window.

'No point in arguing,' said Cheryl, ending the discussion. 'But I'm riding up there with you, okay?'

Lorri held out her arms and was lifted up against the side of the cab. She scrambled up quickly, using a door handle, side mirrors and the open window as footholds, until she could crawl on to the cab roof itself. Cheryl followed her, surprised at how high up they found themselves.

The biggest problem would be holding on. Cheryl seated Lorri with her thighs locked around a flashing orange beacon over the driver's seat. Cheryl sat right behind Lorri and wrapped her arms around her, steadying her feet against a low rail that ran across the front of the cab roof.

'Okay, my man, take it away,' she yelled, slapping the roof beneath her.

The first light was directly ahead of them, conveniently on a level with Lorri's head. Similar ones ran at intervals the whole length of the street.

The truck fired up, its powerful diesel engine shaking as it coughed into life. Pleased the Ford had an automatic gearbox, Ward eased the vehicle forward, steering a course half on, half off the sidewalk.

Atop the cab, Lorri's head soon absorbed the first light. Cheryl leaned back, expecting it to reappear. But it had completely vanished – she might as well have eaten it.

Progress was slow as the truck had to bully its way past all the cars littering the street. At the first intersection, Ward leaned out of his window and shouted, 'Better hang on. I'm going to have to ram this damn Beemer!'

An abandoned silver 318 soft-top blocked both road and sidewalk.

Hugging Lorri, Cheryl braced herself for the impact. They were sitting a good fifteen feet off the ground and any fall could be crippling. Not that Lorri seemed concerned: she had absorbed five of the lights so far and another hovered just ahead.

The truck lurched and there was a loud crash, the screeching of metal and a series of judders until the BMW was pressed up against an office building. The truck carried on across the crowded intersection. Soon afterwards they arrived outside a familiar wrecked Rolls-Royce showroom where a battered grey helicopter was parked precariously on top of a coach outside.

Ward slapped the steering wheel. Of course! *Their Cayuse!* It might be on its last legs, but nothing would get them faster to where they needed to go. He halted the truck, then jumped out and gestured for the woman and her daughter to climb down.

'We got a quicker way!'

CHAPTER 57

The wheelhouse of the *Leanora* stank of booze – the captain had obviously been fortifying himself while awaiting Parvill Rodin's return. An empty pint bottle of Red Label rolled noisily in one corner with each slap of waves on the boat's bow.

'How *are* you going to get out?' asked Kara. She was seated on the high captain's chair, Parvill standing right behind her.

He sneered into her ear. 'You really are one ignorant little bitch.' He darted forward, staring at her intently. 'Or is it all an act?'

Kara was unmoved. 'We're inside the asteroid, so how do we get out?'

He moved to her side and threw an arm over her shoulder, pulling her close to him. 'Dear girl, why *you*, of course. You *again*.' His eyes were cast heavenward.

'I don't understand.'

'You see all those lights out there; every one of them is looking for a home. The beacon has to lead the way and open the door for them. And you are that beacon. When we reach the wall, it'll open for you, we sail on through and all these lights can then go a-hunting.'

'But if I'm the beacon . . .'

'Yes?'

'. . . why are you helping me?'

'Because, my little lighthouse, once we're beyond that wall we're equal again. And, as I told you before, I'm big, you're little.'

'But you can't hurt me now?'

'Now is only for a few seconds more. Look for yourself.'

Kara leaned forward and could see the black emptiness of the perimeter wall filling the whole window of the wheelhouse – as if someone had painted the outside of the glass. But, looking closely, she could make out its details: the clefts, the grain, the angles. They must be so close to it. *Too* close.

'I reckon two minutes,' hissed Parvill. 'And then it's going to get a tad messy for you.'

Hate flared in his eyes, and Kara knew her fate was sealed.

'Why do you want to win?' she asked.

As the tugboat chugged on towards the monstrous wall, Parvill considered her question. 'Because I'd prefer my world to yours.'

'You're not a nice man, Mr Rodin.'

'From you that's a compliment. Now, get ready to meet your maker.'

It still seemed as if they would simply be crashing into a rock wall and instinctively she braced herself for the collision. Parvill, however, felt no such doubts, standing erect at the window and staring out.

The skipper piped up, 'There's no way through!' Suddenly, he started spinning the wheel frantically to port.

'No!' shouted Parvill. 'Keep on course.'

'Look!' shouted the skipper.

Parvill spotted the other vessel too late. As they collided, Kara was hurled forward on to him, smashing his head against the window, before they both fell back on to the cabin floor.

The *Leanora* jerked to a halt. There was a crash, a grinding of metal, the sound of voices screaming, then the boat keeled over to one side, throwing the skipper across the wheelhouse, through the cabin door, where he slammed into the Coast Guard lieutenant and both tumbled overboard into the Hudson – to land in the midst of several children thrashing in the water.

Frank Cantrillo had gone along with Dr Morrow's suggestion of stealing a boat from Bridgeport harbour. Their cross-country trek by Hummer had been time-consuming, but when they reached the waterfront they had found a yacht large enough to carry all seventeen of them – a motorized sloop called *Caroline's Dream*. Soon they were headed for New York City down the Hudson River, engine running at its limit, the children strung out along the deck with spray whipping their eager faces as they sailed steadily towards the black dome enveloping the city. From the water it was an awesome sight, like a giant bowling ball had rolled in from the Atlantic and struck out the skittles of the city's skyscrapers. Despite their mission, most aboard the sloop were apprehensive – not least Dr Morrow, whose reservations grew in proportion to the approaching wall surrounding Manhattan Island.

'What are we going to do now?' he had shouted to Tasmin over the roar of the engine.

'Go inside!'

'How?'

The girl merely shrugged.

The doctor patted her shoulder. 'Thanks for being so reassuring.'

He made his unsteady way back towards Cantrillo at the wheel.

'They say we're going in.'

'Then I suppose we are,' sighed Cantrillo. 'How, I don't know.'

And all the time the asteroid wall was growing, till eventually it was all they could see: a mountain filling the sky, over two miles high. But nowhere could Morrow spot an entrance. He noticed the children had gathered on the fore-deck, all craning forward.

'Is that safe?' Morrow asked.

'How we gonna stop them?' replied Cantrillo. 'This is their idea.'

'You're taking their safety rather lightly, Frank.'

'So what am I supposed to do?' It was said in exas-peration.

'You could turn round, of course.'

Tasmin appeared beside him, startling Morrow. 'Keep straight ahead, Sheriff Frank. Kara's very close.'

'What about that wall?'

'Don't worry, doctor. It knows we're coming.'

Cantrillo and Morrow exchanged glances, then watched in horrified fascination as the boat continued to plough through the water towards a wall so obviously solid that they could now see waves splashing against its base.

'Slow down, Frank,' urged Morrow.

'Can't,' confessed Cantrillo.

He threw himself to the deck as the boat hit the black rock – and sailed through as if it was merely a fogbank.

'Holy shit,' hissed Cantrillo in relief. Then, too late, he saw the other boat.

It was a sky-blue garbage barge, adrift and floating sideways across the river, one hundred feet square and packed with trash twenty feet high. He swerved to avoid it and narrowly succeeded, but then caught sight of a second vessel he had no chance of avoiding at all. *Caroline's Dream* slapped into the other boat's port side at full speed, scraped all along its length, then turned a tight 180-degree circle and smashed nose-first into the middle of the drifting barge.

The tugboat slid past the sloop, then also hit the barge, riding up on to it and becoming stuck fast. Though listing badly under the double impact, the barge managed to remain afloat but now carried two other craft as passengers as it continued its drift oceanwards.

Blood streaming down his face, Cantrillo crawled out on to the deck to find a dozen of the children threshing in the water. Most of them weren't even wearing life jackets, as there hadn't been enough of them to go round. He yelled to them that he was coming to their aid – but Tasmin had grabbed his wrist.

'Leave them. Kara is more important.'

'What?' he cried in disbelief. 'They're *drowning*, girl!'

'Kara is more important.'

He tried to shake off her grip, but her nails dug into his flesh.

'Leave them!' she insisted through clenched teeth.

Already he could feel there was no arguing with her.

Morrow joined them. 'The kids!' he yelled. 'I'll go in after them, if you help haul them aboard!'

'Tasmin says to leave them . . .'

'That's bullshit!' The doctor grabbed a lifebelt and tossed it overboard, then he hurried up the narrow deck and found two more, and hurled these too. He spotted in the water a man in a white Coast Guard uniform, along with another, bearded man. They were both helping the children in difficulties. On the stern of Caroline's Dream sat a small black dinghy with an outboard motor. Morrow debated using it to help the children, but already several were sinking under the surface as they drifted away from the boats. Uncharacteristically, he panicked – and instead jumped after them into the cold, oily water.

'No!' yelled Tasmin, lowering herself over the side of the boat and down on to the barge.

'What the hell?' Cantrillo shouted after her. Then, looking across at the stranded tugboat, he saw Kara Carter being dragged out of the wheelhouse of the tugboat and thrown down on to the garbage, the man with her jumping down after her.

'Hey, you! Leave that girl alone!'

The blond stranger stared at him and Cantrillo felt the hatred. It was like being doused in a bucket of icy vomit. He knew this was the man who intended to kill Kara – in that moment the sheriff somehow understood why Kara was so important and why the other children were of secondary consequence. He knew his place was on that other boat – not in the water – whatever the cost to the children.

The children remaining on *Caroline's Dream* had all gathered around Cantrillo, urging him on.

'Save her,' they shrieked in unison, ignoring their friends in the river.

Cantrillo again watched the blond man dragging Kara towards the bow of the tugboat, then reached for his revolver and clambered down the side of *Caroline's Dream*.

As he settled one foot on the barge's rusted side, a helicopter roared in low from the city, circled the mated boats, then gingerly lowered itself towards the piled-up garbage, a whirlwind of dust and fine debris blinding everyone present.

Cantrillo fell into the barge, cracking his knees on the unyielding deck amid the foul-smelling slop that rippled around the outer edges of the loaded trash. He urged Tasmin to keep well back, squinting against the grit blasted around by the chopper's downdraught, then he began to worm his way along the side of the stinking barge.

Ward had a struggle to maintain control of the Cayuse, its engine coughing like the old-timer it was. He knew that landing on an unstable pile of garbage was out of the question, but Cheryl was insistent that she get on to the vessel. Before its descent had kicked up such a cloud of refuse, Ward had briefly glimpsed the other young girl in Parvill's clutches. He knew there was no point arguing with her mother, but the controls were jerking in his hands, threatening to throw him off and send the chopper crashing downwards.

'You're gonna have to get out *now*!' he yelled into Cheryl's face. 'Can't hold her any longer.'

Cheryl didn't need to hear his words; the expression of panic on his face was enough. She opened her door and leaned outwards. Through the swirling dust, she could see trash bags, cardboard packaging, broken furniture, oil drums, dead electrical equipment, bundles of rags, plastic bottles, glass, ash . . . An evil landscape guaranteed to gash shins and break ankles.

'Out! Out!' screamed Ward, feeling a more violent vibration he suspected to be terminal, like the arrhythmia prior to a heart attack.

Cheryl swiftly unbuckled her belt and turned to the door – and a ten-feet drop on to God knew what. But before she was able to choose her landing spot, the helicopter dipped, she felt a hard slap on her back and she was flying through the air.

As soon as he saw the woman and child disappear, Ward hauled on the controls trying to get the Cayuse higher, but its old engine would no longer comply. The chopper suddenly slid sideways, its rotors clipping a clutch of filing cabinets, sparks flying across the windshield. It then lurched forward, till the jungle of trash filled Ward's vision. Instinctively, he let go of the controls to shield his face. As the machine slammed into the barge's deck, its rotors snapped off and it somersaulted, its still spinning engine burrowing into the garbage. Then, skipping sideways, it rolled over twice before ploughing sideways into the Hudson. The explosion of its fuel tank was smothered by the icy river as it sank into the inky darkness. Shocked and disoriented, Ward was still strapped into his seat.

Lorri had landed on top of Cheryl, but luckily their fall was cushioned by trash bags which burst open spewing their odious contents over and around them. Sensing the violence above them from the disintegrating Cayuse, she pressed Lorri beneath her, burying the two of them in rancid food scraps and evil-smelling waste paper.

As the helicopter's death throes shook the barge, Cheryl couldn't help screaming as the mattress of filth bucked beneath them. Then there was a terrible high-pitched whistling sound as the dying chopper pummelled its way into a watery grave.

As the rotors snapped off, two thirteen-foot sections flew up into the air like javelins, spearing into the river a hundred yards away. A third embedded itself deeply in the cockpit of *Caroline's Dream*. The remaining rotor, however, found more yielding targets.

Parvill Rodin whipped round as the helicopter began to complain, sensing a crash was inevitable. He was looking for somewhere to take cover when its rotors snapped loose. Almost too fast to see, one scythed right towards him and on into the river. He turned to watch it continue its way through threshing children and yelling adults, sliced limbs flailing into the air as it cartwheeled on towards Union City. Only as it finally slapped the water did he realize it had taken his right arm along with it.

Doc Morrow was helping keep some of the children afloat, having seen a young Coast Guard officer swimming over with life jackets. He heard the helicopter destruct behind him just before the whirling rotor blade removed the top half of his body. It then proceeded to decapitate several children and the lieutenant before slipping under the water, its carnage completed.

As the cockpit of the yacht exploded, a large chunk of debris smacked into Tasmin's head, tossing her into the side of the barge where she collapsed, limbs splayed, like a broken doll.

Cantrillo knelt and clapped his hands over his eyes – a pathetic gesture but it was all he could manage. Only when silence had returned did he slowly rise to survey the damage. Out on the river there was incomprehensible horror: bodies were bobbing in the water – headless, limbless – children and adults.

'Jim!' he shouted, leaning over the edge of the barge to look for Morrow. But all he could see were five remaining children struggling to stay afloat.

Cantrillo turned back to inspect the onboard destruction. Glancing down, he sobbed to recognize the broken form of Tasmin. Nearby lay a man with his right arm missing. For the first time in Cantrillo's professional life, horror killed his decisiveness. He didn't know what to do.

Parvill couldn't yet really understand what had happened to him. Seeing Kara still beside him, he reached for her with his good hand. She looked at him blankly, her face white with shock, then she lowered her eyes towards his shoulder.

He followed her gaze to the gaping wound.

There was no pain but he was woozy from loss of blood. He clamped his left hand to the gory mess in a vain attempt to staunch it.

Kara watched in horror as Parvill tried to stop the blood squirting out. She started back from him.

'Don't fucking move,' he hissed with a glare.

The sheer power of his voice rooted her to the spot.

Parvill knew that to succeed he would need to stem his blood loss. Pain he could deal with but his life was pulsing away. All around and above the barge, the lights glowed as regular as throughout the whole city. He at least understood their power.

He reached for Kara with his one bloodied hand, grabbed her hair and hauled her after him along the rim of the barge towards the *Leanora*. There was a light hovering over the side; if he could reach that, he would gain enough extra power to control his appalling wound – at least for a while. But even as he fought on through the slippery debris he heard a shout behind him.

Pausing, he turned to look back over Kara's head to see a sheriff pointing a gun.

'Let the girl go, you bastard!'

He's irrelevant, thought Parvill, facing back to the light.

Cantrillo stepped closer through the putrid mush, one hand on the barge's rusty retaining wall to steady himself. The stench was overpowering and he was breathing in short gasps. He kept his aim unwaveringly on the blond man's head, the children's last cry of 'save her' determining his actions. He was going to save Kara whatever the cost.

'So help me, I'll blow you out of your fucking shoes!'

Parvill was only two steps away from the glowing light, his shoulder continuing to leak his life away, the girl's hair still bunched tightly in his fingers. But he hadn't long before unconsciousness would claim him. He *needed* that light; he could achieve nothing without it.

He edged forward again, his eyes fixed on the rainbow-hued egg floating so tantalizingly close.

A voice suddenly from their left: 'Frank! No! You might hit Kara!'

CARL HUBERMAN

Parvill didn't turn to find out who it was. He used the sudden distraction to step into the light, letting it meld into his forehead.

Instantly, his body began to quiver with new vigour. Staring at his shoulder he could feel arteries constricting, capillaries closing, the blood retreating from the veins sliced open by the rotor blade. And still he felt no pain.

Satisfied, he turned to assess the situation, catching sight of the girl's mother with her other daughter. How the hell had they survived the Empire State Building? But they were both stranded on top of a pile of garbage and armed only with their anger. They were as irrelevant as the damn cop.

He revolved to face the sheriff who was still distracted by the woman. Parvill laughed.

Cantrillo's eyes flicked back to Rodin.

'Let go the girl and get down on your fucking knees.'

'Or what?' countered Parvill, his eyes flaring. He focused his gaze directly on the other man's.

Cantrillo readied his finger on the trigger. But then something strange began to happen.

Parvill's smile broadened as he watched the man's stupefied expression grow.

'Sheriff Frank, don't look at him!' Kara piped up, too late.

Parvill tightened his grip on her hair. 'You, keep quiet. This is between us boys.'

Cantrillo was still staring at him, confused.

'End it all, Frank,' coaxed Parvill. 'End all the pain and all the worry.'

Cantrillo understood the sense in these words and glanced down at his gun.

Through sudden tears, Kara yelled, 'Don't listen to him!'

Parvill tugged again on her hair, making her stumble and fall on to her backside. Then, dragging the girl through the filth, he closed the distance between himself and the sheriff. Once in front of Cantrillo, he let her go and slipped his finger inside the trigger guard of the sheriff's revolver. He raised the gun upwards in one smooth movement, jabbing it into the underside of the confused man's jaw.

Cantrillo seemed totally unable to react.

As Parvill pressed against the sheriff's finger, he watched the top of the man's head detonate in a shower of bone and blood.

Cantrillo remained upright for several moments more, then toppled backwards against a trash bag full of broken glass.

Parvill heard Cheryl Carter's scream much closer than he would have expected and whirled round to find mother and daughter only seconds from reaching Kara, who meanwhile was crawling towards them. If the girls made contact, Parvill knew he would soon be overwhelmed by their combined power. Leaping on to the sheriff's corpse, he wrestled the revolver from his grip and whipped it round to aim at Kara's back.

Cheryl hurled herself over one final heap of garbage, crashing down the side of the barge between Parvill and her children.

Parvill knew he could easily eliminate the woman – she had lost her power – but was distracted by a violent throbbing in his ripped shoulder. Glancing down at it, he saw the blood had begun to flow again. What power he had absorbed must only act to staunch the wound temporarily. He would need to access another light soon.

Unthinkingly, he caught the eye of Lorri – and felt as if he had been punched in the stomach.

Oh God, she's far too powerful . . .

He forced his gaze back to the mother. And spotted his redemption there.

As the three entwined vessels continued drifting downstream with the current, they regularly passed through the grid of lights. One had just appeared to the side of Cheryl Carter, and a moment later it would come to him.

Come on, come on . . . He was consciously resisting the twins' influence, both of whom were now focusing on him.

As finally the light reached him, he stretched up to let it touch the bridge of his nose, suffusing him with new strength. He then returned his aim to Cheryl as she huddled protectively in front of her girls.

'Stupid bitch,' he muttered as he fired.

The impact of the bullet spun Cheryl around and her knees gave way. As she hit the deck, she noticed Kara clutch at her throat. Blood burst through the little girl's fingers and she fell back against the side of the barge.

As Parvill watched the wounded child slither to the deck, a huge wave of relief surged through him. He hadn't been intending to injure the girl – had believed he *couldn't* hurt her – yet she now lay wounded, maybe even dying. And once she was gone, all would finally be his.

But, from the warmth on his shoulder, he realized he

was bleeding again. There would be no triumph if he bled to death.

Lorri shrieked, staring down at her mother, while Kara lay grasping at the base of her neck, her eyes wide with disbelief and pain. She tried to speak but emitted only bubbles of blood. Lorri reached for her hand but a widening of Kara's eyes alerted her to the threat behind her. Lorri spun round to face Parvill and his pistol.

As she rose, she stared into his eyes. She knew she could save Kara, and her mother too, but not if this man now got in the way.

Parvill could feel the world shrinking. Under her intense gaze, his arm was growing weary, his resolve leaking away like the blood from his shoulder.

Some little spark prodded him to look away, and he switched his own gaze to the southern wall of the asteroid, now approaching. If he got outside first he would become the guide, and then his wound would no longer matter. But the little girl was advancing towards him, each step carefully placed amidst the garbage so she wouldn't lose her footing. She was now his only problem, because her power might overwhelm him in his weakened state. Then he saw yet another of the lights floating towards him, too high for the child. If he could absorb that, too, he could certainly get away.

The light was now directly between them. Lorri spotted it, and made a run for it getting ready to jump, but her foot caught in a broken bed frame and she crashed to the ground, banging her head. Parvill snatched at the light, felt its warmth course through him, then turned to head back up the length of the barge.

The pain Cheryl felt in her side was unbelievable. The amount of blood was also scary, pumping through her fingers like a gushing faucet. But then she caught sight of her daughter Kara and realized there was something infinitely worse than her own suffering. She began to crawl towards her, one hand clamped to her side. Now Kara was convulsing, and her mother began scrabbling hand over hand until she was able to cradle the child in her arms, pressing one filthy hand to her daughter's neck to stem the flow.

Parvill had almost reached the end of the barge when he heard Lorri scream again. Thinking himself at a safe distance he turned to look back, raising the pistol.

A shaft of hatred and venom hit him like a laser, making him stagger back. She was now hunched on the edge of the barge, her wide white eyes fixed on him like flashlights. She was mouthing words, but he couldn't hear them. His world began draining of all conscious sound: no more screaming seagulls, no slapping of waves, no distant shouting or car horns or gunshots. Just a roaring silence enveloping his senses – and then his sight also began to fade.

It's shock, just shock, he reassured himself, but the girl's white orbs continued to bore into him as if searching for his core. It was her and her passengers, working together to control him.

He could feel his arm rising just as pain hit his shoulder. Soon the agony was unbearable; he would do anything to stop it.

Anything? whispered a voice.

Yes, yes, anything, he confessed, then cried out as his shoulder seemed to explode with white-hot searing agony.

You hold the answer, said the voice. *Use it.*

What? He could feel the gun in his hand. *Use it?*

Then all the pain will be over.

It lay heavy in his hand, and it was true: shooting himself would end it all.

He felt his arm swivelling to point the sheriff's revolver at his own head. One squeeze, and no more pain. He began to shake. *Her eyes, her eyes.*

The gun hove into his view, its barrel itself like a single black eye ready to open and show him the light.

Oh yes, the light. The beautiful light. The light that will take all this pain away.

But as he switched his gaze fully to the gun, the spell was broken.

Do it, do it, the voice urged again. But Parvill no longer heeded it. He threw the gun away from himself, hearing it splash into the river. And then the real world came flooding back and he forced himself round to climb up on to the stranded yacht a rung at a time, leaning in to the ladder to compensate for having only one hand and steadying himself after each step upward.

Behind him he could hear the girl screaming hatred at him, but he knew that, as long as he avoided her eyes, he would be able to escape.

He glanced up and down the sloping deck, the boat shifting uneasily as the barge beneath it was dragged sideways down river. A boat this size ought to have a dinghy, he thought, so, holding on to the side of the wrecked cabin, he made his unsteady way towards the stern. There he found on the deck a six-foot, inflated black rubber dinghy, complete with a small blue outboard motor. He glanced at the asteroid's perimeter wall which was no more than ten minutes way from the barge. But in this dinghy, just three or four minutes – and then all would be his.

He unlooped the painter from the deck cleat, then used it to haul the dinghy to the rear of the slowly sinking sloop where the deck was only inches above the water. The stern rail could be lifted in part, and once it was removed, he pulled the dinghy as far forward as he could without going overboard himself. Once its very tip was touching the water, he knelt down, put his good shoulder to its rubber rear, and heaved it, inch by inch, down off the deck and into the water.

But suddenly the Hudson grabbed the little craft and it shifted, leaving Parvill sprawling full length on the deck. By now he was bleeding again, leaving a scarlet smear on the fading varnish of the deck. He got to his knees unsteadily. He needed to absorb another light before his last remaining resources were drained, but the dinghy was already drifting away, his only means of escape inching away as he watched. There was no option: he threw himself after it.

As he slammed into it his entire body screamed with pain – his ragged shoulder, stomach, legs, all offering up different agonies.

Then one thing roused him from his growing stupor; brought him back from his black well of agony – the girl, screaming incoherently. She was somewhere behind him, her voice partially muffled by the sounds of the river, but her outrage, her hatred and her powerlessness were plain to him. Hauling his head up, he saw the perimeter wall was close – and with it came salvation. It was now simply a matter of keeping alert until he breached it. He had come so far, taken so many risks, surely he was not going to fail now.

He rolled over on to his back, dragging his feet into the dinghy. *So close, so close . . .*

But suddenly it all went wrong.

There was a sudden bump, and the dinghy lurched sideways. Parvill grabbed one side to steady himself and was astonished to see someone clambering on board. He wore the dark uniform of . . . an airman? A general?

'Ward?' he exclaimed in recognition.

'Fucker!' gasped Ward, reaching for the wounded man's leg.

Parvill swung his foot round and caught him in the face, and Ward slipped back into the river. But Parvill's movement sent him sprawling too, pitching the dinghy back against the barge.

Thrashing about in a rapidly reddening pool in the bottom of the dinghy, Parvill rolled himself on to his back again. He needed another of the lights. Or he wouldn't make it.

It was then that Lorri jumped on top of him, exploding breath from his lungs, her fingers clawing at his eyes.

She was screaming hysterically as he tried to bat her away with his one hand, but the girl grabbed his hair and yanked his head upright, forcing him to gaze directly into her eyes.

It was as if she had squirted acid into his pupils – and beyond them. He tried to cry out, but his voice was lost for ever. He began to stop moving, reacting, thinking . . . Everything he was, everything he had been, everything he had wanted, was all for nothing now. The girl was totally in his head, scouring and scarring and erasing his mind.

Soon nothing else mattered, nothing existed – just him and her. And their conjoining produced a oneness of purpose, together they became a control, *together* they became the pilot.

Ward grabbed a loose cable hanging from the barge and pulled himself up on to the floating shitpile. Getting out of the sinking Cayuse had been easy compared to surviving in the cold river that swallowed it. Time and again he had tried to get a hold on one of the boats, and had failed. Only when the dinghy had glided past, could he summon the reserves of energy needed to try to get on board. For a full two minutes, he coughed up water, then knelt on the stinking deck and stared out over the river. There he beheld a sight that made him doubt his sanity.

Rodin lay on his back, with Lorri Carter on his chest, their faces pressed close together like lovers, her hands cupping his ears. And they were floating fifteen feet above the river, rising slowly. He followed their ascent in awe, leaning further and further backwards until he overbalanced on to a pile of plastic bottles.

Cheryl had edged up against the rusted side of the barge, hugging Kara, her hand holding tight to the ragged hole in her daughter's neck. She had watched in horror as Lorri had clambered over the mounds of trash to reach the other side of the barge, screaming like a demented animal. Cheryl had tried to shout for her to stop, but could only manage a cough which left her groaning in pain as the deep wound jabbed at her insides.

She hugged Kara closer, lost to her horror and misery.

And then she spotted Lorri and Parvill rising in the air – and she finally recovered her scream.

Ward heard the woman shriek but was too mesmerized to do anything but stare in disbelief. As the pair reached a hundred feet above the river's surface, he noticed the gridded lights beginning to rise with them, leaving a darkness pooling around him as if ink was leaking into the hollow of the barge.

Cheryl also saw all the lights rising. *No, no*, her mind screamed. *Please, God, no.*

But nothing now would stop the rise of Erebus.

Soon the myriad lights were above and the perimeter blackness had passed right through them as if they had been submerged in a layer of oil, only to find it perfectly clear and light underneath. The whole sky was jet black: the underside of the departing asteroid.

It had risen slowly at first, but then increased in speed.

As soon as she was able to define its limits, she realized it must be hundreds of feet above them. *My baby, my baby*, was all she could think.

Ward, too, stared at the black orb receding above him. Given its enormous size, he knew it must be accelerating away at a fantastic rate – and with that poor little girl inside it.

They watched Erebus in silence until its distant form was blotted out by clouds. Realizing its progress could not now be halted, Cheryl finally was able to express her horror and anguish and loss. One daughter was up there, locked inside

Erebus with Parvill Rodin; the other lay gravely wounded in her lap.

She howled an ugly braying sound – the cry of a mother for her lost children.

The cry of a mother beyond hope.

At the sound a young girl farther along the barge sat up, her face a hideous mask of blood.

When Ward noticed her, he too began to cry.

FOUR MONTHS LATER

Cheryl was putting Kara and Tasmin to bed. The adoption of Tasmin had been rushed through and the girl was now officially a Carter. Both girls had been suffering with chicken-pox and, although the itching and rash had dissipated, the lethargic legacy of the disease continued to take its ill-tempered toll. Cheryl herself was suffering from a heavy cold, the three making a triumvirate of female misery. Having made sure the drapes were wide open, the night sky visible, she switched off the light and returned to her own bedroom. They were now renting the late Frank Cantrillo's house from his sister.

'They okay?' asked Stanley from the floor, where he lay on his back, raising hand-weights.

Cheryl didn't answer him, but bolted for the bathroom where she scooped up a handful of Kleenex tissues and blew her nose, then dabbed at tear-filled eyes. She tried to kid herself it was her cold, that she should be all cried out after four months, but knew that wasn't so. After what had happened to her daughters, to Tasmin and the others, she doubted she would ever smile again. It had been a miraculous moment when Tasmin had seemingly risen from the dead and staggered across to lay healing hands on both Kara and Cheryl, but the euphoria had been fleeting. The two girls had recovered from their wounds but both had been left physically scarred –

Tasmin with a broad white diagonal line on her forehead now hidden by her hair, Kara by an ugly groove at the base of her neck. As for mental scars, Lorri's absence continued to plague them all.

Cheryl walked back into the bedroom and, skirting Stanley, went to the window. She stared up at the star-strewn blackness. Erebus was still up there, lost or hidden somewhere, with Lorri and that devil Parvill Rodin inside it. She couldn't begin to imagine what was happening to her poor darling.

Rhododendron itself was still shrouded in grief, mourning the loss of its children. Given the circumstances of the tragedy, no blame was attached to anyone – bar the phantoms hiding in their heads. There were still 'infected' children in town, but only Lorri was paying the ultimate price.

Cheryl tore her gaze away from the window and helped Stanley into bed. Surgery had restored much of his mobility, but he was never going to run again and now spent most of his days settled on a chair behind the counter of Evergreen Souvenirs, while Cheryl worked at the local airport helping out a charter firm. Maybe her subconscious aim was to regain her helicopter pilot licence . . .

She removed her robe and leaned towards the Compaq PC sitting on the table in the corner of the bedroom. She stroked the Internet page still displayed on its screen: from a WATCH website relaying its latest discoveries to a suddenly asteroid-wary world. Both Ward and Gaines had dedicated much of their group's dramatically increased financial resources to tracking down the whereabouts of the vanished Erebus – but so far in vain. Reluctantly, Cheryl switched off the computer, then climbed into bed and cuddled up to Stanley.

He wiped the last trace of a tear from her cheek. He gestured at the screen, now as black as the night outside the window.

'Maybe,' he whispered.

'Yeah, maybe,' she agreed, unconvinced. 'Maybe one day . . .'

MATTHEW REILLY

Ice Station

Pan Books   £5.99

At a remote US ice station in Antarctica, a team of scientists has made an amazing discovery. They have found something unbelievable buried deep below the surface – trapped inside a layer of ice 400 million years old.

Something made of metal . . . something which shouldn't be there . . . it's the discovery of a lifetime, a discovery of immeasurable value. And a discovery men will kill for.

Led by the enigmatic Lieutenant Shane Schofield, a crack team of US Marines is rushed to the ice station to secure this bizarre discovery for their own nation. Meanwhile other countries have developed the same idea, and are ready to pursue it swiftly and ruthlessly . . .

'Supersonically paced . . . This is a seriously good book'
Daily Telegraph

SHAUN HUTSON

Warhol's Prophecy

Pan Books   £5.99

*'Everyone will be famous for fifteen minutes,' said Andy Warhol.
And some people will go to any lengths to achieve this . . . Whether
to be revered or reviled, the lure of fame is overpowering for those
without it.*

When five-year-old Becky goes missing in a crowded shopping
centre, it seems her mother's worst nightmare has come true.
But Hailey Gibson's nightmares are only just beginning . . .

After the child is recovered by Adam Walker, Hailey finds
her gratitude to him turning to something warmer. With her
marriage close to ruins, she is even tempted to begin an affair
with this attractive stranger. Besides, Hailey wants revenge
against her husband and his mistress – revenge that could be
contrived with the help of a willing accomplice. And Walker
seems entranced by her, only too happy to please – but what
if he has his own agenda . . .?

'The man who writes what others are afraid even to imagine'
Sunday Times